if you can walk, you can dance

MARION MOLTENO

NIYOGI BOOKS

Published by
NIYOGI BOOKS
D-78, Okhla Industrial Area, Phase-I
New Delhi-110 020, INDIA
Tel: 91-11-26816301, 49327000
Fax: 91-11-26810483, 26813830
email: niyogibooks@gmail.com
website: www.niyogibooksindia.com

First published 1998 by Shola Books, London.
First Indian edition 2017 by Niyogi Books, New Delhi.

Editor: K.E. Priyamvada
Layout Design: Shashi Bhushan Prasad
Cover Design: Misha Oberoi

ISBN: 978-93-85285-61-5
Publication: 2017

Printed at: Niyogi Offset Pvt. Ltd., New Delhi, India

If you can walk, you can dance

If you can talk, you can sing

Zimbabwean saying

BOOK ONE

Chapter 1

It was incredibly hot that last summer, even for December; the very air lethargic with it. We had all got back home by a week before Christmas, all except Edward, of course, who years before had crossed the oceans. And in that heat we still produced heavy midday meals, kitchen steaming, pots clanging, the kind you do for family gatherings but that you'd never think of cooking for yourself once you've left home. Then everyone slumped into after-lunch torpor, staying inside till the worst of the heat would be over. Dad slept, Mom got on with things, the others lazed about, too hot even to talk. Only I was in the garden, moving with the shade. When even that was no defence I climbed over to the neighbours' back yard, to float about in their garden tank, water evaporating around me.

By late afternoon the heat had lifted a little. I climbed back over the fence and stretched myself out on a rug under the maple tree, to lie looking up at the pattern of leaves against the sky. Dad wandered out, no shoes, shirt open and dangling, the waistline of his shorts curving beneath the swell of bare brown belly. He pulled one of the garden chairs over to near where I lay—lowered himself into it—stretched his legs out—and said, 'The nice thing about having a daughter back home is you don't have to make your own tea.'

'*Dad,*' I said, 'I've just settled myself.'

'I'm sixty years old,' he said, 'you're nineteen. There have to be some privileges of age.'

I pulled myself up, biffed his belly in passing, and went inside to the kitchen…Delicious coolth of the stone floor on bare feet as I waited for the small sound of hissing steam through the side where the lid didn't quite fit, the sound of all the years of this particular kettle in this particular kitchen…Out again, to Dad under the maple watching a sparrow…Idle talk over tea till the others began to appear, telling him about things in my life away. Or the bits of it that I felt sure about. Jonas, mainly—

Home was there forever, immutable. I had no concept that there were borders I could choose to cross that would make coming back again impossible. Eden, I suppose; a story as ancient as that. And it is the garden I see first whenever I try now to hold on to it, or rather to that part of me that was formed by it, which feels still the essential core of who I am. The garden, but also its boundaries, asking to be crossed…The lane that ran down one side, where the bushes grew wild and the ground was lethal with paper thorns…Picking my way barefoot after my brother Peter, scared but refusing to be left behind. No one said, 'Don't go out in the lane on your own,' but instinctively I waited for Peter to have the idea…Then the older boys got back from hockey practice, and Peter deserted me and the secret club that until five minutes before had absorbed us equally—

And that other border, the pavement just outside the gate. I used to position myself there each morning, drawing patterns on the gravelly earth while I waited to watch the boys set off for school. In either direction the road stretched long, hot, completely straight, dividing the two known worlds—on this side, the hedged-in gardens, their lawns kept green by being watered through the dry brown winters, on the far side, the untamed veld. A line of pine trees along the pavement marked the border of settled habitation like giant stakes. They were clipped by men who arrived on a lorry with a ladder, to become like trees children draw, straight trunks with lollipop-round heads, punctuating the pavement with circles of shade. I sat within that shade, as close as I could risk to what lay beyond—

—From inside the house all the familiar after-breakfast sounds...'Mom, I've got no socks!'—'For heavens sake Edward, get a move on, do you know what time it is?'...Richard comes cycling out of the gate and past me—the oldest, always first, always steady—his case strapped to the carrier behind him, the special bag Mom made for his flute slung over one shoulder. He lifts a hand off the handlebars to wave. Now the clamour of irritation as Trevor and Edward burst out of the house—'My tyre's flat—where's the pump? I bet Richard's taken the pump again.' Then pedalling down the road, late again, ringing their bells as they pass me. Now Peter, self-conscious in his new uniform, refusing to hold Mom's hand as she walks him down to catch the bus. He carries a schoolcase passed down from Richard to Trevor to Edward and now to him, and whose contents I know precisely, the passionate knowing reserved for things unreachable. A reading book about a farmer called Old Lob. An exercise book covered in regulation brown paper. A wooden pencil case whose top swivels sideways to open a second level for a rubber and a sharpener—

Aunt Ellie says, 'I can't understand why the child plays out there in the dust when there's the whole garden.' But the pavement leads out, to the road—

—Dad—a sudden panic because I left out Dad, in that picture of the boys setting off for school. *Hold on to him*—

Morning, me on the pavement...Dad comes out of the house, leaving even before Richard, at twelve minutes past seven—timed exactly, for he's been walking that same route to the school for fifteen years before I was born, he says. He ruffles my hair as he passes me playing, and I watch him set off. A long stride, easy swing to his arms, completely relaxed in his body. I count the pine trees as he passes them. Three, four—he turns and waves. Eight, nine—he must be passing Aunt Ellie's house now. By twenty-one and twenty-two his tall figure has become so small in the distance that I have to screw up my eyes to keep it from disappearing in the heat. Just as I think he must be nearing the corner I lose him among the diminishing trunks of the pines.

2

I watch as Richard, the oldest of my brothers, prepares to venture into Africa. His bed is piled with penknives and enamel camping mugs, bird books and binoculars, the smell of walking boots being greased, the rough touch of the canvas covering of water bottles.

Dad says, 'What on earth are you taking your flute for?'

Mom says, 'But surely you need more clothes than that?'

We all crowd round as Richard spreads maps out on the living room floor. The only people I know who have travelled beyond the borders have gone on the overnight train down to the coast, from there to sail across the seas, passing the rest of Africa without touching—to land on an island on the edge of Europe to which we seem in every way more connected. But Richard's fingers stay firmly on land as they travel over spindly contour lines, north to places I have never heard anyone talk about. The names are like a poem—Nyika plateau, Zimbabwe ruins, Okavango swamps. They make different rhythms depending on how I say them—*Ny*ika plateau, Zim*bab*we ruins, Okavango swamps—and the rhythms chant themselves in my head for days afterwards, like the *chooka chook-chook* of the train that carries Richard and his friend north. And then the syllables begin to position themselves in patterns of high and low. *Okavango* becomes a bird call, high pitched and insistent. *Zimbabwe* is low and rumbling. *Nyika* is flat and calm…

Richard returns, his walking boots battered and the pages of the bird book coming off its spine. We gather round to see his photographs. Okavango turns suddenly into water and men in dug-out canoes. Zimbabwe becomes a strange building of piled up stones, growing out of the stony earth. But it is the photograph of the Nyika plateau that really catches my imagination—green but treeless, almost featureless except for the shapes of the land, swelling and dipping to the horizon.

'And did you play your flute?' Dad teases. Richard picks it up and begins playing a tune that is unlike any I have heard, like a voice calling, on and on—a yearning sort of call, but over a fast compelling rhythm that makes me want to move. Richard stops and laughs at me. 'Jennie's got it,' he says, and they are all looking at me and laughing, though I don't know what at. Richard says, 'They were dancing to that in the village near where we camped, below Nyika.'

The voice calling, my own body moving to the dance I have never seen…Richard's flute…the green land rolling endlessly… Mom and Dad's faces as they listen—

3

The train that carries me south sets off just before dusk. I lean out of the window waving to the diminishing figures on the platform. Then I pull my head in, pushing up the stiff sash window to keep the fragments of coal dust from getting into my eyes. I sit looking out, watching as light fades over the dry-grass plain. Gradually it gives way to semi desert, seemingly endless—there when I climb into my bunk to sleep, there still when I wake next morning hundreds of miles further on. Now quite suddenly the plateau begins to crack and hump, and the train starts its long descent, down through mountain passes and green valleys, across the last flat sandy expanse, to the foot of the mountain that guards the tip of the continent, sentinel to the sea…

Installed now in the residence…Emerging from the chrysalis of a girls-only school to this campus where young men and women flit careless as butterflies and as alluring, sunning themselves on the wide steps that lead up to the pillars of the university hall. Girls in bright mini-skirts, men in casual shorts, tanned legs stretched out, looking out over spreading suburbs to the bay. Behind us towers the peak, with forest tracks cool and tempting…Studying happens, but almost incidentally, late-night scribbling to get that essay in by the deadline. We move in shoals, like fish when they move from known waters. Into town to explore the harbour at night, weekend gatherings on the beach. Everything seems possible, no one set of choices has yet finally excluded others—

And here is Jonas—A stranger, simply the man whose body presses next to mine in a moving sea of humanity, linking arms to sing *We shall overcome*. His arm, dark brown and not from the sun, hooks too loosely around mine, avoiding any suggestion of intimacy…The singing ends. Up at the front on a temporary platform a young man, tall and suntanned—his very body speaking privilege—addresses all these hundreds of people. I am caught up in his eloquence…

And at the same time I am conscious that the arm is still there, linked with mine Everyone presses close, it's hardly worth trying to move. I turn, smile tentatively. His eyes are solid brown against slightly muddied whites, and there's something in their expression that instinctively assesses. He makes some comment—I respond—he laughs with his whole face, his wide generous mouth. Our talk becomes animated, ignoring the speaker up at the front. 'Jonas,' he says, 'Jennie,' I say, 'both J's,' we say, laughing now at the coincidence that links us when the world is designed to keep us apart. That we touch at all and notice each other's eyes creates an unstated, unstatable awareness of stepping across boundaries…

The crowd is beginning to surge around us, people moving. We're about to get separated. Tomorrow? Yes—Where? Nothing needs saying, but we know public places are out. Anywhere he can move comfortably, I'm going to be far too noticeable. 'The students' union,' he says. Our only possible common ground.

The men in my life come in three kinds, I explain to Dad in that lazy heat under the maple tree, in the idleness of time that will be ours forever. The ones I admire from a distance, like the beautiful man on the platform, challenging injustice—but half the women in the crowd were eyeing him; beyond my reach. Then the ones who invite me out and start groping in the darkened cinema, till I realise I don't know this person and don't specially want to. Jonas is the rare third kind, mutually chosen friend. Warm, real, personal, fallible. All that is the same in us binds, all that is different stimulates. Being with him opens up to me an awareness more powerful than anything I learn from lectures or speeches at demonstrations. We spark off ideas in each other simply by existing—too many to fan into flame, but some catch and are carried high by others around us. We persuade the students' union to set up advice sessions in the township of box houses and potholed lanes where Jonas grew up and still perforce lives, way out of town, where every day there is some battle to be fought with incomprehensible bureaucracies—and the students who journey out weekly get the kind of education Jonas has been giving me. I do the recruiting and practical arrangements, Jonas trains the law students in the facts of life their text books don't admit to. We plan together but divide tasks tactically—some get done more effectively if you are black, some if you are white. It's Jonas who does the township contacts, I who deal with recalcitrant officials. Together we create something neither of us could have done alone—

But only a friend? Dad does not ask, and neither do I. Jonas is Jonas, I am me. Working together we touch a freedom that neither of us would risk disturbing. This friendship matters too much to expose it to the unpredictability of desire.

And then I walk into the students' union building to see Jonas talking to the golden man of that first demonstration—

—They stand outlined against the light from the window. My pulse is suddenly perceptible, but I can't tell who it's speeding up for—maybe the juxtaposition, each tall body speaking in a different way of a thing desired, just out of reach…I join them, trying to feel casual. 'This is Kevin,' Jonas says, 'he's a full-time student organiser, travelling the country between campuses. He's asking about the prison visitors' project'…'Brilliant concept,' Kevin says, and after lectures are over we go to his flat to talk about it. How it started, having to hassle the prison authorities when relatives of political prisoners were being refused the visits they were entitled to; raising funds for families who were missing visits because they couldn't afford the journey…Jonas has to leave before me, he has a long journey home. I stay, while Kevin cooks a meal. 'You're a born organiser,' he tells me. Soon he's lending me books, using me as a sounding board for his own ideas. He urges me to stand for the students' union executive. I am excited, awed; but once I'm on, I discover it's just more of what Jonas and I are already doing. Now we're constantly a threesome, discussing, planning, travelling together to meetings in other towns; and by some unspoken process that none of us ever alludes to, the balance shifts. It becomes evident that Kevin and I are the pair, Jonas the friend.

It doesn't occur to me to ask myself if I like this man. He is Kevin, and he is making it clear that he wants me. I am bowled over.

4

For months—I see it now—we existed in a state of heightened, unadmitted sexual awareness. Not just Jonas and I, Kevin and I, all of us. In the women's residence we sat on each other's beds late into the night listening avidly to what he did or said, or maybe *might* say (or do?) next time. But the talk was of love (Do you *really* love him? Are you sure he's serious?) Desire itself we did not speak of, for we had no words, never having heard any—even I, from a household with no embarrassment about bodies, sharing a bathroom with four brothers whose pale penises dangled innocuous as Dad's hairy scrotum. But that naturalness itself belied the existence of troublesome urges…A huddle in the quadrangle at school…Gwendolyn said, 'Your breasts grow if you let your boyfriend touch them'…Lena said, 'It's not true'…I lay in the bath staring down at my hopeful bumps, thinking I'd be prepared to test the theory but for the regrettable absence of a boyfriend. It was clear to me from my experience of parties (two) that the boys went for the girls who already *had* good breasts, not ones like me who, however developed their minds and imaginations, still had nothing worth buying a bra for…

Now here I was confronted by the possibility of the real thing, and my own body was a stranger, pulse quickening when I least knew how to handle it, or interpret it. Or even who it was that had set it off.

The first time Kevin and I made love I was so bombarded with unfamiliar and arousing sensations that I didn't know whether I liked it or not, only that I was finally doing it. Then he was off travelling again. I longed, I fantasized. He came back—we started to make love—it was sweeping me along, then something in me blocked. I had no idea why, where it was coming from. I just knew I wanted to say 'No'. I could not tell Kevin or he might go away. He had had lovers before—it must be my inexperience that was the problem. I would just try harder. But trying was like hiding, I wasn't sure any more what was real feeling and what the thing I thought I ought to be feeling. I seemed trapped in a sort of dishonesty I would not have believed possible for myself.

The deception wasn't even successful. Kevin sensed—his hands removed themselves. He got up from the bed. I curled up inside, longing for it to be different. 'It's probably the voice of your mother,' he said, 'warning you not to.' That roused me, but not to desire. 'Not *my* mother,' I said. A generic mother, he said, inside every good small-town girl. 'All those messages you've been hearing all your life. Friends, films, women's magazines.' I said, 'I hardly ever *saw* a women's magazine.' But my body seemed to have heard anyway. 'Go on the pill,' he said—and I clutched eagerly at this possible straw, much better than putting that thing on him before my own desire had a chance to surface. But the pill needed a prescription, the prescription needed a visit to a doctor, the doctor needed to know why I needed the pill. He gave me a lecture and handed me some leaflets on sexually transmitted diseases. I left, feeling ill already.

This is nonsense, I told myself; and I returned to face the doctor. And now there was a little round holder of pills in my bag along with my toothbrush as I signed out of the residence and walked down the mountainside to Kevin's flat. But Kevin was so urgent, and though the person inside me still thirsted for that validation of being desired, my body kept up its silent sabotage...Discovering I had forgotten to take the pill. Feeling too tired. Lying too still when he wanted to be passionate...till I finally understood that it wasn't just the voice, the doctor's or anyone else's, it was me, choosing. My body and my spirit choosing NO to Kevin but not knowing how to fit that with wanting what he represented.

This is a mess, I have to get out of it.

December, the long summer break. Having to go home for the holidays seems a regrettable interruption of more important activities, the meetings, the late night discussions. But ten minutes at home and the regret is behind me. The garden—my own room—hours with no pressure. Temperature in the high nineties, the borehole pump working overtime. 'I'm wilting, like my garden,' Mom says, and I think of the Scotland of her childhood stories, and that perhaps her body has never adapted to being transplanted. To me the heat is a native land. I float about in the neighbour's water tank, draped over the inner tube of a tractor tyre—bottom in the water, legs and arms dangling, giving an occasional flip to push my tube and create a small breeze. Large straw hat for shade, I read my way through Engels' *The origin of the family, private property and the state*. It has the jacket of another book—Kevin's copy, secretly lent since of course it is banned. I fantasize about what I will say if anyone from the neighbour's household comes down to the tank and asks me what I am reading. But of course they don't. It would never occur to them that one of Frank and Catriona's children could be involved in anything illegal; and anyway, one book is much like another to them.

I am used to space, I tell myself, space to work things out in my own time. The garden, the water tank, the slow drifting afternoon symbolise that space, the freedom to be. The way Dad's eyes laugh, loving me for what I am; that way he has of giving his complete attention, really listening to learn, not to judge. It's *that* I like in Jonas, that indefinable ease that allows me to be just who I am. Why is it that Kevin seems driven always to demand more, to push through to whatever small hiding-place of self I might have retreated to?

Out of the tank, back over the fence...a rug under the maple tree...talking to Dad...About Jonas. Not about Kevin.

I did talk to Mom about him, once. It was late afternoon, just beginning to get cooler. I was sitting on the grass pulling up the occasional weed near where she dug and planted. It was near the end of my holiday and my mind was already beginning to reorient itself to going back. She said, 'You haven't said much about Kevin,' and it all came out, all the things that bothered me about him. Not the sex itself, but the things about *him* that got expressed in it, the way his needs pushed, denying mine. Trying to work it out for myself by having to explain it to someone else...

Mom dug and shook the earth off bulbs, and finally said, simply, 'It sounds as if you've decided.'

Then I left on the overnight train, and when I arrived Kevin was at the station to meet me, though we hadn't arranged it. And in that moment of greeting there was something vulnerable about his face, as if he hadn't been sure I would come and it really mattered that I did. So I just hugged him hello and thought I would wait a day or two, for the right time.

5

I was definite that I wasn't going to stay the night. But we got into an argument—Kevin started saying things about Jonas, nothing specific but the kind of pointed innuendo I can't stand, about not being so sure any more that Jonas could be trusted. Things had been happening, he said—'What things?' I demanded—but he wouldn't say. I became fiercely defensive, and in the intensity forgot about getting back before the residence locked up for the night.

I should have told him then that I wasn't going to share his bed any more, but it was impossible to think of trying to explain why, with the tension of the argument still between us. So I just said, 'I'm tired,' and before he could suggest anything I turned my back on him, pretending sleep. Tomorrow, I told myself, tomorrow we talk—

—Awake, instantly, staring in the dark…A tapping at the window, someone calling softly, urgently, *'Kevin, Kevin.'* I lie rigid. I can see nothing—total dark…shake Kevin awake…

Now I recognise the voice—Jonas's younger brother. Open the door. He stumbles in, face bloody. 'Police,' he pants. 'Broke the place up. Wouldn't believe he—' His eyes flick round the room. 'He's not here?' I stare at Kevin. Why would Jonas be here? Kevin avoids my eyes—he knows something I don't know. The fear in the room is palpable, almost a smell—

I turn back to Jonas's brother. 'Your face,' I say—so painful I can't bear it. 'Let me wash it.' But he winces to the touch. Then he's gone, to try other places.

The moment the door closes Kevin is tripswitched into frantic activity. He scrabbles to the back of his cupboard to reach a rucksack, opening one drawer, deciding against it, pulling open another. 'My wallet, for Christ's sake where's my wallet?'—Calculating out loud, 'Someone must have tipped him off. I *told* you'—Voice rattling on, words pouring out chaotically. 'He wanted to cut off from the rest of us. I had to hold him back. It would have been crazy, doing anything so public.' His eyes move constantly, like a trapped animal's—

I am staring, watching this stranger whose life and whose bed I have shared, going to pieces before my eyes, and I feel no compassion, only a blind protective anger for Jonas.

'Kevin, what were you doing?'

He looks blankly at me, as if he has forgotten that I don't know. 'Carrying messages.' Words detached, barely linking...Leaders in exile, across the border, north...people in the townships here, forming underground groups...Jonas had the contacts...Gordon tested out border crossings, safer for whites...

All that travelling Kevin was doing; student meetings, he said—His voice cuts across again like a slap—'For Christ's sake, woman, move. *Don't you understand?*'

Eyes staring, shocked now into full concentration—me too. If they're after Jonas and Kevin, there's no way they'll leave me free.

I didn't know, screams someone inside me. But no one's listening.

Chapter 2

The road is as empty as the land we travel through, stretching out ahead of us into the early-morning dark. I sit hunched defensively in the passenger seat and keep looking in the mirror to see if there's anything coming up behind. Nothing but an occasional farm lorry, a few long distance trucks. I tense up as each one approaches; when it passes I return to a numbed state, blocking out the past few hours, unable to think coherently about what might happen next. The fear is so extreme it is almost unfeelable, like water that's either very hot or very cold but you can't tell which.

I try to steady myself by concentrating on the moving shapes of the land, scarcely visible silhouettes of low bushes that come towards us and slip silently past. The distant hills move more slowly than the bushes, but more irrevocably. Rock outline gradually sharpening against the sky, till we are opposite—then gone.

Kevin does most of the driving. Every couple of hours I insist on taking a turn, but I drive badly when I'm tense and his need to be in control is so blatant that I feel attacked every minute I'm behind the wheel. I say, 'Kevin, *please*. Close your eyes, get some rest.' When it gets too much I pull up and hand over to him. Out into that heat again, worse than in the car, but at least it's open. Stretch my legs, touch earth briefly. Then back, trapped again in this moving capsule.

Ahead of us some sheep wander on to the road. Kevin's leg shifts to change gear. I watch the way his thighs fill his tight shorts like sausages coming out of their skins. I move instinctively closer to the window.

A small town—Kevin slows down. It's nine in the morning and we've been travelling five hours on no food. There's one greasy cafe; we buy a couple of buns and a newspaper. While he fills up the car I scan the headlines. Nothing about Jonas or anyone else we know, but that means nothing, it's too soon. Momentarily I see Jonas's face again, but no laugh in his wide mouth now. I hear his voice—'You can't escape it, Jennie, none of us can.'—Eyes unexpectedly hard, like an older brother telling me it's time I grew up—

Kevin is watching me, a question unstated. He won't say Jonas's name. I stuff the newspaper into a bin. 'Nothing there,' I say.

We climb back in, he starts the car. Silence as we drive off again. I go back to staring out of the window, calculating when we'll be level with home. Pointless, because we've left the main road and are keeping much further to the west—a less obvious route if anyone starts trying to track us...The land is drier here than any I have lived in, but still I feel it is being torn from me, or I from it. I'm by-passing home, no chance even to say goodbye.

It's afternoon by the time we reach the city. Fear clamps in again as we approach—the cars, the people, all of them a potential threat. A police car sirens towards us. Kevin swerves, too violently...When it has passed we stare ahead, each dealing silently with our own panic.

We keep to backstreets, stock up on food and water. We need to find a carhire place—too dangerous to keep using Kevin's car, the registration number will give us away...We transfer our clobber, drive both cars off in convoy a few miles out of town in the direction opposite to where we're heading. We abandon his car on an empty stretch of road, then in the hired car turn back east, towards the border.

After a couple of hours we leave the main road. Onto a smaller one that wanders off towards a distant small town…then branching off that before we reach the town, on to what seems like a farm road. I'm supposed to be map reading but the roads don't fit what's on the map. Kevin is tense with irritation. He turns onto a scarcely used track…

Eventually he pulls up, takes the map from me, and climbs out. He spreads it open on the car bonnet and begins calculating with a compass. I get out and go to sit on a stone several feet away, putting necessary distance between us. The numbed shock has begun to recede but I am now fighting an out-of-control hostility, the need to turn on him my misery and confusion at having landed in this appalling situation. I try to summon reason—I know that without his preplanning we wouldn't even have got this far. But it's only because of him that we need to. *He* chose to do what he did, knowing the risks; I wasn't trusted enough to be given the option, but I am being dragged along by the consequences, my life slashed across by my association with him—

He announces that we are not where we should have been but are almost certainly within a few miles of the border. Time to ditch the car and walk. I have no way of knowing whether he's right but it makes no difference. I have no choice but to keep following him.

We stare at the clobber in the back of the car—can't possibly carry it all. Load up Kevin's backpack with the food and water, a slingbag for me with extra clothes. Then out across the bush… Almost it's a relief to be walking; but the car was a protection. We are creatures without a shell now, vulnerable to any bird that circles.

Dusk, light fading fast. Arms and legs torn from pushing through thorn bushes. Exhaustion so extreme we are almost beyond speaking. No idea where we are, but pointless going on. Find somewhere semi-protected for the night. I crouch up against a rock, several yards away from Kevin but close enough to keep at bay the fear of sleeping alone in this place that only the insects have not abandoned. Huddle inside my thin clothes. Mosquitos whine, ominous as helicopters—

I wake, cold and stiff, to a place of boulders and scratchy grass; empty of people. It's not yet dawn. Kevin is sitting up. We do not speak, simply look at each other, taking in what we have woken to. We each move a little way off to pee. Return, to eat, but sparingly—we don't know how long the food may have to last.

Set off again, straight into the sun that hovers eye-height on the horizon…The heat builds up, the hours blur. Mesmeric movement, legs pushing through exhaustion, no choice about each next step. Watch the bumpy movement of Kevin's backpack, sweat streaking the dust down the backs of his legs—muscles taut, veins standing out…Climb down into a valley, struggle up to the top of the next rise. Never any arrival, just another hill beyond that one.

2

It was late afternoon when we saw them. I cannot say how, but I began to be aware that we were no longer alone in this landscape. At almost the same moment I sensed that Kevin too had felt it. We stared at each other, alert as deer but without the instincts that would tell us the precise moment to leap away. We stood motionless, eyes searching the scrubby bushes for a sign of movement. Then it was my ears that told me, not my eyes—voices, down at the bottom of the dip in the land, somewhere around the stream—

—We move to crouching position, Kevin behind a tree, I behind a rock. Now I see them, figures moving about in the water, and the voices become stronger as the slight wind changes direction. There are three of them, and they are women. They stand in the water several feet from each other, their bodies bending supplely from the waist as they beat clothes against rocks and dunk them in the water. The cloths that wrap round their hips for skirts are hitched up, and the moisture on their brown legs catches the slanting sunlight. They call out to each other as if they are much further apart, a loud uninhibited conversation that turns abruptly into song. One begins and after a few notes the others join in. The song lifts, circles the hills like a bird—

I come to, to discover that Kevin is standing up, gesturing to me to follow as he starts down towards them. The song has stopped, they have straighened up and are staring…Now they're talking to each other, fast…We wait a little way from them and try to greet in a way that shows we are friendly. At least our bedraggled state must make it clear that we need help. There is some more discussion, then they sign to us to follow, up the hill on the other side of the stream to a collection of huts…A mangy dog sets up a racket as we get near, then backs, unsure. An old man emerges from one of the huts—legs rough and horny, his body bent from negotiating the low door, not able to fully straighten again.

He seems to have a few words of English. Kevin tries to make him understand that we are hikers who have lost our way. Can he tell us where the nearest town is? My body is rigid, preparing to resist whatever the answer will be—

'Mbabane,' says the man, nodding his head towards the hills. Mbabane, Swaziland. So we have made it.

I see myself as if I am someone else it is happening to. I am standing a little to one side, leaving Kevin to do the talking. I am clearly there, but almost not inside my own body. I don't know what I feel—tired, hungry, miserable, relieved. All of them, none of them. Past feeling.

Eventually I become aware that a group of children has gathered around me, staring and giggling. They are half naked, their brown bodies covered in fine dust. On each small chest hangs a rough necklace made of things that look like seeds. Perhaps charms to keep them safe? Legs and arms skinny, toughened by use. I notice now that the older ones do have clothes—tatty garments hanging loosely off shoulders. It's the little ones who are naked.

The curiosity of so many pairs of eyes begins to penetrate the layers of non-feeling. I am seeing them properly now, these small people, wanting to know about me. I stretch out my hand. They back, still curious but shy. Then one of them dares to say something—the others giggle. I make a silly face, they hoot with laughter. A woman summons them. Reluctantly they move further away.

A younger woman takes me by the hand and leads me down to the stream, to a point behind some bushes, motioning that I may want to wash. She sits on the bank and watches as I take off my outer clothes and stand barefoot in the shallow water, splashing off the dust and grime and sweat. Then it seems absurd to stand like that so I take off my underclothes too and lie down on the rough stones, letting the stream wash over me; an emotional act as much as a physical one, letting go of the awfulness of the past interminable days, letting the water wash it all away. I look up to see my companion still staring at me, fascinated. I smile. She smiles back. What is she noticing? Is this very different from the way she washes, then? Or is it my pale skin that she is so absorbed in studying?

I pat myself half dry with my T-shirt, put my clothes back on my still-damp body, and we climb back up to the huts. By now Kevin has pulled out the last of our food and put it with what the women have prepared. We eat together, Kevin, the old man and I, while the women hover and watch, commenting to each other on our every movement. I ask the old man if they are not going to join us. He says, 'Later, later.' I try not to eat too much, conscious of all those children's eyes. When we have finished the women eat, and after them the children.

It is almost dark now, but no one moves to prepare for sleep. We sit around the light of one small brazier, Kevin and I crosslegged, the others squatting. The tiredness that earlier seemed overwhelming has fallen away, my inner eye and ear racing now to absorb the hours since the sound of the women's voices in the stream lifted me out of isolation and fear…A full moon, the night sky clear…

The voices move quietly around me, accepting my presence without needing to notice it. Someone starts to sing, a simple, meditative phrase, and then other voices answer, call and response. The words scarcely lift on the slow tune, the words have no specific meaning for me…just sound sifting with the moonlight I watch the old man's head, bent as he listens. This place, these people—this is their ordinary reality that I have landed in, arriving from nowhere. Being part of it rescues me from the unreality of all that has been happening to me, connecting me again to where I am, who I am. The flicker of brazier light touches the children's faces, and I am again a child, listening as they listen—

—Standing on a chair near to Aunt Floss, watching the record go round as it creates the sounds and the pictures and the feelings which neither of us needs to speak about…

From somewhere deep inside the house Aunt Maimie's sharp old voice calls, 'Who is it?' but it's only Jennie, so she doesn't bother to come out. I think about how Aunt Maimie is all angles and edges, mouth straight as the lid of a box snapping closed, while everything about Aunt Floss is soft—cheeks soft with powder, voice gentle but a private amusement nestling inside it. She opens the door to me each time I come with quiet graciousness, invites me in to perch, legs dangling, on the old fashioned chairs of the dark living room. She asks whether I would like a glass of lemonade, and she carries it in, two glasses served on a tray with a lace doily. I watch the way her skin hangs in soft folds from the upper part of her thin arms…She says, 'Shall we go to the porch?' and we escape together, to the only part of the house that is truly Aunt Floss's. We sit on wicker armchairs, looking out on to a side garden of sweet peas and nasturtiums, all growing in grateful profusion. She does not ask me what I have been doing, nor give me instructions, we just sit and watch the sweet peas…Wire gauze filters the sunlight…I sit like a grown up, legs carefully crossed…

I say, quite suddenly, 'I'm going now,' and Aunt Floss accepts it as she accepts everything about me. She gets up to accompany me back through the dark rooms. 'Can we see the gramophone first?' I ask, and we go into the room where it stands on a chest of drawers. She puts a chair in place so that I can stand at the right height, and I watch as she lifts the cloth that covers it, embroidered with daffodils. 'What will it be today?' she asks, though she knows the answer. I say, 'The Moonlight one.' She takes it out of its sleeve and puts it on the turntable, but she lets me hold the long brass arm with the needle and lower it on to the edge of the moving black circle—not too far in, or I will miss the first sounds, so quiet they are like silence moving. We stand to listen to it, I on my chair, Aunt Floss next to me, and we wait for the moment when that stillness will become a little dance—

The women are moving about, beginning to spread out grass mats on the floors of the huts. Kevin is to share the old man's hut, I am to sleep in another with two of the women and some of the smaller children…Sleep to the memory of voices in the stream, rising, circling. To Richard's flute calling, my own body swaying to the dance I have never seen. The green land rolling endlessly.

3

The children walk with us to the point where we join the track that leads to the road. We wave down the first lorry that appears. The driver signs to us to climb in at the back…Winding down through the hills, to a collection of buildings clustered in the hollow like pebbles. 'Mbabane', says the notice at the petrol station. We climb off, wave our thanks; the lorry drives on.

I wait outside while Kevin phones Tom to come and pick us up. I have never heard him mention Tom before, but it seems they were at school together. What will he think, us arriving, destitute? I hold my aloneness, willing him to be a long time, wanting no one to come near while I take in that the border is behind us, the nightmare journey over. Safe; but no return. Life can start again; but what kind of a life I have no idea, except that it will have almost no point of connection with the previous one.

I sit in the back of Tom's car, with Kevin in the front doing the explaining. At first I sit tensely, monitoring. Then I am overcome by tiredness and retreat into myself.

We arrive at the house. Tom instructs the Swazi houseservant to get the spare room ready for us. As soon as I feel it is decently possible I leave Tom and Kevin sitting out on the patio drinking and take a quick look around the house. Only one bedroom apart from Tom's and it has a double bed. Tom didn't ask, he just assumed. Or maybe he did ask, when I had cut out.

I am suddenly shaky with misery, and at the same time with relief at having arrived where someone else will take responsibility for seeing that we are fed and can stay quietly out of sight until we hear what has been happening to our friends. I want only to curl up into a ball and sleep, even if it has to be in the same bed as Kevin.

The bed is large. I position myself with my back to him, right over on my side. I wake in the night to the knowledge of having to hide, and realise it's only mosquitos again, whining insidiously right next to my ear. But in that moment of waking and being afraid I saw Jonas again, still fleeing...And then a memory of Kevin talking about him in an unnaturally edgy way, full of innuendo. Not saying anything specific, just, 'I'm not so sure about him any more.'

I turn over. Kevin's body is sprawled, arm flung in a strange position, tense even in sleep. His hair sticks to his forehead with sweat like a boy's, his breathing slightly laboured. He could be one of my brothers, his male half-naked body as familiar as theirs—

NO. I cannot afford to let myself feel those things. I turn my back, shutting him out.

The newspapers arrive in Mbabane from across the border; same day, but late. Tom brings them home and we scour them. The events we have escaped from are front-page news. Five of our friends arrested in one early morning swoop; now in solitary confinement, being questioned.

Still no mention of Jonas.

Keep low, for God's sake keep low, wherever you are.

We stay inside. We are afraid to go anywhere in case we are recognised—in case we have to tell anyone our names, and they connect us with what has been in the papers. In case—

But I don't know what to fear, so the fear is pervasive.

I watch Kevin's face. It is closed up, set rigid to keep his tension under control. I turn away, feeling fiercely resentful. I can't lose the awareness of his fear but he isn't even noticing mine.

Night, and Kevin moves as if to lie close to me. I am out of bed before I even realise it, and have taken myself off to the sofa in the living room. Kevin follows me. 'This is ridiculous,' he says. The strength of my physical recoiling is so overpowering that I do not trust myself to discuss it. I say simply, 'It's finished, Kevin. We're stuck in this hole together and I know we have to help each other get out of it, but I can only cope if you accept that we're separate. *I don't want you to touch me.*' He stares at me, then says, 'For God's sake come back to bed. Tom might come in and see you there.'

I do it, because I haven't the energy to work out what else to do.

We lie on opposite edges again, backs to each other. I do not sleep, just lie there; and in the interminable dark hours the rejection works its way through my whole system, till by morning I know what it is that I accuse him of—that he trapped me, made me feel I could not leave because he needed me—and then kept me ignorant of the one thing that above all others I had a right to know.

Kevin Cartwright and Jennie de Villiers, close associates of those already arrested...thought to have gone underground—

I stare at the words, then hand the newspaper back to Tom, overcome once again by disbelief. Gone underground. Kevin maybe, not me. I see the words as Mom and Dad will be seeing them. I have to let them know I'm safe. Kevin watches me suspiciously. Before I can even speak he says, 'It's not safe to contact anyone.'

His decision again, his judgement; but I do not know how to set myself up against it, for in making that judgement he may know more than he will tell me.

I am beginning to understand that our arrival on foot over the border was not particularly unusual. There are others like us, a straggling eastward trail, like animals migrating from an environment increasingly hostile. The exiles form almost a little colony of their own, incestuously analysing the politics of back home, unable to let go, yet excluded from having a role. It seems the Swaziland authorities know they are here but have decided not to notice. Those who have been here longer have jobs and houses and friends and appear to lead normal lives—except that they are always wary, for every few years someone has disappeared, to reappear in a jail across the border. Here they are apparently free but they experience another kind of imprisonment—no papers to prove that they are allowed to exist, no passports that might let them move—trapped forever in this small landlocked country. People with no future, and even the past is distorted—the stories of how they left are narratives set in concrete, a form they can handle, all sign of real emotion buried. There is a brittleness about them, their surface normality splitting easily to reveal the tension they never lose. Listening to them unnerves me. I cannot live my life like that, always feeling half a person.

There must be another way. Get out, out at least from this house that is no part of who I am. Learn the streets and people's faces of this new place, not trying to claw back what is gone.

It's a strange household, Tom and Kevin and me. Tom had no idea that we might be arriving—how could he? But he accepts his role and seems glad of the company. He and Kevin sit for hours drinking and talking in the evenings. They make gestures of including me, but mostly I opt out. They share a language I don't want to learn, acquired at the elite school that gave Kevin the air of unconscious arrogance that was the cause of most of our tension in the months before Jonas's brother tapping at the window thrust between us something more cataclysmic. Tom has lived half his life in Swaziland but hardly seems to connect. He learnt far too young to direct the activities of people he can see only as uneducated labourers. At weekends he heads for Johannesburg. A few hours' drive, and he re-establishes contact with what he regards as the civilised world; a show, a meal. We have so little in common that had we met in any other circumstances we would scarcely have noticed each other. But he is kind—inarticulately, but exceptionally so; and in my vulnerable state that means more than any other single quality. I feel for him what a stray dog must feel towards the new owner who gives it a home—my gratitude is absolute.

Kevin and I have settled into a sullen truce, like a middle-aged couple who are past feeling warm about each other but are too trapped by the habit of life together to be able to contemplate separation. I don't want to live in the same house as him, much less the same bed, but I have nowhere else to go. He accepts my refusal of all intimacy, but he will not talk about it.

Each time he watches Tom set off for Johannesburg he retreats into a morose state. And as Kevin watches the departing car, I watch Kevin. I try not to but I can't avoid it, or avoid knowing that his state of withdrawal is not healthy. I know I am partly the cause of that, but only partly, and I also know there is nothing I can do about it, so to survive I try to detach myself. There are things he could be doing to help himself, people here who would help him—who are themselves in touch with the exiled leadership he once worked for. With them at least he could talk seriously. But he avoids anyone with a political history. Perhaps he thinks they judge him a coward for having run? Perhaps it's just instinctive self-protection—life has pushed him too far, so he keeps away from people who might expect something?

'You don't even talk to Tom,' I say, one of those moments of desperately trying to shift the weight of him on to anyone else. He stares at me—Tom's about the only person he does speak to. But not about anything real. 'Why cut yourself off from your one possible source of support? This absurd pretence you keep up, about us.'

Kevin turns away and I have no energy to force the issue. Tom is his friend, it's his business what he chooses to tell him.

I leave him, and get out. I have a passionate need to find work, to find my own place, not to have to eat any longer what Tom and Kevin provide for me. But again I am humbled into submission. I have no qualifications. The only money I have ever earned was doing a Saturday job in the children's library in Bloemfontein—where Aunt Ellie was the librarian and there was no question even of an interview. I have never learnt to type, a thing I belatedly realise is more necessary to a woman than any amount of formal education. Even more to the point, I appear to be automatically excluded from the only two categories of work available. Jobs in offices or shops need a work permit, which I cannot get because my presence in the country is not legalised. Jobs in people's homes, like cleaning or cooking or looking after children, cannot be done by white people. Here the issue isn't work permits, but a vast pool of unemployment.

Kevin gets work without trying, taken on as an accountant on the estate Tom's father owns and on which Tom is, at twenty-four, already a senior manager. Kevin knows nothing about accounts, but with patronage no one asks about qualifications or work permits. Tom offers to try to do something similar for me—I cannot accept. Not accepting means I remain totally dependent. Because I am dependent, whatever they do is bound to be wrong. I know I am being childish, I know I can't go on like this, but the determination to find my own way out is now as primitive as my revulsion at being touched by Kevin. It is in fact the same thing—

Out, and up. Out of this house that traps me, the offices that will not have me, up into the hills that rise in all directions around this straggling small town…Hitch a lift to where the buildings give up, and then begin to climb—red-earth dust, boulders, a belt of trees, and over the first hump to the hills beyond. Past the occasional settler farmhouse, small collections of labourers' huts. Women squatting as they scrub pots with ash, children scurrying to stare—*Mlungu*, they call—look, a white person. White people do not walk and get dusty as Swazi do, they drive in cars and look always casually comfortable…

I stop, and squat to be at child's eye level, and try to defuse the strangeness with the few words of Swazi I have learnt. Cautiously at first then with increasing confidence, I hear my own voice echoing the voices around me, the sounds of the women in the hills, who helped me understand that out of this disaster that has overtaken my life something new may open up.

4

I am sitting on a lump of concrete that some builder has carelessly left outside a newly constructed office block. I let the sweat sit on my dusty forehead, not bothering any more to wipe it away. I have reached that point in the day where I wonder if it's worth the effort of going into yet another building to ask about work, when the hills that surround the town are so beautiful, and the sun so beguiling, and the clothes of the women so colourful, and I could so easily be content just sitting here if I could stop bothering about the fact that I will go home to Kevin and Tom's food.

I become aware that someone is standing in front of me. A young Swazi woman, probably my own age but in school uniform with a bag of books. 'You are a dreamer!' she says, and squats facing me as naturally as the women in the hills.

'I'm escaping,' I say, 'taking a break from looking for work.'

The laughter spreads over her mouth. '*Mlungu*, walking the streets, looking for work!'

'I need work,' I say, 'the way anyone else needs work, because I don't have any money.'

She is curious now. 'What kind of work?'

'Anything anyone will pay me for.'

She pats her bag of books. 'You can help me with my English.'

'You don't need any help!'

'Tell my teachers that.' She pulls out an exercise book. An essay on *Adam Bede*, covered in red marks. I read a couple of lines. Her writing is stilted, quite unlike her speech. I cannot imagine this direct, laughing person turning out these passed-down literary comments.

'Why *Adam Bede?*' I ask.

That is clearly a really stupid question. 'It's in the syllabus,' she says. Another curious pause. 'Have you read it?'

'Yes.'

'Did you understand it? All those words?'

'Yes, but English is my language. And I can tell you how to write a better essay about it—write the way you speak.'

She stares. 'You *are* mad.' She leans forward, face right near mine, 'You show me how to write essays like the white kids and I'll ask my uncle to pay you.'

Her name, I learn on the way to her uncle's house, is Charity. The white kids are her fellow students at a school for sons and daughters of the privileged classes, the old white one and the new Swazi one. 'And the politicals,' Charity says—children of varying colours, sent across the border into Swaziland for an education not limited by apartheid. 'You're a political, aren't you?' she says.

I like this woman. 'How did you know?'

'What other *mlungu* sits on the road in the dust looking for work?' She bursts into laughter and so do I—laughing for the first time for weeks, laughing not because anything is funny, but simply in the relief of being with someone warm and natural and female. And then in a second wave, at the absurdity of where I have landed, what I am doing. It goes on and on, we infect each other, become hysterical. Charity can have no idea what has set me off but she laughs as much as I do, till eventually we both come to an end from exhaustion. She says, still breathless, 'There's a teacher at my school—he's a political too. He's mad, like you. He also says things like "Why *Adam Bede*?"'

I am instantly sober. 'And he got a work permit?' Charity knows nothing about work permits. But she takes me to the school to meet the head teacher, who explains with a quiet smile that yes, a full-time teacher would need a work permit, but the school also has a need for part-timers to give extra tuition in English. Then, as if he is having a conversation about the weather, he asks about my university course, unfinished, never now to be finished, and lacking that final piece of paper, of no interest to any normal would-be employer. But this one simply listens politely to the list of courses, then nods in an almost offhand way. He is short of several tutor hours a week, he says. If I would be interested…?

I am interested. I am exhilarated. I dance out of his office to find Charity waiting and she takes me home to celebrate. Her aunt regards me as a waif in need of care. I am. I accept from her what I could not learn to accept with any grace from Kevin or even Tom—food, companionship, a place to sleep. And this is so much more, a household full of people, expansive, generous…I lie in the dark, and feel for the first time in weeks a slight release in my hold on the watchfulness that has become instinctive, necessary defence against the unknown; and all the feelings I have tried so hard to shut down come clamouring to reclaim their space…The child's cry of unfairness at having my home snatched from me before I was ready…My last summer, that I did not properly notice at the time, for I did not know it would be my last—I want it back now, passionately, and all the summers before it. I search my memory for every sensation I can reconstruct…Movement everywhere, shared jokes, laughter, as each brother in turn arrives home and Mom and I make up another bed, get in still larger supplies of food. I help her push furniture around to make room for the extra mattress we have borrowed from Aunt Ellie—where did we all fit when everyone still lived at home? She and I share an unspoken, unnecessary-to-be-spoken, female satisfaction in getting the nest ready, in seeing it filled, in the bustle and noise of too many people needing to use the bathroom at the same time. Richard's flute sounding again in the house, Trevor and Edward's noisy irritations. In the kitchen Radio Bantu turns out Morning Service at full volume, African voices in deep swathes of harmony, *Praise to the Lord, the Almighty, the King of Creation*—chords I can move with, but the words in Tswana, while Annie bangs pots and mashes up potato. Mom has all her end-of-term chores—marking exam papers, reports, but she's also at her most available, as if something in her is released as her brood gradually reassembles. She stops feeling it's so necessary to get everything done and lets herself be persuaded to sit at the piano and play while we gather round and sing, just playing straight off the songs we ask for, making up chords with her left hand as she goes along. The silly songs Dad used to teach us on those journeys down to the coast, three of us squashed in the back and the other two taking their turn in the cousins' car that drove down in convoy with us—more leg room in their car but more fun in ours. Singing *The Darkies' Sunday School*, or the one about a man who took his horse to have its toenails pointed. And the one we saved for the moment when the car groaned its way to the top of the last mountain pass, and we tipped over the edge—and there was the sea stretching out before us—

And what did we see? We saw the sea.
And the Pacific wasn't terrific
And the Atlantic wasn't gigantic—

I go with Dad to the station, a re-enactment from all the years of older brothers coming and going, and I, the youngest, always at home...Decembers with the temperature unrelenting, punctuated only by thunderstorms; or July mornings with the ground trapped in frost—Dad waking me, already in his thick coat, saying, 'Are you sure you want to come?'—a ritual only, for I never missed. Out to the car, the frozen blades of grass cracking with small sharp sounds under our feet. Standing on the platform, hands painful with cold, breath steaming, watching for the train to come puffing its way in. People clambering off, suitcases piling out, porters running about loading luggage on trolleys. Edward's head emerging from a window, a pile of disorderly blond hair ruffled with sleep, a teasing joke in his eyes. Running to the window as he leans out to scoop me up into a hug—

But Edward has gone, left years ago, sailing off to England; and then after some more years to America. His departure seemed to me full of significance, like a parable—the brother who never came back. Mom and Dad waited for his letters with more longing than either of them liked to admit, and when one finally came they shared it around with the aunts, who had hardly heard of the places Edward wrote of, but who told everyone that Frank and Catriona must be *so* proud of that boy, doing so well with all his scholarships. For Mom it wasn't the doing so well that mattered, just the getting of letters.

I was the only one who knew he wasn't coming back. He told me before he left, and he made me swear not to tell the others. If he came back, he said, the army would get him…I saw the army as a relentless metallic monster, needing to be fed young men. 'That's exactly what it is,' said Edward. 'Richard and Trevor were lucky to leave school before the law changed.' But that still left Peter; and each Christmas after that when all of us except Edward gathered round the piano to sing, and someone would say, 'I wonder if Edward will be here next Christmas,' I was the only one who knew he wouldn't; and I remembered what was waiting for Peter…

Watching Peter, marking the changes. He got taller every time you looked, fit and muscular from all that hockey practice, the beginnings of hair on his chest…while I was still small and skinny as a grasshopper, acting the children's parts in the plays Mom and Dad produced. I used to feel his mind was going in a different direction from his body. He was trying to be like the boys at school, moving in the same hip-slouched way, listening to the same records, but it never came naturally to him, I knew—and I knew Peter better than anyone. When his mood changed subtly, I knew it before there were any obvious signs. He had flashes of confidentiality when he sat on my bed late at night and told me things that had happened among his friends at school, and I blossomed in this rare openness and told him about mine. But these were like a momentary return to the level of our childhood secret club, letting each other in on things one wouldn't tell the grownups—

I listened powerless as people around us acted as if it were normal for young men to be taken by the army, almost a necessary initiation into male adulthood. 'The army was called in'—that impersonal statement on the news, which in a couple of years would mean Peter being commanded to fire on young black people in the townships…I couldn't talk to him about it, for the patterns between us were set—I could do nothing except be there if he decided to open up. But how could people not see that their sons and brothers were being trained to kill? And did they think it right that when anyone was honest enough to refuse, he was sent to prison, and when his two years were up, sent straight back again if he still would not submit?

My friend Gwendolyn said pointedly, 'My brother *likes* the army.'

'Peter's different,' I said.

'In what way different?'

I wanted to say, 'You *know* Peter.' But maybe she didn't. Maybe she was taken in by the air he tried to cultivate of being cool, to hide the thoughtful, sensitive things about him—

—December, my last December, and Peter is there before me. Lying on his bed for hours just lying, not reading. Back from the army, but not on leave; a breakdown, they said. Discharged, medically unfit...I hear Dad saying, 'Jennie, tell Peter dinner's ready.' Peter gets up and comes to sit at the table as one who has been ordered. He eats almost nothing, says nothing. If we chat on, it is as if we are ignoring his depression. If we don't, it makes things worse, turning on him the artificial spotlight of our silence.

He cannot talk about what happened. But I am too used to tuning in, I cannot lose the habit. What he does not describe I begin to see for myself, the men who all these months have ruled his life. They have legs of immense, packed power, booted feet planted, belted hips threatening. And I see without needing to have been there how Peter did what they told him to do, but to the letter, and took his real self away deep inside where they couldn't reach him; retreated so far in his misery that after a few months his tormentors could find no one left inside this shell to command—

It wasn't just Peter who was different, it was all of us, all five of us who grew up in the island of sanity Mom and Dad created just by being who they are. We all learnt to defend ourselves from lies, to reject those who fanned hatred. But there was a cost—and Peter had to pay, for all of us. Another ancient story, but far more troubling than Edward's; the unspoilt youth, sacrificed so the rest of the village could be spared...And now I too—

No—it cannot be happening this way. I try to fill my ears with the chords that will hold it all together. Mom—I must find Mom—I go from room to room, searching. She is in the kitchen, waiting for the kettle to boil; standing alone, staring at nothing. 'Mom?' I ask. We look at each other silently for a moment. She says, as if we are already in the middle of a conversation, 'Peter must *know* we don't think him a failure.' But it's a question more than a statement, a miserable, self-blaming question that she cannot ask him direct. I put my arms around her as if I were the parent, she the child. She accepts it silently, her head buried up against mine. 'I understand why all that awfulness was too much for him. But I don't know why he's not getting better. It's over a month now that he's been back—'

My hand is stroking her hair, grey and oddly dry to the touch. There is nothing to say. She moves as if to detach herself, as if it is wrong to be putting her burdens on me. 'Stay a moment more,' I say, and I keep holding. Her. Peter, as he was before. Dad in the garden under the maple tree. Stay a moment more.

5

'Tom was circling the whole bloody town looking for you,' Kevin shouts. I shout back, becoming the adolescent he thinks me, 'No one asked Tom to be responsible for me.' Then my words come back to accuse me, for I ask Tom precisely that, every day, by continuing to live here, eating his food. I go to find him. 'I'm sorry,' I say, and I really am. 'It just happened—I didn't know myself I was going to stay.' He says, 'Forget it,' but there's something evasive about his manner. I see now that he has today's paper, folded open, and he's hoping I won't notice. I see the words STUDENTS CHARGED. I hold out my hand. He passes it to me…Black law student arrested after massive police alert…Jonas Nkosane, thought to be the key figure in a country-wide network recruiting white students to a banned organisation, was arrested while attempting to escape to Botswana—

My eyes sting, I can hardly hold the words—

Police have urged parents not to protect those still in hiding—

I look up. Kevin is standing there, eyes waiting for me, flashing the warning—No letters, no messages.

It's not safe, I know it. To keep silent is not Kevin's decision only, it is mine too. But the misery of not knowing is theirs.

I walk out into the hills that have become my place of retreat. I have been trying so laboriously to put it all away where it can no longer damage me, the life I have lost, the hurt I have caused in leaving, the pain of knowing that Jonas is left behind, to carry the punishment I have evaded. Punishment for what? For wanting so simple a thing, that we should live well together, with equal dignity...I see his eyes, and feel overwhelmed that I allowed myself to be allied with Kevin and not with him. *I didn't choose*, I call out silently across the chasms that separate us. It just seemed to happen, like so many other things...His eyes follow me, and his voice—'You can't escape it Jennie'...I had no idea what he was talking about but I was afraid, for the words connected with things I had seen and heard but had never fully faced up to, that no one would ever explain—

—There in the night-dark of childhood fear, as I press my nose against the window-pane, to watch the still darker figures appearing noiselessly round the corner of the house, into the outhouse where Gertruida sleeps...I can tell from the way their bodies move that most of them are men, and I don't understand where they come from. The only African men I see are labourers, arriving when a roof needs mending, a new tap fitted; and Gertruida who works in the house stands at the kitchen door when they're taking a tea break, and talks in that expansive, uninhibited way that fascinates me and that I know the white adults don't like. When the job is done, the men go away again, somewhere else. Yet here they are almost every Saturday night, appearing silently in the dark...

I sleep, but warily; and wake again only a few hours later, to the noise of loud laughter, louder arguments...Then Dad's voice, cold to the point of rudeness when the neighbour arrives, and I know that something serious is happening because Dad's talking to him at the door instead of inviting him in. Complaints about rowdy servants are charged with menace in a way that complaints about rowdy children can never be...Gertruida's voice, bad-tempered for days afterwards, taking it out on me when no one else is there, but still no one tells me what it's about...

Another night, suppertime, and the police arrive. *Goeie naand, meneer de Villiers*—'Good evening, Mr de Villiers'—one of them went to Dad's school, he says, and I hear in his voice the habit of respect struggling uncomfortably with his duty. Dad is unnaturally controlled as he says, 'I see no reason for you to search her room. I guarantee there will be no further complaints.'

Gertruida goes on leave; we all take turns making supper. But then Dad is driving her things to Bochabela township, and a woman called Annie moves in. I keep my distance, from Annie, from Dad...Now he is taking me on his lap, saying, 'Jennie, we need to talk.' Do I understand why Gertruida had to leave? he asks No, I do not. She was brewing *skokiaan*, he explains. (I see the cardboard boxes under her bed, and hear her voice sharply telling me to leave them alone.) It's against the law for Africans to buy alcohol, so women like Gertruida brew it secretly. The law is wrong, but once the police knew, Gertruida was in danger. If he hadn't asked her to leave, she and her friends might have been put in jail...

His voice is calm, rational, but it does not blot out those other sounds, the loud laughter of the parties Mom and Dad have, when the play one of them has been acting in or producing is over, and Mom plays old-time favourites and everyone sings *Foggy Foggy*

Dew in raucous voices. And I sing too, watching in fascination as the men get drunker and begin to droop sentimentally over other men's wives. And when I can keep awake no longer I go to bed to the sound of singing and laughing, louder by far than Gertruida's parties. But the neighbours never complain, or the police come—

I don't want them to come. But I don't want the burden of that unfairness. And I am angry with Dad that he cannot take it away—

I have arrived—I don't know how—at the road by which Kevin and I first came in to town. I stand for a few moments taking it in, then wave to a passing lorry, heading out. It stops, picks me up. 'Where to?' the driver asks. I hear myself say, 'I don't know the name of the place, but I'll recognise it when we get there.' And now for the first time I realise where I am going. The driver looks at me strangely but accepts it, drives on. We bump over the uneven road, the hills lurch drunkenly through the windscreen. It's a relief, being on the move. I shift position, supporting myself against the jolting as I feel in my pocket to check if I have any money on me. A few coins, one small note. This is crazy...The noise of the engine blots out all possibility of speech. It throbs, a low heavy rhythm, becoming repeated words—Jonas is in prison. And I am free...

It would not help if I were there too. But still.

Jonas chose to do what he was doing, knowing. Would I have chosen? *Should* I have chosen, if they had given me the chance? Chosen to be where Jonas is now? How could anyone choose that? Surely you only choose to act if you convince yourself it will never come to that? But something stopped them asking me. Telling me, even. Jonas was right to keep me ignorant, and Kevin wrong. That's irrational, I know, but it's what I feel...It was days after we had arrived in Swaziland before I confronted him—'I want to know why,' I demanded, cold now with the anger I had tried too long to suppress. His eyes blanked out, iron guards against pain. I saw it, but I couldn't listen to it now. 'Kevin, tell me.'

He said, 'It was Gordon. He thought you were too—' He couldn't bring himself to say it. 'Gordon was in charge of the network. We all agreed to accept his decisions on security.'

'Too *what?*'

'Naive,' he said reluctantly. 'That you might not realise how dangerous it was.'

It was Gordon who thought it, but Kevin's voice I heard it from. *Too naive*—my indignation swept over them both, flailing powerless at being relegated to the status of a child, a girl child, by these people who thought themselves men—

—The driver shifts gear as the road becomes steeper. I jolt back to alertness, not to miss the point where the small track joins the road. 'I think it's somewhere near here,' I say. He glances at me, eyebrows raised, but he says nothing. Is he suspicious, or just protective? Do I give *everyone* the message that I am naive? *That's not who I am,* I want to say...But who am I? How did I get here? I, who spent my childhood drifting around the garden and the veld, making patterns with leaves and twigs, listening to sounds that no one else noticed...Watching...Maybe that was part of it, born into a world already peopled by larger creatures who moved constantly, and I always watching, listening...

Watching from the safety of the apricot tree as Trevor leads his backyard cricketers up on to the garage roof, to prance about on the corrugated iron—a deafening noise and a calculated one, to get back at the stuffy neighbours. Peter hangs about at the base of the ladder. He wants to go up but Trevor shouts at him, he's too small. If Mom sees, she'll say it's dangerous and stop them all... Now Edward is going up—he doesn't want to, but it takes less effort to give in to Trevor than to resist when he's in that marshalling-the-troops mood. Something's going to happen—Edward is long and gangly, limbs growing too fast for his instincts to keep up with.

The roof slopes, the other boys dance wildly. Edward slips, falls from the roof. The boys shout in panic, people come running, Peter retreats to join me in the apricot tree. The ambulance arrives, lights swirling…Now it is gone, taking Edward and Mom with it, and I watch in even greater awe as Dad's rare anger sweeps over Trevor, and I wonder why it doesn't annihilate him…

Then the days go by, and Edward's plaster of Paris slowly fills up with maths equations and messages from his friends, and Trevor bounces back to test the limits yet again—

—Watching, noticing, learning those other limits…Aunt Ellie reads her church magazine and gets cross with the self righteousness—'They've no idea what loving your neighbour means'—but she doesn't stop going to church…Mom reads the papers out a sense of duty that she ought to stay informed, but she says the world is in such a mess she can't think of anything she can do about it, and goes out to the garden to thin the irises…In the bathroom where Dad is shaving the radio drones on—'Police have fired on crowds assembled outside parliament.' Snap—the voice is cut off. Dad mutters angrily…I push it to the back of my mind through the scramble of breakfast, gathering up the books I need for the day, getting my bike out of the garage. Alone cycling to school the voice returns, hatefully detached, as if announcing an upturn in the price of wheat. Why do we all accept it, as if it's normal for the police to shoot people?…In the history lesson I ask why Africans don't have the vote. Miss Joubert is afraid even to have heard, let alone answer. 'We have to stick to the syllabus,' she says. The next lesson I sit at the back of the class, ostentatiously reading a novel, and Miss Joubert is too cowardly to prevent me. At break my friends gather round, admiring my defiance but uncomprehending. 'You can't let the natives take everything away from us,' they say—

—The lorry rounds a corner and suddenly I see the track. I call out but we are past it already. The driver pulls up. 'Sure you know where you're going?' he asks. 'Yes,' I say. 'It's fine. Honestly.' I climb out, thank him. I want him to go, before he can ask any more questions...Now I am alone at the roadside, in the dust of the disappearing lorry. I start to walk. Now that I'm here it's all printed on my brain, every detail of this track. I can't remember how it's going to be past where I can see, but with each hundred yards further the next bit comes back to me. Just let my feet go where they are going—

—'We have to stick to the syllabus,' they all say. Don't ask, don't question. It's naive to think you can do anything, just learn the facts in the book...I can't do it, and I can't understand how everyone else can, even my brothers...What's happened to Richard, who used to come home in university holidays when I was still a child, lighting my imagination with stories of torchlight parades? Thousands of voices raised together singing *Nkosi Sikelele Afrika*, God bless Africa—African hymn become the symbol of the liberation of the spirit...Now even his political spark seems to have gone dormant. Trevor and Edward never had one. Peter's preoccupied, in front of the mirror seeing if Brylcreem will make his hair stay down...

I have to do something, now. I lie awake in the dark running through the options...Every few months electricity pylons get blown up. That means people sitting together at night planning how to do it, instead of lying alone uselessly as I do. Where do they find each other? And where do you get explosives? And *me*, doing something so dangerous, so illegal?...A letter to the paper, maybe? All right, it isn't much, but you have to start somewhere...But they all know Dad, someone's bound to ask, 'Do you think it's OK to print this letter from Frank de Villiers' daughter?' And they'll give him a ring to check, and Dad will come and talk to me about it—making it deliberately light, perhaps, teasing me as if I were still a little girl; or he'll sit down seriously with me and say that he honours my strong feelings and high principles, and of course he agrees with what I wrote, but it won't change anything, so maybe I should think about it a little first. And though I'll accuse him of double standards, and retire to my room indignantly, of course I'll give in—with his face looking so serious, and all that tolerance...It'll have to be something separate from Dad, from the whole family. And better if I don't do it alone. Maybe I can persuade Gwendolyn?

The plan comes to me. We will write to the Prime Minister, Gwendolyn and I. He's always making speeches about the youth being the country's future. All right, we'll tell him what the youth think. He's a horrible man but maybe there's some remnant of conscience in him that can be shocked into action if someone with no political advantage to gain stands up and says, Listen, this is wrong—

I compose the letter, and show it to Gwendolyn. It isn't as difficult as I'd expected to persuade her to sign it—it seems no more risky than talking back to one of the teachers. Easier, in a way—if he writes a stinging reply it still won't be as bad as being shouted at directly. We choose a time to post it when few people are around, the after-lunch haze. We stand a little away from the pillar box and look up and down the street first. Gwendolyn says, 'I'm not holding it.' I say, 'It won't make any difference, we both signed it.' She says, 'You made me, I would never have thought of it myself,' which is so clearly true that I don't continue arguing but drop it in quickly before her panic can begin to affect me.

Now we wait. To Annie, who took Gertruida's place in our kitchen, I say, 'If there's a letter for me, please hide it in my room. I don't want Mom or Dad to see.' I want to tell her what the letter will be, for suddenly we seem on the same side, Annie and I. But even without my telling she seems surprisingly co-operative. Perhaps she thinks I have a boyfriend.

For two weeks nothing happens. Then I am summoned to the headmistress's office. Her face is blotchy-red, her voice hysterical.

The accusations fly at me like slaps—'Leading an otherwise sensible girl like Gwendolyn into this Outrageous Behaviour'—My pulse is pounding. All I can think is, Gwendolyn's gone and told her parents—I *should* have done it alone—'Dragging the School's Name into the Mud. Do you not realise we may be Banned from Participation in National Events?'—She vests in each word the weight of a pronouncement from on high—'Do you think the government will believe that a pair of schoolgirls would be capable of coming up with a letter like that?'—I am trembling, but the unreasonableness of this last attack rallies my indignation. 'You don't even know what's in it,' I say, 'and *no one* helped me.' That I dare to defend myself infuriates her further. I realise—She's afraid! The headmistress, afraid.

For days Gwendolyn and I avoid each other. It's all morally too confusing. She got me into trouble, but then I got her into trouble first. Where we expected to make an impact there has been none, and instead we have unleashed a terrifying battery of adult wrath much closer to home. When the headmistress phones Dad I can hear her voice all the way from my room, and Dad's voice cold—'It is entirely up to me how I will handle the matter.' I wait for his footseps to come towards my room. He says, 'I expect you heard that.' I nod. He says quietly, 'It sounds like you've had a lot to deal with,' and puts his arms round me while I pour out a confusion of defiance and panic and tears, feeling far guiltier than if he had shouted and banned me from going out after school for a week, as Gwendolyn's father did. Dad listens, listening to learn, to understand what I thought, and felt, and how it happened. Then he says all the things I knew he would say, about honouring my strong convictions, but maybe—

—I stop walking. It's there, the collection of huts, I know it's there, over that next hill. And now that I am almost there I feel foolish; I don't know why I have come. If I had thought about it properly first I would have brought presents, to thank them. I have come again as I came last time, with nothing except myself, asking for help. And not even the words to do it with.

There are people at the huts, and they see me coming. They point, and exclaim. The women talk excitedly and seem to have forgotten I don't understand. The children have almost lost their shyness. They hover during the greetings, and follow me wherever I move, and this time no one tries to draw them away. One of the older ones starts to point to things and tells me their names. The others gather and are convulsed at my attempts to say the words. The women take up the game; half-testing, they gesture that I can help prepare the food. When I take the wooden ladle and start stirring, they hold on to each other with laughter. The laughter is pointed but it also feels like an acceptance, the way it did the first night when they sat by the fire, talking over me, just letting me be there.

No way of getting back before dark, so I sleep again on the floor of the hut, sleep with a sense of homecoming that comforts the ache of knowing how totally I am cut off from where I really belong.

6

With Jonas arrested something shifted inside me. While he was still trying to hide, so was I—from the reality of what had become of us. Now he was in the worst place it was possible to be, and I was stuck here, and nothing could be done except to try and deal with what was.

With my first earnings from the school I negotiated with Tom a ridiculously small amount that was all he would accept towards my keep. The rest I saved towards the unknown, unimaginable moment when something might change and it might be necessary to move again—fast, and this time alone. Meanwhile Charity's aunt's constantly changing household was there whenever I needed a break, or female company, or the coming and going of people of all ages. No one had any privacy or would even have understood the concept, and I slept on whichever bit of floor seemed at the time convenient. But it was like sleeping in the hut in the hills, the ground received me, and I emerged ready to return to Tom's house; calmer and with a modicum of graciousness.

Charity shows me a photo of herself in her first town school uniform—a group of small girls of ten or eleven, and amongst them this buxom young woman, full breasts squashed into the same straight up and down pinafore…We are the same age, almost exactly, but she is still struggling to catch up with the formal education that for me was simply part of the structure of childhood. In this house we shed the absurdity that classifies me as the adult, her teacher, while she still is bound by school rules. The years before she ever got to school have given her a down-to-earth maturity that is way beyond mine. She grew up in a village, given in infancy to her grandmother to comfort her. 'That's why I am called Charity,' she says, 'child given in love.' And because her grandmother had no desire to lose her to school, as she had lost the others, Charity stayed in the village, learning the things that mattered—to carry water, gather firewood, take care of younger cousins—while her town brothers and sisters, or cousins, she was never sure which, sat in straight rows and copied the alphabet…'My aunt used to visit the village, and always brought me something. Then one day she told me, you are coming back with me, to go to school. And I learnt that she was my mother!'…Charity takes it all as it comes, the being-given, the being-taken-away. I listen to learn, I who am still fighting my own sense of having being prematurely removed. Learning from her, and from the others whom I tutor in the school—

New people, new issues. The effect is so invigorating that it cannot be dulled even by the domination of the syllabus, which insists that I train Charity and her friends to express opinions they cannot possibly feel, in vocabulary they will never hear used.

Their lives suggest material for scores of essays more stimulating than those the teachers set. I do what seems to me the obvious thing, and try at least to link what they have to study with the reality they experience. But real issues are dangerous, it seems, even here; the headteacher is not pleased to discover that we have been comparing witchcraft in Swaziland (which is Superstition) to that in *Macbeth* (which is Literature.) In any case, he says, these are not questions that will come up in the exam. So we drag ourselves back to the syllabus, and wait till the bell has gone to talk about the rest.

Reality, unreality. We live, Kevin and I and the others who have fled, in a strange state of suspension, never clear which level of life is the real one. Because we have to, we make a new present, which is in fact the only one we have. Though at first we do not think of these as our people—for ours are the other side of the border—these here are the only ones we ever see, the ones we meet and talk to each day; and so they become in the end perhaps more important than the ones we are missing, who dominate our dreams and fears, our hidden sense of guilt and failure. At one moment the real world for me is Charity and the school, and the delight of waking to the mist that covers the morning, watching it drift and concentrate into strands of cloud and then gradually lift away, opening up the hills—

Then each new day's newspapers arrive and we are yanked back to where our lives are really being decided. We scour the reports to piece together the details of a past we only half understood while we lived it, a future we have only half escaped. For Kevin the very act of reading about the trial churns up all he still cannot resolve in himself. Perhaps it would have been better to be with the others now, taking responsibility. They at least are publicly known to have acted on what they believed; he cannot raise his head. He never talks about Jonas; each new detail uncovered makes it clear that Jonas knew more than he did, was in it before him—that in fact he, Kevin, was naive. The one person who seems to have known it all is Nick, a man Kevin thought his friend, a reliable colleague—as perhaps then he was. Now he stands in the witness box giving evidence against all the others. Once the trial is over he will be taken under armed guard and put on a plane, out of the country, never to return; freedom in return for betrayal. Kevin's eyes are wild—'I hope he rots in hell,' he says—but Nick evokes more than curses. Fear, of himself, of what he might have done if *he* had been tortured.

My pain is less existential, more for the people I know. I scan the page first for any reference to Jonas. Then Leonie, a woman I met at a conference, once—but here's a photo of her appearing in court, and she is so altered, thin faced and drawn, her suffering so obvious it gets inside me and almost feels my own. And with each new report I think of Mom and Dad reading it, their only way of connecting with me.

Gradually the balance between caution and acceptance settles within me, and I know that whatever the risk I have to let Mom and Dad know I am safe. Nothing needs to be written; Tom can see Richard when he's next in Johannesburg, and Richard will be visiting Bloemfontein. Tom will do it if I ask him, and not tell Kevin.

Wherever I look there are hills. *This* now is the shape of my land. Childhood was the edge of a town that grew out of the dusty veld, stretching flat in all directions. For the first moments of adulthood I perched on a mountain side with the sea behind me, on the southern tip of the continent, looking north. Now I am part of that once unknown interior to which I looked, and I am surrounded on all sides by hills. Hills where I walk, hills where I sat with the women on the ground, legs splayed, preparing food—

—It is time to go back. I have begun to understand that those women who first received me have already taken me beyond the limitations of my own narrow experience—they who scratch the simplest of livings out of a landscape that does not look as if it can sustain life, with their men nowhere to be seen. Gone to the mines, presumably, which is only another kind of imprisonment. I want to learn how they manage with almost nothing—for having nothing, as I now do, I have begun to understand that finally the only security is in yourself. I think of them singing as they work, in the stream, in the fields, winnowing grain with that deft flick of the wrist that holds the flat baskets, singing so naturally that they forget about me squatting there in the dust listening, my body absorbing the rhythms that move theirs, learning the pace of time.

This time I prepare for the visit; town-bought food for the women, clothes for the children. 'Do you want to come?' I ask Kevin. I don't want him to, but encountering them was his experience as much as mine and I don't feel I have the right to keep it to myself. He says, 'I can't face it.' I don't understand—there is no burden in going, just pleasure. Then I see he cannot think of the people without remembering what took us there. It is his own history he cannot face.

But Charity comes; and with her to interpret, all that was potential comes vividly to life. She slips without self-consciousness into being one among the younger women, bending her knees in respect to greet her seniors. I am grateful for the chance to watch while they talk, the attention off me. The greetings seem to take a long time—I see now how unnecessarily sudden I must seem. Then she explains who this strange white woman is who appears out of nowhere and then disappears again. They listen, faces wide with interest, but they do not seem to think the story unusual; evading oppressive authorities is nothing new. What interests them more is what we can tell them of Mbabane. 'They're asking if you're going to keep coming,' Charity says, and one of the women points to the clothes I brought the children, volubly lifting the cloth that winds round her waist, showing how faded it is. The presents have opened a door I am not going to know how to close—impossible to explain to people who have as little as these that I don't have lots of money. Charity is embarrassed for them. 'They shouldn't ask you like that,' she says, and it is a while before she will interpret again.

Later I ask if they can teach me the song they were singing in the stream the day Kevin and I arrived. They laugh—There are so many songs, they say. Was it this one? No? Maybe this? Then they forget about finding my song and sing another, and Charity joins them in a voice that seems never to have known the Beatles. Their bodies move—the dance is part of the song—and the children giggle hysterically as I try to follow, this *mlungu* earnestly trying to do the hip swaying and feet rhythms and shoulder-and-breast shaking that every girl knows from childhood how to do. The singing too—I can see I am going to have to learn a new way of using my voice. Mine seems to have an unnatural damper that stops it lifting as theirs do, opening out to carry over the stream and the hills. Once I almost free it, and I recognise the sound immediately, something that is natural to me, not their way that I am borrowing. *This* is the way I should always have been singing, but for the accident of having lived too much inside buildings.

I leave Charity with the other women and go and sit near the old man. He seems to have an odd position in the village—they respect him because he is old but he is half recluse, speaking little, preferring to sit on his own and play the *mbira*, a little wooden box that he holds in both hands, pressing down with his thumbs on the metal strips that are set like piano keys across its top. He accepts me sitting silently next to him, listening as he plays. I don't feel it disturbs him, because it is obvious *he* chooses when he will be disturbed.

After a while Charity comes to squat next to me. She says, 'No one else around here plays those.'

'How did he get it?'

She asks him. Patiently, one question, then a suitable pause before the next. Eventually she tells me, 'He's travelled a lot. Down to the coast, Mozambique, up to Rhodesia, with men he met in the mines.'

The old man goes on playing as she speaks. I have the feeling he could have understood but he's not interested in tuning in. His mind is off elsewhere, following the mesmeric patterns of sound that his thumbs draw out of this simple box. Some women come and stand near us. They start explaining. 'They say he's got more of them,' Charity relays. 'Some small like this one, one big, inside a calabash. Every time he came back he brought another. Other people bring back radios and saucepans from the mines, this one goes off to Rhodesia and brings back another mbira!'

The thumbs move so fast I can hardly follow them. It is like watching a drummer, the rhythms dancing and crossing. Charity says, 'They say someone bewitched him with mbira music and now he can't let it go.' And I too long to get inside those rhythms, to feel in my own thumbs how they work—

Back to Mbabane…To Tom's house, and the newspapers, and the long wait for the trial that never comes to an end. To another night on the edge of the bed that Kevin and I share but do not share; to the future that cannot be planned and so is best pushed out of sight—

I become aware—I don't know how—that something is changing in Kevin's state. I see it each time Tom goes to Johannesburg, a greater restlessness, waiting for his return. Messages being carried, that I am not being told about? I am caught in a morass of contradictory feelings. Suspicion—but then I hid from Kevin the one message I asked Tom to take. Indignation that Kevin allows himself something he will not allow me—then an internal voice that says, There is no reason why he should tell me, I am constantly making it clear that we are separate…But I have learnt the hard way that what he does cannot but affect me—

Put it aside. Nothing I can do but wait, and be alert. Back to the day' s work—to the school, and the syllabus someone else has set. And then put that aside, and get on with making my own connections.

In the kitchen of Charity's aunt's house, I practise speaking with the house servant, Simangele. She wants to learn English, I want to learn kiSwati, so we have set up a mutually satisfying trade in basic phrases. She is Charity's distant cousin, I discover, though her position in the house is hardly different from that of the servants I grew up with. She watches, envious, as I write the sounds of the phrases I am trying to learn—and it becomes obvious that what she wants most is to be able to *read*. We begin with the letters that make up her name; but when I try to move on to simple kiSwati words, she dismisses this as firmly as Charity dismissed my 'Why *Adam Bede?*' It is English she wants to read, whether she understands it or not. Writing is about access to that other world, she doesn't want to learn something that will keep her where she is. The Mahlalela household laughs at us both, at me for my impractical notions of education, and at her for thinking she can get anywhere other than their kitchen. We pay no attention, Simangele and I. We keep teaching each other and enjoy ourselves.

Now Mrs Mahlalela herself develops ideas about how to fill my time. She produces a second student for me from the hospital, an orderly who starts to come in the afternoons before going on night duty. Then a young boy who works in her garden, hacking away at the grass with a long-bladed panga—he had to leave school because his parents couldn't pay the fees. 'He should learn something,' Mrs Mahlalele says firmly, as if he has been deliberately wasting the gifts God gave him. 'He can't spend his whole life cutting the grass.'

The classes grow. We move from the kitchen to group under the trees, and from there to an outhouse when it rains. There are too many now for me to handle, so I ask around to find others who can teach—and find them among the wives of expatriates—road engineers, agriculturalists. The wives have servants to take care of the children, and little to do while their men are at work. The first I recruit—Marilyn, a Canadian—says, 'But I've no idea how to teach.' I say, 'Neither did I until a few months ago,' but I am realising now, that's not true. It seems I know instinctively, just from having grown up as Mom and Dad's child, the way boys whose fathers are mechanics know how cars work without needing formal training. Yet I too have never till now taught anyone to read or write, nor maths, which is what the boy who works in the garden passionately wants, nor any of the other things each new student comes up with. The basic principle, formed in reaction against everything I know about schools—the one I lived through and what Charity has to put up with now—is that there is *no syllabus*. We teach people things they themselves decide they want to learn, and we work out as we go along how to do it, watching to see what works. Charity and her friends do the kiSwati bits, and the *mlungus* do the English. When I am sitting with Simangele and the others, watching their discovery that they can do this thing which they have always assumed was beyond them, I feel happy in a way that lifts me clear of any miseries of my own. I begin to recapture a sense of possibilities. Perhaps after all we *can* try to remake the world.

Mlungu, mlungu, the children still call in the hills above Mbabane. I ask Charity, 'How long will it take to get past being *mlungu?*'

'And be what?' she asks.

'*Umuntfu*, maybe.' Not a white person, just a person. Charity laughs and tells me how the old people used to frighten the children by saying, '*Mlungu* will come and get you!' I carry in my skin the sins of people who aren't even my ancestors—the traders who exploited them, the missionaries who told them they were immoral, the government officials who imposed a hut tax that drove men to the mines, changing forever the fabric of family life. Charity just laughs and says, 'You want to change history?'

7

The trial is over. Jonas, seven years, Leonie four. Gordon, thirteen. We have known for weeks now that it would end this way but it casts us both into depression. For once I actually seek Kevin's company, the only person with whom it is possible to share what this means. But by late afternoon I know have to get out.

I walk blindly, not noticing time or place, until I see that the light is fading. Within ten minutes I can see almost nothing except the trees right in front of me. I stop, not knowing what to do. I want to cry, but there are no tears. I want to shout, but there is no one who will hear. I am alone, and I do not know what will become of me. For so long life has been suspended while we waited for the trial to end—but what did we think would change then for us? There is nothing now to wait for. I try to summon the energy to start finding my way back but I feel weighted by listlessness. I search my memory for things that can sustain me; all I can find is the people I have failed. My own people, whom I have found no way to tell all that keeps me close to them while I seem so totally cut off. Jonas, trying to help me grow up, but no one else can do it for you. Why did I back off from loving him when there was still a chance? I was afraid, afraid of so many things I refused even to give names to—

Ahead of me through the trees something moves. My breath waits. An animal of some sort? That wouldn't bother me. A person—that would be different. I sit absolutely still, watching, waiting—

I must stop this. I have to find the things in me that are strong. I have to survive, to build something new. But I cannot think, there are too many small sounds that come at me from strange directions. Night fear is creeping over me, night, and the image of what they have been doing to Jonas. Night, and the weight of all the nights he will sleep in a cell—

It is Tom who finds me, and loads me into his car as if I am a runaway child. My body is shivering, my mind numb. He takes me home. Kevin is asleep, with the smell of alcohol permeating the room. The numbness has begun to recede. I try to thank Tom. He brushes it aside in embarrassment. 'You'd better get warm,' he says.

By morning it is possible to think rationally. Their case is finished, but ours remains open. Return will always remain impossible, and our safety questionable while we are so near the border. But there seems less chance of active surveillance. It is agreed that we will still avoid the post office, but that Tom can carry letters…Reality, unreality—Nothing that matters can be written about. No reference to who among those convicted are my friends, to what has been my connection with them; nothing of how we walked across the border. And Kevin? I remember my last real conversation with Mom—'It sounds as if you've decided,' she said, and the next she heard was the newspaper telling her Kevin and I had disappeared together. What did she make of it all? That I'd changed my mind? Has she been thinking, 'At least she's not alone'? It will not help to disturb that comforting image. So much has changed in me, so much thinking and feeling to try to communicate, but it has to be done elliptically—

Late at night. Letter written, and I am churned up with unaccustomed feeling. I look up to see Kevin watching me. He says, 'There's something I need to tell you. I've applied for a British passport.'

I am speechless.

'My father was born in Britain,' he says. *Now* I see—the messages to and from Johannesburg—birth certificates—and this accident in the fifty-year-old past now miraculously gives him the possibility of a future. Within weeks he will have in his hands that small navy blue book that will open up all borders, except the one that is forever behind us. He will be free to move—while I am stuck, still without any piece of paper to allow me to be where I am, let alone go anywhere else—

A momentary surge of hope—Mom was born in Scotland, perhaps I too? But in the morning the High Commission regrets to inform me that the right to nationality passes only through fathers. I stare in disbelief. All those cliches about motherland, mother country, mother tongue, all the things that make up identity, but when it's rights only the men get them. I walk out, no energy even to argue.

What got into me, to allow myself to drift on climbing hills and learning Swazi dances and helping people practise how to write their names, as if all were now taken care of? Why do I have to keep kick-starting myself into growing up? *There is no one else*—if I don't act nothing will be resolved. But what?

'You could marry Kevin,' Tom says, as if it is obvious. And now I see that it should have been, that this is what Kevin has been offering, but couldn't say. Marry Kevin! It is without question the thing I most do not want to do. But already my fierce, instinctive *No!* is being held back by the knowledge that I am caught. It is only by marrying him that I can begin to extricate myself from what my disastrous relationship with him has landed me in—

'I need to think,' I say.

Tom sets off with the letters. He will give them to Richard, who will take them to Bloemfontein when he is able. Another weekend Tom will collect a reply—but Richard said, 'Wait,' and scribbled an instant response, and looked out some photos to send me—

I retreat to the hill behind the house, to devour them alone. The photos are mostly from the last time we were together. I study the faces avidly, taking in details I once hardly bothered to notice. Peter looking grey and strained. Richard, long nose, thoughtful eyes, like that old photo of our Scots grandfather whom I never knew. He's lying on the lawn talking with his new love Patricia, the first time she had met any of us—and she's now his wife, with a child on the way…They've been laughing together until the camera caught them, but Patricia has looked up and her eyes have the beginnings of that reserved expression she had with the rest of us—

And now the feelings of the time come sweeping back to me, no simple nostalgia, but complex adult feelings. I see again how we must have appeared to Patricia. The noise and excitement of each new arrival, everyone hugging, talking, laughing—of course we hugged her too, but it wasn't her style. We asked about her family; she had grown up an only child—and now it was obvious she was besieged by sheer numbers. The jokes that didn't need explaining—but they did to her. The songs she didn't know the words of, so that music, our way of including everyone, left her out. Dad just carried on as normal; since Richard had chosen her, she was a member of the family already. But Mom felt responsible for making things go well and that made its own kind of anxious tension. I wondered if I was being like Mom, and I wished I could be meeting her on her own, separate from all this, but she was years older and for once I was shy. Anyway Richard wasn't giving anyone the chance. I didn't want to admit it but I was hurt. He didn't *do* anything hurtful, except not noticing that I had grown up—

Move on. A photo of Trevor, exuding health, lounging back in the garden chair as we sat eating supper outside, while his girlfriend never-quite-partner Jill stands behind him, curling her arms around his neck. Buxom and bouncy, she smiles glowingly, announcing to the camera her and Trevor's oneness…But she listened to the plans for Richard and Patricia's wedding with scarcely concealed envy. She joked about only ever seeing Trevor in white—in his doctor's coat, busy, or a distant figure on the cricket field. Trevor laughed and let it flow over him He seemed not to register what she was feeling, or to take it all as if it required nothing of him in return. He let Jill dangle herself around him, or sit at his feet, her soft sexual shape instinctively moulding itself against his muscular thighs. She met Trevor's every need—what cause had he to stir himself? He would go on accepting the drinks she poured for him and the meals she cooked for him, and then wander off to play another game of cricket, and she would go on longing for him to affirm and claim her…I can't bear looking at the photo, it prods at memories of how I was with Kevin in the first weeks. *Never* like this, surely?…

Leave it, it's the life that is finished. Useless to revisit it. Richard's letter—'All of us who love you have felt heavy at what life has handed out to you. But also proud, that you were indignant enough not to accept things that had to be rejected'…I feel crying starting, in my throat. Skip to the end, brief news of the lives I have been cut off from…Trevor, a new job…Edward, last heard of walking in the Grand Canyon…Peter, moved to East London, getting treatment but still far from better, not wanting any contact. Doesn't write or phone…Back to the first page, Richard's voice speaking directly to me while he made Tom wait, urgent to say what had remained unsaid for so long. 'Don't ever wonder if it was pointless. None of us know whether the little we are able to do makes any difference, but we need to do it just the same. If there are consequences we couldn't have foreseen, well, that just has to be accepted. The important thing is to live as a whole human being, not to let anyone stop you responding fully to the people and situations around you'—

Move on, move on.

Kevin and I sit to negotiate. Even after marrying it will be a year before I would be entitled to my own passport. That will mean him staying here all that time, when without me he would be free to go. But he says it's OK, he has no immediate plans for moving...I know I should feel grateful, but I cannot shake off the fear that I am putting myself even further under his control—and that he wants that more than he will admit—

I do not want to marry anyone. I want, passionately, to be left to be alone.

Another weekend, and Tom returns with a suitcase of my clothes, some of my books, and a fat envelope from Mom and Dad. Mom says, 'It wouldn't be possible to tell you what it meant to us to get your letter. Whatever happens, you know the love that is here for you, so draw on it.' Dad's voice, knowing me—'It seems you judge yourself to have been immature. Maybe, but that's where we all start. It's the journey that matters.'

No use resisting. There's only one route out, so take it.

The only witnesses to the cold ceremony in the registry office are Tom and my friend Marilyn from the classes. She suggests we go back to her house for tea afterwards. I know she will bake cakes to make it all nice, and I can't face the thought. But I am trying my best to be sensible.

Tea. Kevin and Tom leave; I stay on, and it is night before I return to Tom's house. No one in—they must have gone out drinking. I go to bed, grateful not to have to talk. I blank out almost immediately—

And am woken from a dream in which I am being pushed into a police van. I am kicking and screaming and wondering why no one seems to hear when the street is full of people. They all walk past as if what is happening to me is quite normal. My eyes flip open, to a smell of alcohol on Kevin's breath and his hands all over me, his body pressing. He seems not to realise that I have been asleep, and is unable to adjust to my being now awake and resisting violently. At first I cannot believe this is happening. We have been here before, Kevin and I, him asking with his pressing body, me pushing him away and removing myself, unable to speak in the strength of my rejection. He knows it, knows there is no point, knows it only makes things angry and difficult between us for weeks afterwards, that each time he has done it he has pushed me further away and it has taken longer before we can be civilised with each other again. In that first moment of waking I am angry with him for being so stupid as to try it again, and it is some minutes before I realise that what is happening now is something quite different—that he has pinioned me and I cannot get free of him, that there is a dreadful force in his thighs and hands as they hold me down, in his heaving body. A force that has nothing to do with desire, that is brutal, tearing my tense dry flesh. We flail against each other, each driven by a primitive need—to dominate, to escape. I scream continuously—

Suddenly Kevin lurches, groans, falls off me. I see Tom standing there, fists clenched. He yanks me off the bed into a standing position. I stare at him, almost unable to register. Then I am out of the room, and cowering on the corner of the sofa.

Tom appears. He stands a little away from me, looking at a loss. Silence now from the other room. I don't know what has happened between them and I don't want to know. I hear my voice sounding cold and definite—someone else's voice—as I say, 'Your car. I need to go.' He leaves the room and comes back with his keys and a selection of my clothes. He turns away while I dress, but waits. He doesn't ask where I am going but only says, 'Are you OK to drive yourself?' I have no energy for unnecessary words. I say, 'I'll be at Marilyn's.'

8

After that there was no question of sharing a bed with Kevin. Marilyn could hardly believe that I had gone on doing so all these months. She listened and rocked me in her arms as I cried, and tucked me up in bed like a child, but despite her unconditional support she was shocked that I had not sorted out my living arrangements better long before this. She never said, as I am sure others did when the story began to creep out, 'Well, what did she expect?' but she too found it hard to understand how I could have been so foolish. I tried to explain but it's difficult to get across to someone who has lived always the kind of sheltered life I did before Kevin and I had to leave—that when life thrusts you into a bizarre situation you cannot proceed on normal rules of logic, so you lose all sense of which of the things that used to seem obvious still apply.

With other people, nothing could have made me talk about it. The people who visited Marilyn's house and seemed surprised to find me there; people I met in town, who found ways to mention that they had seen Kevin. I despised them for their unspoken curiosity, was convinced they were waiting for a chance to judge, when they could know nothing about what either Kevin or I had felt, or what circumstances had pushed us into.

The only people apart from Marilyn and her husband Fred who ever knew about it from my telling were Charity and her aunt, and that was weeks later. They took an entirely practical view. Men are like that, it happens all the time. You protect yourself if you can, accommodate to what you can't change, and get on with life.

We are sitting together after dinner. Marilyn is writing a letter. Fred puts on a record and hands me the sleeve. It's his way of helping—he has been giving me silent messages of concern via Bach each evening. My eye drifts over the text—'reads' would be too large a word. The unaccompanied cello suites—I have never heard them, like most of Fred's music. This one gets to me, even more than the others. One instrument only, yet creating a dialogue with itself, and so many moods. I feel calmed by the mind behind these constantly moving sounds, so sure, knowing itself.

Fred says, 'I saw Tom today.'

I look up. I feel nothing.

'He says Kevin was drunk. Didn't know what he was doing.' Marilyn's eyes flash scorn but she says nothing. I realise, this is a planned conversation. Fred goes on. 'He very much regrets what happened.'

I receive this information coldly. 'Kevin used to tell me about his father. How he always swore that he was sorry, that he didn't know what had got in to him, on the mornings after the nights when he was violent.'

Fred does not give up. 'He is still willing to go ahead with the passport thing if you want to.'

I walk out of the room and go for a walk on the hill behind their house. I do not think, I just escape.

A week later I succumb to Marilyn and Fred's gentle pressure and allow them to arrange yet another meal at which Kevin and I will both be present. Tom guarantees that at no time will I be alone with Kevin. I see again Tom's towering body, his clenched fists, Kevin groaning from the blow…As if remembering lessons from an earlier life I realise that I have not thanked Tom. I ask Fred to take him a message from me.

We eat once again in civilised distance. Marilyn and Fred take care of the talking—all I have to do is be there, get used to it. After coffee they leave the three of us in the living room to negotiate a new arrangement. To maintain the fiction of the marriage I will leave my things where they are at Tom's house, and I will eat there most evenings, this being the time other people are likely to drop by and notice whether I am there or not. But I will sleep elsewhere, and these arrangements will be no concern of Tom and Kevin's. I will continue to pay Tom my contribution to the housekeeping—he looks pained and starts to protest, but then must see something in my face that makes him stop. He looks out of his depth, like an awkward boy confronted by adult emotions he doesn't understand. I feel a flush of intense affection for him, which has the effect of making me able to relax slightly with them both, as if his kindness redeems Kevin.

We begin again.

For weeks my state of mind fluctuates wildly between blanking it out, and being overcome. That Kevin and I no longer sleep in the same house liberates me and I acquire the fresh energy of a young animal. I am convinced that it's all finished, that life is now sane, normal. Marilyn's house runs on lines that create a sense of safety. She has a baby with soft chubby legs and breath that smells of milk, and I wake to the small sounds of a three-year-old peeping round the bedroom door, and Marilyn's voice some way behind saying, 'Leave her, Charlie, you can play with her later.' He sees my eyes are open, takes this as licence to ignore the voice, and comes bundling on to my tummy to be tickled. Childhood songs that have dropped from my consciousness for all the years since I was Charlie's age emerge from somewhere inside me now that they are required. We go for little walks, the baby tied on to my back with a brightly printed cloth, Charlie tugging at my hand if I stop to take in the view. He brushes carelessly past wildflowers of astonishing beauty, then suddenly applies complete concentration to the way an ant carries a fragment of grass. We collect a little pile of stones and examine the qualities of each new find. Weight, sharpness or smoothness, the colour and shine. I learn to see as he is seeing, to open up to that fascination with solid objects that adults lose because we are so ready to classify and generalise. For Charlie each rock is unique. I feel the continuities running through me—Charlie—the child I have been—the child I may one day have. The adult I am and yet am always about to become. The things I am cut off from but carry within me, a stream that runs underground whether I see it or not.

Marilyn says, 'You're lovely with Charlie, Jennie.' I am glad there is something small I can give her, in return for all she gives me. I say, 'It's mutual. Charlie's lovely for me.'

There are moments of lightness when the future begins to dance before me—open-ended possibilities—all the people I have not yet met, all the things there are still to experience. The passport that has dangled always out of my reach comes each week a little nearer.

Maybe I'll travel, I think. I observe Marilyn's life, wondering what mine will be. She has Ruth, the house servant, to tote the baby around, pick up after Charlie, prepare the children's food, wash the nappies, a line-full every day. Fred comes home to meals exquisitely prepared, a house calm and pleasant, and a wife who isn't tired from having made it so. They eat dinner by candlelight, the children tucked up in another part of the house. Then Fred listens to Bach and Schubert while Marilyn reads books on childcare. It is aeons removed from the life I have been living, or any I can envisage myself making. But it is loving, and I am grateful for their quiet assumption that I can be part of it whenever I need to be.

Then without warning the weight is back, pressing on me again, and no one else's borrowed calm can help me lift it. All it takes is a slight shift in the temperature over dinner in Tom's house, a small difference of opinion with Kevin that flares into a potential argument before I have realised it is happening, too sudden to take evasive action. The precarious balance inside me suddenly tips, and I can no longer bear to sit at the same table as him. Adrenalin starts surging through me, telling me against all reason to scream, to run. I force myself to stay quiet until the meal is over—I am not going to create a scene, not show how vulnerable I feel. The moment we get up from the table I am off, escaping again to Marilyn's.

Marilyn knows. She is sitting there with Fred in the living room, and for a few minutes we all three talk as if my sudden tense arrival is perfectly normal. Then she says something innocuous like, 'Let's go and see if the bed's made up,' though we all three know it always is. We go through to the spare bedroom, she comes in with me and closes the door, and I go straight to the bed, feeling I cannot stand one minute longer. She sits and holds me to her as I sob in my confusions that seem to be taking so long to work their way out. When I have cried myself out she brings a damp cloth for me to wipe my face, and tucks me up in bed. I manage a small laugh and say, It's so stupid to keep going on like this.'

She says, 'Don't worry if it's stupid. If you need to, you need to.'

I am lucky, I tell myself, repeating it, repeating it. I am one of the ones who got away. I parade before myself the people who have gone down in the flood, Jonas, Leonie, Gordon. I am out. I am free. If I have been made neurotic by having Kevin invade my body, think of what has been done to them, body and mind. But I feel I am becoming unbalanced, constantly being revisited by fragments from way back. They do not feel like stray memories—they follow me, will not leave me alone. I remember the lane at the side of our garden, I see pictures of myself and Peter as young children, playing carefully among the tumbleweed, or looking across to the low lying stretch of wasteland that each year's summer rains turned into a surreal lake, trees and bushes stranded, and then when the water subsided was strewn with debris and weird patterns of congealing mud—

—And now the sense of threat takes form, and I remember coming back across that wasteland once with Aunt Ellie and seeing a strange man sitting among the bushes, bottle in his hand, everything about him bedraggled and uncared for. I was afraid, because of the way he looked at us as we came towards him—I had no words for it, but I knew he hated us. But I also felt guilty for being afraid, for I knew Aunt Ellie would think I should feel sorry for him for being poor. As we got nearer he spat out some words that I did not understand. I looked quickly up at Aunt Ellie, knowing she would not tolerate rudeness. But she said nothing, just pulled me over to the far side of her vast skirt and marched me past—

—I tell Marilyn about the memory. Then I hear myself saying, 'I met that man again once,' though I didn't, and haven't ever before thought that I did. 'I don't know why I said that. It was another man, years later.' But even that I had forgotten until this moment. And in one sense he was the same, the age-old man who emerges from the bushes, the man whose lurking presence makes adults teach their girl children to be afraid before they are old enough to ask the reason, let alone understand; to accept the boundaries and be timid…

I was alone when I saw him. I must have been about twelve, cycling home after school. The road had houses down one side only, and they were all closed up in the after-lunch heat, no one about. On the other side was a drainage ditch maybe five foot deep, which flooded after thunderstoms but for the rest of the year was dry and empty. A man emerged out of the ditch. I saw him long before I reached him, his head slowly rising above ground level, looking fixedly in my direction. Then lifting himself out on to the side, to stand waiting for me to get nearer. I see it in terrifying clarity, his every movement prolonged unbearably. Slowly, painfully slowly, I cycled towards him. I wonder now why I did not turn and ride off in the other direction, but I went on cycling, mesmerised, a bird before a snake…It is now, now, and he stands and waits, and though he is so still I feel as I watch him as I felt flailing ineffectually beneath Kevin's heaving body. Now I can see the rough face, his mouth hanging slightly open, his hand—and I am now so near that if he chose he could reach out that hand and grab me with it as he lunges towards me—reaching instead down to his crotch and slowly, deliberate opening his fly to fetch out a swollen penis and point it at me—

The moment I passed him time began to whirr in an out-of-control way. I was shaking when I reached home. I told no one, just retreated to my room and lay on my bed, hugging my knees up against my chest, rocking the panic away. For days and nights that penis loomed, massively swollen, red veins protruding. To avoid it I left for school ten minutes early to go round the longer way, but because I was not on my normal route each bit of the way reminded me of why I was here. At night I read late, delaying the moment of switching off the light till my eyes were heavy. But as soon as it was dark I was alert again, listening to the branches of the climbing rose scratch and whine against the closed window pane, and lurid visions of penises of all descriptions would begin thrusting towards me.

I made myself return to the road. I cycled slowly until I came near the spot, reserving my strength—and then furiously past it, escaping now where before I had been too panicked to try to save myself. He was not there, the man—and without him the threat subsided, became almost pathetic, this mindless organ with no other outlet for lust than to be pointed for so brief a moment at a passing girl on a bike; and holding it, a lonely man with nowhere to sleep but the drainage ditch.

It is my own life. I did it. Whatever was done to me, it is only I who can now move it forward. But there is such a huge weight I have to move first, of accepting all that is past before I can start again. Of accepting that there is no point hating Kevin, who has been as little in control of his reactions as I have been of mine. Nothing has changed in my body. It is still mine, still smooth-skinned and good to touch, with nicely shaped breasts, and legs that can walk where I need to, and not just that, but dance. And a time will come when I will stop feeling as if Kevin has left his mark all over my whole life, which I shall never be able to wash out.

9

This time I could hardly claim that I was rushed into leaving. But I was so absorbed in taking leave of the past that I did not know how to imagine a different future. In the end it was probably just as well that Kevin made his decision and left me no choice.

He announced it one evening at dinner. Tom and I stared. There had been no build-up, we had not known he was even thinking of it, but here he was telling us he was leaving for Britain in three weeks, flight booked. He had had my name entered on his passport. As his wife I was free to move, to leave, to enter; separate from him no one would allow me to exist. Four months and we could each have done our own thing, but he had come to the end of some process of his own and he couldn't wait. I just sat there looking at him, thinking, OK, so that's what comes next.

But I hated everything about leaving. Hated saying goodbye to Charity and everyone in her house, knowing I would never see them again. To Marilyn and Fred and Charlie and the baby—'We'll stop in London on our way back to Canada,' Marilyn promised. But a day at most, and in two year's time. Leaving the school, which I suddenly realised I had become fond of, and even more the classes under the trees. Marilyn promised to keep them going but I knew things would dribble to a halt within a few months. Who would do it all? Finding substitute teachers when someone's child was ill? Preparing teaching materials? Sweet-talking employers into giving their servants time off for the classes? Marilyn didn't have the cheek and the others didn't have the commitment. I left knowing I had created nothing that would continue. In the end that was a useful thing to have learnt, but at the time it just felt miserable.

And the village. I understood now—I had known all along, but somehow never seen so clearly—that in years to come it was *this* experience more than any other that I would look back to as the one that really changed me. It was these people who helped me become *umuntfu*, simply a person, by accepting me—not just as a stranger who was entitled to hospitality, but something more difficult, a woman who kept coming back and yet had no clear role. Already grown, but needing constant instruction; less use than a child in anything that involved words; in practical matters manifestly incompetent, unable to tell edible wild plants from poisonous ones, or to catch a chicken, which even the small children could do, let alone pluck and prepare it for cooking. But they let me come, and let me be. And because so much of the time I didn't understand what was being said, I spent hours letting the sounds flow over me, hearing them as one might hear music. Listening to meanings beyond words.

It was the old man who really taught me that. We hardly exchanged three sentences in all the times I went there, but more than the others he freed me of the burden of my strangeness. He had left history behind him and found another level at which to live, one he could see I wanted to learn, for it must have been clear that it was not idle curiosity that made me come each time to sit and listen to him play the mbira. And on about the third visit he finally rewarded my patience—stopped playing, and silently passed the mbira to me—

—Slowly I feel my way along the keys. They go up alternately left and right, but tuned to a scale my ear doesn't expect. He takes it back and plays a sequence of five notes, repeating it while I watch his fingers and let the pattern and rhythm lodge in my ears. Then he passes it back and I try to pick out the same notes. He waits till I have got it, and then tries me on another, more complicated. I begin, but lose it. Back again to him—the same phrase, but he's made it simpler, the main shape showing through.

The women are at work a short way off, hoeing. One of them starts up with a song, just to keep the work going along—

'*That's it*,' *I* shout. Work stops, people gather. 'The song,' I say, my kiSwati suddenly unusually fluent in my excitement, 'the one you were singing the day I came!'

And they sing it again for me now, and then again as I sit there in the dust with my notebook, recording the syllables that later Charity will translate…*ku-LE*, it begins, touching the first low note only long enough to lift off it with a yodelling sweep, to land on one high above, and then hold it, reaching out to someone beyond the hills. Then dropping low, finding no one—*zon ta* a *ba*...Now up again, but this time with less conviction—*'bo-li-BA*...and dropping in steadier steps—*mba li nga sho-o ni*... I feel immensely privileged to be learning it right here where it was designed to be sung, with my ears, my voice, my body, till its rhythms and patterns become part of me, lifting and bending as they did on that first day of my new life—

ku-LE--zo nta-a ba
'bo-li-BA--mba li nga sho-o ni
On those distant hills, catch the sun before it sets,
you who are mourned...
I am now just a song that everyone sings.
I loved a young man but they took him,
gone to seek work on the mines...

They took him. Gone.

And now I was going away, from all that had been. Lying in those last days reading in Marilyn's garden, I saw the one I grew up in. I saw Mom out at the front, pondering over the shapes of flower beds—the back lawn, where Trevor and his band of neighbourhood boys played cricket in the summer, hockey in the winter—the washing line where on Saturdays I used to help Gertruida peg rows and rows of the boys' socks on the lower line that I could just reach. The garden absorbed all those different energies, all those unsynchronised states of being. It combined in satisfying proportions areas that had been allocated a purpose and those that were left open, to be used as the mood took you—as one would like life to be, in fact...My inner eye settles quietly on each area in turn. The garage, bikes piled up against each other, old trunks, tools. Bulbs waiting to be replanted—dead as old onions yet hiding flowers inside them. Behind that a coal shed, restocked at the beginning of each winter by men whose eye-whites loomed out of faces made blacker by coal dust as they loped down past the garage, bent forward under the weight of the sacks that pressed down on their heads and backs. Gertruida's room, and after her, Annie's, where on their afternoons off the servants from neighbouring houses would gather and talk in Tswana in a full-throated uninhibited way, and I would listen to the rising-falling pattern of sound and make it into private little songs that ran in my head. At the back door, the tomato plants Aunt Ellie brought from the farm—I remember still the smell of their leaves, pungent if I twisted them in my fingers…

Tom came to find me. 'I just wondered,' he said awkwardly, 'whether there's anything you needed from home. Because I'm free next weekend.' I put my arms around him and couldn't find any words; two of us, inarticulate together. When he returned from Bloemfontein he brought, along with the letters and a suitcase of my things, a bottle of stewed apricots from Aunt Ellie…

I see the apricot tree, the first tree I learnt to climb, for its branches were low and there were lots of places to hold on to. It had been there since before Richard was born, and the adults kept saying it could not be expected to go on producing. Year after year it surprised them. For all of one weekend other activities ceased while we picked and carried baskets into the kitchen, where Mom and Aunt Ellie washed and cut and boiled and stirred—to emerge on Sunday evening from the sticky steam and display rows of glowing bottles along the top shelf in the pantry. The intense colour gleaming through glass seemed almost magical, so rich a transformation from the soft shy bloom of the fruit on the tree…

The day before I left I phoned them. I hadn't felt safe enough even in my last letter to tell them that the marriage to Kevin was not a real one; not until I was on that plane, and had landed in Britain, and been let in. We were doing quite well, laughing a little—Dad finding things to tease me about—until Mom said, 'We're just so grateful you've got Kevin,' and I was too choked to go on.

'Child, you're so sure of your welcome,' Aunt Ellie said once—and why would I not be sure, when welcome was there waiting for me to be born into? There was nothing I ever had to do to merit acceptance. It was a childhood I am only now beginning to understand was immeasurably privileged, in the love, the humour, the tolerance, the indignation at injustice, in being left to find my own rhythm within that assured welcome, unfettered by arbitrary rules. To fill my mouth with mulberries from the tree that grew higher than the house, nourished by the borehole whose huge piston plunged up and down to pump water from hundreds of feet below...Purple juice dripping, staining fingers, clothes, mouths. Collecting leaves to fill the shoeboxes where silkworms spun their bright yellow thread over cardboard hearts—

I am saying goodbye. To the place on the pavement beneath the pine trees that edged my world on one side, to the lane with the tumbleweed that edged the other. To the freedom to move within those safe boundaries, and the knowledge that even when you step just beyond them, home will always be there to retreat to. To my brothers, who have gone off to other adulthoods, in different directions from mine. To Mom and Dad, who will be forever there where they belong, and whom I will never again be able to reach. To the child I was before I was faced with the consequences of my own choices.

It is so obvious that there is no point in crying, that I simply sit holding the memories to me, rocking them to keep them safe.

My last day, and the road to the village. I have been going for so long now that I have learnt the pattern of the seasons, the dances that go with the harvest, the song the children sing when it starts to rain—the *ngqo-ngqo* sound to beat the clouds away... Farewell gifts this time. Clothes for everyone, and plastic buckets for the women. I tried to resist the plastic but Charity said firmly, 'It's what they want.' Their present to me is a flat winnowing basket, so that I will not forget how to prepare grain once I get to England. For the old man Charity suggested a radio but that I refused. 'If he had wanted one he would have got one when he was on the mines. He makes his own music.' I have brought him instead a new blanket—it gets cold in the hills at night. He accepts it with a nod, then calls Charity to interpret. People have told him I am going far away—is that right? Yes, Charity says, it is right. He says, 'When you travel with the mbira you will never be alone. It will speak to you, first with your voice and then with its own.' And he puts it into my hands, his own mbira.

'Go on,' says Charity, 'I told you, he has plenty others.'

All the way back to town I hold it reverentially, this small, silent piece of hollow wood, that I have only to touch to bring back the sounds of these hills. On the morning I have to leave I wake early, and walk a little way away from the house where I won't disturb those still sleeping, and while the mist sifts and lifts around me I play over and again the tunes I have been taught, so that my thumbs will remember them.

Chapter 3

Flying in, above the clouds. Then the plane comes down through them and we land on tarmac wet with rain and the lifeless shine of oil. I have been making silent speeches about being positive, not wasting emotional energy fighting what is happening. Think about what you may be going to, not what you're leaving—

But I don't know what I'm going to; and by the time we emerge from the airport it's four o'clock and already dark. I didn't know such a thing was possible.

We take a train to Nottingham. This is the last journey we will ever make together, I tell myself. We have to have a shared address for four months at least—I don't know where I am going to be, and Kevin does, so his address will be ours. But I will not live in it, not for one night. We will find him a place, I will memorise where everything is and then take the train back to London to find something of my own.

The future is hurtling towards us—we have to sort things out before it becomes the present. Kevin will post on my mail. We will meet for a meal once a month so we will know enough about each other's daily lives to be able to answer questions intelligently if challenged. The story will be that I have a job in London so we commute to see each other at weekends. It's difficult to see how we're going to make that stick since I can't think what job I'm likely to get except the most menial. I'm struggling not to feel paranoid about being discovered and deported. At Nottingham station there are a couple of policemen—I turn instinctively to avoid them. Kevin says, 'Jennie, for heavens sake,' embarrassed to be associated with me. It's easy for him, he's legal regardless of whether anyone believes we're really married.

A night in a room above a pub; separate beds. The only other essential was that it should be cheap. It is, and with good reason. An electric bulb dangles dangerously from a ceiling grimy with years of coal dust. The basin is coming away from the wall. The gas heater swallows coins alarmingly before it will work, and then smells and only warms us if we sit right up close.

Something odd is beginning to happen to me—I want to laugh. At us, here, in this bizarre place. At Kevin having to dress for his interview as if he is coming from the kind of house managers live in. He does, in fact, but that's skipping a couple of stages. Kevin doesn't see the joke. OK, so this is the policeman incident reversed—I can see the ridiculous side because it's not me going for the interview.

While he's out I begin sniffing around the streets, a mole emerging into daylight. I ask the woman at the newsagent how you find a place to live. She and the man who's buying a paper give me lengthy advice, pleased to find someone ignorant enough to instruct. At lunchtime I sit in a smoky cafe that's smaller than a Swazi hut inside and eat baked beans on toast while I listen to the conversation of the men at the next table and try to glean fragments about the lives they lead. One's a truck driver, another digs up the roads, but why I can't tell. I have to strain to follow—not just the accent; we hardly seem to share a vocabulary. Then out again into the grey, wet streets, practising silently. Another new language to learn.

Kevin gets the job. It was all fixed up beforehand by a friend of his father; he'd have had to do something really stupid not to get it.

Now my turn. A bedsit in London, definitely the cheapest possible. Money is a looming crisis—most of what I managed to save in Swaziland has gone on the airfare…A temporary flip into panic the first time I have to give my name. Jennie de Villiers, I say, and then think, Christ, what if the Home Office checks up on this? I don't live with Kevin—at least I should use his name. But I can't bring myself to, whatever the risk.

Finding a job turns out to be easier than I'd expected. I join the ranks of early morning cleaners, setting out in the five o'clock dark. I share the bus with Jamaican, Irish, Spanish women, heavy legs and tired faces—I am losing my defining whiteness but discovering in its place what being female signifies. My employer is Burbage and Crighton, Cleaning Services. The glossy leaflets show perfect office environments, kept spotless by smiling women with hoovers; the depot itself is a grotty hole under the arches of a railway bridge. The office I clean is all echoing corridors—only the night watchman there when I arrive, and I am gone (leaving office as in brochure) before the first secretaries get in. Then in the evenings I reappear to empty the waste-paper baskets of the drafts of letters and used tissues and remains of take-away lunch. I fill the spaces with these ghostly presences, reading torn-up notes and opening drawers to get clues. Sometimes there are men in suits still shifting papers doggedly at seven-thirty in the evening. I make up stories about them, and about the wives whose dinners are spoiling. The men never see me.

Between shifts I do all the things I assume one does in London. Queueing for matinee tickets along with the students and tourists; working out how to get from Temple to Covent Garden by tube and then discovering it would have taken half the time to walk. Hours in art galleries and museums trying to feel excited by the fact that I am here, doing this, and actually just wishing my legs didn't ache.

It is weeks now since I have spoken to anyone beyond chatting to the woman next to me on the bus. You can keep sane quite a long time on small interactions—a laugh in the corner shop, helping someone with a pushchair up the stairs at the station. I play a game of memorising all the ways it's possible to comment on the weather—part of the language learning exercise. But there is no disguising that I am terribly lonely, afraid even to let myself think about the people I have lost, who live where there is always light and sun. I wander the streets among tourists who emerge from cinemas and restaurants, senses bombarded, appetites jaded; to Leicester Square where the young and hopeful hover on the edge of a world of swirling lights that costs more to enter than they can raise, and the old and derelict doss down in the square, beyond caring. Surrounded by people yet alone, I see myself as if from the outside, watching—as I was the other time I had to start again from nothing. You think you move forward but it's like a dance, round and round, back to where you began.

On the steps of St Martin-in-the-Fields a signboard announces *Free lunch-hour concerts*. A string quartet. Corelli, Albinoni—I have never heard of them, nor watched this kind of music being made. I take my place to wait, feeling as new as the first time I sat on my haunches in the village as the women danced. And I am transported, clear out of this time and place, into a sense of proportion, of depth and lightness. The sound lifts off the strings and moves through my own body and mind, evoking things that have been, possibilities to come, all twining together. Long after it is over I sit in the emptying church feeling the sounds still soaring, and I a part of that great lift of the spirit—

—And come to, to discover everyone else has gone, except for a man up at the front doing something with candles.

Out, on to the rainy pavement, people bustling, traffic milling. It has gone, gone before I could catch hold of it. I cannot remember a single phrase of the music, and I want to cry for the loss.

Alone in my rented room, I channel my longing through my hands that hold the mbira, and I feel Charity near me, squatting in the dust in that life that is now beyond reach—yet another one; so little point of connection with this one that I doubt sometimes my ability to hold on to what it meant. But the mbira holds it for me, this piece of a tree carved by the hands of a man I will never know—somewhere north, the old man said, but he couldn't remember where. No one now to teach me tunes so I let my hands discover their own patterns, like a dance. Letting go rather than doing, letting the wave carry me. If I mean to repeat a pattern and misjudge the distance, something else emerges, and maybe it's more interesting. There are days when nothing co-ordinates and my hands seem to have no rhythms in them. Then I retreat into yesterday's patterns, repeated for comfort. On other days my hands hardly seem to exist—it is the wave that is the music, an energy, an elemental force that I sense is there and need somehow to link in to.

The Burbage and Crighton hoover starts depositing a trail of dust out of the back. I sweep it up with a dustpan and leave a note for the supervisor. By the next day the hoover has developed indigestion and is spewing out of the back faster than it sucks in at the front. The supervisor arrives, says, 'I've had a complaint, you can go.'

There's something about jobs like that, you don't look for the same kind twice. Waitressing next—harder work than cleaning but a lot more fun because there's company, Portuguese waitresses and washer-uppers who avoid policemen just as instinctively as I do. That lasts three weeks. Then one of the regular customers says he gave me a twenty pound note when he'd only given me ten. *I know* he's just getting at me because I didn't respond to the greasy way he chatted me up. By the time he summons the manager I've already gone too far and he's saying, 'I've never been spoken to like that, she ought to be sacked'—

Reality hits me. I have visions of the manager calling the police. I get in first and say he can have his job.

I am shaking when I get out into the street, but I also have a heady sense of freedom. Confronting authority isn't new but I've never done it this personally. *And* I'm getting my evenings back. I celebrate by queueing for cheap tickets and seeing within the space of a few weeks two plays, my first opera and twelve concerts—lunchtime, evening, the lot. And especially string quartets. Free if possible, cheap if not, restricted views from behind pillars if necessary. My anxiety about having to live as cheaply as possible competes with my passion to hear all that lies hidden in those beautifully shaped wooden boxes, gleaming silently until the strings are touched with the bow, then releasing sound that rises and fills all the spaces…

Franco's Sandwich Bar it is, this time. Leicester Square, a ten-hour day, with a break mid-afternoon that's just too short to make it worth going anywhere. So I bring a book and sit on the grass along with all the pigeon droppings, and every day I see, on a bench opposite, this same young woman with a face I am sure I know. By day four I realise it's exactly like one of those Indian miniature paintings in the British Museum—oval eyes, long nose, black hair that frames her face and is taken smoothly back to a long tail of a plait. With a face like that it's amazing she doesn't get hassled…something about her that must be keeping them off, a protective, private misery.

There seems no point in continuing to sit on opposite sides of the square every day at three-fifteen. She looks startled when she sees me coming towards her. I say, 'Hi. We always seem to have our break together.' She lets a cautious smile out and says, 'I've been seeing you every day, but I wouldn't have had the courage.'

It wasn't courage so much as need.

We meet every day. 'Which way are you going?' we ask each other, and find we can take the same bus part of the way. Jaswinder says she's been terrified of that journey home every night. Alone, everything about central London terrifies her. With someone to keep her company she is lively and full of affection. She has lived in London since she was twelve but is less fitted to cope on her own than I who have only been here a matter of months, for until she left home she had never gone anywhere alone. She left because she didn't want to get married, she says, at least not yet. She didn't want to end up like her older sisters, having children too young and just working in the factory down the road, married to men who worked in the same factory. She wanted to get some qualifications—surely her dad should have been pleased? She could earn more money then, and he could make a better marriage for her. But he just kept on shouting at her about bringing disgrace on the family. So here she is—miserable, in a little room like mine, working in a job that's as boring as the factory, and missing her mom and her sisters dreadfully. Two runaways together, both missing our moms, both anxious about money; but being two transforms everything.

I give the counter a final wipe and look up to see Jaswinder waiting for me in the road outside. Something odd—I usually get off before her. The moment I get near she starts telling me—the dropped pile of plates, the angry manager—I hardly need to hear the details, I know it all—she's been sacked. It's her first time. I say, 'Forget them, Jas—you'll find another job,' but she can't see past this week's rent. I say, 'Try your family, maybe they're missing you as much as you miss them,' but she just says, again and again, 'You don't understand, you don't know them.' In the bus she is weeping, wiping her dishevelled black hair off her face with a frantic sweep of her arm. I say, 'Come back to my place.' We sit on my bed talking, and she becomes a little calmer. It occurs to me that it's crazy for her to have to go back to her room alone. I say, 'Sleep here.' It's a big bed but I wonder if she will feel awkward sharing. But she says, 'That's how we always slept at home, me and my sisters,' and as we go to sleep, 'I hate living by myself.' In the morning I say, 'Share my room, then at least you won't have to worry about rent.' When I get back from work that night she has done it, given notice in her old room and moved in.

The landlady is knocking on the door at eight the next morning. At first I have no idea what has upset her—she's normally a mild little woman, and I have the impression she has had to psych herself up to the confrontation. 'It's a room for one,' she blurts, 'I'm not having you cheating me.'

I don't want to have to move, not again. 'I'm paying the rent,' I say, 'and it won't be any extra trouble for you.'

Her voice becomes hysterical. 'I know these Pakistanis—you let one of them in and there are ten before you turn around. This is a respectable house.' Jaswinder is saying, 'I'm not Pakistani,' and I'm saying, equally indignantly, 'If by respectable you mean white—' But she's not listening. She's making quite sure I get the point. 'There's only one bed,' she says, 'it's disgusting.'

We are surprised into silence. She realises she's scored a winner and takes herself off. Jaswinder and I turn to each other, awkward for the first time. For a moment we say nothing, each gauging the other's eyes. Then we both start laughing. I say, 'Come on, let's get out of here. We'll find somewhere.'

Now we meet it on every doorstep. No one will rent one room to two young women. So simple a device for saving money, denied us.

'What we need,' I fantasize, 'is a place where the people who live in the house make the rules.'

Jaswinder isn't given to fantasy. 'The only way you get that is by owning it yourself.'

'I don't know. There was this Portuguese woman I met, Maria, in that restaurant I told you about. She lives in this house with a whole lot of other women and the landlord never comes near them—'

Maria says, 'Come.'

2

The house is a vast Victorian sprawl of rooms—unexpected angles, cupboards under the stairs, scullery, outhouse, ragged back garden.

Five floors, if you count the basement that Jaswinder moves into, and my attic. It's in such poor repair that no one but a collective would have it, so the rent for both of us together is less than either of us was paying before. And we get all this space, all this company.

There are supposed to be eight of us, but there are plenty of mornings when I go down to find someone I've never seen before in the kitchen, peering into the fridge to see what she can find for breakfast. The systems all look as if they've been cobbled together by a set of hopeful amateurs, electric flex trailing, pipes disappearing into and emerging from strange places. The landlord can never be found when there is a real emergency, like the boiler erupting, or whatever it is boilers do—steam everywhere and filthy water from rusty pipes all over the bathroom floor. We rush around with mops and buckets and back copies of *The Daily Worker* and *Women's Own*—the political range in the house reflected even in our domestic crises—while a tall woman called Paula with a wild mop of hair trips switches and closes off gas pipes and gets going with a wrench. Jaswinder and I look on in bemused admiration. There seems no practical task Paula does not know how to deal with.

The attic is the smallest room in the house, but also the best retreat. I have to slide into bed and crawl out again to avoid bumping my head—it's just high enough at the head end for me to sit up to write a letter. I hang an African cloth on the one upright wall, arrange my books all the way round the skirting board, and sit crosslegged on the bed to play my mbira, leaving the rest of the world somewhere down there below. It's also surprisingly light. There's a dormer window that opens if I bang it but doesn't close again unless I summon help from Paula, and I pull the long metal thing that is supposed to hold it in position when open while she presses the top of the window frame up against the hinge from which it is gradually separating. Paula says, 'We ought to fix the damn thing,' but she forgets as soon as she's down on the floor below again, and I haven't the least idea how to. I could find out of course, but there are too many things I'm busy finding out, swollen window frames will have to wait; so I just live with it not quite closed. The rain doesn't usually get in, nothing that can't be contained by a towel wedged into the crack. When Jaswinder comes to sit on my bed and chat she says, 'It's freezing up here, how can you put up with it?' But I'd rather have it open and be cold. It's the one thing I can't get used to about London, being inside the whole time. I need the window open so I can stick my head out and look out over the roofs and chimneys, at the sparrows chirping determinedly on their television aerials. They make me laugh, they're so oblivious of their surroundings—claiming territory as if they were in a wood. In Jaswinder's room in the basement it's like being a mole, peering up through the always-closed window at the feet that walk by on the pavement. And the fug of heat—Jane's threatening to rig up a special meter on Jaswinder's gas heater so that the rest of us don't have to share the bills. I don't mind about the bills—Jaswinder does far more than her share of the cooking, in a class of its own, and she's the only one apart from me who ever cleans the kitchen without waiting for a house meeting to decide whose turn it is. She can have her heater on all day as far as I'm concerned.

Meals are either scrappy, individual, or huge and collective. When someone has the urge to cook we sit for hours talking—and I soaking it all in. Maria's plump arms sweep as she tells us about her latest poem, dark eyes intense with a passion that's political as much as aesthetic. It's the freedom to write her poetry that keeps her in London, working for half the going rate because the restaurant owner knows she hasn't got a work permit and can't go back to Portugal. Jane's the only one who can read her poems and she says they're far too subtle to translate. From Maria I get the impression of a vast canvas, encompassing everything—Love, Life, Liberty. Jane's idiom is different—'They're about being free inside yourself,' she says, 'whatever the bastards try to do to you.' Maria shows me the underground journal that circulates in

Lisbon, and prints whatever her fluent pen produces. My mind flips continents—I wonder what Gordon, who thought *me* naive, would make of Maria, who is convinced they're making a revolution with their poems and stories…Then I think, look where Gordon landed, however acute his political judgement. Maria might turn out to be right after all.

Meal over, Jane and I head for the station. 'Where did you learn Portuguese?' I ask. 'School holidays,' she says. 'My dad's in the army and Portugal's Our Oldest Ally'—a cheerful half-mocking air, making it clear none of that was *her* responsibility. 'In the army' turns out to mean her dad's a Colonel, and 'school' was a converted stately home set in thirty acres. She walked out from under, like a tortoise discovering life could be more fun without that shell weighing her down. Now, small and slim-bodied, she moves agile as squirrels on the common, ideas leaping easily while I follow, getting her to explain things she takes for granted. 'Define bastard,' I say.

She laughs, enjoying being challenged. 'People who walk over other people. Not always male, but frequently.' She sounds as if she'd like to take them all on, all five foot two of her. She stops as we pass a boarded-up house. 'And people who own property they don't need but won't let other people use. Any decent society would make it a crime.' She is eyeing the house affectionately, head tilted to one side. 'That was our rehearsal space a year ago.'

'This house?'

'The very one. Paula and I squatted it, for our theatre group. She fixed the plumbing and the electrics, and we had a glorious six months. Till the police threw us out.'

'You mean, physically?'

'Very physically. Dragging us by the hair—in Paula's case, that is; by the arms in mine'—she caricatures an attempt to grab her own hair—too short to get hold of. 'It wasn't even as if the neighbours minded. They don't like the house being empty.'

Paula was philosophical, she says. 'You know what Paula's like. Things go wrong, you fix them.' But Jane still hates that landlord—

And anyone else who keeps others out of places she thinks ought to be public, like those squares with lovely gardens that only the people in the neighbouring houses have keys to. Walking down the street with Jane, every railing is a challenge. She can climb anything, and slip round a corner and be lost among the dustbins like a cat before you can work out where she's gone.

This is the new life, the one I couldn't imagine as I wandered in the hills above Mbabane, or watched Marilyn's life and wondered what mine would be—

I'm leaning up against a post in St Pancras station. Scaffolding everywhere—they are redoing the station concourse. The Nottingham train has just come in. I watch the line of passengers stream past the ticket barrier and wait for one of them to be Kevin. The usual tense mixture of feelings about this meeting—a strong resistance against being pulled back to something that has no connection with my present life, and yet—and yet Kevin is still, as in Swaziland, the only person who connects me with what I have left behind.

And here he is walking towards me. Dapper suit, sober tie, briefcase. We stand a couple of feet from each other.

'Where are we eating?' he begins.

I say to myself, 'Don't rise,' for innocent as it sounds this is a loaded comment. Anywhere I suggest is beneath consideration, yet he knows there's no way I could afford to eat in the kind of restaurant he regards as normal. He says, 'I want a decent meal, I'm tired,' but he is taking in my jeans and old duffel coat and plimsolls (which I notice for the first time have developed a hole around my big toe), and that look of faint disgust is in his eyes again. I say, 'I'm tired of this, Kevin. You choose where we eat, and you pay.'

And so I sit here in my tatty plimsolls and eat lobster. If he's ashamed of me in his posh restaurant, let him choose a sensible one. I say aloud, conciliatory, 'I could cook for us in the house.'

Kevin pours the wine. No comment.

'We could eat in my room,' I say. 'You wouldn't have to talk to the others.' But he's intimidated by the very idea of them. He can't get away from them, because the deal was that we each need to know about the other's life. I get the trials of having to take on a new secretary and the tensions on the squash club committee, and he gets Paula and the boiler, and Eva who ran away from a violent husband and has had her child taken away from her because she's now Paula's partner. But he doesn't want to know about this other Britain I am discovering, so far removed from the one he now inhabits. He protects himself against having to think, shielding behind a set of ready-made opinions he must be picking up from his new colleagues. 'Your bra-burning friends,' he calls the women in the house—and this is the man who started me off reading *The Second Sex*.

'So how's your sugar daddy?' Paula asks when I get in. 'I see you dressed the part!'

'Good for his soul,' I say. 'Keeps him humble.'

A woman's voice sings from her record player, deep but secretive, something suggestive that the voice won't share—

But sometimes you leave since there's nothing to lose
You might not have chosen but still opt to choose
And there's no returning

singing the life of young women alone in London, but African rhythms jut out unexpectedly. A piano played with verve, off-beat. I pick up the record sleeve, asking, 'Who's got this wonderful voice?' Paula is amazed. Other things that are new to me she accepts as natural in one recently come from Africa; but that I have never heard Sasha McKinley! For the rest of the evening—till Eva gets back—she proceeds to fill this terrible gap.

Curious now, she asks about that other life of mine, the home that is thousands of miles away across oceans. I try to describe it as we sit on the floor surrounded by her records, but I hardly know where to begin. It was a quality more than a nameable set of events. The feeling of lazy after-school hours in the garden, with the sound of Richard practising his flute floating out of the window…She listens, absorbed. She's an extraordinarily creative listener, Paula—you can almost see things going into her mind and being reassembled, to come out again in a quick humorous challenge to think. 'How did you get like that?' I ask. She laughs—'Survival, I expect.' And she tells me about her childhood, on a council estate in Newcastle; being passed around a succession of neighbours, but mostly just being left to cope on her own, while her mother was out working. 'Mostly night work,' she says, and her eyes say, you work out what kind—as she as a child was left to do. Her father? 'A tall dark stranger,' she says, 'gone before I was born.' Her arms lift and she ruffles her hands through her long frizzy hair. 'From Africa; fantastic dancer, my mother used to tell me. One week's leave from his ship, then off again'…Her mother was all she had, 'But I never had her,' she says, 'not what I longed for from her.' Cuddles when she felt in the mood, slaps when she got in the way—and then her mother was out, with no idea when she would be back. The adult Paula talks calmly about it, but it's no surprise that she has set up a collective house, leaving nothing to chance. Or that she has eyes so alert there's no hiding from them.

'What does your mother do now?'

'Much the same, except she's conned a man into looking after her since I left. He's not keen on me and it's mutual. So I stay away.'

'Does she want to see you?'

'Who can tell? Certainly not me. And it's a long time since I last tried to find out.' She flings her hair back, and sings with Sasha—

The journey you take is the path that you choose
The blue sky is blue but it's also the blues

My own home arrives every fortnight, with Mom's neat handwriting filling the sheets of blue airmail paper with the satisfying detail of the life that I need to know will forever continue in my absence. The agapanthus that she has put in down one side of the back lawn, now that it is so many years since anyone needed it for cricket…Photos of Richard's growing family—the child who was born the first year I was in Swaziland now cutting her third birthday cake, while her younger brother stares at me out of the photo, firmly positioned on his short legs. I stick the photos on my wall, feeling suddenly horribly deprived that I can never know these two. And still little news of Peter, who hardly phones, and never writes—

Kirsty comes in, a seven-year-old, Eva's child. She watches as I paste up the photos, and wants to know about these other children and why they never come to stay. She lives with her father and Eva gets her only once a month, but these are the times when the house is most like a home to me. She's a real child of the collective, friends with us all. She makes chapatis with Jaswinder, gets Jane to teach her to vault railings, watches documentaries on telly cuddled up against Maria. She has a room on the floor below mine—an odd shaped boxroom with a high-level bed built by Paula, that keeps the floor clear for a sprawl of toys and games that don't have to be cleared up at bedtime. I wake to the sound of her feet on the bare boards as she goes to Eva and Paula's room—a pause as she checks, and if they're still sleeping, the feet patter up the stairs to the attic. 'Let's play our story game,' she says now, settling on my bed. I listen for the stairs before we start, feeling Eva's breath on my back. She's tense these days—smoking too much and eating for comfort, things like jam doughnuts that leave her pasty-faced and irritable; and too often when she wonders where Kirsty's got to, she finds her in my room.

But no sounds from below. 'OK,' I say. 'You start.'

'There's this girl called Javier,' Kirsty begins.

'*Javier?*' I ask. 'What kind of a name is that?'

'Her name,' says Kirsty firmly. 'She lives in a tower at the edge of a wild moor, and her neighbours are two foxes. Now it's your turn.'

'One day she was walking across the moor at dawn...'

And so we go—your turn, my turn, co-creating. The story grows like an amoeba. Strange new bulges form and move and then are reabsorbed as we each in turn feel the heady power of creating whatever life we choose, and then the next moment have to watch our creation turned on its head, direction changed, thrust into some new unexpected landscape.

November it was when Kevin and I arrived. Just four months, I thought, till I get my own passport. No point thinking further ahead. December, January, February—but it seemed we had not understood the complexity of the regulations. March, April...In May Jaswinder and I moved into the women's house, and still I was meeting Kevin for the once a month meal. November again, and all I've had from the Home Office is a duplicated leaflet—due to staff shortages there are delays in processing applications in the London office. I'll be lucky if it's two years. The future recedes—

And who cares? For it's an extraordinary time to be twenty-four, and free. Free from fear of arrest, free to be alone, to run to catch a bus, and sit up at the top looking down on the world going by, till it is time to hop off again to meet a friend—everything to discover and nothing to avoid except the puddles in the pavement...I have arrived from another continent to discover that while I was walking across the border with Kevin, here in London and Paris the students were rising. I hear people talk of '68 as a time of upheaval, and I remember that yes, of course, I did read something about it, but I was so intent on scouring the papers to find clues to the much nearer dramas in South Africa that I hardly took it in that thousands of miles away there were barricades in the streets and nothing would ever be the same again. Now I am learning it all like a story I nearly missed. I read voraciously—Kate Millet on sexual politics, Noam Chomsky on

American imperialism—reading with the same passion to make my own judgements that fired me when I discovered that Kevin had known things that I did not, and out of that knowledge had made decisions that determined my future. I go with Paula and Jane to rehearsals of their experimental theatre group—no working from parts others have scripted for them, they devise their own to express the life that is in *them*. On my days off I'm in the library, tracking articles in obscure journals to find out what is happening in South Africa. When Kevin and I meet he gets it all—the green movement and the red brigade, radical feminism and socialist feminism, alternative theatre, alternative everything. His own adaptation process is taking him the other way. Each month he cuts himself off more from what he has been—in his vocabulary, his accent, the books he reads, the politics he affects. These days most of what he knows about South Africa he hears from me. I tell him because I have to talk to someone; and though he resists—I want to smile at the sight of him so obviously not wanting to be drawn back politically, as I don't personally—yet we both get there after about an hour of irritating each other. Once it's over I feel oddly released. He doesn't share my continuing need to know, but at least he understands the language.

Meanwhile the house swells to take in new waifs, and then has rooms left empty as those who have been there longer grow beyond wanting to put up with everyone else's coffee cups and cigarette ends. Women come in single, form couples, develop bitter jealousies. Weeks of tense silence break suddenly into angry denunciations, and someone storms out. I watch the loves and jealousies around me with detachment, feeling only relief not to be so driven. The effect of Kevin seems to have been to turn me off the idea of desire altogether, and I celebrate daily the freedom to be on my own, to make my own connections with where I am, this Alice Through the Looking Glass inversion of the home I grew up in. A childhood filled with brothers—and here I live entirely among women. There connected on all sides by a web of kin—elderly aunts round the corner, young cousins who visited, and Aunt Ellie's family stories to make us constantly aware that we belonged, that we had this uncle's nose and that grandmother's way of speaking—and here there are no old people, and only Kirsty to represent the children. All those I live with act in the confidence of agelessness, refusing the baggage their families have handed on to them, living as though they came alone into the world and can remake it along the lines they choose...But personal need weaves complex patterns around the values we espouse. We debate whether lovers who are not part of the household (but who spend almost as many nights here as those who are) ought to contribute to house costs. And—most intransigent problem of all—what to do about men? It's a women's house not a lesbian one, but there's no getting past the fact that Jane's succession of women lovers are more easily welcomed at the communal dinner table than Maria's Latin men, who may be her comrades in the struggle against fascism but are also the embodiment of *machismo*. And even the self-consciously non-sexist men whom other women bring home get strange looks if they appear for breakfast too many mornings in succession. We are in fact an inversion of the world outside, for here lesbian coupledom can be incorporated into the house style, heterosexual coupledom cannot. And all couples tend to be impermanent formations. The important thing is to find yourself, which leaves less energy for finding the other person—

—The days lengthen. I clear out the garden, learning the patterns of time, as once I did in the village. January, dead branches, sodden grass. February, crocuses popping out of the silent earth. March, forsythia down in the overgrown corner. April, primroses along the side of the railway line...Time passing, and I begin to be restless, knowing it is time I worked out something more meaningful to do with my life than waitressing...New leaf on the trees that I pass on the common, which Jane tells me are called

Swedish whitebeam—soft white like a dusting of powder on the underside of each curled leaf, then opening to become a small green fan…I stand beneath it and stare at this miracle of new, perfect life, and I too am poised, ready now to open out—

To what, I don't know. But something that will hold from the centre, like the shapes of the music that lifted with the arching stone of that first string quartet, or the voices of the women in the stream, rising in the air of the hills.

3

Down the stairs past Paula's room—

The place where you settle is what you become

The more your heart beats the more it's a drum -

Walk to the station, to that rhythm now lodged in my feet—thinking, what *should* I become? In the underground, the sound of Vivaldi on a busker's flute—sharp clear notes bouncing like summer hail in the acoustics of the tunnel, opening up to space and light—Like *that*, I answer—full of joy and conviction. Then home again, to a medley of sounds emerging from bedrooms, from communal living rooms—some muffled by closed doors, some decidedly unmuffled, volume on full to get that real gutsy feeling. Lifting the spirits or irritating them, depending on if it's your music or someone else's. 'Who left that damn thing on?' someone demands, coming in to a now-empty kitchen where the radio is still churning out disc jockey patter. Click, it is off. She goes back to her room, to her own music.

The goods you once purchased are no longer stocked

You're somebody else but no one is shocked

It's all in the learning

mocks the voice of Sasha McKinley.

I wander into each room in turn, drawn by the sounds. Maria's *fado* songs from Lisbon—guitar strings plucking, voice yearning.

Jaswinder's Indian film songs—lovers' hearts pierced forever, moths drawn irresistibly to candles. She explains the words, laughing with me at the absurdity, but part of her suspends disbelief, and she is caught by the swooping sentimental strings, the cloying, almost whining quality to the voice that drives the others in the house to slam doors. To Jaswinder it isn't whiny or shrill, it's beautiful—and that in itself I find interesting. Do we hear only what we have been trained to hear? But that doesn't seem to work for me—I feel open to it all, and asking something else beyond. The only kind of music I don't like is Eva's—such thumping rhythms I can't see what there is to keep her listening.

'You're the only one without your own music,' Paula says, 'and the most music-obsessed.' It's true. I've been accumulating sounds in each place I've been and then having to leave them behind. It's too soon to be defining or limiting, I want to hear it all.

I stand in the foyer of the community centre, to meet Paula after her rehearsal. While I wait I read the posters on the notice board. Saxophone players and rock groups and all-women singing groups clamber over each other. An all-night concert of Indian classical music—the *all-night* intrigues me, and so does the picture of the musician. He is dressed in a long white shirt embroidered at the neck and sits crosslegged on a carpet, caressing the strings of a deep bellied instrument. The absorbtion in his face is almost like sound itself. I am thinking, Here's *another* kind of music-making I've never heard before—and I feel Paula's arm on my shoulder. Her eyes follow mine. 'Ravi Shankar,' she says; clearly a name she knows. I feel overwhelmed suddenly by all that has been kept from me, angry that I should have spent twelve years in a school so limiting it exposed me to *nothing* of all that the cultures of the world have to share.

Paula is watching me. 'Do you want to go?' I'm about to say, 'You know I can't'—I'm waitressing still, so evenings are out. Then I see it *starts* at 11.30. If I can just get off early for once—

—Now it's here, the sound itself, and the world falls away. The restaurant, and my anger, and even Paula sitting next to me. Just the sound of that first quiet run of notes constantly rippling, inducing a state of consciousness that is alert, calm, tuned in to receive and respond…Then the pull of longing on the strings of the sitar, exploring regions between the sounds, setting up vibrations of feeling that I cannot name.

Next day I wander about in a daze of lack of sleep, but the quality keeps sifting back, lighting everything I see. It has woken in me again, a private, passionate intensity that sends me journeying across London in any spare hours I can grab from work, to fill my spirit with this new kind of music. Saturday morning sessions at the Indian Cultural Centre—I try and persuade someone to come with me—There's a shehnai player visiting, I say, and it's so beautiful I want them to experience it. 'What's a shehnai?' asks Paula. 'It's a thing you blow,' I say, 'with a wooden body and a brass bell shape at the end, and it sounds like a human voice with no words, really gets inside you.' But Paula and Jane can't come because they're rehearsing, and Maria says there's no way she's going anywhere at ten on a Saturday morning, and Jaswinder says she doesn't go for that classical stuff, she prefers music with words. Eva's shoulders lift the way they do when I'm being enthusiastic—that's OK, I wasn't imagining Eva would want to come. But once I'm there I forget Eva's shoulders and all the rest of them, it is I who need to be here—

—Week after week. Now it is the tabla that absorbs me, as I watch the hands that tap the taut skins of two small drums, hands that talk to each other as they subdivide the beat, doubling this side, adding a triple that, then faster, moving past each other…Linking to rhythms inside me, then dancing away in patterns so complex that my ear can barely hold on…He laughs and starts again, showing us how he built it up out of a few simple elements…slowly, slowly, till the rhythms are in our ears. 'But you must feel it in your own body,' he says, and teaches us to beat sixteen time as we listen. We move one finger at a time to tick off the groups of four beats. In the middle we throw one beat away with a wave of the hand. 'Why that beat?' I ask, for it was certainly not the strongest. 'Ah, but it marks our movement towards the strongest,' he says. 'Music never rests. It is like the present moment, a constant becoming'—

An internal metronome ticks off not just months, but years. 1969, the trial. 1971, arriving in London. 1973 now, and Jonas has two and a half years still to go. I fantasize sometimes about meeting him again, being able to talk at last, about what it all really meant. But where? I can't see him leaving, and I can't return…Gordon still has more than eight years. I'll be in my thirties before the whole saga ends—

'Did you hear?' Kevin says, 'Leonie's out.'

That's a jolt. But of course, her sentence was the shortest. 'They wouldn't give her a passport,' Kevin is saying, 'so she's taken an exit permit.' Permit to leave, never to return. 'Where did she go?' I ask. But of that he has no idea. Perhaps here, I think. London is where people go when they leave, the automatic first stop. Perhaps I'll bump into her…Movement, unpredictability, in a situation I have got used to thinking is half the world away.

We sit over a slow Saturday breakfast, analysing Paula and Jane's latest show. I am trying to get them to explain to me what they planned beforehand and how much they improvise. It all goes so fast—Jane's agile body moving in minutes from one vivid caricature to another, Paula drawing the audience in to help her create ludicrous scenes that mock the establishment and celebrate the power of laughter, her repartee flying as wild as her mop of hair—'You're the ideal audience,' Jane laughs, 'no defences.' She tips her chair back. 'Have you told your Mum and Dad about us yet?' She's laughing at me still, for writing letters home every fortnight. 'Sure I have,' I say, unabashed. 'They were producing plays long before you were thought of. I grew up doing the children's parts.'

They stare. 'You never told us,' says Paula. 'What kind of plays?'

'All sorts. Terence Rattigan. Noel Coward. I was a lion cub once in a play about Darius of Persia. And a junior angel in The Zeal of Thy House.'

Kirsty stops seeing how many teaspoons she can pile on top of each other without them tipping over. 'Did you have wings?'

'Huge ones, made of paper feathers on a wire frame. And my brother was a choir boy, with a long red robe and a white sort of bib thing over it. We did it in the cathedral and he fainted because one of the priests swung the incense burner too hard.'

Kirsty waits for more. This is better than stories about foxes on the moor. Paula says, 'Canterbury Cathedral, in the middle of Africa—I like it!' Jane says, 'No wonder you think we're revolutionary!'

Eva gets up from the table and walks out. The chair stares emptily at us—I register only now that she's been sitting there through all that banter, face closed. Paula says quickly, 'I think she heard the post arrive.' Eva comes back, letters in hand. Paula's expression relaxes a little. 'Another letter for Jennie,' says Eva, and she hands it to me, making it sound like something I've done on purpose.

OK, so what's it today? Kirsty again, probably, Kirsty listening to my stupid story. It's *Kirsty* who chooses, not me. And of course she's not choosing me over her mum, not in any fundamental sense. If Eva would just sometimes do things at a child's level—What am I supposed to do? Like Kirsty's last weekend—she was up in my room long before Eva was awake, saying, 'Let's go to the swings.' Do I say, No, because your mom doesn't like you to have fun with me? Eva wouldn't even have known except that we took a different route back, following like detectives some wonderful full-harmonied hymn singing that was floating over the Sunday morning air—nothing like the drone that's all you usually get if you walk past a church. We tracked it down to a small chapel. Kirsty tried to read the notice at the entrance.

'It's all funny writing,' she said, and I showed her the English words underneath, Welsh Chapel. When we got back Eva was up, and resentful, and it didn't help that Kirsty started telling her excitedly about the church—

Anyway, it's more than Kirsty, it's my mere existence. I feel attacked by an unspoken jealousy that I can do nothing to evade. We both have boring, badly paid jobs but I'm trying to work out some way of getting beyond this, while for Eva it's all there has ever been. And now, 'Another letter for Jennie'—so that's another charge—I have parents who accept what I have become, where Eva's mother will hardly see her since she moved in with Paula.

I let the letter lie unopened on my lap while we finish eating our toast—or muesli—or last night's cold bulgar wheat. The communal breakfast table gives scope for all diets, as it does theoretically for all ways of being, personal and political. But we have to co-exist. If Eva can't cope with me being what I am I have no choice but to adjust.

I remove myself, to dig viciously in the garden. I think about Paula, warily watching Eva's moods, while Eva watches to check that Paula isn't enjoying herself with anyone else. I just don't understand what keeps Paula with her. 'The two of you never even seem to talk,' I said to her once, and then thought maybe I'd gone too far.

But she just said, 'Not everyone wants to put things into words as passionately as you do.'

That was balking, and she knew it. 'Come on Paula.'

'You never see Eva the way she really is, because she never lets you.' Then, flinging her hair back, 'There isn't a day I don't feel passionate about her, however crabby she's being.' For a moment her face looked lost. I hate seeing her vulnerable but I love her for not trying to hide it—

—What I find hard to take, I tell myself as I yank up weeds, is being resented for who I am. I *hate* trying to keep out of Kirsty's way. It feels unloving, unnatural. It goes against all my instincts about being with children…That's the whole trouble, I tell myself as I scour the dishes everyone else left last night and that are now glued up with spaghetti. The whole trouble is that being with children comes naturally to me, more than it does to the others. I don't know why, and I don't do it deliberately, so I don't see why—

Stop. This is getting out of control. Everything Eva does is beginning to irritate me, like everything I do irritates her…I've been here before, with Kevin, and I never want to be in that state again…And thinking about that time brings back other things. I see Charlie and his pile of stones, each unique…Marilyn saying, 'You're lovely with Charlie,' and me saying, 'Charlie's lovely for me.'…It's not just Eva's need pushing this—

Time I did something about it, then. Find some other children to be with, and get out of Eva's hair. And then I realise, there are people who would actually *pay* me to do what I would do for pleasure. And all this time I've been washing and cleaning and serving food, and it never occurred to me that I could be doing the one bit of women's work I really like.

Goodbye to waitressing, forever.

4

The child lives a short bus ride away. A two-year-old called Michael, a slow moving child who stares at me solemnly on our first meeting. His mother, Felicity, is angular, competent, tense—about to take off. She's a solicitor, and Michael's father Dave is some kind of financial whatever you call it—investor, advisor—I've no idea really. It's Michael who decides for me that this is the job I'll take.

I wake each morning and feel I'm on holiday, not going to work. They have a small garden—oppressively neat, but I negotiate our right to dig and mess about in one corner. On good days we go to the swings, on rainy days to the library or puppets at the arts centre. Even walking there is interesting, each small step illuminated by Michael's concentration on what we pass on the way. In autumn we collect leaves on the common. In early December I wake to a freak drop in temperature—snow coming in at my dormer window—and look out on a world born new in white, and I feel like singing to know I don't have to go and shut myself in some grotty laundrette or quick-food booth, but can take Michael out on the common and kick snow and squash it into balls that he tries to throw and that drop six inches from him, exploding into brilliant white fragments. Then home to cocoa, and sitting with him cuddled into my lap as we study the patterns of snowflakes on the windows. When he wakes from his afternoon sleep and it's already almost dark, we tear up old newspaper and make our own snow storm, which we only just manage to clear up before his mum comes home. Felicity gives precise instructions on how I should prepare his food and where I should hang his coat but for the rest it's up to me to keep him happy in whatever way I can devise.

And there's the company of women, too. In a hut at the far end of the common I discover an institution with the delightful name of a One o'Clock Club, where after lunch each day mums sit and chat while the children play. The common backs on to homes of all types—a council estate on one side, large Victorian houses like Michael's parents' on the other. Here among the mums there are no discussions of feminist rights, nor even much question of individual preference—their days are simply organised around attending to the needs of others. To me, being with children is fun, but I know I will hand Michael over at the end of the day—the mums conserve their energy, knowing they will be asked to spend more than they have. I am underpaid but I have only myself to support—the mums are constantly calculating, burdened by how much things cost. There are other childminders but they are also mums, coping with other people's children as well as their own. The tiredest are the older ones, still wiping runny noses years after their own children have left home. Their usual reaction to anything the children say is, 'Not now.'

The women all seem to know each other. Arriving as a newcomer with Michael is the opposite experience from arriving in a Swazi village; there anyone new is a focus of curiosity, here it seems I will be inducted by being ignored. But down at toddler level life runs on different social principles, much closer to the village experience. The children stare openly as I join them on the floor. I offer one of them a block. She takes it and adds it to the pile we're constructing. Within a couple of minutes there's a little group round me, and we've got a great game going, and soon a little action song…I see the rain has stopped. 'Let's go outside,' I say to Michacl, and the children start to trail after, not wanting to miss the action. Before they get near the door they are scooped up and dumped firmly back…I push Michael on the swing, and a little girl comes running over and pleads 'Me, me!' so of course I give her a turn—till her mum emerges at the door of the building and calls sharply, 'Josie !' I stop the swing, but Josie holds on tight, wanting more. Her mum comes over, looks right past me and yanks the child off, scolding her for some misdemeanour as mysterious to her as to me.

It seems I'm only going to discover the rules by breaking them. 'You'd think a civil word costs money, wouldn't you?'

It's a woman over at the next set of swings—and the voice is Irish, and the face is laughing. She assures me cheerfully that she's as foreign as I am. 'My name's Colleen,' she says, 'you probably guessed.' She has five children of her own, one not yet at school, 'And a couple of other people's to keep me from being idle.' With a down-to-earth, unfussy warmth she joins me with the little cluster of children who gravitate to Michael and me, oblivious of the social code, which itself blurs and relaxes as the days pass. Colleen and I gather up the ones we are responsible for and go back to her comfortably untidy house, with photos above the fireplace of her husband and overgrown son and four freckled daughters, dancing at the Irish community centre. And a week later I'm there with them—the fiddle jigs unstoppably, my feet leap, my body spins round in an exhilaration that's been missing for far too long. The music gets faster and faster—I dance the pulse of that far-off life into this new one.

Then back next day to walking at Michael's pace—

—Slow.

Michael is turning out to be a challenge in more ways than I expected. Everything that has to be learnt he takes in laboriously—each stage visible as he assimilates it, as if someone had slowed down the film. I watch his mouth limp silently after mine as I sing *The Grand Old Duke of York*—his very body concentrates, his legs stiff, his toes curled up as he tries to clap. I had never realised before how complicated such apparently simple actions are—ear, brain, muscle co-ordination—amazing that each small body finds its own way to learn all that. He watches my feet intently as we stomp home along the pavement—

We went into the SHOP
To shelter from the RAIN
We took a LICK from a lollipop STICK
And then went on AGAIN—

Singing is the only way to get him to walk at anything like normal child-pace. Something about the rhythm. If he is sad, what works best is just to hold him and rock him All children are like that, but with him it's so noticable, he's got me wondering why it should be so. Does the pulse release a tension in him, get through to his own physical pulses, perhaps? Lungs expanding, blood pumping? It even works with language—he struggles to get hold of new words, but if I sing them it seems to open up that channel of his brain. It's more than just a physical thing, I'm sure it's the *feelings* music makes happen in him that help him learn—

—'And the more I notice what makes him different,' I tell Paula, 'the more I discover he's just a slow, visible version of what happens in all of us.'

'In you especially,' she says. She is half lying across my bed, idly plinking at the mbira. Our usual time—evening, before Eva gets back. I listen to the patterns that come off her thumbs—different from anything I would produce. 'I wish you could have heard the old man in the village,' I say. The others used to say he was bewitched.'

'And what did you think?'

'That he understood something the rest of us didn't.'

She puts it down, and looks straight at me. 'Have you always felt this way, Jennie?'

I hardly know how to answer. The source is deep in me, there in my earliest fragmentary memories—standing with Aunt Floss to listen to the sound of Moonlight; being allowed to stay up late in my pyjamas as the family gathered round the piano to sing; Richard's Pied Piper tune dancing before me through childhood. But only in adulthood have I become aware of the power of music to connect me to other levels of experience…Paula is watching my face as I try to tell her. The awareness that's often between us these days has become suddenly heightened. I feel the strength of her wanting me to be able to use what is in me—

And suddenly I think of her African father, the fantastic dancer, and all the things she is linked to but knows nothing about—and I jump up and start showing her how to tie a cloth around her hips the way the women do, and get her to move so the cloth jerks up and down as she dances. Extremely sensual it is, especially the breast shaking, which she does better than me, being better equipped by nature, and I show my appreciation as they do in the village—*ululululu*—tongue flapping, hand moving rapidly against my mouth to vibrate the highpitched, almost birdlike sound. Jane and Jaswinder come running up the stairs to find out what's going on—

The others are gone, back to their rooms. Paula and I stand facing each other, panting, recognising that something has shifted.

'You *are* bewitched,' she says, 'and you're doing nothing with it.'

'I want to,' I say. 'But I don't know what.'

Just experiment, you'll find something…It's easy for Paula to talk, she's found her thing…Just decide you're not going to let it go, she says, it's part of who you are…But what do I *do* with who I am? If I had started when I was a child…I would only have had to say, 'I want to learn the flute too,' and I could have been *making* the music that I now journey across London to hear. But now?—

Jane and I are in the kitchen. From upstairs, the voice of Sasha McKinley.

You could have loved better, you could have loved more
You could have relaxed on the sand by the shore

Jane listens, says, 'That woman's pretty acute.' Then, 'You and Paula dancing last night—'

'Good, wasn't it? And there's plenty more where that came from.' Then I realise she's watching me curiously.

'You're amazing,' she says.

'What way?'

'The things you don't see. Has it never occurred to you—'

'What?'

'That you want something more from Paula?'

I stare at her, caught completely off balance. Her eyebrows are slightly raised, smile hovering. I realise the question must seem obvious to everyone else. I pull myself back from my instinctive *No!* and say steadily, 'What I have with her is exactly what I need. All the pleasure of an intimate relationship, and none of the tension.'

'Except the tension that Eva can't believe that's all it is.'

That pushes me over into indignation. 'That's ridiculous,' I say. Jane just keeps looking at me with an expression that says, Carry on, there's more to think about…I say, 'If that were really going on, I'd have felt it myself.' But she's making me feel uneasy, defensive. She's right, there is something changing inside me, coming to a head, but she's giving it the wrong name…

A shrill voice floats up from the basement—*Tumhe yaad ho ky na yaad ho*—the deserted lover, yearning—I am yours, whether you remember or not—and Jaswinder sings as she washes her long black hair in henna, and chooses her clothes with care before she sets off for the launderette, where she will meet the same old clients and their dirty washing—

Paula comes in and bangs the door shut. 'That sound's going to drive me demented,' she says. 'I wish Jas would just find a man and be done with it.' Jane and I start laughing. 'What's the joke?' Paula asks, but she's got something of her own to tell and isn't waiting for an answer. 'Look what I've found.' She hands me a leaflet—'A music workshop on Saturday. And you're coming with me.'

A draughty community-centre hall. Probably thirty people waiting about, bald men, mums with kids, longhaired youths, none of us knowing what's going to happen. 'I don't know any more than you do,' Paula said, 'except that it's the kind of group that works with music the way Jane and I do with theatre. Starting with people, not with something written down'—

We form into groups, move to different rooms. Paula's not in my group and I hardly see her for the rest of the day. I'm with a boy with an electric guitar and a plump woman called Mabel, holding a violin she says she hasn't touched since she gave up lessons in grade three. I have no instrument but my voice—'The original and best,' says one of the musicians, who has joined our group to start us off; a large man with a Scots voice. I am beguiled by the sound—the *rr* of *original* rolls relaxedly, and *best* has a slow, calm vowel. But the comfort is momentary. 'I can't read music,' I say. He laughs, 'We'll not be reading anything today,' and *today* ends in an even purer vowel. 'We'll be taking it from the air!' He brings a couple of shy ten- and eleven-year-olds to join us, and gives them things they can shake—a rattle in a gourd from Africa, a bamboo pipe from the Andes that tips slowly to rustle like rain. 'All we're going to do,' he says, 'is see what kind of music we can make together, starting from sounds that come naturally to each of us.' We stare at each other in disbelief—we are going to make up the music? But before anyone has time to panic he has us sitting in a circle and he's saying, 'Let's start with some rhythms. Close your eyes'—and through the quiet receiving dark his clapping hands invite us to join. The pulse changes and we follow. So simple, but the blanking out of sight is unexpectedly powerful, for knowing we are not being observed we lose the need to be self-conscious, or to let our eyes make rapid judgements about the others...The clapping stops. We open our eyes—to look now with relaxed curiosity at the people who have, like us, been part of that single yet constantly changing pulse...

He lets the silence be for a moment, then smiles and says, 'I think I forgot to say—I'm Neil. I'll be moving between you and one of the other groups. While I'm gone, start by having a go at each others' instruments.' And he's off, taking that ease with him, leaving us with a space to fill...

The shakers are fun, and the children love holding the guitar. Mabel's violin is impossible, but we laugh at our own scratchy attempts, and that has the effect of making Mabel forget to feel anxious. She says, 'Now you're supposed to share your voice around, Jennie!' But that feels suddenly easy, for we've each got our own and the clapping has given me an idea. I start to teach them the simple kiSwati words they need for the chorus—

ku-la-pha s'khon'
ku-la-pha s'khon'

clapping and shifting feet in time. At first they protest that they can't do it, but the tune's simple, and it's got such a perky rhythm it's impossible to keep still to. 'What does it mean?' asks one of the children. 'It's a song young girls sing when they've been kept away from the boys and now they're allowed to mix with them again.

Something like, Here we are, you guys, take a look at us!' The children giggle at the sight of Mabel with her rolling movements and me with my uninhibited ones saying, 'Here we are'—until Jim, the boy with the guitar, suddenly decides to take charge. He gets the children to help him clear the chairs out of the way, and finally here we all are stamping around in a circle, me doing the lead voice, them clapping and chorusing away—

The dance ends. We look up to see Neil is back, standing just inside the doorway and watching us with amusement. He has a cello with him. Breathless and laughing, we pull the chairs back into a circle and watch as he twiddles the adjusters on his cello, head inclined, tuning the strings. The wood gleams…He lifts his head and says, 'You appear to have tuned in to each other already. Now for a little improvising.' He puts his bow lightly on the string and plays a pattern of two notes, over and again. 'Come in when you're ready. With whatever sound you like.'

No one moves. It is absurd to think we can. The cello notes are so clear and full, how can we barge in with our untrained noises? He says nothing and isn't looking at anyone in particular—the two notes just keep moving on, same notes, same rhythm, becoming the environment in which we exist…Tentatively I start to sing with them, just ah-ing the same two notes. Then that feels limiting and I find other notes that sound good with his; then a little hop in them, trippling in one of my mbira rhythms. Neil nods, eyes smiling, and keeps playing his same two notes while he looks around at the others—a slight pressure of his eyes meeting theirs now. My voice experiments more confidently. The guitar jumps in, Jim on a chord. He pulls a face, tries another—and when he's found one, starts plucking an accompaniment. Instantly the nature of the music changes, and his rhythm releases the children, shaking and rattling. Now it's only Mabel we're missing. We all look at her, willing her to join us. She laughs in embarrassment but by now there is so much other sound that it is safe, and she plunges in. The voices of guitar and violin are all around mine, swooping and chasing in a crazy medley while I sail—kites all of us, with that persistent two-note line on the cello pulling at us, holding us in the air—

The cello slows down, and stops. It is like the wind dropping, and all the kites fall to the ground. We stare at each other—our disbelief has disappeared. We have made music.

It was like that the whole day, a constant series of surprises, simple but profound. For weeks afterwards I felt that going to that workshop had changed the course of my life, but there was nothing to show for it except what changed inside me. Just holding Mabel's violin set off the strangest feeling, quite powerfully sad. It followed me for days afterwards, till sitting in a bus I remembered suddenly a story Mom used to tell about her father. He lived in a village called Auchterrnuchty—I can hear her voice digging deep into the *ch-* sound, her vowels broadening. Her father was the last of eight children in a labourer's family, and he had left school to work in the fields before he was ten—strange, it has already the sound of folk memory, retold for children. But it was Mom telling it, so it must be true…Her father as a young boy longed for a fiddle, she said. Each week he kept back a few pennies before handing over what he had earned to his mother, until eventually he had enough to buy the fiddle he had seen in the pawn shop. When he brought it home his mother was so angry that she broke it over his head—

That story fascinated me, and appalled me. So many things mixed up in it, frightening feelings—about being poor, the same kind of despairing poverty I saw in the faces of the men who knocked at the back door asking if we had any work. Impossible to take in that this had been the normal state of my own family, just one generation away. And his mother—however much she needed the money, how could she have smashed the thing through which his spirit longed to fly free?—

I stood holding Mabel's violin, not wanting to give it back.

Neil's a composer, I heard one of the musicians tell someone during the lunch break. I watched him across the hall of people, curious…In his mid-thirties, I'd guess. Large-bodied, quiet, but a sense of knowing himself well. Rumpled corduroy trousers, comfortable sweater…I felt I was seeing the man for the first time, though he had been with us half the morning. Somehow he released us to go straight to what was fundamental…Then the afternoon, the whole group together—punctuating what he was saying with short demonstrations on his cello—snatches of what he had heard each of the groups improvising. This rhythm, that line of a song. Fragments of our kite song lifting off his cello like birdsong, and gone as soon—we wanted more but he laughed and would not give it to us. 'It's you making the music,' he said, and we went back to our groups to shape those fragmentary beginnings…That skill of the instinctive teacher, to make it seem simple enough not to frighten, challenging enough to entice—

—The day is almost over. A moment of awe as we realise, it is now, now that we bring it all together. The musicians begin. Seeing them together I realise now that they make up a string quartet, and what they play is spun from strands of what each of our groups has produced, that they have somehow managed to weave together in between helping us with our own improvisations. We listen, amazed, at this beautiful thing that we have helped to make…The violins become still, and the viola. Just the cello is left, a quiet, repetitive phrase. Neil says nothing but the phrase does its own speaking—and the group that created it realises, 'It's our turn.' They gather their breath and their instruments, and begin. He keeps playing with them until the sound strengthens, then he fades off. Their piece is quite different from ours; so is the next group's and the next, an infinite variety of possibilities emerging from a single creative process.

Now our turn. The cello phrase pulls, quiet but insistent, waiting for me…I hear my voice before I know I have begun, and then I lose all sense of strangeness. I have come home, to some home that was inside me all along, and now sings.

5

And now what do I do with it?

For days, nothing, except try to take it in. Paula's picked up some ideas for her theatre improvisations. Mabel said she was going to try and keep going with her violin again, maybe playing with her granddaughter—I don't know if she has, I didn't think to take anyone's phone number. I keep hearing Neil's cello—encountered once, become intimate in a day, then gone, out of reach, off into the vast anonymity of London. I ask Paula to tell me if she ever sees any more workshops organised by the same group. 'It was a one-off, not a regular group,' she says, and smiles a challenge—'Over to you.'

But sometimes you leave since there's nothing to lose
You might not have chosen but still opt to choose…

I can't work out what's going on in me. Nothing I could put in words, just a restless excitement that has been let loose, intensifying the diffuse casting about of the past months, years… There's an energy now in all I do with Michael, a purpose. We experiment with all the things that make sounds, anything we find around the house or pick up outside. Striking pieces of metal or wood or glass, and listening—while I watch the expression on his face that announces which sounds he responds to most. We blow—a whistle that came out of a Christmas cracker, a comb covered with tissue paper. Blades of grass stretched taut between my clenched thumbs. Pots, pans, tins—he is thorough, and once he has discovered that a pan sounds different if we bang it with wooden spoons or steel ones, or tap it with our hands, he needs to test out the principle on every other pan his mother's kitchen possesses.

The women in the house are amused—mealtimes become equally experimental. Wet fingers zing around the tops of glasses, hilarity as we root around for pieces of hose pipe of different lengths and compete with each other trumpeting on them. Jane finds, sorting through a box of old papers, a penny whistle that she says I can have, for she never uses it. For several days I am absorbed in working out where to put my fingers to get the different notes. Then suddenly they know where to go and I can play any nursery rhyme the children in the one o'clock club ask for. The mbira lies untouched for weeks while I make up tunes of a different kind. The mbira is metallic and sonorous—to me its rhythms are like faint echos of the vibrations of rocks deep in the earth. The penny whistle comes from another element altogether, high and chirpy—the tunes it calls out of me circle like birdsong, or jive like the *kwela* music of the streets of Johannesburg. I feel beneath my notes, unsounded, the rhythmic pull of a double bass, improvised by street-wise children who have no possibility of buying anything. An oil drum, a tall stick nailed to it like a mast, a piece of wire stretched from the top of the stick to the rim of the drum, forming the string...The energy pulls across time and continents and lodges in my own body, leaving me once again restless with undefined music that needs to be made through me. I try to make a small version for the children, with an empty oil can I cadge from a filling station. But it produces only a floppy *doump-doump* sound you couldn't possibly dance to.

Now I become determined to discover what essential quality it is that makes a stringed instrument work—to devise in its simplest form something that will evoke those connecting vibrations in the children. We whrrrr with elastic. We stretch rubber bands over cardboard boxes. But there is no sounding box, no bow, I cannot get the tension right. I wanted to keep it within a child's reach, but I've simplified in the wrong way, for what's the point if the sound is dull and disappointing? There must be a way for them to experience the real thing, but at their level—like Neil made it possible for us to do. I think of how the cello string vibrating made everything else fall quiet, carrying me on its sensuous movement, to release my own music. A capacity of the spirit all of us have, which only needs opening up to let it fly free—

But I do not know how to make that happen again now that I am on my own, let alone help these children discover it for themselves.

Around me the women talk to each other, hungry for adult time. They hardly seem aware of what's going on between the children, intervening only to instruct or prevent—'Get down, you'll fall,' or 'Mark, don't touch, that's not yours'—until Mark does it once too often and his mum is out of her seat and yanking him away so that his arm nearly comes out of its socket. '*How* many times must I tell you?' she says. 'Now sit down next to me and *behave*.' She carries on her conversation about the new bus passes, oblivous of Mark, who is by now snivelling and resentfully poking her leg...A child called Sarah is climbing over me, saying, 'Rosies, Jennie, let's do rosies.' We do it—holding hands, round in a ring, all falling down—Mark too, and he's laughing with them all. They get excited by being near each other but they hardly know how to be together. Maybe that's why the singing and holding hands in a circle keeps going, generation after generation; music as ritual, a way we initiate children into understanding how to be part of a larger group...

A health visitor arrives, and talks to each of the mums. I like the unobtrusive way she watches the children. She sees without my needing to say anything that Michael is slow. 'It's helpful talking about it,' I say. 'I can't with his mother.'...Felicity's so super-efficient, she engenders tension in him within minutes of taking him over. 'Oh come on, Michael, *move*,' she says, and you can just see him clamming up. She's afraid, and it's easier to deny, to pretend that he is being slow from wilfulness. Dave is gentler, but he feels at a loss. Felicity has professionalised motherhood, making of it a science of exact measurements of food and only one right way to do up shoelaces…The health visitor says, 'It would be good if you could talk to them. But you've got something good going for him here, anyway, helping him learn alongside the others.'

'I love watching them discover what they can do,' I say, opening up to the pleasure of someone who understands…I'd like to help music-making seem natural to them, I tell her, before school gets hold of them and makes them believe it's something you only do if you're particularly talented; or that the way to start is by staring at little black marks on paper…

'Those awful piano lessons,' she agrees. 'My teacher used to hit my knuckles with a ruler when I played a wrong note.'

'Mine too! But I only lasted two lessons. I couldn't understand why some notes were supposed to be wrong, and she didn't try to tell me, so I refused to go back. I knew even then it should be easy.'

When she is gone I think, it's the same old thing, rejecting the syllabus. I was right about the ruler, but maybe too hasty about the system. There *are* patterns to be learnt—

Maybe it's not too late. Maybe I should stop trying to invent everything myself, and go and find out what others have understood before me.

I start reading, working my way through the couple of shelves called Music in the local library. A biography of Wagner, a history of opera—I read, but it's not what I was looking for. This is all information *about*—like reading a history of a country's literature when what you want is to be able to speak the language. Jane says, 'There must be a specialist music library.' I find it, on a Saturday so I can do it without Michael. Shelves and shelves of scores…I wander along them, picking them up and feeling intimidated. They contain mysteries I have no way of getting access to. I remember Simangele in Mbabane, and how reading and writing were to her all the doors that would not open. Now here I stand, as illiterate and just as frustrated...A librarian has been watching me, and eventually asks if I want help. I explain my incompetence and say, lamely, 'I was hoping to find something more basic, about how music works, in people's lives.' She looks doubtful, but finds me one or two books with alarmingly technical titles. I take them home, but they have lost me before chapter two.

Another spate of concert going. I look for unknown groups, contemporary composers—I keep thinking I might find Neil's name, but he's gone underground...Does he work always through people, or does he compose things that get performed?...I am pushing at the edges now, rebellious at the concert ritual that makes the audience unnaturally passive, the performers distant. We sit like worshippers in a medieval cathedral, cut off by elaborate screens from the sacrament that is being conducted on the other side. No way of connecting this with what the children experience, or could be part of. They're too young, people would say—but how can you be too young? Music is a human capacity, there from the start—it's only the form our society presents it in which excludes. What Neil did sidestepped these divisions, brought to our own musical culture the kind of meaning that dance has in the village, where no one needs to be silent and keep unnaturally still while the voices call and rhythms urge you to move, where nothing is written down, so no one is excluded because they can't read—if the love of music is in you, it can find a way out, whoever you are; where the musical thoughts of people long dead and whose names are forgotten move through the thumbs of the old man with his mbira, yet he constantly creates as he plays, so that what is old is also always becoming new—

That's where I need to be looking, to music across cultures. That's the way to understand the musical impulse that's common to us all—The librarian decides it's time to send me somewhere else.

School of Oriental and African Studies says the notice cut in stone above the entrance. SOAS, say the students who stand about talking to each other or rush down corridors, late for lectures. It's strange walking back into a university, and arriving with a child…I make my way to the library, and negotiate whether I who am not a student will be allowed to borrow books. Then for as long as Michael can last I move slowly along the shelves, overwhelmed by all the knowledge that is gathered in these dull-covered books. All possible subjects, all possible peoples…But music seems hardly to feature. A chapter here. A monograph there. I must be looking in the wrong place…I come home with a book on Indian musical instruments, and one on something called a gamelan from Indonesia. I chose it because of the photo that caught my eye—a big group of people sitting on the floor surrounded by brass gongs of all sizes, with little padded mallets raised to strike them—as if they themselves are the individual keys of a vast piano, and to make one tune they all have to be linked into the same imaginative concept, the same rhythm.

More visits, more books. Michael becomes a familiar figure. A couple of the women students smile in solidarity—maybe they have children and know what it's like trying to study while your attention is being demanded elsewhere. But the books stop short always of the nameless thing I am trying to understand more fully, that will connect these complex musical systems with the instinctive music in the children, in me. In the child I was, with sounds arranging themselves in patterns—Okavango swamps, Zimbabwe ruins, Nyika plateau—and my body moving to the tunes Richard played. In the untutored young woman, learning to use my voice in the hills. All of us in that community hall, discovering that making the kind of music people play in concerts can be as communal, as spontaneous as learning to dance…I join the queue to get my books checked out…It was we who made the music, but we could not have done it without Neil creating the space, the acknowledgement of our own creative spirit. That's what I'd like to be able to do with the children. But I need some framework other than working with Michael alone, or the one o'clock club. I could open up so much more to them if I had time and space set aside... Books in my bag, proceed slowly with Michael out of the library, along the corridor...A music-making workshop for children! Why not? Where mothers would bring the children, so there would be no need to tactfully wait for moments as they occur. I could work out things at a child's level that would take them through the same kinds of processes Neil took us through, to let them use that amazing power of concentration they have, to experience their own capacity to absorb and make music, so that they have it as a resource in themselves, as natural as breathing. It doesn't matter what they produce, it was the *process* that was so powerful, opening up what was in me, who I have been, what I may become—

I look up, and there is—my past suddenly reappearing. Leonie, ahead of me down the corridor, walking through the swing doors and into the crush of students who talk in animated groups as they emerge from the common room...Leonie, out of prison, the prison Kevin and I might have been in if a farmer in a passing landrover had seen us walking through the bush—

It can't be her. She had long hair, straight, and this woman has hair short and oddly stiff. But it's her, I'd know that walk anywhere, a sort of lope like a giraffe. Panic has started working its way up from the base of my spine. I *don't want to go back* into all that. I slow down...She's going out of the building now—I'm picking Michael up on to my hip and running, afraid that she'll be gone before I can catch up with her. Along the pavement behind her—'*Leonie!*'

She turns. She doesn't recognise me. I have advance notice of her presence, she has none of mine, but it's bizarre nevertheless. The only other person in London who has been part of the events that drove us both into exile—and we stand looking at each other and she doesn't know who I am. Michael wriggles to get down. 'I'm Jennie,' I say, 'Jennie de Villiers. Student union conference, Durban, 1967:

Her eyes flicker but do not relax. She remembers now; but what does she remember? A time before adult life began? Someone full of naive energy, new to the executive where she, Leonie, had done two years already? And who knows what her interrogators chose to tell her? 'Hi,' she says, voice cold. Her gaze takes in Michael. 'What are you doing here?'

We find a cafe. She does not talk about prison and I don't ask, but its effects are obvious. She is mistrustful, of everyone and everything. She hates living in London, she says. She has registered to do a PhD, and it's totally isolating. Hours alone in the library.

As we are going she says, 'When shall we meet next?' She's been behaving as if she cannot trust me, yet she still wants to hold on—

'There's something about her I find really disturbing,' I tell Paula and Jane, trying to explain across chasms of such different life experiences. 'She's cut off *inside*. Like she can't find who she is, so can't go forward.'

Paula asks, 'Too close?'

Maybe. A distorted mirror—

We arrange to meet in the students' common room. I ask about her PhD, and tell her about what brings me to the library. But our purposes hardly connect—she's only here because she can't think of anything else to do. I think, if she could only talk about what happened to her—But she is jammed closed…I carry her like a responsibility, thinking of things that might lift her out of herself.

I suggest some Latin American music—vigorous rhythms, haunting Andean pipes. But then a group of Chilean singers comes on stage, and a woman steps forward to tell us they are going to sing the songs of Victor Jara, whose voice the military thought they could silence by murdering him. She speaks simply, directly, but her own voice is eloquent of a knowledge of suffering; resilience—

I don't sing for love of singing
or because I have a good voice.
I sing because my guitar

has both feeling and reason...

Leonie can't cope. We leave at the interval and go back to her room, hardly speaking.

She starts as soon as we are inside. The worst was the isolation, she says. After the questioning was over, that is—and she moves on past the questioning, too painful to touch. On to the interminable months of the trial, the years inside. White prisoners are segregated from black, politicals from criminals, men from women. She was the only white woman political in her prison—that meant being alone most of the time. 'When you read other people's prison accounts,' she says, 'they always talk about the sense of solidarity. I had no one'—

—Walking back alone from her room to the underground... Round and round in my head, strands of thought that seem unconnected, but everything connects...Leonie, me.... me, Michael...

I sing because my guitar has both feeling and reason—

It was the Chilean woman's voice that opened her to her own feelings, in a way that all our talking before had not done...Leonie has confronted me again with the self I was in Swaziland, trying to connect...She is trapped still, but she could be free; it is her unreadiness that traps her. Four years she has lost, years I have been able to spend coming to terms with myself. Time now to *move*. The essential things I needed to understand—about music, about children—are obvious already. Time to weave something definite from all those strands of thought and experience.

Tomorrow I'll talk to Felicity. She's going to need to understand that what I'll be doing isn't taking my time and attention away from Michael, but something that comes out of trying to work out what will help him. But she isn't even at the point of admitting that he needs help. I've kept putting off talking to her about it, and now they've gone and put his name down for an appalling prep school, where the boys are all expected to do the same thing at the same time, rows of square pegs in neat grey uniforms, a place that would flatten him into frightened passivity in two hours. She can't face the fact that there will be no future of him doing brilliantly at school, of being successful, as she is successful. They're going to need some professional, whose credentials they will recognise, to sit quietly with them and help them accept Michael as he is, and work out what he needs; and to see that what I'm suggesting can be part of that—

I sleep lightly, waiting for tomorrow to come.

Felicity is half an hour late getting home. We talk briefly. She is tense, but that's nothing new. I can't wait for the right time, there will never be one. 'There was a health visitor at the one o'clock club,' I hear myself saying. Felicity waits, unencouraging. I push on. 'She's been a couple of times, and watched the children. She was talking about developmental tests—'

She interrupts, icy in her rejection. 'Jennie, I will thank you not to teach me how to care for my own child. If you don't mind my saying so you have a tendency to overstep the mark. I have not asked you to take Michael off to see health visitors—'

'I didn't take him to see anyone. I told you, she was there. She saw for herself.'

'It's time you went,' she says. Her voice is hard, her body stiff. I stare at her. Indignation surges through me like a rising temperature. I turn to pick up my things and walk out, slamming the door behind me. On the pavement I realise I didn't even say goodbye to Michael.

'It's time you went'—does she mean today, or forever? I should go back, find out. I can't, I shall say something unforgiveable, and then if she wasn't meaning to sack me before, she will now…I stand for a moment in indecision, then start walking furiously around the block. She's his mother, OK. I know I have to curb myself from getting too involved, the last thing I want is a repeat of Eva. But he needs both of us, no one could do it round the clock. I can be patient with him precisely because I can stay that little bit detached. If he were my child maybe I'd feel it like she does, feel his limitations as something too hard to face. Maybe. I'm not sure. It hardly matters. *She* feels those things, and if she were with him all day her tension would communicate itself to him and damage him more. *He needs me*, I want to shout. *Don't be so stupid*—I'm not holding on for my own sake, but for his—

I have arrived back at Felicity's front door, at the shiny brass letters announcing 27. The house, the child, they're all supposed to reflect status and confidence and importance. I hate them for putting all that on Michael. I wheel around and head for the bus.

I am too confused to face anyone else. Shut myself in my room, pretend sleep when Paula looks in. She goes. My head throbs, won't let me sleep. When the house is quiet I get up, get dressed again, go out into the streets, to walk off the tension. It's drizzling. I screw my eyes up against it, then deliberately relax the muscles. Grimacing like that doesn't keep off the rain—just get wet. It's what's happening, just accept it…Shiny oil slicks on the wet tar. Debris from the evening's take away meals—greasy paper with some uneaten chips on the pavement. The unshaven old man who roams about with carrier bags of stuff he's picked up off skips is wandering still. A couple of youths lounge at the end of an alleyway ahead of me. I don't know why, but I don't feel scared. Perhaps I should. Perhaps I'm losing my instinct for self-preservation…Or perhaps it's under attack in some more fundamental way, making the young men who stand there, watching me pass, seem irrelevant… They're cutting me off from a child I know how to help, from all the children, trying to block what I know I can do, something I've put love and life and thought and effort into.

I am going to fight, to stop them doing it.

6

I arrived for work next morning as if there was no issue. Dave opened the door to me. That figured; she was avoiding me.

'Felicity had an early meeting,' he said, and in ten minutes he too was gone.

All day my mind was hyper-alert. Everything that happened with the children suggested ideas for the music workshop, and I kept saying to myself, Hold it, make sure first that things are OK with Michael—

The next day it was Felicity again. She was brisk, and did not look me in the eye. Then Dave again. A couple of embarrassed false starts, then, 'Felicity is terribly upset. I hope you understand that it's because she's so—We both are—About Michael.'

'It's OK,' I said.

He rushed on. 'It's difficult for her to—I've been trying to get her to talk about it for a long time. I don't know what—And you must know how grateful we are to you. So creative, so patient. We've had other childminders before, they don't stay long—'

'I want to stay,' I said firmly. 'And there are things I think I can set up, that will help him. But that will only be a part.'

Dave swallowed. 'We've spoken to our doctor. He has referred us to a child development specialist.'

Begin—like rolling downhill, brake off—

Start by tracking down Neil. So obvious, really—and why in all the weeks of trailing around libraries did that not occur to me? But as soon as it's for the children I just do it—go to the community centre where the workshop was—they look up his phone number. On the phone I say, 'I was at your workshop. I've got an idea for music-making with children—can I come and talk about it?' He says, 'Sure,' and gives me his address. Simple as that.

It's a collective house. That's no surprise. People coming and going, unwashed coffee cups, and in the living space the smell of smoking, spills of wine on the carpet. The woman who lets us in—I have Michael with me—yells up the stairs—'Neil, someone for you,' then turns back to us and says, 'Go on up.'

We take the stairs at Michael's pace. He needs to peer at the gaps between the bare boards, concentrating as each step creaks. I am so used to how large every small experience is for him that I take it for granted—and then I look up to see Neil waiting on the first floor landing, watching us in amusement. We reach the landing. Big features, warm natural smile. Especially in the eyes.

'I'm Jennie de Villiers,' I say. 'This is Michael.'

'Now I see the face, I remember. You'll be the one who sang.'

'That's it. With those kids who went wild on the rattles.'

'A pleasurable experience, the whole workshop. Come on in.'

His room is a complete contrast to the living space downstairs—open, calm. A huge room that goes from the front of the house to the back, windows at both ends, high ceiling. A double bed mattress on the floor at the far end, the rest is work space. Books, sheet music, a desk with piles of paper. A cello on its side—chair behind it, music stand in front of it—he must have been playing before we came. A violin, or is it a viola? in its open case on the floor under the window.

I come to, realising I am staring as Michael does. 'This is a fantastic room.'

He looks amused. 'What way, fantastic?'

'The feeling of music about to happen. Did we interrupt you playing?'

'Not specially,' he says. I am taking in the lilt, more than what he's saying—the *no* sound for 'not'—'Some coffee, before you tell me your idea?'

I accept the coffee, and the distraction of settling Michael on to my lap. I am beginning to lose courage, to wonder how, I got here. It's nothing Neil's done or said, it's me, a sudden onset of inadequacy from seeing all these signs of his musical life, of which I know nothing. I make myself push past the feeling…'I don't have a very clear idea of what kind of activities we'd need,' I begin. 'But I know the effect I want it to have.'

'A good sign.'

'Oh?'

'The reverse is less useful—teachers who tell me exactly what I should be doing, and they've not thought why.'

His relaxation has banished the moment of awe. I laugh and say, 'I'm not a school teacher! It's for children this size.'

His face makes a 'Well—that's new!' expression. 'In that case I'm a novice. The youngest person I know is ten.'

I am curious. 'Who's that?'

'Child of a friend of mine.' He looks at Michael, speculatively. Michael stares back from the security of my lap. They keep looking at each other in silence till Neil says, 'OK laddie, you win.' He turns to me. 'It's not often anyone sizes me up quite so openly.'

'He's thorough, Michael. He only understands things if you let him wrap all his five senses around them. He has to stare at it and listen to it and pick it up and preferably taste it and then he's fine, he's taken in what it is.'

'You left out smell. Shall I offer him my sweaty feet?' To my delight and Michael's solemn absorption he does it, *slipping off* his Indian sandals and putting out one foot to twiddle his toes invitingly in front of Michael. But too close. Michael's body retreats into mine.

'Back off a bit! He doesn't like being rushed.'

Neil says, 'You're *sure* he's old enough to make music?'

Instantly I am on my guard again. He is laughing at me—at Michael—and I won't have it. 'Listen,' I say, 'I can't read a note of music and if anyone had told me before that workshop that you were going to get me to compose, I'd have said they needed their head examined.'

'There is a wee difference—'

'No there isn't. It's just because you don't know young children that you think that.' I am indignant now and in full flood, as if this is one of my older brothers not taking me seriously. 'You know yourself, the musical impulse is inborn—there can't *be* a time that's too soon to help it develop. The problem is, before anyone encourages it, it gets killed off by disbelief. If we *assumed* all children were going to be able to make music, like we assume they're going to learn to speak, they would do it. It's just a question of working out what will encourage that capacity and what will depress it.'

I note with satisfaction that he's listening now without that amused look. He pushes back his chair, stretches out his legs and says, 'Perhaps you'd better tell me how all this started. And where you've got to.'

'It was the workshop—' I break off. 'That's why I assumed you would understand. I'm sorry if I sounded like I was preaching.'

'No, no, you were perfectly right to be firm.' I am beguiled again by the sound—*perfectly right to be fir-rm*—the roll of the *rrs* underlining the concession. 'Go ahead, I'm listening.'

Where to begin? The workshop, the feeling of starting again, the children—When I use the word 'childminding' his face registers yet another new piece of information. Of course, he must have thought Michael was mine. Now there's a rush of thoughts, all wanting to come out, about the challenge to find the kind of situations that will let them be musical, in any way it's possible for a child of two or three to be. The particular challenges of Michael—'It's no different from what you were doing with us, creating the safe space, and the stimulus.'

He rocks back on his chair. 'There *is* a difference, you know.'

'Of course there is. We'd have to think harder and observe more, to find out what level the challenge needs to be.'

I have a feeling of unusual lightness, a confidence in what I know and that he doesn't yet, and that I'm going to be able to make him see. The mirror image of the feeling I had at the workshop when it was him taking us through the necessary steps to discovering what was already in us. Now it's me, for him; this man who knows no one younger than ten but who looked at Michael the way he did, taking in the whole small person that he is. It's obvious he's going to be able to work with children. All he needs is to be convinced.

He is not. He is saying, 'I can't see it working, not with people as young as this. Of course you're right he can *respond* to music. But *make* it?'

'That's what I'm talking about.'

He shakes his head. 'You'll not get much past the banging of tambourines.' His eyes are amused again. 'You've no cause to look indignant, I'm not saying anything about intelligence. In the workshop you drew on all the music you've ever heard and made your own from those elements. He's just not heard enough.'

'He's been listening since birth. How do you think he learnt how to speak? He takes in our words and comes up with sentences of his own that no one ever said before, that express what *he* wants to say. I don't see why it couldn't be the same with sounds.'

'You underestimate the complexity. To make music requires some ability to organise sounds—and for that you've to have a vision, however inarticulate, of what the sounds might be like once organised. Which requires a great deal more life experience than that young lad's had. Otherwise the concept of music you're working with is not very different from noise.' He interrupts himself and starts laughing.

'What's the joke?'

'Sorry. I was just thinking, there *is* a concept of music that's not far off that. You've heard of John Cage, maybe?'

'No.'

'No, no reason why you should have. Of little interest except to other musicians, but a big name in the world I emerged into after music college. He tried to persuade people that music was whatever sound happened in a structured space. By that definition it's immaterial whether the child can consciously plan. We may be at the forefront of experimental music here!'

'I don't get it.'

'Example—there's this piece called 4'33'. Four minutes thirty three seconds, that's how long it takes to perform. There are no notes written, and the only musical instruction is *Tacet*—Keep quiet.'

I stare. 'So where's the music?'

'What happens in the space. Those four minutes thirty three seconds while the audience watches the performer keep quiet.'

'But that's absurd!'

'Of course it is. That's the point.' He is enjoying himself. I think, Are there really music students who take this kind of thing seriously?

Michael is beginning to shift in my lap—my time for uninterrupted adult conversation is almost up. And we still haven't started. 'OK,' Neil is saying, 'try this one.' He moves to the cello, positions it between his knees, gets his bow ready. Now that there is some movement Michael is still again, watching. Neil's bow moves. One long continuous note. The lowest string, deep and sonorous, vibrating over its whole length without any fingers pressing down on it. The bow pulls slowly, right to the tip and back again all the way. The string's vibration is almost visible, a haze with no clear edges. All the air around us seems to move in the same buzzing drone—on and on, mesmeric—

Something has changed, some invisible electricity. The child's body feels almost as if it is part of the sound, vibrating. He is staring at the cello with total concentration. Neil is watching too, his eyes fixed on the child's. The sound is everywhere now, in us, around us, holding us. The only thing that moves is the bowing arm and that constantly vibrating string.

The sound fades. The bow is still. The string rests.

Silence, like no other I have experienced. Space.

Small sounds creep back. A car starting outside. Cups clanking in the kitchen downstairs. A bird making a chuck-chuck-chuck noise. Michael's head moves slightly at each sound. Then the spaces begin to fill up—someone calls, a telephone rings. Michael wriggles, climbs off my lap and stands a few feet from the cello, staring at it.

I move too, to kneel next to him. He puts out one hand to grip my sleeve and with the other points at the cello.

'You want more?' I ask.

He lurches down on to me, knocking me into a sitting position, and climbs on to my lap, waiting. I look up—Neil is waiting. The cello begins. This time it is the next string up and he moves it gently, a warm, caressing sound that begins to throb—and I see his bow is no longer moving steadily but in little waves, slower, faster, slower. I sway with the pulse, forwards, backwards, to help Michael feel it more strongly. He moves with me, slightly lagging. Neil watches and makes the pulse firmer. Then his bow begins to hop and the sound is broken up into skipping. Michael's backward-forward push becomes jerkier—more awake—and now it's almost as if it's Michael creating the rhythm, the bow following. The skip becomes a dance—the child wriggles round to look delightedly up into my face. I take his hands in mine and clap them in time.

The dance stops. I look up. 'Why are you stopping?' I laugh. 'We were just getting into it!'

'You're right about him listening. I've never played to a more appreciative audience.' He looks speculatively at us both for a moment, then says, 'Now there's another composition that challenges the categories somewhat.'

'That was a *composed* piece?'

'La Monte Young. The score says, Hold for as long as possible.' I start laughing. He asks, mildly, 'And was that one absurd?'

'It makes a lot more sense than the silence one.'

'But this one gave you silence too?'

Now he's got me thinking. Was the silence part of what was composed? I become aware that he is watching me, waiting for my answer, but it's not a pressure, more like he's really curious to know how I experienced it. I say, tentatively, 'You *feel* it's silence, but then you begin to hear—so many small sounds—'

He says, 'It's a profound mystery we're touching on. We need silence to shape the sound, and sound to shape the silence. Neither exists without the other.'

Michael puts his fingers into my mouth. I lift them out to say, 'I'm being recalled to duty! How would you feel about him touching the string?'

Neil puts his bow down and leads Michael's hand to the string and curls the small fingers round the string—'Come, it's waiting to sing,' he says. Michael pulls. Only a small whirr, but the delight at having made it himself spreads over his face and leaps instantly into Neil's. Michael laughs and does it again, a little firmer, louder. Then again and again, till it is zinging madly and we are all three falling about laughing.

I say, 'The instructions on that piece say, As wildly as you can. Composer, Michael Palmer.'

Neil says, 'OK, you're on.'

Chapter 4

The idea took off like Michael's composition, zinging away faster than we could keep up with it. Neil only needed someone to bounce him into opening his mind that one step wider than it already was and he was bubbling with ideas. Seeing the possibilities came naturally to me but I hadn't the musical experience to develop them. Neil had all that and in addition a real warmth of feeling about people that made him want to open up to them the things he loved in music. And he couldn't resist a challenge. 'Experimental music is a question of trying to *hear* things in a new way, but we start far too late. We can't escape from what we've experienced.' The more we talked, the more excited he got at the idea of what might be possible with children whose every reaction was bound to be spontaneous.

My days with Michael became suddenly busier. With Colleen from the one o'clock club I did the rounds of local playgroups. Megan, the health visitor who had seen that Michael needed special help, said there were four other young children she knew of locally that we ought to invite specially. Each time I had to explain the idea it became clearer. At the arts centre a lanky young man called Lawrie who ran puppet workshops listened to us with his whole body swaying like a reed—I kept wondering where his centre of gravity was and whether if we went on talking long enough the momentum would reach the point where he fell over. But we didn't need to go on. He suddenly stopped moving, announced that it was a great idea, and leaned across to look up in the centre diary the first free Saturday. Three months ahead. That sounded forever but he said, 'You'll need some lead-in time.' And money for hiring the hall—I hadn't even thought of that. Lawrie swayed and said, 'I've got a small budget for new initiatives. Only a one-off—won't break the bank.'

Megan looked at our growing list of takers and said, 'It's mad to do all this just for one Saturday. It really needs to be something regular. Enough for them all to feel these are normal activities. Once a week for a term, I'd say.' But that meant a lot more money. Lawrie said, 'Apply for an Arts Council grant,' and then, as he began to do some rough calculations, 'What's Neil's fee?'

I hadn't even thought to ask—

—And now I see that it's not going to work, he's too busy. He gets out his diary. I see the pages already scrawled over. Someone phones, something about Max's score. Phone down, he says, 'So how many sessions are you thinking of?' then before I can answer someone arrives to see him, to rearrange a session of something called The Group. I think, 'You're on' was for one Saturday, there's no way he'll agree to every week. He's flipping ahead in his diary, saying, 'Thursday mornings might be possible,' but I can see half the Thursdays are already booked.

'What about all those other things?' I ask.

'They're not your problem,' he says calmly. 'Some of this clutter I need to ditch anyway. As long as we finish by mid-April. Then I've a term's residency in Manchester.'

'What's a residency?'

'I reside, they pay me. The deal is I produce something for the orchestra.'

I am instantly curious. 'You'll be composing for an orchestra? A normal piece?'

He looks up, eyes laughing. 'You can't imagine me doing anything normal?'

'I mean—is it like, you do the composing, and they play, and other people come and listen? I didn't know you did that.'

'I do, for the rare groups who're willing to court bankruptcy to try my music. It's not what your Normal Audience expects.' He is amused. 'You regard this as a sell out?'

'No, I'm just—After your workshop I kept wondering what type of music someone like you composed. Now I'm here, asking you!'

He says drily, 'Musicians do what someone's prepared to pay them to do. In between I make space to do the kind a thing we're doing together now, that keeps me alive and challenged. If it pays, I'm grateful, otherwise I do it anyway. Just occasionally someone asks me to write the music I have in me and let other people hear it. For that I drop other things and run.'

'I'd like to hear some.'

'You'll have to wait a while—performances don't happen as often as composers would like.'

We worked together in the evenings, in his room. After a day dictated by Michael's pace there was an excitement in going *fast*, like the pleasure of sound after silence. His ideas started always from the nature of music, mine from the nature of children. I would show him things I'd already tried doing with Michael. He listened, analysed, theorised—and suddenly I understood why. He put an idea to me—some new way of testing the limits of what we hear and feel and respond to. At first it sounded far too abstract. I said, 'Tell me how you'd use that if it were with a group of adults.' Instead of telling, he made me do it. As soon as I had felt it in my body I could see how we could turn it into an activity that would work for children.

When the others who lived in the house came in, Neil drew them momentarily into what we were doing. I began to know their names, and odd scraps of information. Tania, a cellist in the BBC symphony orchestra—a woman Neil's age, I guessed, mid-thirties. She was the one who appeared most often. I wondered occasionally if she was checking up on us. Then someone called Mike, making arrangements for the mysterious entity called The Group—

—'What's The Group?' I ask, when Mike has gone. Neil is amused at my direct questions but always answers straight. 'Five or six people who meet to explore composition.' Then, vehemently, 'To be perfectly precise they're a band of self-absorbed tossers. They like to think they challenge elitism in music but they're only interested in esoteric experimentation no non-musician can understand.' He gets up and waves his arms about aggressively, as if the irritation needs out. 'I'm scunnered the day,' he says—he's almost forgotten he's talking to me. Then he notices me and laughs. 'In English, *fed up*. Only that doesn't say it anything like as well.'

'What keeps you with them, the self-absorbed tossers?'

He looks at me curiously. 'You know what a tosser is, then?'

'I could take a guess.'

His scunnered feeling seems to be diminishing. More calmly he says, 'I stay with them because we do things that interest me, musically. It's when I'm confronted by people like you who've no training but who passionately want to use music that I get impatient with them.' He looks directly at me, struck by a new thought. 'And what have *you* been up to, since the workshop? You said it woke things up in you.'

'It did. But over so soon. I didn't know where to go with all that energy.'

'So? Where *did* you go?'

'Here,' I say, surprised that he needs to ask. 'Doing this.'

'This is for the children. I'm asking about you.'

I retreat, defensive. 'Listening and thinking, mostly. And reading.'

'What?'

'About music in other cultures.'

His mouth moves slightly, that characteristic registering of something new. But he leaves that on one side. 'I thought what you took away was the discovery that *you* could make music.'

'I get that by being with the children. Singing, playing silly music games.' It doesn't seem enough of an answer. His waiting presses me for more. 'I play for myself,' I admit. 'But I can't read music so I just mess about. Things that come into my head.'

Now he is looking at me in that directed, speculative way he turned on Michael the first day. 'When you sat there telling me off for not trusting to the creative instinct in children, you'd a passionate zeal about everyone having music in them. Now you're talking about your own musical activities as messing about. Why the apologies?'

I feel cornered. Then my resistance suddenly collapses and I am grateful at being pushed to be more honest. 'Because I long to be able to make real music and I can't. Like watching people fly, and my own wings are clipped.'

'Because you can't read music?'

'That. But also because I didn't start learning an instrument when I was a child.'

'But you said you play now?'

I say nothing.

'Go on, tell me.'

'The penny whistle. And the mbira.'

Again his face moves, to register surprise.

'And what would you want to play?'

'Everything! There isn't an instrument I've heard that I wouldn't like to get my hands on.'

'Be specific. What are the recurrent fantasies?'

'The shehnai. Or the tabla—the way they talk to each other, work each other up—the rhythm driving, the song pulling. Or being in a gamelan orchestra, knowing I'm only a small part of that whole sound but if my gong is missing the music doesn't work. An African xylophone, the kind with gourds for sound boxes hanging beneath each wooden strip—playing like mad while everyone dances.' I am laughing at myself but also watching him to check that he's not laughing at me. 'And nearer to home, to be part of a string quartet!'

'This sounds a trifle like greed.'

'It is. It's ridiculous and insatiable and I don't know where it comes from. So what I do instead is roam around London listening to other people play and it stirs my longing even more. Then I go home and piddle away on the mbira. I'm not knocking the mbira, you should hear what the man I got it from can do with it—'

'Where was that?'

'In a village in Swaziland. I didn't know then but further north where he got it they use them to summon the spirits of ancestors. When it's played properly it's completely mesmeric. But there's not much I can do with it, especially alone, in an attic in Britain.'

He says, more to himself than to me, 'A viola, I imagine.'

'What about a viola?'

'That's what you should be playing, in your string quartet.'

'Why a viola?'

'Because it seems your most obvious passion is to get into the middle of the chord.' He uncrosses his legs that have been stretched out in front of him, pushes his chair back and goes over to pick up the viola that lies in its open case under the window. He holds it out towards me. 'Have a go.' I want to take it but something in me resists. I'm sure he's laughing at me and I wish I had never told him.

He is not laughing, not even smiling. His hand is still stretched out, holding the viola. 'Take it,' he commands—the voice of a father talking to a recalcitrant child. I take it. It's heavier than I had expected. I hold it tentatively, afraid to damage it. He says, 'Experiment with how to hold it. I'll be back in a minute,' and leaves the room. With no one watching, my nervousness disappears. I let the viola lie in my lap, steadying it with one hand while with the other I stroke its wooden belly, touch the strings. A small sound escapes, startling me. Just from a touch! I sit still looking at it, waiting for it to speak again. It lies looking back at me, doing nothing. Cautiously now I try lifting it to put under my chin. Which hand do you hold it by? How stupid that I can't remember—so many hours I have sat watching string players! I try it both sides—they both feel odd. Like something live nuzzling up, close enough to whisper. I hold it there, get used to it. My arm has to bend round underneath its neck in what feels an extraordinarily abnormal position. It begins to ache. Carefully I touch the strings again. A little buzz of sound, vibrating through the wood, into my neck. It tickles—

The door opens. Too soon. Much too soon.

He is carrying another viola. He stands in front of me for a moment, assessing the position of my head, my outstretched arm. Then he notices my face and starts laughing. 'You've no need to look so defensive. I'm not about to take it away!'

Hold it in my lap, comfortably, like a child...Then under one arm like a banjo...'Talk to it,' he says, 'walk about with it. It's just a beautiful box with strings. Touch them like Michael did, find out how much plucking it takes to make them really sing.' Then he gets me swinging my arms about, big limbering up movements, and when the viola's in place again under my chin my arm finds its position much more naturally. 'It's meant to be a pleasure,' he says. If you get achy muscles, you're working the wrong way. All we're going to do is channel your body's instinct to move to music, so the movements become precise, directed to making specific sounds...Never rigid, never forced—just finding the stillness within the dynamic'...

My hand holds the bow now, resting on one of the strings. The position of stillness, waiting for the movement to happen. Neil picks up the other viola and his bowing arm starts to make long smooth movements...'Listen to the steadiness of it—Nothing dramatic, just as simple as you can. Like a pulse, in your own body'...Then he stops talking and lets the viola speak, saying the same thing, till I feel it coming from inside me, almost…'The fundamental thing about music is that it structures time. That's what creates the sense of security when you listen to Bach. The sounds can move fast or slow'—his bow is doing it as he speaks—'high or low—tense, exciting—or gentle, peaceful—but the net of structured time that holds them is always there…' Arm and hand an extension of his voice, his mind…'OK, let's try it together. Just on that one string, and nothing to think about with the other hand.' Tentatively I move my arm, following his as Michael follows me when he is trying to walk in time. The sound of the string being set in motion so near my ear is distracting. It scratches unevenly, measuring my lack of control. Instantly I stop—my sound is spoiling his—but the rhythm of his constant sound holds on to me, will not let me go…let your arm find its own natural weight and pace—a pendulum.' He keeps watching till our arms are synchronised. The sound becomes diffused, like a background drone…His voice joins the pulse now, walking on the rhythm of our bow strokes—'Now I'm—stopping but—you keep—going—' I concentrate so hard that of course I falter. He waits till the pulse becomes sure again, then through the mesmeric push-pull of my bowing arm his voice comes at me—'Just keep steady. You are the net that holds the tune I'll be playing—'

And he is off, the tune dancing high, light, free. Bouncing back on to my rhythmic beat, touching base then off again, dividing time in energetic little bursts or pulling it out in long smooth swoops—to land exactly where my pulse has got to.

He stops. By now my arm is moving by itself. It keeps going for several beats. Then my mind reasserts itself and I bring it to a halt—

I look up to see him watching me. 'So,' he says, tone matter of fact now. I lift the viola carefully down and watch the warm glow of its deep brown wood, silent now. Reluctantly I go over to the window to put it back in its case. From behind me Neil says, 'We'll have another go next time.'

I swivel round, not sure I have understood. He is packing up the viola he has been playing. He looks up and laughs. 'I presume you want to do more?'

'You know I do!'

'Well then. You'll be needing this to practise on. It doesn't make quite the sound of the other but it's good enough. It's the one I use when I'm working in schools, so the children aren't tempted to get their sticky fingers over mine.'

'Like Michael did on your cello!'

'That was an exception,' he admits, smiling 'But worth it.' He closes the viola case and passes it over to me. 'Go on, take it. We'll see how we're going by the time the children's workshops finish.'

I lie with eyes open in the dark, too alert to sleep. My mind floats back to Marilyn's garden in Swaziland and to the thoughts I had then about how my future life might be, before I had any idea I would one day be in London or live in a collective house or look after children for a living—or discover music. I remember watching Marilyn's life, so neatly organised that it left no room for any new possibility to arise unexpectedly. She writes every couple of months and I write back. They have renewed their contract in Swaziland so the promised meeting in London never happened. Her letters are the only link I now have with Swaziland and it all feels very far away. The love is there, but it's difficult now to find the substance to carry it. Charity never writes. Having taught her, I know how alien the written word is to the real Charity. It doesn't matter fundamentally; if we ever landed in the same place again we would begin again, immediately. But I wonder what she is doing these days. What she thinks about. The direction of my own life has changed so much that she would hardly recognise me. Or would she? Maybe there's more the same than I can see.

I get out of bed and go to stand at the dormer window, pushing it open to look out over the roofs of London—the night lights down on the pavement—a few late buses and cars moving along the streets. This is now where I am. Definitely here, itinerant no longer. Here in London, here in adulthood. I had not known until now that the final arrival still lay ahead of me but each new present moment changes the past, shows up things that were not clear before. I have discovered the thing I can do, a talent I have that was there all the time but I never thought it was something I could start to build a life around...The excitement of thinking something out from my own experience, then sharing the idea, seeing the other person's face open up as it grows in their own mind, and then—

Every one suddenly burst out singing
and I was filled with such delight
as prisoned birds must find in freedom winging—

—winging with it, for the song is their own. There's a quality that's different from anything I've done before...The classes under the trees gave up within a month of my leaving, and as for the prison visiting scheme, that won't have survived Jonas' arrest and my flight by more than a couple of weeks. No one else felt responsible for anything except their turn on the rota. This time the idea was born in my head but it's no longer just mine. I've learnt to let it grow strong by letting it fly free—

as prisoned birds must find in freedom
winging wildly across the white
orchards and dark-green fields, on—on—and out of sight.

2

It rained that January, day after day. Sometimes just a continuous wetness descending, hardly visible. 'That's not rain,' Neil said, 'just a wee smirr.' But I would emerge from his house on to a pavement shiny with the reflections of street lights and by the time the bus arrived my clothes would be clinging damply, my anorak dripping water down on to my trousers. On the day of the first session I woke to the sound of rain and thought, Oh God, half of them won't come. But they were there, all fifteen children on our list and two we hadn't expected, the foyer a flurry of small bodies milling about, of mums shaking out umbrellas and removing wellingtons—and then there we all were in the hall. The numbers of people made me excited—and Neil was unexpectedly ill at ease. After all the theorising they were suddenly far too real, these constantly moving beings—and so young. I didn't know how I knew that was what he was feeling because all that showed was an apparently calm detachment, watching from the side while Colleen and I started them off with clapping games. As he was in the orchestra workshop, creating the space and then letting us do it. Then it was his turn—and mine to watch, as he sat on the floor with the circle of children. The detachment lightened and then was cast aside as he led them into feeling time-spaces that they themselves created and shaped, through stopping and starting, sound and silence—those first elements in making music—

—'Always begin with rhythm,' he says, 'the most basic physical experience.' But not as I had been struggling to do with Michael, helping him arrive at a rhythm decided with no reference to him. Here it is *their* bodies that evolve the rhythms, they who set the pace. Neil watches and judges when they are fully released, then—'Now *listen* as hard as you can to the other sounds—' And no matter how unco-ordinated their banging and moving has been, when they start listening a pulse begins to emerge—'Now see if you can hear Becky's rhythm—' And each in turn they discover the excitement of watching others march or hop to the sound they are making, and the equal pleasure of letting themselves be absorbed into the collective sound.

The rhythms become more specific. They pass a big ball around—whoever gets it calls out their own name. We call the name back as embryo music, clapping its rhythm—*Sa*rah *Pen*fold, *Jon*athan Mac*Don*ald—and the rhythm asks them to stomp to *Sa*rah *Pen*fold, to skip to *Jon*athan Mac*Don*ald...It becomes a ritual incantation, not just rhythm now but pitch, as the voices slide closer to each other in the age-old chanting tune of childhood—

You ca-an't catch me
Jo-na-than Mac-do-nald.

Neil's cello comes to every session. It lies on its side in a corner of the room and the children watch it as if expecting it to sing on its own at any moment. A moment of excitement spins around the group when he picks it up—they gather, pushing and fluttering like sparrows after crumbs. Neil says quietly to the children nearest him, 'Close your eyes,' and then just waits as gradually they each notice and follow, and the hall becomes silent with their concentration. Then he produces from his cello one simple pattern of sound, lingering over it till it becomes like a friend. A child breaks the silence to say, 'It's a curly one. 'OK,' he says, 'How about this one?' That one's heavy—and the next jumpy. Their eyes are open now, alert. Neil's hands keep producing an extraordinary carnival of sound textures, almost detachedly, and all the time he's watching. Just when I am thinking, 'He needs to stop now, it's enough,' the note begins to swirl up, swirl down and he says, 'Now you get inside it—see if you can become part of it.' I think, 'That's absurd, they haven't an idea what he's saying'—but I'm wrong. Joining the sound appears to be an ordinary idea to them. Some of them say *Woohoowoohoo,* trying to rise and fall with the note. Michael sits and rocks. One slices the air with her arms—bowing. Another dips like a small aeroplane, arms out to the sides, his whole body becoming the vibrating string...

He watches their responses with the same total involvement he watches mine in our viola lessons, constantly adapting what he does to what has just happened. There is no talking down and in an odd way no concessions because they are so young. The activities we have planned together take off in unexpected directions once he is actually with the children—

'Indeterminacy in action,' he says to me afterwards, and from his amused tone I know we're on to more musical theory. 'The composer sets the framework, the actual musical happenings are decided by chance. Or in this case by what that collection of uninhibited individualists chooses to do with it!' I love the way he laughs at the children and at the musical theorists, and yet takes both seriously—

There was a world out there where it rained and buses ran and people hurried by without seeing each other. And another here inside, full of life and stimulus and music. For weeks I didn't read a newspaper. In South Africa black people were ignoring the law and joining unions; a rising tide of strikes, one of the most significant changes in a decade and I wasn't noticing. Right here in front of me as I walked to the arts centre, the headlines shouted elections. At the kitchen table Jane and Eva argued about whether there was any point voting Labour. I do remember that, but it was about the time I started viola lessons so the details washed over me, like the rain—

—Paula comes into my room where I am practising. She drapes herself on the bed. I put the viola down, reluctant to stop, but I don't turn down time alone with Paula. 'How's it going?' she asks.

'Brilliant,' I say. 'I mean—not me, the viola. It's extraordinary how difficult it is to get one simple note out of it, the way you hear it in your head before you start. There's so much to think about.'

'Like what?'

'Not holding the weight in your shoulder, but letting it down into the bow arm. Holding this other hand curved round the neck, but soft, no strain in the fingers. Neil says you have to feel like you're holding a bird in your palm—' I pick up her hand and mould it to the shape. She lets me do it and then her hand flies off, out of mine—

A moment's silence. I don't know why, but I feel awkward, as if what I've been saying isn't really an answer to what she asked.

She says, 'Jane says—before all this—she asked you if—'

'Yes,' I say, aware of her sharp eyes. 'If I wanted more from you than I have.'

'I wondered too, for a while. Not any more.'

I capitulate—flop down on the bed next to her—we both start laughing. She ruffles my hair and says, 'Go on Jennie, *tell* me.'

My laughing is stilled—the stillness within the dynamic, Neil would say. 'There's nothing to tell. Just that I feel light and free, and excited every day.'

My absorption changed the ambience of the house. Everyone felt it, no one liked it. Paula laughed at me but even with her, things were subtly different. When we did get time to talk it was like paddling away in separate canoes, calling to each other over the noise of rapids. With the others it felt like a collective jealousy, if such a thing can exist. Of course they would have denied it—there was no reason why my sudden involvement should be more a threat than anyone else's. The internal dramas of the theatre group loomed as large in Paula and Jane's minds as the viola and Neil did in mine; Maria was out as much, drinking and talking into the small hours with her Portuguese friends while they analysed events back home. But everyone was used to that. With me it was different. Through all the coupling and uncoupling I had been there, unattached, not wanting to be attached. The house and all the women in it had been the whole content of my emotional life and it seemed they had come to rely on that almost as a conventional household relies on the mother and wife always to be there, making it home while they feel free to come and go. It was not that I had done anything special the rest of them didn't—just that they'd got used to how I was. Now I was out almost all the time. A week could go by without my overlapping with Jane or Maria, and when we found ourselves in the kitchen together getting breakfast they said, 'Hello stranger,' and joked about whether I was planning to move into the arts centre—

—'Where do you sleep these days?' Jaswinder asks. 'Where do you think?' I say. She's envious in a more pointed way than the others, and there is no way to calm it. If I tell her it's not Neil I'm absorbed in but the music, she doesn't believe me and feels hurt that I'm not being straight with her. If I leave her to think what she's going to think anyway, she sees only that I've found what she so badly wants. And I used to claim not even to want it. That's the rub, it seems, that I have changed. But we are all changing all the time—why is it a problem? I feel momentarily hurt, as if they are unfairly demanding of me what none of them expects of themselves.

And Eva. Since they all think I am in love, and with a *man*, I am presumably no longer a threat. But though her manner is less aggressive it's also more offhand, as if this proves that she was right about me all along. Kirsty picks up the change, her antennae sensitive as a radio aerial—

—A Saturday morning, an unusual flash of mild air. I'm out in the garden early, clearing dead winter undergrowth and uncovering the first snowdrops. Kirsty comes to squat next to me. She has learnt to choose her times with me much as Paula does, when Eva won't notice, but neither of us says anything about why that is necessary. She watches a while then says, 'If you wanted to, we could go to the swings.' I look up, interested. It's months since I've done anything like that with her. Now it seems she feels it can safely be risked. As if we are two adults talking about the children she says, tolerantly, 'Mom and Paula are so lazy they never want to get out of bed.'

I straighten up and say, 'Come on then, we'll do it quick!' And we're off, and back before anyone else stirs.

I field the innuendos and try not to think too precisely about what might be happening. What is clear is that I have become for Neil what the children are, an absorbing musical experiment. He allows me to discover the possibilities of the viola as directly as he lets the children discover time. He puts no written music in front of me—we do everything by ear, by hand, by eye. He demonstrates, I watch. He talks me through the action, constantly raising images in words but making the sound at the same time. All my senses are involved before ever my hands attempt to create the sound, and then it's never just them but my whole body—moving arms, rotating neck, flexing knees. Breathing steadily—'No muscle moves without the breath.' Swirling the bow around in the air, stabbing things with it. 'It's an extension of your arm. Move it till you lose the sense that it's separate. When your mind sends messages to the arm, they'll be travelling right through to the tip of the bow, the most delicate control.' At last I bring it to rest on the string, but still before I move it I listen to the feeling, letting my arm discover its weight in each position on the string. It is like learning the steps of a slow, highly disciplined dance form.

And finally, we move. By the time that happens my whole body is longing for the sound and it is an inexpressible release when it comes. All the conscious awareness of breath and muscles falls away, but it must still be going on somewhere for the sound comes full and free. Sometimes when I am practising at home I am greedy to get to the sound sooner and I cut the preliminaries, and am instantly tripped up with a scratchy, uneven sound that I can find no way to control. Who knows which tense muscles are responsible? I put down the viola in frustration—Why can't I do it properly when I'm alone? I love the lessons but I want to be independent, to be able to make music now, on my own. But the viola sets the pace. If I try to cut corners it refuses to co-operate. I start again, humbled into accepting that this thing will not be hurried.

He is there even in my practising, creating the space. I am so dazzled by the fact that he is willing to give me all this extra time that I practice all the hours I am not spending with Michael or in meetings preparing for the workshops. I wake unnaturally early and in the four o'clock dark I sit up in bed and practice silent finger exercises. There is an element of challenge in making sure I never let him feel that this is a waste of his time, for then he may decide it's enough, I can now go off and find an ordinary teacher. He has any number of other musical things to do that have much greater claim on his time than I do. I know it can't last—and I want to get the maximum out of it while it does. Each new thing he introduces me to I have made my own by the time we next meet. He checks it out—a brief nod as if to say, 'Fine, we've done that one,' and then we start in on the next thing. Sometimes he laughs, as if it's a bet we've had that he's pleased to have lost again.

He delights in letting me feel the power of what I can be part of even with so little technical experience. 'Music that lives comes out of interaction,' he says—rhythm and counter rhythm, melody and harmony, the sound out there and your own mind. There's always some kind of co-ordination, simultaneous perception—'A shared consciousness,' he calls it—and from the first sound I produced on the viola we are making music together, my mind creating the pattern of sound, choosing the order, changing the rhythm, using the bow on the string as aggressively or as delicately as I know how, and Neil's mind weaving around mine on the cello or the violin so that my simple note is transformed into something that moves, that dances, that laughs or cries. When I say, 'But it's really you doing it,' he says, 'OK, just listen to what my part sounds like alone'—and he is right, it is thin and empty by comparison—

—We are improvising together. He says, 'Hold on, this needs another player.' He goes downstairs to see who is around, and comes back with Tania. She takes over his cello while he picks up a violin. He says, 'We've a slow pulse going here that's waiting to be interrupted. Cut across it with something gritty.'

We begin, Neil and I, moving together, as we were before. Suddenly the lowest string of Tania's cello is angrily vibrating, changing instantly the quality of what we are doing. I have to hold on to stay in there and the tension gets into my notes. Neil's sound keeps weaving around mine, rescuing it…

We stop. I look at Tania. It is like getting off a roller-coaster and noticing for the first time the stranger you have been sitting next to, whose hand you have been clinging to as you screamed and the air rushed past. Tania says, 'You're a wizard, Neil,' and goes off, back to whatever she was doing before Neil summoned her. The roller-coaster feeling disappears, replaced by the unpleasant sense that I have been put down. The innuendo in her voice was 'How clever you are, Neil, to extract real music from such a beginner.' He is, but he never makes me feel that. Everyone is a musician to Neil—me, the children, all equally valuable—

—Paula thinks I have gone overboard with admiration. She knows what he's like because it was she who took me to that original workshop. 'Sure I liked the way he worked,' she says calmly. 'But he's just a musician. He's not God. Take it easy.'

I am taking it easy. Easy, like flying—

Neil carries on, oblivious to the edge in Tania's remark. Maybe I imagined it. What does it matter, anyway?

Mom's fortnightly letters bring me my distant family neatly packaged in her familiar handwriting. They have become like people in a novel, real when you are reading about them but never there at breakfast time. I notice the change and think, 'It's time'. They *aren't* part of my daily life any more, it's right that my emotions have caught up with fact. Not just the fact of distance but of being an adult. Too much of my early life was dominated by the example of my brothers—whether I longed to follow or was deciding to reject, it was still they who set the course simply by being there first.

Having them drop away has brought a new kind of freedom. There are no precedents. I have neither the childish eagerness to be like someone else, nor the defensive *I will not let you decide things for me* of that time with Kevin and Tom in Swaziland. This is *my* life now, only mine. There are no voices exercising subtle control. I am free. I am creating myself, the way Neil and I create music.

But for the ten minutes that I am reading Mom's letter, or an occasional one from Dad or Richard, I discover I am not as detached as I had thought. My brothers may not be commenting on my life choices but I have definite opinions about theirs. Trevor has gone to America—a research post at a medical institute in Connecticut. 'What about Jill?' I write. 'I'm afraid that's over,' Mom replies. 'Trevor thought it wasn't fair to her to try to keep it going over a long gap.' That *I'm afraid* is the nearest Mom can get to criticism. I feel no such restraint. I fume privately, and not so privately—to Jaswinder as we push our trolley around the supermarket, doing an emergency stock-up for the house which has run out of everything. 'For years he lets Jill trail along while it's convenient to him and then when more exciting things offer off he goes alone—and *then* he has the nerve to say it's out of consideration for her.' A few months later, and Trevor is getting married, to an American woman whose father happens to be a senior consultant. 'That's it,' I announce to the sparrows outside my dormer window. 'That's what it's all about.'

But when the time comes to write to him for his wedding I find I am remembering things from a time before adult issues crept up on us. All his boyhood I was so much younger, and as a girl so useless for most purposes that interested him, but he turned that into a kind of privileged status, teasing me and carrying me around on his shoulders, letting me help him oil his new bat that he wouldn't let Peter or Edward near. I returned the compliment with uncritical admiration, always willing to run his messages, trotting off to ask Mom for an old curtain to string across the living room while Trevor organised us all into performing a play. He always found a way to include me, even when I was too small to be trusted with speaking parts. One year I was a dog whose only function was to be lost and then found again…

And now that I have started remembering, they all stand out clear and separate as pop-up characters. Edward getting irritated with Trevor being so bossy, and disappearing at the moment the play was about to start, so that I was sent to look for him. Or the time Richard got interested in medieval music and couldn't be dragged away from his flute practice, so Trevor rewrote the whole play around a wandering troubadour. Richard composed a ballad specially—*World Premiere*, the handwritten programmes announced that year—copied out with pens from the calligraphy set Peter had been given for Christmas and for once let me use. *World Premiere*, with thin strokes up, thick ones down, leaning drunkenly to one side—

—World premiere. The first time ever. The excitement of knowing we are creating something that has never been done before…'You're all on a tuppeny hurl,' Neil says, and laughs when one of the children picks up the two-syllable sound of his *hur-rl* and starts tossing it back at him—*Hur-rl, hur-rl, hur-rl*—'Riding high,' Neil interprets, while Colleen catches the hands of the hur-rl hur-rling child and whir-rls around the room with him.

Megan is there at every session, watching the children who are her special concern, the ones who seem to have developmental delays. She sits for half an hour after they have all gone, making detailed notes. The next day we meet and talk through what she has observed. How each child participated, the ones who always play safe and choose the same rhythm instrument, the ones who were suddenly stimulated today to attempt something new. Which activity it was that got Trudy finally clapping. I feed that back to Neil for us to think about for the next session. The children are unaware that they are being observed and equally unaware that some are more the focus of that attention than others. There are no labels, no levels. Each child creates what comes from within. Each sound they make is equally part of the music. What is going on here is like a metaphor of essential life processes, life as it could be. I am as absorbed as Neil is in the nature of music itself, in what it expresses of things for which we have no words. It is because it is so unspecific that it can be a vehicle for the individuality of each child here, and yet provide the aura in which divisions disappear.

At one session Megan arrives with a child psychologist, doing research on perception in children with learning difficulties. He sits to one side and watches silently, and at the end asks if he can fix a time to interview me. The following week he is there again and now he says that he would like to use some of what we are doing here as part of an article he is writing. Can he be introduced to the parents? I say to Megan, 'Try Michael's.' It might help them, the status of it. At the next session Michael's father, Dave, takes a morning off work to come and see for himself what goes on at the sessions. They have heard about it at each stage, of course, but it was Jennie's thing, like the one o'clock club. Now it becomes their thing. Dave wants to know each time what activities we did, how Michael responded. It's always he who gets back for Michael on music session days. He must be organising his diary around it.

The potential of what we are achieving almost spins me away. In my daydreaming moments I am playing in string quartets and giving lectures in child development institutes. In real life Megan asks whether I have thought of training in child psychology and starts giving me leaflets about courses. Late at night in my attic I read through the small print. At first I am excited—possibilities open out in all directions. Then the stodgy quality of the language gets up my nose and I think, Why would I want to go and sit in lectures listening to people drone on and refer to each other's articles? We are *doing* it here, without degrees and certificates—they're just talking about it. *They* can come and learn from *us*.

3

The session is over, the last of the mess cleared up. The only children left are those of the clearer-uppers. They run wildly up and down the now empty space, released from the concentration of the past two hours. We gather them up and go over to the arts centre cafeteria to check we all know what's planned for the next session. Colleen says, 'It's time we got on to tunes. Enough of this whole body stuff!' Neil appears to listen but I know he is so absorbed by taking music one element at a time that if we don't push him he'll keep them exploring the qualities of sounds for the whole term. But the very rhythms suggest tunes, the tunes ask to be sung.

I challenge him when we're alone. 'Why do you want to keep tunes out? That's the whole pleasure of music.'

'And its most learned aspect. All the elements that define western music are there in the simplest nursery song. The expected pattern of tones, the harmonies, the shape of a phrase, the rhythms. Humankind has made sublime music in that framework but it's not the only way. Once you've trained those children's ears to think it is, they're unlikely ever to unlearn it. Our function is to give them space to experiment.'

'Neil, it's like you're telling them not to run.'

'On the contrary, I'm giving them the freedom to run. Every child in that group sways to music by nature, but watch when the mothers start with a tune—you can see on the children's faces, 'This I have to *learn*.' Then instead of being able to be spontaneous they're struggling to follow. Do that before they've had time to discover the processes for themselves and you'll be deadening what's so alive in them.' He's gathering up the sheets of paper we've been using for scribbling ideas. I get the viola out of its case and wait till he looks up.

'Neil, I want to learn to read music.'

He says nothing, then turns back to the pile of paper. 'Go on then, learn.' A moment later he looks up again and puts the papers to one side. 'You'll find books in any music shop.'

'So that means you won't teach me?'

'There's no need. The system's perfectly simple. Someone of your intelligence and motivation can get fluent at the basics in a week.' Then, 'Why do you want to learn?'

The answer is so obvious that I think he is laying traps for me. 'You know why.'

'The question is perfectly genuine.'

Now I'm cross. 'I want to read for the same reason anyone else does—because there's music there and I can't get at it.'

'You'll do it sometime and it'll be no problem. But there's no hurry. In your illiterate state you're a natural musical creator. We could carry on the way we're going and within a year you'd have enough control over the sound you get out of your viola that you could take off, making music straight from your spirit to your hands. You've no more real need to be able to read than your old man with the mbira.'

'I do. You did. I want to be able to play *with other people*. I want to be able to get together with anyone, not just you, and there's music in front of us and we can just play it.'

'*Other* people's music.'

'That'll do me fine.'

He's off, full flood. 'What in God's name do you think we've been doing all this time? *Real* music starts inside you, not with mindlessly repeating the thoughts of others...here you are, an instinctive musician, and all you want to do is follow a track laid out for you'...etcetera, etcetera.

I interrupt. 'You can read. Are you following a track laid out for you?' He stares. I say, 'You're treating me like a child.'

He gives a short, tense laugh. 'Far from it.'

He gets up, starts sorting through a pile of manuscripts, then spreads three of them in front of me. One looks like a drawing of a snail, another has shapes that swirl, cloud patterns with words inside them. Another is a list of instructions with a small diagram next to each. 'Written music,' he says. He fetches down a printed score—Mozart—opens it at random. 'And here's another kind.'

'Neil—'

'They're codes, Jennie, that's all they are. You can't write sound so you have to represent it some other way. Interpret the codes and you can *turn* them into sound. *Any* of them. This isn't talking down, it's what some of the most creative musicians working today are experimenting with—because it's a *more* effective way of representing the sounds they are imagining than the taught code. If they'd tried to record it in conventional notation it would have come out in a fixed form and what they're aiming for is something far more fluid, that allows for creativity at each stage. The taught code works for Mozart, it wouldn't work for this.' There's a tension in him today that's more than just this argument. He moves, a backwards jerk of his chair as if staying sitting has become suddenly intolerable, scoops up the scores and starts shoving them back on to the shelf with far more physical push than the simple activity requires. 'It's like any orthodoxy,' he says, turning back to face me, let it run for a few centuries and what started as something that came from deep inside the human spirit turns into a set of holy texts that stultify thinking Then people who yearn after the real experience as you do get palmed off with a set of rigid theological propositions—they absorb this extraordinary concept of music as something that's already been written down and all that's left for them to do is learn to read it.' Then, slightly more calmly, 'You're lucky to have come to music-making late, and in your own way.

You'll learn to read other people's music soon enough—but find your own first. Keep away from the holy books as long as you can.'

—Something's happened, something's going on that he's not saying. And it's evoked a reaction in me—we've hit my obstinate streak. I say, 'You're leaving something out. I *want* to play Mozart. Like the children want to sing Three Blind Mice.'—

Let him theorise with his snail notations, I tell myself angrily as I wait for the bus home. He thinks I can go straight to where he and his friends have got to without learning first all they have chosen to put aside, but I'm not interested in short cuts. I'm like Michael, I want the *whole* experience. I'll do it on my own if he won't do it with me.

But there's no time to get to a music shop just now.

There were other things that happened, confusing in a different way, because I couldn't understand why they upset me so much. Tania's 'You're a wizard, Neil.' The more I thought about it the more I knew I was right, she *was* putting me down. Why? And all that accidental popping in, almost as if she were threatened seeing Neil and me making music. What was there about me that could possibly threaten her, a professional musician? Why did she need to be so patronising?

Then another time. Neil said, 'We've a companion for your lesson. This is Juan'—

—The ten year old. So this is the youngest person he knew till I introduced him to the children. I watch for clues. Most of the time Juan lies on Neil's bed reading comics. Once he comes over to ask Neil something—in Spanish. Neil puts his arm around the boy's shoulders as they speak for a moment. His own Spanish is relaxed and fluent, definitely not the kind you learn at school. Disorienting, having the Scots obliterated from his voice, as if he has suddenly become someone else...Juan goes off downstairs and comes back with some bread and cheese...That one small interaction, and whole chapters of the man's unknown life announce themselves.

His arm resting on the child's shoulder in that vague way of a father whose mind is elsewhere...'The child of a friend,' he said, but they are so obviously used to each other, Neil must be at least a frequent father-substitute...Juan lies again sprawled over the double bed—Who else uses that bed? Why did it not occur to me that Neil might have a partner, even if not a resident-one?

Juan's mother arrives to collect him. 'Teresa, Jennie,' Neil introduces. Full, round figure, character written all over her face. She scoops Juan into a hug and at the same time talks over his head to Neil, at an immense rate, all in Spanish...Warm, definite, no-nonsense. A sense of humour. And something more—familiar. I have seen her before—Where?

She bursts out laughing at something she's been telling him. Neil smiles in a way I now know well—warm, but keeping his distance. I am irrationally relieved, and then immediately feel a revival of confused feelings. Neil gives her and then Juan a hug, and they leave.

I ask—I can't stop myself—'I'm sure I've seen her before—'

'Quite possible,' he says. 'She's been performing all over London.'

Now I remember, the concert with Leonie, the Victor Jara songs. 'She's Chilean?'

'She is.'

'I've heard them sing. They're very powerful.'

He nods. 'It's an object lesson for people who think technique is all. Teresa's group does nothing very extraordinary musically but their absolute conviction moves mountains.'

'I went to hear them with a friend who'd just been released from prison in South Africa. It was too much for her.'

His eyes flicker interest but he doesn't ask. 'Teresa's husband is in prison in Chile. With faint prospect of ever being released.' I have the impression he is about to say more, but something makes him change his mind.

I am jealous. Absurd. But true.

What do they have that I want—Tania? Teresa? Maybe nothing. No, that's not true. They are part of his life, regularly. I am in a box, confined to viola lessons and the children's workshops. Whatever their relationship to him, it's already obvious that they have a level of intimacy that I'm not going to be allowed to have—

—Paula says, 'How was the lesson?'

I say, 'Fine,' closing off further questions. I can't see past the expression on her face that says, *He's not God. Take it easy*. I don't want to hear her caution.

'And today—' with a flourish Neil sets a music stand in front of me and places on it a sheet of paper, 'today we unravel the mysteries of the Written Sound.'

I start laughing. 'What's got into you?'

'I decided I couldn't forego the pleasure of showing you how simple it is.' And then, the nearest thing to an apology, 'I only wanted to be sure you'd got a certain distance without it, so you'd not be tempted to use it as a substitute.'

'And if I do?'

'Then you're on your own!'

I look at the page. I might have guessed—not the expected series of black notes with tails, but a thick continuous line that starts with a sudden jagged peak, then rises and falls in gentle swoops. '*Neil*—'

He cuts me short—'Listen.' His bow hits the cello string with a crash, zooms up high, drops way down and then slips into a smooth, easy flow. He stops and laughs at me watching his cello bow. 'Listen again but this time look as well—at what I've been to such bother to prepare!' And of course, it is a sound version of that shape on the page, zooming high to start as the line does, dropping steeply, then climbing gradually to follow the soft lines of the humps.

'OK,' he says, 'now we play it together.'

'I couldn't possibly.'

'It's very similar to what we were playing three days ago.' 'But *you* played the tune, all I did was the rhythm.'

'So do the same now. Just listen to the tune again and put your bow on the G string while you do it. Whatever rhythm it wants.'

'What about what's on the paper?'

'Forget that for the moment. Let's go.' And his bow drops again, attacking the cello for that first dramatic peak. I wait till the tune has smoothed out and then I start with my viola, accompanying him.

'OK—now watch—' and he marks on the paper, slashes across the wavy line for each place I had put my beat. Like marking a rail track on a map. 'Now we'll play it again—and watch time moving on the picture while you're doing it.'

By the next lesson the slashes across the line have turned into bar lines, the wavy line gradually separates out into notes. The marks become more precise, adding one element at a time—now length of note; now exact pitch. Patiently, humorously, he woos me into losing my awe of written music. I am like a child being led but at the same time an adult watching that process with detachment, noticing how he handles the task. 'Just stop fashing yourself, and let your eyes follow what your ear's already doing.' He is right, we skate over the first stages with no difficulty. It's so simple, why did I ever think it would be a problem? Then I want to skip the step-by-step bit and go straight to the music on his shelves. Immediately it rears up at me again—a page of dense black notes, scurrying through rhythms my eye can't make sense of, let alone my ear hear. 'Take it easy,' he says. 'Your brain's too impatient. It's your old enemy, greed.'

But what's tripping me up isn't greed, it's a kind of rebellion. The things that come easily to me are those I am given space to explore myself, with no rules that I am expected to obey. As soon as there's a system someone else has devised, I instinctively balk.

It's that deep refusal to accept a syllabus again, but taken to a ridiculous extreme because I *know* this is one I need.

Neil is amused. 'I never thought I'd be saying this to a student of mine but you need a *modicum* of intellectual obedience. It's no harder than learning your tables.'

'Which I could never see the sense in. I learnt how to do maths without them eventually. My teachers couldn't understand how.'

'The only maths you'll be needing for this is dividing by two and three, and your body does that instinctively. Put down your viola.' He begins to clap a rhythm. 'Join me.' And once we've got it going, 'Now fit in a few beats to each of mine. Two, three, combinations, whatever you like.' He gives me time to experiment till one pattern seems established. 'OK—this is what you've invented.' He scribbles it down on music paper, a pattern of quavers and triplets, looking very complicated. 'Now play it, any string.' I do it—not as easily as before, for I have to slow down to let my eyes follow what the rest of me already knows. But still they are doing it and I feel amazed. 'Now keep that going when I come in,' he says. The tune he weaves around me feels already familiar, as if grown from that same rhythm. He plays the same couple of lines again and again till the two rhythmic patterns begin to feel like one, yet held separate. When we put our bows down I say, excited, 'Write that tune for me, the one you were playing.' He writes—I play it back—hesitantly, but I do it.

He listens, intrigued. 'So there we have it,' he says. 'All you need is to learn first with your body, and your brain follows.'

My lesson is over. I loosen the bow hairs and wipe the resin off the strings. I say, 'I've been thinking some more about tunes.'

'Aye?'

When he says that, I know he's half-mocking, waiting to be entertained. I ignore the tone. 'What you said about western scales and how our ears are trained. I don't think it works like that.'

He stretches back in his chair, legs out. 'Proceed.'

'OK, so it's a system and our ears learn to take it for granted. But music *requires* a system. I don't see that being trained in one stops you enjoying others.'

'It'd be nice if you were right but I'm afraid the evidence is against you. Ask any concert programmer. Try to include anything that was composed since the war and the audiences fall away. Why do you think composers are poor?'

'People are conservative, they feel safe with what they're used to. That's true in any society. Those children are going to think conventional western music is normal and maybe they'll think other cultures' music strange. But it's not inevitable. If we just help them to feel the excitement of music it doesn't matter what kind it is. I don't think there's only one way to make a tune and I was sung to from birth. Western nursery rhymes.'

'You're unusual.'

'In what way?'

'You're a cultural hybrid. Not many of my viola students also play the mbira. I doubt very much if the only music you heard as a child was nursery rhymes.'

'I first heard an mbira when I was twenty-one years old, and I had not the slightest difficulty responding to it.'

'Yes,' he says drily. 'That's what I mean. You're unusual in your openness, to all kinds of music.'

'And what about you?'

'*What* about me?'

'What music were *you* hearing as a child, the age of these children?'

He laughs. 'The organ in the kirk and my mother playing Handel on the piano. And drunken strains of Auld Lang Syne at New Year.'

'So no mbiras in your childhood, but it hasn't stopped you from experimenting.'

'The kind of musical education I had,' his voice is suddenly hard, each syllable separately edged, 'nearly cut me off from music altogether.'

The change of tone is so abrupt that I am momentarily silenced. After a moment I say cautiously, 'I don't think I've ever heard you angry before.'

He says, more calmly now, 'I stopped playing for almost a year after I left music college. Everything that matters about my music has come from starting again, differently.' He stops and looks directly at me. 'How old are you?'

'Twenty-four.'

'I was only a year younger when I started the cello. That's one reason I know adults can learn, often in more creative ways than children—*certainly* than children the way they're usually expected to learn. All my childhood I played the violin, and I was taught in so formalistic a way I wonder sometimes how I emerged with any musical sense at all. All technique, divorced from anything else. It was only when I'd given it up—thrown it all away, like getting rid of a straitjacket, and had a year without playing at all—that I could begin to discover what music was about. I taught myself the cello, working it out from first principles.' He gives a short laugh. 'Bizarre. I couldn't have done it on a violin. Nothing to do with the instrument, just set in the way my hands had been taught to think about it.'

'But you play it so—'

'The hands remember. Ever ride a bike? You can go for years without climbing on one but your muscles never forget. It's not the body that sticks but the spirit. I still can't think or feel on the violin the way I do on the cello.'

I'm trying to imagine Neil not making music for a whole year. Like thinking of a bird not flying. 'What *was* it? That made you throw over what you'd been taught?'

He says, in a tone I now know is dismissive, 'It's a long story.' And that's it. Door shut.

4

Memories swirl around like debris of forgotten lives in slow-moving water. Dreams. Sounds…In my dream I am back at Great Brak River and it is summer, perpetual summer. I am standing in my bathing costume on the big flat rock where the river joins the ocean, and the current swirls around it and the sea foams up against it, spraying me where I stand. The boys are diving off into the frothing waves, then clambering back up, bodies brown with sun and slithery with sea water, their hair dripping in wet strands over their foreheads. I am standing back, well away from the edge—longing to be doing it with them, but afraid. Richard stands waist high in the water, arms stretched up to me and calls, 'Jump, Jennie, I'll catch you!' Now he is standing behind me as I stare at the black notes that dance tantalisingly just beyond my comprehension—O God, four flats, I hadn't even noticed, and that bit in the fourth bar that jumps around so—I could work it out if I had time, and no pressure of anyone saying, 'It's just a run of semi-quavers, of course you can do it'—

—Neil asks, 'Jennie, do you remember anything about how you learnt to read—words, I mean?'

I think for a moment. Yes, I do. Sitting on the *stoep* with Mom getting me to sound out the syllables from Old Lob, Peter's reading book. It was Mom who taught me, because I was so desperate to follow the boys to school. And I remember too crying in frustration because I thought I was doing it, I could recite the story without even looking at the page. But for some reason Mom didn't think that was enough…Staring at the black marks, knowing there was some mystery hidden in them that the others could see but that refused to make itself evident to me…

I look up, to Neil, waiting. I laugh and say, 'Mainly what I remember is that it was something my brothers could all do, from before I could remember. And I couldn't!'

'So you're the youngest. That figures.'

'What do you mean?'

'Oh, nothing very specific.' He turns to his desk, looking for something. With his back to me he says, 'Just that there are moments when you behave like my young brother used to.' And then firmly, before I can probe, he puts in my hands a new handwritten sheet of music. 'A wee dance to try at home. Very simple, I promise'—

It kept happening. Those half-jocular but firm dismissals. We would be surfing along next to each other, equally full of energy, equally stimulated—and suddenly, 'That's it. Off you go now.' It was so obvious that he enjoyed my directness, liked me challenging him, liked the equality there was between us, but when he distanced himself in that sudden way it was as if he needed to retreat to something more—more controlled. He was still warm, but from within a role, like a father enjoying a child who shows unusual spark. I did not want to be a child. I did not want to be simply his musical experiment.

I heard Michael's mother, Felicity, saying, 'If you don't mind my saying so you have a tendency to overstep the mark.' I *did* mind. I minded Neil saying so.

A voice singing through my dreams

You could have sung laughter,
the note's on the score

I wake. It's a Sunday afternoon and I'm curled up on the sofa in the living room with Maria next to me watching telly, and the song's coming from Paula's room, upstairs. Maria says, 'You're exhausted, Jennie. You need to stop running for a while.'—

—He is taking me firmly on, into the next wave. No more paddling about where it's safe. Not my own notes now, written down, but pieces he makes up for each lesson to pick up on the things that emerged in our last one, turning them out as effortlessly as we create new activities for the children.

'Ready?' His bow is poised. 'Let's away!'

We're off—his dancing triplet setting off time so that I have no choice but to follow. And now, miraculously, some level beneath the conscious takes over and my body seems to be doing it for me. The bow moves steadily, the fingers find the notes. The pulse carries us along like the pull of oars...

It is finished. Neil lays his cello down, gets up and waves his arms around, freeing them from responsibility. 'Was that so painful, then?' 'It was brilliant,' I exult. 'I can't believe I did it.'

He brings his arms to rest. 'You'd save us both a lot a bother if you'd take note of the fact that you can now read music, and stop behaving as if I'm suggesting you climb Everest every time I put anything on your music stand.'

But from the top of Everest the high plateau stretches endless...A Swaziland memory now—Simangele learning to read words. When she had finally cracked the code and understood that squiggles on paper are just ways of recording sound, and could read with rising excitement the little books I made for her which told the story of her own life and daily doings, she thought she had done it then, and was cast into depression by the discovery that when she picked up the newspaper there were still so many words she could not sound out or understand...I want to do what people can do who have been reading music for years, just look at the page and hear it, lift my bow unhesitatingly and let it sing. What we have done is the easy part. Getting fluent will take a lifetime.

He leaves me no space to be depressed. Before I can lose courage he has scribbled down the phone numbers of two people whom he instructs me to meet, and to join a group they have formed which plays simple string music together. I protest that it is impossible. He says, 'Jennie, *do* it,' the way he said on the first day he held out a viola to me, 'Take it.' And I do it, because he has told me to. Extraordinary—almost no one tells me what to do. They must sense before they try that it's going to be no good. And if they don't notice and start giving me instructions I automatically want to do the opposite. And here I am, doing it like an obedient child and not even minding. Loving that he knows what I need, and knows that my resistance is only fear, and that I long to be released from it.

So now that's another evening every fortnight. Paula is intrigued. 'A string quartet? But you've only just started playing!'

'Tell me what you mean by a string quartet,' I say—and I am laughing, realising that I'm taking Neil's part and she's taking mine. But she's too quick. 'OK,' she says, 'so it's any four people playing strings together—but you know what I mean. What *kind* of music can you play? Mozart? Handel?'

'Yes, actually, very simple arrangements. But mostly things Neil writes for us. The group's got a stack of stuff he did when he started them off. He knows what kinds of things we can manage. Each part's simple, but with four lines of music you get wonderful sounds.'

'So he's teaching them too?' Paula asks. She doesn't need to spell it out. She is warning me again—Maybe your status with Neil isn't as special as you want to believe?

I choose to answer her words not her thought. 'He taught them for a short while in a group last year. They've gone on playing together.'

'So who is the group?'

'People with children at a primary school where they asked him to do a series of sessions, starting the children on stringed instruments. He said he would if the parents and teachers learned too.' I can see she is impressed despite herself. I go on, gathering momentum. 'He said the adults had to experience it the way the children did otherwise they'd kill it for them, nagging them to practice scales.'

Paula shakes her head. 'He never puts a bloody foot wrong.' Enough. I've had it. 'Paula,' I say, really upset now, 'you're being a pain in the arse. Like you can't cope with me growing up.'

She looks shocked. 'You're 180 degrees out. I love what's happening to you—the music, the children, the work. But Neil's—Jennie, it's like I'm watching you go overboard and it doesn't seem likely to me he's going to be there to rescue you. And I'd miss you if you drowned.'

I am crying now, and I don't know what I feel except that I'm glad her arms are holding me. After a bit she ruffles my hair and says, 'Thursday tomorrow, isn't it? Can I come and see for myself?'

She comes. Of course she is a natural with the children, throws herself into it, hair flying. When the session is over she and Neil stand talking animatedly. I leave them to it, aware of them both all the time we are clearing up, feeling airy with happiness to have them both there, both so alive. When they have finished I walk with her out of the arts centre and to the bus stop. She gives me a hug and says, with none of that cautious edge to her voice anymore, 'Brilliant stuff, kiddo, no denying it. Even God's doing well.'

'Piss off,' I laugh. The bus comes, and she bounces on to it.

He is pulling, taking my hand as we move out to meet the waves and the surf breaks deliciously over us—out deeper to where I can no longer stand. 'Don't worry, I've got you'—then with a sudden tense movement he lets go and swims off on his own—

—An argument that afterwards seemed so pointless. Something about song being essentially an interaction, that you couldn't conceive of songs that didn't involve two people's minds in some way—Impossible now to remember why it would have seemed worth arguing about, but the chemistry between us made him state it more extremely than he felt it, and flipped me into challenging—'Neil, you're such a purist. *Lots* of singing is alone. In the bath. Singing to yourself.'

'Sing for me, then.'

'Oh come on.'

'Go on, sing. Whatever comes into your head.'

I stare at him and think, Right, I'm going to win this one. And I sing the song I heard first from the voices of the Swazi women in the stream, sing with that over-the-hills quality in my voice that I took such pains to acquire and have hardly used since I've been in London—

ku-LE—zo nta-a ba…

'bo li BA mba li nga sho-o ni

He listens—as always, with total attention. There is a moment of feeling decidedly pleased with myself at having put in front of him something outside his experience. Then I forget about him, for that song always works on me in a way that is beyond sound, connecting me to those other voices that freed mine—

The song ends. My awareness returns, this place, this room. Neil sitting silent. Letting it be silent, after the sound.

Eventually he says, simply, 'You have a beautiful voice, Jennie.' I say nothing, stilled by the wonder of having moved him.

But then he is gone, breaking the moment. In a voice now practical he says, 'Describe for me what you're seeing as you sing.'

The suddenness of the switch leaves me—'abandoned' is the only word I can find. It takes me a moment to calm the feeling and find my way back to the argument that made him say, 'Sing'. The fight comes back into me, rescuing me. I say, 'I see a woman in a stream in Swaziland, beating her washing against a rock.' I'm tampering with the truth. It's not one woman but three, and I hear their effortless harmonising. One voice leads but the other two are part of it, so much that the women laughed when I was learning it and asked how I thought I would sing it alone. But I am like an obstinate child now, determined to make my point regardless of the truth.

He says, 'While you sing, your ear listens to her still.' I have no answer. He says, 'It's a song of longing, isn't it?'

'Yes. For a lover who left her, to go away to the mines.'

'There's your answer then.' But the fight has gone out of his voice. He gets up and moves to the window. His back to me he says, 'Jennie, I'm tired. Let's pack it up for tonight.'

5

The last workshop session is over. The children have triumphantly orchestrated their way through the coming together of sound and movement that Neil has finally let loose in them. Tunes too, but their own. The photographers from the local press have been and gone. The child psychologist has taken away reams of Megan's notes to analyse. Lawrie is saying, 'We need to meet soon to work out how we are going to follow this up next term. Too much impetus to let it drop.' Colleen is saying, 'Are you doing anything special over Easter? Why don't we get together with the kids—maybe a day in Brighton?'

Everyone talking of the next thing, as if life just goes on normally from here.

My last viola lesson. 'We'll see how we're going by the time the workshops finish,' Neil said. Now they have ended. In three days he is off to Manchester for his term's residency, and to get to work finally on his new commission.

'Do you know yet what you're going to do with it?' I ask.

It's germinating,' he says. 'I've the sound of Andean pipes weaving around in there. Teresa's group will work with me on it.'

On to the next experiment.

There's no point even thinking about what might happen when the term is over and he comes back to London. He has never let me talk about paying him for the lessons; and anyway I know he wouldn't give the time. I have gleaned enough about his life by now to know he has an instinctive resistance against letting anything bind him. I see now that there was nothing special in the way he took on me and the children—spontaneously is how he likes to do things. Someone arriving out of the blue with a musical challenge, that's what he needs to keep his diary free for—more new possibilities, walking in through the door. Anything that encroaches on his freedom to respond is a threat. Any long-term work commitment, any relationship that might demand something of him. Whether it is Teresa or Tania or other women I have not encountered who share his bed, I am sure now that he allows none of them to be regular, to begin to think that they have claims on him

'He's just a musician,' Paula said, and she was more spot-on than she knew. For all his natural ease with people, it's not the people themselves that interest him. I think it is me he is laughing at, or arguing with, or wooing gently from fear, and yes, it is Jennie he sees, but only the Jennie who brings a particular kind of challenge, a particularly intriguing bundle of musical characteristics.

He's gone far enough with that one now. He has analysed, got me over the hurdles, set me on course. It is obvious now how it will go on and the challenge is over.

'Your viola.' Packed in its case, last lesson over. I hold it out to him. He backs away, will not take it. '*Your* viola,' he says.

'Neil—'

'Cut the speeches. You know it's yours.'

I am as tentative about keeping it as I was the first day he put it in my hands. 'You need a spare, you told me you do.'

'If I decide I need another I can get it off the proceeds of the Arts Council that you've so kindly put my way.' He pushes it firmly back towards me. 'For the Lord's sake, Jennie, take it and be done. Do you think I put all this time into you only to leave you without an instrument?'

I take it back and feel such a confusion of gratitude and abandonment that I do not know what to do with myself. Then my body decides for me and I am giving him a goodbye hug. He returns it, holding me for a moment, then putting me back in my place, separate. And now his voice is light once more—'I expect to come across you again in the middle of Africa, making extraordinary fusion music with your viola and a choir of mbiras.'

The whole intense three months of it, finished. The children and childminders and mothers who were strangers to each other in January, and then for twelve weeks part of the same intimate adventure—chanting each other's names and learning to know the little quirks of how each body and temperament expresses itself—dispersed.

Back to the closed houses and separate lives of a city.

Colleen and I meet a couple more times with Lawrie to sort out the accounts. Once Megan joins us and we talk about possible next stages. A weekly activity group for children with learning difficulties? But the whole beauty of our music-making was that those children were centrally *included* and could take part each at their own level within the wider group. No labelling. And anyway who would do it? They look at me. I know I could but I also know I don't want to. Not without Neil.

Without Neil the spark has gone. Only now he is no longer here do I discover how fundamentally I have been energised and sustained by his enormous spirit. The intense arguments about the nature of music. The undemonstrative but total concentration that he gave the children—and me. The way he knew at each stage exactly what I was ready for, when to go slowly, when to push. The sense of flying when we played together and it worked, his line intertwining with mine. The way he laughed at me, enjoying me challenging him but conceding nothing. The way his arm lay lightly on Juan's shoulders. The energy of his large body, leaping around the arts centre hall with the children. And sticking out his toes to Michael, that first day.

Everything's so bloody empty, I can't bear it.

I practise my viola compulsively. It doesn't work alone. Of course it doesn't. Music is a shared consciousness. I don't want to share it with anyone else—I have been spoilt by being allowed to touch, even so briefly, the real thing. I pull out the pile of music he's written out for me ever since the day of the first swooping line—'I wanted to be sure you'd not be tempted to use it as a substitute.' Well now I am and there's nothing he can do to stop me.

I go back to the beginning and play them all, to summon in my mind the sound of the cello part. Where's that song he arranged, the one he put in my hands as I was packing up, right near the end? 'A wee piece for your next quartet session,' he said—nothing more, but when he says 'a wee' anything, it's in self-mocking, a barrier against the real feeling. I took it, knowing it was for me. That moment of excitement each time he put something new in front of me, knowing no one else had ever played this piece before, or heard it. That these marks on the page were going to turn into sound following no pattern I recognised, but touching close enough to things known to stir up feelings, unpredictable—

The water is wide, I cannot get o'er
Neither have I wings to fly—

A setting of a folksong, coming so soon after he had said, 'You have a beautiful voice, Jennie.' He is talking through the moment, not letting it be silent. 'You want to feel the sound come from far away, from over the water,' he's saying. 'That means keeping your bow well over the fingerboard, lightest of touches. Except when you get a fragment of the tune, then you let it carry like a voice.' He notices that I'm still looking at the words. 'You know it?' he asks. I don't. He plays the tune for me. His cello sound gets right inside me, creating a stillness I do not want to break. He nods, smiling. 'Definitely one for you to learn to sing. *Waly, waly*, it's called—been cropping up all over the country since the 18th century and everyone thinks it's their own. But you can have it on soundest authority, it's Scots.' I'm laughing at him now, but he insists—'From a lost ballad, *Lord Jamie Douglas*. All anyone's found is fragments, but that refrain's there.'

The water is wide, I cannot get o'er

Neither have I wings to fly
Give me a boat that can carry two
And both shall cross, my true love and I.
I leaned my back against an oak
Thinking it was a mighty tree
But first it bent and then it broke—

Why are folk songs always about that?

For a couple of weeks life drags on. Michael is difficult. Eva drives me up the wall. Even Jaswinder with her infernal film songs. The romanticism irritates me unbelievably. I wish she would snap out of it and stop being such a wimp. Paula has a new Linda Ronstadt LP she's mad about. I feel zero interest.

I am detached from everyone in the house. These people who used to be so central to me. Now I am back at meal times, every day, but there's a strong residue of resentment. I feel like an outsider trying to push in on other people's conversations. OK, so I haven't been contributing much—so what? Everyone has phases like that.

Sod them all. I'm going to bed.

I am tired. Really, really tired.

Paula appears in my room. I'm in bed already but with the light still on. She perches on the bed next to me, looking at me. 'What are you staring at?' I ask. I hate the sound of my voice. Why can't I even be normal with Paula?

'You.' She moves to come and lie propped up on an elbow next to me. She says nothing but with her free hand starts stroking my hair. I lie stiff under it for a few moments, and then the relief of having someone know me and take care of me is too great and I start to cry. She goes on stroking me, holding me, saying nothing, until I have cried myself out. Then she says, 'It's the pits, loving people who won't love you back.' And I start crying all over again.

I don't know what's the matter with me. I seem to have lost

my resilience. I feel tired all the time. There have been worse things than this happen to me and I've always found a way to bounce back.

I remember the night I thought I had been sacked from looking after Michael...walking the streets, thinking, *They're taking my life away from me again*...How many lives can you create, and lose, and still have enérgy to start again?

I can't concentrate. I can't think clearly. I think, How old am I? and it takes me a couple of minutes to work it out. So I'm twenty-five. My birthday happened and I didn't notice. The house insisted on making me a cake and doing the happy birthday bit, but it was as if I wasn't there. Jaswinder has taken to making *khir* for dessert again, which has always been my favourite. I feel a dim stirring of love for her and make myself say how lovely it is. But I can hardly get it down.

I start thinking about Peter again. Peter in that last summer I was at home; lying on his bed all day, having to be *called* for meals and everyone trying to pretend it was normal him just sitting there, hardly eating, saying nothing. Once, just once when we were alone late at night, he suddenly started to talk. Not about the army—he said he could hardly remember what had happened—but vaguely, about not knowing any more who he was or what he could do. Or whether it was worth trying to find out, because he wouldn't be able to do it anyway. I know the others in the house are watching me now as we watched Peter, trying not to make it too obvious how anxious they are. I know, but it doesn't reach me.

I keep playing my viola. That alone stays. But I have gone back to a time before written music. I tell the quartet group I am not well and won't be coming for a few weeks. Even on my own I cannot play if there is a music stand with something on it. It has to be just me and the viola, no one looking over my shoulder. No one urging me on. No one teaching me anything, challenging me, making it easy or laughing or—or *anything*.

The viola does not intrude, it makes possible. I do not try to play anything in particular. I move the bow and let my fingers choose whatever notes my sub-conscious directs. And for days, no rhythm. 'The fundamental thing about music is that it structures time,' Neil said. He is wrong. The most basic impulse is from a state before time. Just sound. The qualities of sound take over. I listen intently to the effect of each small change in the pressure of fingers on bow, angle of bow hairs on string, type of bow stroke. My hand and arm learn to make the bow shiver, bounce, attack, touch lightly and then speed. My spirit absorbs the sound.

A phone call from Kevin. 'There's a registered letter from the Home Office, addressed to you. Do you want me to open it and read it to you, or post it?'

'Open it,' I say.

When I put the phone down I stand staring at the wall.

Jane flips down the stairs, sees me, stops. 'Jennie—?'

I look at her, blank. 'I've got a passport,' I say. I feel completely flat, unable to react. 'I'm British.'

Jane hugs me and dances about, the others come out of their rooms and exclaim. I try to respond and be pleased that they are so pleased for me. But it washes over me.

On the phone I had said to Kevin—awkwardly, not knowing how to finish this gracefully—'Do you want to meet for a last meal?'

He didn't.

No. Well, neither do I.

He said, 'I have a partner. She'd like to get married. We need to start fixing up about a divorce.'

More negotiations. I thought we were done. But of course.

'Sarah—my partner—She hasn't found it easy that I've had to keep meeting you. My solicitor will be writing to you about the divorce.' Solicitor. So I'll have to find one too. Me, with a solicitor.

So much history, coming to an end.

I wanted to put the phone down, but I couldn't just end like that. I said, 'Thanks, Kevin. I know it's been a drag for you, having to wait so long.'

He said, 'Forget it.'

Forget it. Forget the whole long story. It's finished now.

I arrive at Michael's house every day and I take care of him. Minimal care. I do the same things we have done a hundred times before. Finally I recognise what it is I have seen on the faces of the mums who just carry on, because there is no option.

Dave starts talking about September. Michael will start in a special nursery school they have had recommended. That means they'll only need me half time, to collect him in the afternoons and be with him till they get back. Can I stay? For Michael's sake they want the continuity. But obviously I have to think about my work position. They'd only be paying me for a couple of hours a day.

'Let me think about it,' I say. Other children there are in plenty. But am I going to be a childminder forever? The next day I say, 'I'm confused. I think I need a break, to sort myself out.'

Dave looks worried. 'What length break?'

'Maybe a fortnight.'

He says, 'I'll get on to the agency. I'm sure they can fix something.' Then—the most personal thing he has ever said to me—'I'm sure it took a lot out of you, the music.'

It certainly did.

'If it's any compensation,' he continues awkwardly, 'it gave me something I'll always be grateful for.'

OK, so that does help. Being reminded of what the point of it all was. To know that I did something that was for people. For a different way of living, and accepting each other.

A fortnight without anyone requiring anything of me.

For the first two days I do little but sleep. I wake, go for long walks alone on the common, come back to my attic, sleep again. On the third day I take a train out into the country to find hills

They are not like the Swazi ones—these are domesticated, plotted and pieced like the Gerard Manley Hopkins poem. Farm houses nestling up against the downs. A white sprinkling of blossom on the blackthorn. A soft dampness underfoot. I begin to hear sounds. Unidentifiable chirps in the hedgerows tipped with green. A distant tractor. A lark, constantly hovering, sound travelling—

across the white
orchards and dark green fields; on, on…

I crouch next to wildflowers and stare at them as I once did with Charlie. Stare for a long time, back to that long-ago person I once was, the Jennie of the gypsy life. A small bag of possessions at Charity's, another at Marilyn's, a toothbrush in my shoulder bag with my books and papers, in case I decided to stay overnight somewhere else. The ultimate in having no home, no roots, and it brought its own kind of freedom. I search back, trying to summon again that quality of self-sufficiency, of having things to give. *This little piggy* while Charlie squealed with tickling delight. Waking on Sunday to Mrs Mahlalela's friends arriving, in church-uniform dresses of white and blue, then off to sing hymns at the gathering point at the end of the road. The sound followed them back up, wafting in that special

African harmony, dense chords like an organ of natural sounds, and something in the voices that seemed always about to lift out of the tune and fly free. Nothing like the church Aunt Ellie used to go to in her brown felt hat, where the hymns dragged, too heavy to lift—

I remember now a Saturday when I climbed out of Mbabane to go walking in the hills, and realised I had gone too far to get back before nightfall. It seemed very simple—I would find somewhere. I could ask for shelter at the next house I passed and walk back tomorrow. It turned out to be a European-style farmhouse, a rambling building with thick whitewashed walls, lived in by a couple old enough to be my grandparents. They took me in the way farm people do; I was on their doorstep and night had come, so of course I should sleep there. They fed me and showed me photos of their grandchildren and put on 78s with scratchy Victorian songs, ones I'd heard about but never heard—*Pale hands I loved beside the Shalimar, and Believe me if all those endearing young charms*. I was enchanted, and got them to play them again and again so I could learn the words. They loved it. 'We thought you young people only liked that awful noisy stuff they call music these days,' they said. Finally they said it was their bed time, and showed me into a spare room that smelt musty and had things dropping out of the thatch, and I slept on a carved wooden bed that had been shipped out from Scotland and carried all the way up from the coast, God knows how.

And woke early, before they were stirring, to an awareness of goodness that was like air fresh after rain. A calm knowledge of resources in myself—

—Which now I cannot find.

The light is different—the day must be coming to an end. I look at my watch and see in mild surprise that it is seven-thirty. I had not noticed that the days have got that much longer already. Why have I been inside so long? What kind of an artificial life have I been living, obsessively searching after something that turned out not to be there, when the real world is here, waiting to be received?

I get home late. The only person I speak to is Jane, to borrow her wildflower book. She says, 'Take these too,' maps marking public footpaths. The next day I leave early and am out in the hills before the traffic has got going on the village roads. I set out across the fields on the public footpath, feeling my chest expand in the space. Most of the day I spend standing still beneath a tree, staring up at the pattern of leaves against the sky, or crouched next to a collection of wildflowers. I try to look them up. 'Narrow lobes, tipped with bristle, seed capsule rounded, petals overlap, blotch at base.' The words are odd but they help my eyes to see.

The detail absorbs me.

I do not think about my life or what I am going to do with it.

The fortnight is over. I go back to work. It is manageable now, but just that. There is no prospect, nothing to work towards.

Through the blankness I am aware that the people around me are loving me, willing me to become whole again. Kirsty pulls up weeds around the plants in the garden that she knows I used to tend, and devises little activities to tempt me to join her. Jane brings home some Andean pipes she found in a craft market and says, 'I'm sure you can work out how to play them.' I can't, because they make me think of Teresa. Maria tells me bits of news from Southern Africa, as if trying to wean me back into noticing what's happening to the world. Jaswinder cooks and puts little bowls of flowers in my attic. Each time something like that happens I get a little better at responding properly, till their love releases mine and I can begin to live again.

Paula is there, throughout, but oddly the least able to find ways through to me. Perhaps that's because our friendship has had so much talking in it. And that kind of talking, about what you're thinking and feeling, is the one thing I can't attempt.

Eventually it becomes possible to think about Neil without too much pain. I let him back in, cautiously. He slips in every time I sing with Michael. He begins once again to be there, observing and smiling in that detached but still involved way, as I play with the children in the one o'clock club—the games that we first tried out in the workshop. They are an instinctive part of my repertoire now, and Colleen's. Now there are two of us I don't feel any more that the mums will think I'm trying to take over.

'You have a tendency to overstep the mark, Jennie.'

OK, so Felicity was right. But there are other ways of saying the same thing. Overstepping the mark is what we did when we challenged the apartheid government. Overstepping the mark is not accepting the limits of class and colour that were put around you by birth, and refusing to be boxed off from your fellow human beings.

Overstepping the mark is walking across any border, intellectual or spiritual. It's Neil, refusing to be limited by the canons of classical music. It's me, walking into the life of a busy composer and expecting him to give time to working with young children—

And not wanting to be put back in my place when it's all over.

Maybe it would be easier to be the kind of person who accepts the limits…I remember now, from childhood, a card pasted inside Mom's wardrobe door, and I standing on tiptoe to read the words—

> *Grant me the serenity to accept the things I cannot change*
> *the courage to change the things I can*
> *and the wisdom to know the difference…*

It never occurred to me to wonder what the words meant to her, what experience had made her paste that up, to see each day as she took out her clothes. Which of those qualities did she think she needed to practise? Wisdom she had—but she was forty when I was born. What do I know of what it took to make her wise? Serenity? She who seemed to me always the fixed, calm point of the world? But maybe serenity had to be cultivated, along with the agapanthus…Courage—it could have been that.

It's wisdom I'm after. So elusive. Year after year, life after life, almost touching it with outstretched hand, the tip of a bow—and then it's gone, where I can no longer find it. And without it, it's pointless to wish for serenity.

Finally I begin even to let him come back when I am playing my viola. I begin again to play in the way we played together and I find I can do it without too marked a sense of loss. Rhythm comes back and remembered harmony—his line and mine. It eases up, begins to be pleasurable. I get out the pieces of paper again but that's too much. *Keep away from the holy books*. I'm not letting the things he wrote for me become my holy books. The viola is for me, I'm keeping it clear of all that.

I start going to the quartet group again. That means facing the pieces he transcribed and arranged for us. Except for *The water is wide*, which I won't play, the rest are manageable now, with the others there to dilute the effect. The structure of the music begins to delight me again, that wonderful facility he has of creating such vivid effects from such simple elements.

In the house the others see that I am coming back and they stop looking so anxious. We start to talk about him again in a way that normalises things. Using his name is like saying, It happened, it's over. Facing it, so I can begin to start again somewhere else.

Paula says, 'Think about those sweaty toes. It wouldn't surprise me if he farts in bed. Men who live alone till they're middle aged are pigs to have around the house. My mother's bloke is like that.'

'I don't know,' says Jane, 'I've got this uncle, not married, and worse than having a granny nagging at you. Everything has to be done exactly the way he does it or he freaks out.'

But I loved his free wiggling toes. And I've seen how he lives.

'All this floating about on music stuff,' says Jane. 'Bad for the system. What do you know about the man himself?'

'He's probably boring as hell when he's not talking about music,' says Paula. 'All these dedicated artists are.'

They're doing their best. Occasionally they make me laugh.

'The problem with you,' Paula says, 'is those brothers of yours. Too much damned adoration in early life.'

Leonie phones. 'Haven't heard from you for ages—what have you been doing?' What *have* I been doing? How do I describe, even to myself, what it was that took over my life for all those months? All that's left of it is a cardboard box stuffed with paper—piles of spare leaflets that I was going to put up in local shops but that were never needed because before I got to doing it we had more children than we could handle. Bumph from the Arts Council. A photocopy of Neil's CV—I had seen it on Lawrie's desk—he'd asked for one for the grant application. I'd made myself a copy when no one else was near the photocopier. Strange reading it, so anonymous, as uninformative as programme notes—and yet there was I, who spent hours with Neil each week, scouring it for clues to the life I would never be let in on. Born in Dundee, 1938. That makes him thirty-six now. 1950, I was scarcely walking and Neil was thirteen, winning prizes for composition; seventeen when an orchestra gave the first public performance of one of his works—and I a child of six, setting off to school for the first time, finally able to read *Old Lob*. Music college in Glasgow. A violin concerto. A song cycle based on medieval Scots sources. Then an unexplained gap in the dates; no compositions for four years. He stayed silent for *four years?* What happened?

I hear his voice, light, dismissive, 'It's a long story.'

I shove it back in the box.

A letter from the child psychologist. Bumph on the course Megan wanted me to take. It feels an age ago that I sat up in bed in the small hours reading this same prospectus, imagining myself already on the course. Perhaps I should consider it after all. This must be temporary, what's happening to me. Perhaps that's what courses are for, to give you a structure, to tide you over the time when inspiration fails. But as soon as I try to imagine myself going every day to lectures, to listen to boring people spout on, I feel tired. I bin the prospectus.

It's gone. Lost. The intensity, the desire for life that made me study Michael's every response, and leap hurdles of understanding in so short a time. It is as if I have been a dancer, moving with speed and delicacy and precision, and I stand now listless. The same body, but it has no urge to move.

BOOK TWO

The water is wide, I cannot get o'er

Neither have I wings to fly

Give me a boat—

Chapter 1

Fragments of those days, surviving like memories fixed by photos around the things that were being said and done at that instant. Paula standing in the doorway, looking at me as I looked at those finished pieces of paper, each of us surveying the wreckage. Coming to sit next to me on the floor—

'It's time I did something with my life,' I said.

She nodded. 'I was thinking of taking a couple of days off. Do you fancy a night in a youth hostel?' As if it were an ordinary thing to do, she and I going off together. And I too bound up in my needs to have the energy to ask what she had said to Eva…

The youth hostel, where we heated baked beans in frying pans buckled with years of use, and played draughts with a couple of women in their seventies who had walked further that day than we had. Sleeping in creaky bunk beds, Paula on the lower one and me above. Waking in the night to the sound of an owl hooting, and seeing through the curtainless window the moon sailing past, clear and dazzling…

Climbing next morning a ridge that dropped suddenly to a valley, and near the crest sitting perched on a wooden fence covered with lichen, while I taught Paula songs I had learnt in Guides—

Land of the silver birch, home of the beaver,
where still the mighty moose wanders at will—

and then stomping down a path beneath beech trees to the songs she had learnt on the Aldermaston marches—

Och, och, there's a monster in the loch,
and we dinna want Polaris—

Footpath across a field, over a stile. Paula pauses at the top. From where I stand waiting to follow, her body is outlined against the sky. 'Jennie, do you remember when you first came, how you spent hours reading journals in the library?'

Sure I remember. Sexual politics, Vietnam, the coup in Chile—

'I don't understand what's happened to your politics. You don't even read the paper now. Where's it gone?' She drops down on the other side of the stile. 'It's like the music wiped it all out of you.'

I follow, up and over. How to explain? I hear Richard's words—There will be things to be indignant about wherever you go… 'To me they're the same kind of energy, the music, the politics. Something that gets set alight inside me when I feel connected to the people I'm with. Like electricty that you can use to heat baths but also to light lamps.'

She laughs, freeing something in me. I say, 'The problem is what you do when the electricity itself cuts out.'

The path leads into a clump of beech trees. Sun filtering, brown leaves damply carpeting. She says, 'Talk to me, Jennie. Tell me what's going on in you.'

I feel stuck, no way to say it. 'It wasn't just Neil. I mean, not just him, the man.'

'What then?'

'The way he lives—really *living* his engagement with music, and that creating ways for others to experience possibilities in their own lives. I want that quality—for myself, and to be able to use it like that. It felt like we were *both* doing it, constantly stimulating each other, *seeing* everyone take off because of our work. Effortless as surfing—but—'

'But?'

'But now I see it was he who created the wave. On my own I can't think how.'

I realise I have stopped walking in the concentration of trying to put words round the confusion of feelings. Paula is standing looking at me, a slight smile hovering. I feel known and accepted. I say, 'I want to live like that again.'

She says simply, 'You will'…

We lie now on our backs in the corner of a field, grass nodding above our heads. After a while Paula rolls over on to her front, pulls up a grass stalk and starts peeling the outer layers. I say, 'I feel like I've been on a long journey and still I'm at the starting point. I'm twenty-five and I'm not going to be a childminder forever. I need to get some kind of a qualification.'

'To do what?'

'I don't know.'

She stares. 'That's absurd.'

'You went to drama school.'

'Because I knew what I wanted to do. If you want to do something different, fine. Work out what it is and start doing it. Maybe it needs a qualification, maybe it doesn't.' Her face has the expression it gets just before she flings a challenge at the audience. 'You're feeling vulnerable, so the old family values creep up on you.'

'Meaning?'

'Richard, university lecturer; Trevor, consultant; Edward, brilliant economist. We won't mention Peter, because it's not his fault. But here's Jennie, just a childminder.'

I sit up, indignant. 'You haven't the least idea what you're talking about. No one put any of that on me.' I glare at her. 'You've known since you were so high that you want to parade in front of other people and make them laugh. There's nothing *virtuous* about being so clear, you're just bloody lucky. There isn't anything I know how to do except get angry with the way people exploit other people. And look where that got me.'

She says steadily, 'I don't just make people laugh, I make them think. And there are five thousand things you have the capacity to do.' She waits for me to calm down. 'You're OK just the way you are, Jennie. When you want someone to love you and they don't, it's easy to start assuming that you have to change yourself. You don't. Just start from who you are.'

Her voice calms me but I can't talk more now. 'Let's walk,' I say.

A stone bridge over a stream. Water like clear cider, burbling over smooth stones. We lean over the side, dropping twigs into the water, watching them disappear under us.

I say, 'There's something else. My passport.'

She turns her head, waiting.

'It means I could move again.'

She straightens up, both hands lifting to push her hair back. 'What makes you think moving will change anything?'

'If I could get myself back to Africa—'

'Africa?' She drops her arms, body tense. 'That's pretty melodramatic.'

'It only sounds like that to you because it's at the edge of your mental map. The place fathers come from and disappear to.' Her face stiffens, and I feel sorry, I didn't mean it to hit. 'It's the opposite for me, Paula. It would be starting from who I am.'

'No! You've gone too far along the road here. You'd be starting again now, in yet another new place. And this time there's not even someone else throwing you out, you'd be doing it to yourself.' She turns abruptly back to looking at the water, then notices that she is still holding a twig. She hurls it into the stream. It is caught behind a stone, swirls gently, refusing to be the vehicle for her vehemence. We both watch it, then simultaneously look up at each other and start laughing. She says, her voice now matter-of-fact, 'Anyway I don't want you to go.'

'I know. I don't either.' I put my arms around her, a quick hug. 'You could come and visit me. You could all come!'

'Talk about daydreaming!' She hugs me back hard, the way Kirsty does at the end of her weekends with us. We stand quiet, each gettting used to what is happening. Eventually I say, 'There are bits of me that have gone dormant living here, Paula, bits I can't even name. Like a plant that you think is doing OK in a pot, but maybe if you transplant it back into the kind of earth it came from it'll spread all over the place.'

She looks thoughtful, then announces, 'Sex.'

'Paula—'

'This dormant bit. Plants flourishing. Clear sexual imagery. You just need a lover. Forget that useless Neil and find a real one.'

'Cut it out. I thought we were having a serious discussion.'

'I'm extremely serious. There are parts of you you never explore and you know it. Get yourself a lover and you'll stop talking about going back to Africa. You need a man, like Jaswinder does, but you're more afraid to admit it.'

My eyes are watching a distant bird circling. I know she's probably right because I feel my mind blocking off. 'Listen, there are patterns in life and you can't just ignore them. There are things about your life with your mom that come into why you need Eva. I don't understand them but I accept that if that's what you need, that's what's right for you. For me right now it's not sex, it's probably not even being loved. Or not only that. There are still undone things from way back. I spent my childhood barefoot in the lane and playing in the veld—and look at me, I know more names of English wild flowers from just a few years here than I did from all those years surrounded by South African ones. I grew up listening to Beethoven on a record player and all the time there were African women out at the back singing and I never learnt the songs. That's one of the reasons Neil had so powerful an effect on me—it wasn't just him, it was what he enabled me to take back for myself. To listen to what's *there*, to respond to the sounds that mean something to me, not just the ones I've been told I should listen to.'

'You learnt that here. Stay here and do something with it.'

'I'm trying to make sense of my *whole* life, not just this bit of it.'

Lunch in a village pub. We take our food out to the garden at the back and Paula distracts me by describing the latest goings on in her theatre group. We spread out the map to work out the way back to the station. Paula suddenly looks up and says, 'Why don't we make it another night?'

'You serious? I thought you had rehearsals?'

'I'll phone Jane. The others are always having crises, I don't see why I can't once in a while.'

She goes into the pub to phone. When she comes out her face is closed.

'What happened?'

'Eva didn't come home last night. Didn't tell anyone where she was going.'

I feel at a loss. Paula tosses her hair. 'She's probably just punishing me for coming away with you, She'll get over it.'

We stayed the extra night, but now it was each of us helping the other fend off tension. Eva was not home when we got back, nor did she come that night. Paula phoned around all their friends, trying not to show that she was becoming frantic. Two days later Eva walked in half way through the morning—I wasn't there but I heard it all when I came back that evening. She walked into the bedroom she had shared with Paula and announced that she was leaving to join another woman in another house. It turned out she had been involved with this other woman for months, spending days with her while Paula was out rehearsing. All those months she had been so crabby and suspicious, and now we understood it was her own defection that was making her tense.

She packed and she left. It was horrible, watching Paula alternately fighting to get her to make sense of it and then giving up and looking panicked and miserable. Eva's back seemed always turned defensively as she went around the house collecting her things, speaking to the rest of us as little as possible and to me not at all.

And of course in leaving she took with her Kirsty's weekends and all the accumulation of little things Kirsty had filled the house with over the years. I defied the angry No Entry notices of her eyes and said, 'Eva, let Kirsty come and collect them herself so she can say goodbye.' It was a totally stupid thing to say because of course once I had said it that's the last thing Eva would let happen. Suddenly I got wildly angry and said things I probably ought to have regretted. About how she was doing to Kirsty what the court decision had done, breaking her relationships without giving her any choice in the matter, and how did she think Kirsty was going to be able to trust anyone if Eva didn't give her a chance to see we were still her friends?

That night Paula came into my bed, her body heaving as she sobbed like an abandoned child. I held her as Marilyn had once done for me when I ran away from Kevin and from myself. Paula kept coming for a couple of weeks. Most nights she said, 'I'm going to be all right tonight, I just don't want to be alone.' I said, 'Stop apologising, come on in.' As soon as she was next to me and could feel someone was looking after her, she would begin sobbing again. I stroked her hair and her arms and her back, until the sobs got slower and more like hiccoughs, then stopped altogether. I lay awake long afterwards, seeing pictures of her as a child, alone in the flat all those nights when her mom was out working; and I hated her mom along with Eva, and all people who hurt the people they're supposed to love, whether they can help it or not.

2

For months Paula was listless. It was a state I had so recently inhabited that it took no special insight to recognise what she needed from me, which was simply to be there, unquestioning, and wait until she was ready to emerge. She made little sign of noticing whether I was there or not. I did not need it. I wanted only for her to become strong again, the way I knew she could be. She carried on with her work, but found it hard to summon any of her usual enthusiasm—and her kind of work required a constant flow of fresh inspiration. She said once that she was beginning to see why a script might occasionally be useful.

We had become for each other the one fixed point in a life in which too much seemed to be changing. She was to me and I to her the sister neither of us had had, but without the potential rivalry of sisters. Jane gave up trying to fathom why there was no sexual element to it, and I began to see that in fact there was—that sexual loving is a wider thing than I had once understood, and present to some degree in almost any real closeness. The touching and hugging was not incidental—to withhold it would have seemed as unloving as to avoid touching a child. We became so tuned to each other's thinking that, like lovers, we often started speaking at the same moment, with the same words. I could feel I was growing more like her, relying on my own strength, daydreaming less. And she grew more like me in some ways, beginning to admit to things in her past that she would previously have dismissed as irrelevant. Being more often simply loving, not needing always to challenge and spark.

In an odd way it seemed helpful to her that I too was at a transition stage of my life, and perhaps one more fundamental. I remember especially a day I'd got her to come out walking again and she got me to tell her about Africa, trying to learn what it was that was drawing me. We had climbed half way up the north downs and turned to get our breath. We stood together looking down over the neat, parcelled English countryside that we were leaving below us, and I wondered what she would see if she landed among the hills of Swaziland. I said. 'They're not like these hills, emptier. There's a lot of dust. Most people are poor. In the villages the kids run around barefoot and their clothes are tatty, like they've been handed on too many times and washed too often. But there's something about the way people live—'

'That village—tell me why you liked it.'

'The people. The directness. The feeling of doing without all the clobber of my usual life and being closer to the basic rhythms. Collecting firewood before you can cook anything. Walking to the stream to collect water. Feeling in my own body what work goes into the simplest but most essential things, weaving mats, winnowing grain.' Her sceptical look made me laugh. 'OK, they're tedious as hell if you have to do them every day. But—'

We turned and set off on the path up again. 'That school you taught at—'

The school…It seemed so long ago, much further than the village. But she was right, that too was part of what was working its way out in me. 'It was an idealistic experiment, black kids and white in the same classes. My friends went to prison in South Africa for wanting something so simple. But those children learnt as little about their own history as I had. They were part of a fantastically rich musical tradition and the school didn't even *acknowledge* that it existed. Everything it offered them to nourish the spirit came from cultures far away. If that's what you're fed on how do you discover that creativity is something that comes from inside you?'

'If you go back to Africa, what happens to finding a way to work with music?'

'I don't know. It's like trying to invent a life again from first principles.' I heard my own voice unconsciously echoing Neil's, the time he talked about starting again on the cello. I felt winded by a recurrence of the pain of being abandoned. Then gradually that gave way to an awareness that what made his voice powerful at moments like this was that it was also mine. I was touching something he and I both understood without need of words. 'Neil kept pushing me back to working out why I wanted music, to find what is basic and real in me. And I see now the final push was to remove himself, to leave me just with who I am.'

'Jennie, wouldn't it help if you could let yourself feel angry, just once? You never say a thing about him that doesn't leave him in the right. And that leaves you put down.'

'The problem is I don't know what to be angry about. He didn't ask me to love him.' Paula made a noise like a small snort. I said, 'I used to get mad at him when he was teaching me, an irrational indignation wooshing through me if I thought he wasn't taking me seriously. But it wasn't him, it was what I was putting on to him.'

Her hand was firm on mine. 'You're better off with him gone.'

It was my explorations in the SOAS library that suggested a way—'An African studies degree?' Paula flipped through the course prospectus. 'What would you learn?'

'All the things no one taught me first time round. How people in Africa lived and thought before white people arrived. What stories they told, what music they made—and still do.'

'And what will you do with all that?'

But it was more about being than doing.

My application was late but I talked my way into seeing the head of department. Waiting to see him in a corridor decorated by handwoven West African fabrics I felt suddenly convinced that this was what I wanted to do, and urgent to make him see that I couldn't possibly wait about another year to start, and that life experience and motivation mattered more than conventional admission requirements. All that adrenalin surging around, and he turned out to be mild and reasonable. Without my asking he suggested that my almost finished degree would count as the equivalent of one year off this one, provided—he looked down at my CV—'There's a language requirement, of course,' he said.

'I speak Swazi,' I said, hoping he wouldn't test me, so many years it was, and so inadequate my command.

'Yes, yes,' he said, as if my speaking it were to be taken for granted. 'Just a matter of a formal certificate. Regrettably Swazi isn't one for which we could provide an examiner. Do you think you could pass a first year exam in another African language by September?'

Four months—

No time now to think, or mope. It was the new life full speed, or not at all. I came home with a pile of course books I had collected in an initial raid on the library. How to decide on a language? That was like deciding where I might eventually go, and it was much too soon...Paula shook her head at the strange words and long grammatical explanations. 'You're crazy,' she said. 'I'd never have the patience.' I said, 'Not even to get to places like this?' and together we stared at an illustrated history of Zanzibar... buildings with carved wooden doors, old as a medieval European city, islands ringed by coral reefs—light green sea of the lagoon, changing suddenly to deep blue. She stopped at a picture of Dar es Salaam harbour—huge steamers alongside fishermen's boats carved from trees. She said, 'Maybe this is where my Dad comes from.'

'Could be. Swahili's the language of the earliest trading ships. We could learn it together!'

'No way,' she laughed, but the fantasy intrigued her for all that. She picked up the other language books. 'Chichewa—where's that?'

I showed her on the map, finger travelling south to Malawi, Zambia. 'Nearer home,' she nodded—my home, this time. And she was right, Chichewa it was.

Summer, my last few months with Michael; and in the time I had alone, hours of study, learning a language this time with no one to talk to, just books and tapes. Solitary intense activity made its own kind of healing, gathering my spirit together before having to go out and deal with the world again...September, suddenly an autumn touch to the air, and I was handing Michael over...The Chichewa exam...A last quiet breath, and now it was October, plunging into the crowded corridors and bodies pushing, voices calling...

Get yourself a lover, Paula had said, and I knew now for myself that it was overdue. For years I had kept that part of myself alive by simple hugs with the women I lived with. I had let myself be wooed only by Michael and other small warm-bodied beings whose every emotion was physically expressed, exploring my face with their fingers, climbing on to my lap for cuddles. But now my survival instinct told me that while hibernation might have served its purpose after Kevin, a second retreat would be disastrous. Desire unreturned might be painful, but the awareness of desire was the road to life. I could not again confine it to the subliminal regions.

And here I was surrounded by young, intelligent people all involved in the process of finding mates. I was conscious of each male body I passed in the corridors or brushed up against in the crowded students' common room. While Dr Anderson droned on with the same tutorials he had been turning out since the end of empire removed him from the remoter regions of the Nuer, I was noticing the way the tall student opposite me raised his arms behind his head when he was making a point, or the dark-haired one sloped back in his chair, legs stretched out, the way Neil used to. There was even one with a Scots voice, though not really like Neil's—a diluted, compromise-English version. Still, anything that connected with him had instant evocative power. I didn't hide from that, but tried to teach myself to let the things I loved in him become objects of desire in themselves which I could respond to in other men. And presumably my eyes were giving out whatever it is eyes give out when one is in this state, for there was no lack of response.

Still something in me stopped it going beyond the stage of mild flirtation. 'You scared?' asked Paula, but I didn't think it was that. Perhaps simply lack of conviction. When you haven't been able to get something you long for intensely, anything less doesn't feel worth disturbing your life for. I was twenty-five and had sorted a lot of things out; most of my fellow students were five, six years younger, straight from school, with no more life experience than

I had had at eighteen. The Asian or African students were older, with a wider view of the world, but most were sons and daughters of privileged families, and knew they would go back to a life as part of a ruling elite; the British students at least had had to step outside of what was expected of them in choosing to come to SOAS. I ended up spending my time mostly with postgraduates, people who had come by long and complicated routes, arguing their way past unwilling bureaucracies, living on almost nothing. Studying, finally, things they cared passionately about, and knew more about than their lecturers, though maybe not in such academic ways.

Student political life was in the doldrums. I occasionally attended student meetings just to see what the atmosphere was like, and would sit perched on a table at the back where I could watch the people as much as listen to the speaker. But I usually slipped away early, protective of my time in the library which always had to compete with the need to earn against an insecure future. I knew I could once again end up stuck if I didn't have the money to move myself from one country to another. I had gone back to Lawrie at the arts centre and taken on organising Saturday and holiday events for children. At first I did it purely to earn, but the children got to me, revitalising a part that still no one else could reach. Whenever it seemed practical I collected Michael to take with me, and it would have been hard to tell which of us was more delighted at each reunion. At first Felicity tried to insist on paying me but Dave stepped in and let it happen the way I wanted it, me just being Michael's friend.

It was in every way a different experience from the days of being a student in Cape Town, and the contrast served to measure all that had changed in me. In those days essays were dashed off at midnight, having scanned three books hastily and lifted a few quotes to try to clothe the scanty body of facts. Now I read to learn, to think, to argue with the author, to follow a detective trail from one book to the next. It did not occur to me to write an essay unless I was ready with something that needed saying; and there was no problem with deadlines.

'You're so lucky,' said Jaswinder, not once but often. She was right, of course, but I assumed it was the chance to study she was talking about. In the Leicester Square days she had staked her life on the dream of going to college, and here I was doing it. 'Why don't you too?' I said. There were further education courses everywhere, and she could have got a grant just as I had. But she was unresponsive. I remembered Neil saying, 'Jennie, do it,' and decided maybe Jaswinder needed someone to do that for her. So I grabbed time away from the library to go round collecting prospectuses and tried a couple of times to get her to go through them with me, till it became clear that it wasn't the studying she was after, it was the students. And specifically, the men. And more specifically, young Indian men, of whom SOAS had, of course, more than its share—

—The idea comes sudden, fully formed—Why don't I bring someone home for her? I don't understand why men aren't queueing up for her. Maybe growing up as she did blocked the instinctive giving out of signals? Perhaps she can't find someone herself, having expected always that her family would?

In the common room I look with new eyes at anyone male and Indian. There is something to disqualify each of them. The cultured lot who talk about books and arty films—I'm not taking one of *them* home to condescend to Jaswinder. The political radicals, interested primarily in the sound of their own voices. A handful who have grown up in Britain—like Jaswinder herself, children of immigrant parents without social pretensions, but they're disqualified on the grounds of sexism. It shines out of them, unembarrassed, that assumption of their right to special treatment because they are male. Even Jaswinder in her current mood wouldn't be able to cope.

Then, in the first week of my second term—I have more or less given up, and here is a possible candidate. He's from East

Africa, just starting an MA. He's Muslim and Jaswinder is a Sikh, but neither of them is interested in religion. He's clearly from a privileged background but he has an easy way about him, unpretentious. Nice looking too…We get talking. A sense of humour, fun to be with. We talk about how we got here, our families. I like the affectionate way he describes his mother and sisters. I feel like a traditional parent going through my checklist, and we seem to be doing well.

His name is Muhib. 'Does it mean anything?' I ask.

'Afraid so,' his eyes are laughing. 'It means lover—as in lover of mankind, but also straight 'lover' . Like in Indian film songs!'

The perfect entry. I tell him I live in a house with Indian film songs playing constantly, along with Sasha McKinley and Portuguese guitars. He is entertained. I say, 'Do you want to come and meet them?' He says, 'Why not?'

He comes. Jaswinder pulls out all the stops with her cooking. He says it's the best meal he's had since he left Nairobi. Jaswinder never takes her eyes off him. He is on the phone next day—

For me.

3

It seemed to be our year for emotional disasters. I made it clear to Muhib that he needed to cool off if we were to remain friends, but it took him a week to accept that and each time the phone rang Jaswinder disappeared into her basement so she wouldn't have to hear. Her envy flared more violently than before, burned itself out, and left her with a major depression. I hadn't said anything to her about why I was bringing him home, but she knew. I had waved before her, delicate as a chiffon scarf, the hope that there might be a way of getting back to at least some of those qualities of living that felt familiar, while still keeping the freedoms she had won. The dream wafted, then was whipped away, exposing the same old drudgery. Off to the launderette for ever and ever, world without end.

Eventually her pragmatism reasserted itself. Dreams had never come true for her, the romantic promises of the film songs were all lies. Just stop thinking about it and get on. She had flashes of cheerfulness again. Then one evening she got up from the table where we were having a communal meal and came round to where I was sitting, and gave me a hug. I hugged her back and started crying. She said, 'Forget it, it's all so stupid,' and then we were laughing and all the others laughing with us.

Forget it—it's all so stupid...For more months than I liked to admit to anyone else I was subject to recurring waves of vulnerable, angry feelings. It was like being caught in an old film that should long ago have been junked. I would speak my part and Neil was never there to answer his. He must have felt what was going on—the pleasure had been so obviously mutual. So why—? Why end it so firmly? 'I expect to come across you in the middle of Africa '—When we lived in the same city? When he knew I would have taken any occasion he cared to invent for continuing to work with him? When, if he wanted to make something of our friendship, all he had to do was pick up the phone? And if he'd lost my number, phone the arts centre to get it?

There was no escaping it, he was choosing that we should have no further contact. But then he'd kept me at arm's length the entire time, all the time he was wooing me with his musical voice and inviting me in to argue with him and challenge him in ways he so clearly enjoyed. Deciding when he wanted me, and how much, and then when he had had enough just shutting the door with no bloody explanation. And why didn't I challenge that? I wanted him and I knew it, so what kept me from taking the lead that he wouldn't?

No answers; and I was left washed up on a pointless shore of logic. It might all be true, but it got me nowhere. And eventually another kind of truth would come creeping back, to lap gently—the knowledge that however unsatisfactorily unfinished our relationship, this was a man I loved, whom once I was lucky enough to be close to, and who during that short time immensely enriched my life.

Neil or no Neil, my viola had become part of me, as deeply structured into my sense of who I was as the knowledge that I could earn my own living, and make my own assessments of the books I read and the interpretations of life they offered. The viola linked me to another way of knowing and being, wordless but more sure, intangible yet precise. I had no teacher and wanted none: it was for myself I played. But Neil had been right when he said my clearest passion was to get into the middle of the chord, and once a month I indulged in that intense pleasure by playing with the group he had introduced me to. It had assumed an amoeba-like existence, constantly changing shape. On a wet night there may be only three or four of us, the next month ten. We met in a rambling house on three floors, the home of a woman whose grown-up children had moved out. On full nights we split into trios or quartets, each choosing music at a level we could manage from the collection that they had been accumulating over the years. We played for pleasure, not to progress, but the simple act of making sounds together, and having to listen, trained a responsive awareness that cannot be learnt alone, and that drew me constantly to want to give fuller expression to the spirit within than I could technically manage.

'You need a teacher,' said one of my friends in the group, and offered to put me in touch with hers. I resisted, as instinctively as I had balked at finding a lover. When I realised I was not prepared to explain why, I knew it was time to jolt myself forward.

The teacher was everything I would not have chosen. Musically conventional, doing everything from the page. Unimpressed to hear that I improvised for pleasure—'No wonder your reading is slow.' She insisted on putting me through standard technical discipline.

To my surprise, I obeyed. Even more surprising, it worked. The apparently boring exercises weren't tedious because I could see they were helping my fingers and arms to produce the kind of sounds my ear was asking for. She pushed me on to solo viola pieces so difficult it took most of my practice time each week just to work out the notes. If I had been just that bit less sure of my own music I'd have gone under. As it was, she was for the moment precisely what I needed—and in that recognition I felt something beginning to shift off my shoulders, a yoke I had been *choosing* to keep there.

'I'd like to hear your music,' I had said.

'You'll have to wait,' he had said—

—In the arts centre cafeteria I overheard a couple of women talking about a string playing project some composer had set up with young children in East End schools. I was sitting at the next table—they didn't know I was listening or that I knew their unnamed but unmistakable composer…'You should see the way the children concentrate,' one of them said, 'and so confident, even though they've only just started'…I soaked it up as personally as if it were meant for me. And maybe I *was* part of what he was doing? Maybe what he learnt by working with me had moved him on, as I had moved on—to find my own thing but different from what I would have looked for if we had never met?

Lawrie was in the foyer stacking publicity leaflets. He handed me one, an event with the string project children performing and Neil directing. Lawrie said, 'Shall we go?' It was ridiculous not to. While Neil and I were both in London, both involved with children's music, the chances were we would encounter each other anyway, so I might as well choose the time…But the very strength of my desire warned me that it was too soon, too dangerous to stir all those feelings and then have to spend months dealing with them again, alone…When I got home I phoned Lawrie—'I've discovered I'm doing something that night,' I said, 'I'm really sorry to miss it.' Which was true.

Paula said, 'You're making too big a thing of it. Go, get past it.'

But I wouldn't. I didn't say, I only want to meet him again when I've got far enough with my own life to feel calm, to make a real equality possible. But Paula knew.

The whole of creation is dancing, the whole universe—
galaxies, stars, their satellites, they turn and come together,
draw apart, and come together again...

I was doing my own exploring now, kinds of music Neil could never have introduced me to. The SOAS noticeboard was cluttered with posters of events I could have heard about nowhere else—visiting musicians and dancers who were unknown to most people in the west. Their small groups of adherents gathered in classrooms or people's homes, to listen and be connected again to the pulse within themselves of the universal song. Often I was the only outsider, among Koreans this week, Uzbeks the next. I stayed afterwards to talk to the musicians. They let me hold their instruments and showed me how to produce a few notes, and I received from the masters of each style impromptu lectures on its complexities. They had no idea how to estimate what I knew, and everything came expressed in its own terms, that often seemed to have no connection with how a western trained musical mind would conceive them. It was like trying to learn many different languages at once, and never getting past the beginning stages in any. Yet I discovered that breadth generated its own kind of understanding. The essential musical elements began to arrange themselves in patterns across traditions, and gradually I learnt how to pinpoint what it was important to ask, and could more easily make sense of the answers.

Music begins as a rhythmical stirring in the body

wrote the ethno-musicologist. *Yes*, I said out loud, sitting there in the library reading his words years after he had written them, and on another continent. The student at the table opposite me looked at me strangely and returned to his own book...

Back in the arts centre I danced with children with faces from all over the world and watched the ways their bodies moved. An African child and a Vietnamese one, same impulse to move in rhythm, but subtle differences in hand movement and hip fluidity…'It's a profound mystery we're touching on,' Neil once said—sound and silence, how neither exists without the other. And here was another profound mystery, one I had known instinctively all along but that now struggled to formulate itself—that we come to understand what is the same in all of us through becoming aware of what is different. I had an image of babies across London being sung to in a hundred languages and styles, and then growing old enough to go to a school where they all learnt *I'm a little teapot short and stout,* tipping themselves awkwardly to one side, not quite in rhythm with the learnt words—

—And that night I dreamt I was walking through rice fields with the arts centre children, and we were following the Korean dance-drummers whom I had seen the week before, as they summoned people to a celebration. Each drummer wore a hat with a long white ribbon flying from a tall aerial that spun round as he jerked his head in small movements—rhythm made visible. The white flash whirls round, so fast it made wheels of light as the drummers moved towards each other and away. Their heads scarcely shifted but the ribbons beckoned and flirted, flipping themselves away before they could be caught. The children's eyes followed, their bodies alert with excitement. 'You should see how they concentrate,' said a voice behind me—

The next day I went straight from lectures to find Lawrie. 'I've got an idea,' I said. He listened and swayed as he had done when he listened to that first idea, over a year before…'There is a whole *world* of singing and dancing that comes to London anyway,' I told him. 'All we have to do is find out in advance, add on a day to their schedules and bring them here, for the children to experience. Korean dancers one week, Andean pipes the next—'

This time he was sceptical. 'Too much sitting still for the kids.'

'They won't just be sitting. They'll be part of it—learning the dance steps, holding the instruments, trying on the hats and seeing how you make the ribbons dance.'

Lawrie kept swaying. 'And the musicians—you think they'll be able to handle that? Probably not used to bringing it down to children's level.'

'That's OK,' I said. 'I can take care of that.'

And now I began to see, still hazy but emerging from the constantly moving shapes, a concept of what might lie ahead, not just for the arts centre events, but for me...The children, the adults; people from one culture, people from another; musicians, and people with no musical training...all potentially involved in the same process, but moving right past each other unless someone could connect them. And that I could do instinctively, with that part of me that was both child and adult, that belonged to all cultures yet to none, that had been living musically since my first breath yet had only just begun to understand the spirit within.

4

Saturday, mid-morning. Jane and I are out at the back. I'm lying on a rug, reading. She's become inspired by the weather and is cutting the grass. The kitchen door stands open—Jaswinder's in there, talking to one of the new women who has just joined the house. I hear the front door bell but I go on reading. Someone will get it. A couple of minutes later Jaswinder appears. 'It's a man for you, Jennie.'

We are all three looking at each other in amazement, Jane, Jaswinder and I. Since Muhib any men in my life stay firmly at the university, there are none who call at the door. I get myself upright and follow Jaswinder back in. My pulse is racing—something inside me that I had thought had gone dead has woken to violent life and is charging around so fast that it takes concentration to walk evenly. This is ridiculous. There is no way it can be Neil. He's never even been near the house—

I turn the corner into the hallway. It is Edward.

Edward. Here on my doorstep. Edward, the brother who went overseas half a lifetime ago, the brother who lived on only in letters that came as rarely as in the days of sailing ships…Everything flicks backwards, and the Jennie of that other time flings herself at the brother who has come home unexpectedly, while from all over the house women emerge to see what's going on.

'I'm on my way to Zurich,' he says, 'for a meeting.' What kind of meeting? I have become like the aunts in Bloemfontein, knowing only that Edward is doing something very clever with economics. Of the letters I remember only the holidays—the Grand Canyon, skiing in Vermont. Once from the Alps, saying there had been a blizzard in the night and people were being advised against walking alone, but he had decided to go anyway. Then for three months we heard nothing. When he finally wrote again he had forgotten all about the Alps and was suprised Mom and Dad had worried…

I'll find out about the work later. He's got two days, he says, and I start thinking about mattresses on the floor. He laughs and says, 'You come to my hotel.' I grab a jacket—we're off. I'm heading for the underground but Edward is summoning a taxi. The hotel has marble floors and men in uniform who open doors before we get to them. Edward decides it's dinner time—he shepherds me out past the uniformed men into a restaurant that makes the ones Kevin used to take me to seem drab. I am bemused rather than rebellious. What is a brother of mine doing at this level of luxury? Then I flip that picture and realise he is seeing a sister who lives with a bizarre collection of women in a house that's falling apart, and he's feeding me up as if this is the only decent meal I am likely to get this week.

We talk almost continuously, for two days minus a few hours for sleep. We remind each other of the time he fell off the garage roof; of summer night suppers in the garden, and how he taught me the names of the stars. We compare notes about the others. We have all become lazy about writing to each other, for Mom's letters do the basics for us.

But Edward and Trevor are on the same continent, and it's clear he does little to diminish the distance. Perhaps he is glad that adulthood gives him a wide berth? I talk about Richard, and I see in Edward's eyes that he remembers someone different. Richard and I write only occasionally, but the quality of the man is immediately present, however short the note. Does Edward not feel it? And Peter—of course, he never *saw*, for he had left before Peter went to the army. All he has had to go on was what Mom has let herself say in her letters.

'Peter's taking a while to get over it'...'We don't hear much from Peter' and it seems that in all these years he has not properly heard the misery that lies behind those quiet phrases.

'And with you?' he asks. 'Do you and he write?'

'He doesn't, I do.'

'And you keep writing, when he doesn't reply?'

'Usually just a card, every few months. Like a message in a bottle, just in case it gets picked up.'

Edward is amazed at my perseverance. I can't explain what it is. 'It's something to do with him having gone under, while I got out.' And I find myself describing something I have never talked to anyone about, not even Paula, how in Swaziland I used to go walking on my own, away from everyone, till I found a quiet place to sit looking out over the land that connected me to Peter, and to Jonas; and sitting there I talked to each of them, and hoped that they would know.

Edward looks amazed. 'It's bizarre, how we've all turned out,' he says. And then, switching firmly to the practical, 'Let's phone Mom and Dad.' And for ten phenomenally expensive minutes there we suddenly are together, all four of us, almost in the same room. When the phone is down I want to cry, and Edward puts his arms around me, the way big brothers are supposed to—

—But it's a good thing it's only two days because by half way through Sunday we're touching present reality again. 'Tell me about your work,' I say. Over his wine he launches into macro-statistics and GNPs, juggling his variables like glittering balls, careless of who gets hurt when they drop. I look at him as if he's a stranger and think, 'This man is ambitious!' The sort of brother who could tell you the capital cities and names of prime ministers of all countries—a phenomenon, but never a threat—and now the boy who resented Trevor organising him has taken himself off to advise companies on how to organise whole populations. I challenge him on wage levels, he throws back rates of return. I brandish unequal terms of trade, he responds with the trickle-down theory of growth. Across all those years and all that distance we are waving banners at each other, each parading our own regalia.

And then he is gone. Flying in, flying out. I feel like one of those barefoot children in Swaziland who used to run from their village huts to the roadside, to watch the cars zoom past. Dust myself off—

—To discover I have changed. Something that had got stuck has become dislodged. After years of keeping my childhood safe where it could never change, one bit of it has broken off and come crashing like a meteorite into the adult life that I have become so used to, facing me with the fact that nothing stands still, not even the past. And I have been jolted not only by Edward but also by my own reaction when he was announced—'It's a man for you, Jennie'—that instant rush of adrenalin. Am I never going to get past thinking that if there is a man for me, it has to be Neil?

Move, girl, move. Life is passing.

A sudden spurt of haildrop beats on the wooden drum, a voice leaping through the rhythms, rich and sensual—

ton te-ge-de-gen
ga-za-ge-ze-gen

The drummer is a Ghanaian called Kwesi. Tall, vigorous, immensely alive, a research student who takes some tutorials and breathes life into an otherwise moribund course on African music. The tones are like those of his language, he tells us. Through them the drummer speaks, beating the rising-falling patterns of meaning—

Turn and be sure
Stop and turn around—

'Hold your own beat, but hear them all.' His voice comes strong over the noise of three simultaneous rhythms. 'Yours on its own is nothing. It is only when they link that you get the power'...

To the other students the drumming is light relief; to me Kwesi offers an initiation into a deep magic I have experimented with imprecisely, and with longing. He gives us each a rhythm pattern and sets us off like clockwork mice. There's no unifying main beat, and it's not a question of subdividing or syncopating—each of us is separate. 'It's not part playing,' he says, 'it's apart playing.' I beat mine and listen for the hidden pulse that throbs though no one plays it...But the rhythms around me are beginning to lose themselves, converge, collapse in a heap. We come out of the tutorial. The students who are waiting to use the room after us grin and say, 'Sounds like you're having fun!' The air among the academic staff is that if it's fun it must be intellectually lightweight. That kind of attitude is the antithesis of what I have come back to university for, to learn things that will help me live in a more aware, involved way. Kwesi does that with his drumming and they haven't the wit to see it. Or maybe it threatens them because they don't have his flair.

He and I go off to have coffee together, and he tells me stories about how he learnt drumming...I bring in my mbira, and we sit on the grass in Russell Square and he teaches me to play patterns on it that fit like another rhythm instrument into his drumming...

But it goes no further. Kwesi's in no hurry to limit his options. There are other young women in plenty, perhaps not so fired by the beat but equally responsive to his charm.

Now I am sitting near the back of a darkened lecture theatre, listening to an elderly Indian who chants Urdu poetry in a strange drone. He sits cross-legged on a carpet, in a long embroidered shirt and white baggy trousers. The audience—Urdu speakers all, it seems—move their heads sideways and say 'Wah, wah' at particularly fine lines. Through the words that mean nothing to me I hear the rhymes and the metre of the rising-falling tune, something between Gregorian chant and bees on a hot afternoon…My attention wanders. I become aware of the person sitting next to me. A faint but warm sense of his body's presence. Without turning my head I can see only a pair of legs stretched forward comfortably…I begin to feel I know those legs, but I am trapped, looking ahead, and I don't want to do anything obvious.

Curiosity wins. I turn—

It is Muhib, once lover-designate of Jaswinder. And he has turned to look at me at precisely the same moment.

Within a week we are lying together. It feels sudden, and yet long overdue, for we chose each other months ago though I would not let myself see it then. Even now I will not take him home, despite the teasing of the women in the house and Jaswinder saying, 'Don't be silly, Jennie.' Instead we use the flat he shares with a friend, who is out most of the time. The lovemaking is so unlike my experience with Kevin that I need a new vocabulary for it. Muhib is considerate, exploratory, constantly aware of how I am responding. Each time I feel more whole, more alive to my own sensuality. Balm to the soul, to be desired in the body.

Our delight in each other creates an aura that surrounds us like the music that he puts on the moment we get into the flat. We do not so much listen as exist within it, an element like light or air. The sound of shehnai or sarod creates the space in which we sit on the floor to eat, or lie together after lovemaking. At other times we become animatedly analytical, and he guides me in ways of listening I have not yet discovered…First the drone of the accompanying tampura, focus simply on that...Not as you listen to a tune, don't expect anything of it, just let it settle in your body. A sort of musical breath...Now let it go, become unaware of it...And now open up to the sitar. No need to listen actively, just let it in... Feel how he's pulling one string at a time, so slowly—that's to let it begin happening in you, to let you feel the whole vibration, let it move around inside you...Now feel, there's just the suggestion of a pulse—you can't call it a rhythm yet, but beginning to move like a wave, to and fro...Now it is a rhythm—a quiet one at first. But the music quickens, becomes more complex. Notes chase each other, pressing against the limits, trying to express the inexpressible, building up until it is a wild outburst the senses can no longer encompass—and then just as you want to cry out, 'Stop, stop, I can't bear it,' it falls away again, spent and calm.

For weeks we passionately communicate all the details of our past lives. It seems significant that we are both of Africa but not African. For me he offers the stimulus of things I have already chosen to absorb myself in. He moves between Nairobi and London, crossing continents as naturally as a migrating bird. He is at home in the Swahili of Nairobi streets, the English of Shakespeare, the Urdu poetry that was passed on to him by parents who carried their love of it in that first migration to East Africa. He sings it as the man in baggy trousers did the day we sat next to each other and felt, each at the same moment before we knew who the other was, that sudden pull of chemistry—

I give myself entire to love, and love of life possesses me

I worship lightning, and lament all that it has destroyed-

Nothing destroyed, but something—missing. Something so vague I cannot formulate it, but I see it first in Paula's eyes when she hears me talk of him, and I know her eyes are only the mirror of what she is hearing. What can be missing? His mind, moving effortlessly; his body, a delight; his temperament, easy going, fun to be with. But—

It's the love of life bit. It's there as enjoyment, but instinctively I look for more—for depth. Nothing has ever been a struggle for him, that's what it is, there's nothing he has ever committed himself to. A path was laid out for him, and all he has done with his life is to follow it. I see photos of his older sisters. They were at university in Britain before him and are now married, back in Nairobi, gracious against the background of wealthy homes. What kind of life will Muhib go back to? And I, if I am connected to him?

No need to think about tomorrow, today is enough. But from Muhib himself I learn a new concept of time. In Urdu, he tells me, tomorrow and yesterday share the same word—*kal*—a day away from today, in either direction. I see it immediately, a constant cycle of cause and effect, around the constantly moving present. Until our bodies chose each other, my tomorrow was being formed by my own yesterday; there was a logic to it, a balance that gave to each today a centred calm. Now I am in danger of losing that. When I think only of today, I follow my desire and I have no doubts. But to be drawn into the cycle of his yesterday and tomorrow, which has so little to do with mine?

Chemistry reasserts itself. Time is ours, the present is all.

5

Maria's was the first future to happen. The year I went back to study, Portugal erupted. The army refused to go on fighting wars in Africa, as she always said they would, and in London it seemed that all the Portuguese waiters were milling about in our kitchen, tuning in to the radio and singing revolutionary songs. By half way through my first year Portugal was gearing up for elections, and the phone was ringing for Maria—they needed her back. The group of women who had been circulating their illicit journal of stories and poems were holding meetings, women's issues were on the agenda, and people were asking for her to read her poems. We knew she would be going any minute and we suddenly felt we had never celebrated her enough. Jane decided this was no time for subtleties and that some of the poems could be translated after all. We made her a huge card with a collage of her own words, in Portuguese and in English. Life and love and liberty—'We'd like them all,' said Paula, 'but sometimes they have to take turns.'

Maria understood that for me her departure meant more than it did for the others. As she left she said, 'It'll be your turn next.'

'Next may be a long time away!' I laughed. Too long to believe in. Change in South Africa would come, I knew, but not soon enough to be relevant for me. I went back to studying Chichewa and learning the rhythms of African drums.

Listen, really listen. Create within yourself an echo
of the drum, then you will start to dance…

The new anthropology tutor, Derek, looked around the tutorial group. 'The point is,' he said, 'it's not a musician speaking, it's a chief. So do we conclude he is talking about dance as dance, or is it a metaphor for other forms of social participation?'

'Like?'

'Think of the metaphors we might use, about our own ways of being part of the whole social group.'…Being tuned in to each other…Keeping in step…Part of my mind watched, assessing the man. A thin, angular young man, awkward except when teaching. But he seemed released by his absorption in ideas…'I know nothing about music,' he was saying. 'When I set out to do field work I had no idea I'd come back with boxes of tapes. But once I got there, no option. Every significant occasion in their lives is marked by music. And not music to listen to, as we would here, it's total participation stuff. In the villages to the south of the Nyika plateau—'

The words nudged at the edges of my consciousness. Something dislodged, something from way back. A rhythm hovered now in the recesses of my brain, but elusive, I couldn't pin it down. For days its stubbornly unrevealed presence nearly drove me mad—

Till I woke one morning with the tune dancing off Richard's flute, as if it had never been lost.

I went to find Derek. 'Those tapes you were talking about, they're from the Nyika plateau?'

'Not the plateau itself. Far too high and inhospitable, no one lives there. From a village a little way southwest.'

'And that was where you did your field work?'

'I spent two years there,' he said, 'and it changed the way I see life.' He was looking at me curiously now. 'Why?'

'Tell me about it.'

There was nothing, it turned out, that he loved to talk about more.

An evening in Derek's flat, listening to the tapes. Then another, for we had hardly got a quarter of the way through. Derek kept pressing the pause button, explaining what people had been doing at the time they sang that, or when the women's voices began, or when the drumming changed. Then he began copying them for me, saying, 'I wish you'd have a go analysing them, musically I mean. There are bound to be musical structures that connect with the social functions of the dance.'

Hours now with the tapes in my attic, late into the night. I tried to sing with them, echoing the syllables in this language I didn't understand but that occasionally seemed to slide close to the Chichewa I was learning. Moving with the rhythms, trying to feel them by being part of them...Their subtleties still eluded me, still constantly just beyond what my ear could hold or my mind interpret...The intricate web of patterns—the call of the first voice, overlapping with the chorus that had a rhythm that seemed not to link in to the first, and beneath that the rattles, the ankle bells, the clapping, all fitting in different ways around what the drums have built up. Starting from the whole and with no one to put the leading threads in my hands, the fabric seemed impossible to untangle. 'I need to *see* the music being made,' I told Derek. 'My ear can't separate who's doing what.'

'Come as my research assistant next time,' he laughed.

It was a joke, but my fantasy held it…A village in the shadow of that high, uninhabited plateau, where the grass waves over land that dips and rises, green to the horizon…I saw myself there, learning in my own body as I danced, watching to see who moved to create which beat; and through that connecting rhythm, getting closer to the underlying pulse to which all of humankind dances—

—Paula comes in. I turn down the volume. She says, 'Give me a break, turn it off.'

'For someone who plays Linda Ronstadt as loud as you do—' 'That's real music. This stuff of yours just goes on and on.'

'What's got into you tonight?'

'Dunno.' Then, curiosity lifting her grumpiness, 'What kind of a song is it, anyway?'

'A pounding song,' I say. Two women's voices against a thudding double beat—*du-dum*—pause—*du-dum*. No other accompaniment than they make with their pounding sticks, lifting and dropping. The rhythm of all work songs, of women with hoes above the head and down again, lifting their arms, curving their backs; of men stripped to the waist, brown backs glistening with sweat…I hand Paula the broomstick I've been using to get the right feel as I sing. 'Have a go.' Up to the ceiling, thump it down on to a cushion—

Galu, galu,
Mwagaluka mwaonachi?

'It's a song of complaint against her man,' I tell her—

Ignore me. Ignore me.
What have you seen, to ignore me?

'She's beating it out of her system while she pounds!'

'Imagine singing while you're working this hard,' she says.

'Derek told me when he was new in the village he asked them if it wouldn't be easier if they saved their breath. They didn't understand the question. They said, 'If we didn't sing we'd have less breath for the work!'

We're both laughing. She throws the broomstick across the room and comes to sit with me on the bed. She asks, 'What keeps you at it, Jennie?'

'I don't know, I just love it. Each step pulls me on to the next one, trying to feel how the rhythm works. It's amazing how doing it changes your perception. I've discovered it's the up movement that needs the real muscle action, so that's what you feel as the beat, even though it's the downbeat that makes the sound. So the main beat's internal—what you hear is its echo.'

'And your voice—how do you get it to do that, that projecting kind of sound?'

'Make it all one texture.' She tries. It's what I learnt in Swaziland but I don't know how to describe it. I try again, 'Think yourself outside, with masses of space around you. Aim for a distant hilltop.'

'I like that,' she says. 'I think that's just what I'll do.'

A distant hilltop...Africa is still continents away, but time is getting nearer. Only half a year till I've finished this degree, and then? Derek keeps telling me I'll be wasting a natural talent if I don't go on with anthropology. Muhib keeps hoping I won't decide anything, that we can just go on as we are until he's ready to move—

Muhib's parents arrive for a visit to London; a regular event, it seems. They take us out to a meal. His father is urbane, tolerant, but too fond of the sound of his own voice. I hear Muhib's voice in ten years time, sounding just like that. His mother is definite, more of a force than her husband, wearing her sari in a way that looks practical rather than elegant. I ask about her work—it is obvious somehow that she doesn't stay home supervising the servants. 'I'm a lawyer, my dear.' She looks at Muhib in mock reproof. 'You told her nothing about your family?'

'I told her lots,' he says calmly. 'She never asked about that.'

'And I thought I brought you up with some respect for women,' she says, giving him an affectionate touch on the cheek.

'You're as mentally idle as your father.' She turns to me. 'Look out for yourself with this one, my dear. The men in this family are charming but they take all the good things for granted.' Muhib's father smiles in a detached way. He has heard all this before and lets it wash over him—

—I am amazed that I needed her to put words on it. His easy radicalism connects with nothing real. His views on life were provided for before he had time to be aware that he needed them. I have merely slotted into that, fulfilment of the next stage. That I refused him first time round heightened my desirability, for he is not used to being denied. The passion of the first months was in fact a long celebration of having got what he wanted.

And now he's relaxing into it. There is nothing remarkable in having a woman who loves him. It's what he has always had, what life owes him…I remember Trevor lounging in a garden chair while Jill draped herself around him, her very body pleading for attention. Trevor idly dangling her along while it suited him… Never, I am never going to be another Jill…I see Paula, sobbing against me in the night, her need for Eva unassuaged…Me, almost going under after Neil left…

Never again. And certainly not for Muhib. Desire of the body cannot be separated from desire of the spirit. I need to feel both for the same person, otherwise I'd rather be alone.

Muhib is uncomprehending. I say, 'Friends, yes; lovers, no.' He says, 'That's absurd Jennie. Why leave out the best part?' I say, 'There's nothing wrong with today, it's tomorrow I'm thinking about. I want to stop before it all get's too intertwined to disentangle without pain.' He says, '*Now* is when we live.'

And since I've said that to myself, it's difficult to think of a reply. But I do it anyway.

Paula says, 'It never works, thinking you can stay friends with ex-lovers.' But I know Muhib better; after a couple of weeks he will accept my terms, out of idleness; it will be easier than thinking seriously about why the rest is ending. And from my side there's something I can't cancel and don't want to, and that's gratitude. The loving was kind and his pleasure in me real. I grew in that light and warmth, to find my own natural delight. Mine now, part of me wherever I go, and whoever it might be who goes with me.

6

June 1976. Final exams, through the hottest summer Britain has known for half a century, and suddenly South Africa is in the news. I watch on the television as black school students storm police stations, symbol of their physical oppression, and burn their schools, even more potent symbols of their intellectual subjection—

—I am summoned by their anger, their determination not to accept what limits them. Summoned back to the child who listened to the sounds of Gertruida's party, and hated the police who drove her out. The rebellious schoolgirl, asking questions in history lessons that Miss Joubert was afraid even to have heard, let alone answer. And here are these school students, no older than I was then, confronting not just their teachers but the whole aparatus of the state—and nothing to fight with but the stones they pick up from the roadside. Police swarming, people running, arms, legs flailing, bodies struggling as they are dragged off—but there are more to take their places. Paula sits with me to watch the army going into the townships—we stare at fresh-faced white conscripts of eighteen, successors to Peter who look out of hard, panicky eyes at the debris left behind after they have been ordered to shoot. A war of scarcely grown-up children, through whom society channels its hate, its failure.

Now the news is of prisons overflowing and people fleeing across the border. Kevin comes back into my dreams for the first time for years, as I drag myself behind him into Swaziland…A reporter holds a microphone up to the group of tense young men who have managed to get to Botswana. 'What will you do now?' he asks, while their faces look blank with delayed shock. One of them says nothing, just stares at the camera—straight at me, looking for some response. The rest talk at once, but not an answer, simply an outburst of frustration. We are stuck, they say, we have to move on. 'To Zambia,' says one, where the liberation movements are based...I think of the journey that will mean, north through the Kalahari desert, the Okavango swamps, north across the Zambezi river, and the names thud in my mind like Kwesi's drumbeats—

ton re-be-ge-den

We are going far away—Be sure

It will not be freedom they will find there, but more waiting around, wondering what they will do with their lives.

Nothing ends. It just keeps starting, over and over again.

I'm going. And I'm sure.

'Zambia?' The woman in the overseas recruiting agency raises her eyebrows sceptically. 'Pretty difficult these days.'

'How do you mean?'

'Wars on three of their borders. Shortages in the shops, everything going down hill. The only money comes from copper and the price has dropped.' She starts looking at my CV. 'Kenya would be a lot easier. Wonderful beaches, they say.'

'I want to go to Zambia.'

She shrugs and pulls papers out of the file. 'Head of the English department, Luapula secondary school.'

I say, incredulous. 'I'm not even a trained teacher.'

'But your Swaziland experience—I told you, we can't recruit.'

'I'm not going back to English teaching.' That would defeat the whole point. 'And not in a school,' I say while I'm about it. I can hear the head teacher already—'That's not in the syllabus, Miss de Villiers.'

But it seems there is nothing else anyone will pay me to do. Sod them all, I'll just go, and find something myself when I get there.

'You'd really be better off trying Kenya,' she says. 'We could find you something short-term if you're not sure you want to stay.'

'And they'd pay my fare?' Perhaps it makes sense. I'd get to Africa right away, earn, live simply, and save to get myself on to Zambia. Then arrive by land, crossing real borders...'How about this?' She has found a three-month job between someone leaving and someone else arriving. Project administrator in an organisation called Local Community Projects International. Absurd—how can a project be both local and international at the same time? But the waiting has been too long already. I care only that I should get there.

The contract is signed, my ticket booked, my jabs are done. Only a week till I leave.

Goodbyes. Michael. Lawrie and the people at the arts centre. Derek, who provides me with precise directions how to reach his village if I should ever get to Malawi. The house—cocoa late at night in the kitchen, or sitting on each other's beds. There was always an indefinite amount of time and now suddenly it has become precious.

Megan phones, Megan the health visitor who was part of the children's workshops. I have been occasionally to have a meal with her family—husband and two teenage children. She regards me as a talented waif who needs a regular dose of home comfort to remind me that the straight world is there to come back to if I will ever consider it. Occasionally I return the compliment by persuading her to escape from her mother-wife-worker duties and do something entirely for her own pleasure—a meal, a concert in town. 'Let me plan it this time,' she says, and I leave it to her gladly as I scoot up and down to the attic several times a day, discovering yet more things to sort out before I go. The next day she's on the phone again. 'I found something delightful. Have you seen the Proms programme?' The Proms programme is the last thing I would have time to notice right now. She laughs and says, 'I'll post it to you.'

It arrives. I glance, hurriedly, at the one she's marked. Berlioz, Rodriguez—and a new commission by Neil MacPherson. And he's conducting.

OK, so it's going to happen. Maybe I won't even see him to speak to—there'll be hundreds of people—thousands, maybe. We'll be lost in the crowd. And if I do, maybe it's not a bad thing. Perhaps this will help finish off a phase of life. I want to start again clear, not carrying baggage like last time.

I imagine standing in the crowd nearby, waiting to catch his attention. His eyes sweep over me, only belatedly recognising me. Maybe not quite able to place me. Or embarrassment. Or its opposite—a few ordinary words, as if we were once vague acquaintances—

It's running out of control already. Oh Christ, I want to just leave, without opening up all that.

Megan and I meet at five-thirty in the queue that's already snaking down the steps behind the Albert Hall and disappearing round the corner. She's been to the Proms before but sitting in one of the amphitheatre of seats, never joining the promenaders queueing for standing tickets. She has come equipped as for a siege—a thermos of coffee, a picnic supper of rolls and salad. She says, 'Thank goodness we got here early. How near the front do you think we'll get?' I feel an absurd panic that it's going to be too near. She gives no sign of knowing that I might ever have had complicated feelings about Neil. Maybe she doesn't know, though it seems unlikely—at the time it was happening I was beyond taking any pains to hide. Perhaps she knew and has just assumed I got over it.

Megan is saying, 'I've never seen anyone I know conducting.' Nor have I. 'All we'll see is his back.' She chatters on. 'You know the way he was with the children? That way he had of releasing them, just by taking it for granted they were going to be able to do wonderful things? Do you think he'll be like that with an orchestra?'

We stake out our small space on the promenade floor, surrounded by other people fanatical enough to be prepared to stand for two and a half hours to hear music played. Is it the Berlioz and Rodriguez they've come for? Or have all these hundreds of people heard about Neil and want to hear his music? I have no idea what to expect. Who knows what may have happened to his musical expression in two years? Someone who thinks as actively as he does, constantly responding to each new stimulus—

Megan has been glancing at the programme and now passes it to me. 'It'll make more sense to you than me,' she says. It's a piece called *Exile*. Whose exile? Exile from what? Why would he, who had never had to flee, choose such an image? I dig into each word of the programme notes. They connect with no Neil I know. 'A voluntary exile, choosing to inhabit territory most people do not let themselves explore.' I can't imagine Neil saying that. It's probably not him, it's the programme-note writer. Then I remember the four years' silence, in which he composed nothing; Neil saying, 'Everything that matters about my music comes from having started again'...I begin to feel overwhelmed by all I do not know about him. I pass the programme back to Megan, laughing to try to defuse what is building up. 'I'm not sure I'm going to be able to cope with this!'

Applause around us—he is there, coming towards us, looking right over our heads to the circling sea of clapping hands. He turns, arms raised. Silence. He lowers his arms. I wait, suspended, one with those who sit poised in the orchestra, waiting for his arms to move again and release the tension, free the sound—

He turns towards the lead cello. With the smallest movement of his head, he motions to it to begin. A single long sustained note, deep down, on and on; vibrating within me till I have become absorbed into the sound and it is impossible to hide.

The applause is over. Neil has left the rostrum for the last time. Interval. Megan turns to me, her face laughing, and says, 'I love the clothes—he hasn't changed!'

I scarcely noticed. Of course she's right—the conductor for the Rodriguez wore the usual—formal suit. Neil was himself. No jacket, his arms sweeping freely; but no attempt to create an alternative style either. Just Neil, in a shirt.

We are moving out, propelled by the crowding promenaders into the corridors and out into the night street for fresh air. Megan says, as if it is so obvious we don't even need to agree it, 'Let's go and find him,' and heads off for the door marked 'Artists' Entrance'. Leave it, I want to say. But I just follow.

He is there—people milling, talking animatedly around him The cello soloist is getting most of the attention. Neil looks oddly lost in the middle of all that hubbub. He hasn't seen us but he's facing in our direction, his head slightly inclined forward as he listens to someone—that's the same, too, I'd forgotten it—he's tall, it's an instinctive way of giving others his full attention. We are near enough now to see his face clearly—and I realise that he is tired. It's more than the tiredness after intense concentration, something more basic than that. I have seen it in him only once before, and it moves me. 'Let's go,' I say quietly to Megan, touching her arm to stop her going nearer. 'There's too much going on—'

But he has seen us. His head lifted, his eyes register—a moment's disbelief, shock almost—and then vivid pleasure. There is absolutely no mistaking it.

He excuses himself from the group and comes over to us.

Chapter 2

So fast, a film spinning out of control. Expressions of amazement, delight, laughter, hugs all round—His voice again, the Scots lilt almost wiping me out with joy, the illusion of being back again as we once were—Where've you been all this time?—How's the viola?—Your viola!—Nairobi! When are you leaving? Jennie this is absurd! You can't suddenly appear like this after two years and then say you're away to Nairobi…

So he knew how long it was, without having to work it out.

It's the suddenness that makes things happen. He had no preparation, as I had, no chance to think what he would do or take defensive action. He says, 'Hold on a minute,' pushes through the people, is back a moment later with a bag and pullover. 'Let's away,' he says, and we are out crossing the road, all three of us, to sit on the grass in Kensington Gardens, still light in the long mid-summer evening. Groups of people stand with their interval drinks, talking. Phrases waft out at me…Stunning last movement…But does it go anywhere?…I'm sitting with Megan and Neil on either side of me, talking across me. I don't notice what I'm saying, if anything. I've gone blank with joy, just being here—

The interval is nearly over. People beginning to wander back. Neil says, 'What are you doing afterwards?'

Megan says, 'I'll need to get back. But you stay and talk some more, Jennie.' Then—I don't know what makes her say it, she's not a manipulative woman but she must have seen, on our faces. 'Actually, my feet are killing me,' she says, 'I think I'll skip the second half.' She gets up, bag on shoulder. She says, 'It's been a lovely evening and we heard what we came to hear. You two have lots to talk about.'

And she's gone. They're all gone, back into the hall for the rest of the concert. Neil and I look at each other, momentarily embarrassed at having been organised. Then the absurdity of it gets to us both at the same moment and we laugh. Another pause. He says, 'I have to go to Glasgow tomorrow.'

'So I'm not the only one who's leaving soon!'

'I'm away for a week,' he protests. 'That hardly signifies.' Then immediately he starts plying me with questions. When exactly am I going? What will I be doing? What have I been doing in the last two years? Do I still play the viola—alone? with others? And what other music have I been involved with?

I answer, bubbling, as he is, but I am confused. We are talking as if there has been no break in time, the intimacy and the spark still there, instantly available. But in an hour he's asked more questions than he ever did all those months we worked together—a need to know that he never would admit to before, in the days when I gathered scraps of information about him and tried to piece them together. Exhilarating, but unnerving. It may stop as suddenly as it started.

The light's beginning to fade. I see him glance towards the Albert Hall and know he's thinking, They'll be coming out soon. He says, 'Let's walk,' and we set off across the park under the darkening trees, heading nowhere, just away. The movement and the sense that we are moving to where we will not be disturbed have a steadying effect. We are talking more calmly. Everything I ask he answers straight, none of those closed-door moments of two years ago. All the things I remember with love are still there. A momentary teasing in his eyes, his pleasure when I challenge. We talk lightly, seriously, calmly, humorously, the moods of weeks happening all in half an hour; then that look of tiredness on his face that I saw before he knew we were there returns—momentarily settles—then is banished. We are behaving like people who have known each other for years and yet we have to ask the most basic questions. All those months of working together we existed entirely in the present, no past or future allowed to intrude. Now we have leapfrogged into another present moment, but even briefer. The real past is still too dangerous to explore, the future already allocated, elsewhere.

I say, 'Tonight's music—I'm sure I'd have known it was yours, even if no one had told me. But I've no idea how.'

'Try,' he says emphatically, and his pleasure in pushing me to find it for myself makes me able to, the way it always did.

'For a start, the long cello note.'

He stops walking. He is looking straight at me. He says, 'That was Michael's note. It's been hovering for years, waiting to be used.'

It's out now, stated. We stand silently absorbing what has been admitted. He says quietly, 'Being with you is better even than I'd remembered.'

He has only said what is obvious to both of us. Something moves in his eyes—I don't know what it is but I become afraid he is going to disappear again, closing a door with no notice. Before he can do it I say, 'You knew it was two years since we'd seen each other.'

He nods. 'I gather you didn't need to count either.'

'An internal calendar. It keeps certain things going even when I tell it not to.'

'Your face—' I don't know what to expect. I feel momentarily afraid, of being exposed. He says, 'It looked as if you'd been trying to put a mask on it all day, and had given up.'

The fear dissipates. I start laughing, at myself, at this incredible thing that is happening. 'It's amazing, being known so well.'

'And amazing for me. That you still feel that way.' His voice is—gentle. The love in it threatens to overwhelm me. I pull away, move instinctively further from him, searching for something to cling on to with which to protect myself against that voice. 'If it meant something to you, why didn't you do something? Two bloody years ago? You knew where to find me.'

He does not answer but puts out his hands to take mine. It's a movement of asking, not answering. Asking for acceptance. Maybe for help. He too is afraid.

He says, 'There's too much we've never talked about, Jennie.'

Beneath the words, regardless of them almost, a current surges. This time I know myself better and know it is the chemistry of desire, not just of the body but for the whole person. I have taken his hands, receiving their size and warmth. 'I need to understand what's been happening to you, Neil. Then. And since. And before.'

'You still want everything, all at once!' Then the amused tone gives way, and he says, 'You are quite right to.'

'It was you stopping us talking properly last time, Neil.'

'I'm aware of that.'

The admission halts me. 'All this time I have assumed—'

'What?'

'That you didn't want it. What you could see I was feeling.'

'Not didn't want.' His hands tighten on mine in emphasis. 'Couldn't handle.'

'Why? It never made sense. I *knew* the pleasure was mutual.'

'From the moment you started tearing me off a strip for not trusting to the musical potential in children.' His eyes are amused again. 'It's not a common experience, being faced with such a frontal attack from a stranger.'

'You didn't appear to mind.'

'It's what made me interested.' He hesitates, searching for how to get into something difficult. 'It was the other bit I backed away from.'

'Meaning?'

'The need.'

Fear returns; then coming to my rescue, indignation. He's letting his memory distort the equality there was between us. 'It was never need. It may have been longing, for what I couldn't have. They're different.' But they're not. Not then, not now. 'Neil, just tell me. I want to know what you felt.'

'I felt that you were very desirable, and very careless about your own safety. And since I knew I could not get involved with you personally, I felt I had to create a little distance.'

'You succeeded.' I pull away from his hands, surprised at the bitterness in my voice, the confused, hurt feelings of two years ago, suddenly here again.

He does not answer my tone but goes on steadily. 'I also thought there might be some confusion in your own mind, arising from your first passionate encounter with the viola. The vibes were a little overwhelming. For both of us.'

His words are taking away from me the self I have built up over these years, the self that is undefeated and strong. I need to stop myself slipping back into need. 'I don't like this,' I say.

'Which part of this?'

'The picture you are reconstructing. You as a mature man, watching me as a young woman, going overboard. And you being so kindly concerned. In fact,'—the passion is growing now—'I don't just not like it. I hate it.'

'You may hate it. It's what happened.'

'And I hate you being so bloody calm.'

'Calm is not what I'm feeling, Jennie.'

We are stuck again, staring at each other, not knowing how to proceed. And it's obvious now that I am looking at him properly that he is far from calm—it's only his words that he has managed to hold steady. His eyes are troubled, in a way I cannot bear. I put my hand out to touch his face. He reaches up to my hand, puts his over it, holds it there. I become aware that it is now completely dark and we are still standing here under the trees. Somewhere behind us, the sound of traffic. Night lights on the streets. The crowd must have come out of the hall—streamed past us—gone home—and we haven't noticed. 'Neil, I'm confused. It's been such a long time with one set of pictures in my head, and now—'

'What I said about need—I didn't say it right. You didn't ask for anything that didn't grow naturally out of how we were together. It was me not being able to handle it. Even musically—the rate you were progressing, I thought it quite possible you would soon discover you no longer needed me—'

'The Holy Books.'

He acknowledges it, a self-deprecating smile. 'But not just music. You. The way you were. Are. I kept trying to say—let's keep it at this level, no further—and everything we did together just kept moving us on, beyond where I could do anything to stop it. There are things I should have told you right from the start but I didn't know it was going to be necessary. And by the time it was—by that time I was trying to avoid talking personally altogether.'

I stand very still, waiting.

'Jennie, what did you think was going on?'

'I didn't know, I just lived each day and loved it. And then I realised, something has changed, it's not me on the outside looking at you, but us, everything we did was us—' Tania saying, Neil, you're a wizard…'And then I caught myself feeling jealous.'

'Jealous? Of?'

'Anyone who seemed to be part of your life when I couldn't be. Tania. Teresa.'

'And did you think I was involved with either of them?'

'I didn't know. It scarcely mattered. You let them in, in a way you wouldn't let me in.' I wait for him to tell me. He says nothing. 'Go on, Neil. Were you?'

'Teresa and I have been partners for almost three years.'

I suppose I should have known. The way he was with Juan… But what I am chiefly taking in is the present tense. 'Have been' means 'we still are'…I look up. He is watching me, waiting for my reaction. I have none. I feel blank. He says quietly, 'It's not your standard partnership, Jennie. We've never lived together in the same house.

There has to be a certain amount of discretion. But still it was there, and—I knew I should have made it clearer. I don't know what stopped me.' He breaks off. 'We can't stand here all night.'

We start walking again, heading for the lights. He walks next to me but separate, a definite space between us. Then within a few yards he thinks better of it, puts his arm around me and we walk together. Moving helps. Feeling less vulnerable, doing something.

'Tell me now, Neil. Properly.'

'Teresa has a husband. I did tell you that. You may have forgotten.'

'I haven't. In prison in Chile.'

'If there were a change of regime and he were freed she'd be with him tomorrow. Meanwhile she's a warm-hearted woman, with a life to live and no prospect of seeing him again. It's not the easiest situation in which to make clear decisions about partnerships.'

'And you? What would you want, if she could decide?'

'Decide?' He doesn't seem to understand the question. 'I haven't said it right. She knows what she wants—she wants him back. She's not available for anything really intimate, or long-term. But we were close friends and—it would have been a pointless added strain to cut out of her life everything that—she's a woman of strong principles but also quite practical about what's possible and what isn't.' He pauses again to check whether he should go on. Then, 'She was new in Britain, dealing with a hundred problems and at the same time trying to be a creative musician and a good mother to Juan. I was taking care of him a lot of the time when she was performing. She was grateful that I gave him time when the other people she was surrounded by just talked over his head at her. When she had to go on tour she felt more comfortable leaving him with me than with anyone else. It was easy for me to do. His school was just round the corner. And he's been very good for me. Teresa was in and out because of Juan, coming back to me at the end of each day, off-loading. I admired her courage, and liked her, and was happy that what I could give her was helpful. I wasn't looking for intimacy, but maybe because of that there's been something I've had with no one else, being there for each other, in a way we can both rely on completely. We realised one day we were in fact each other's partners. Then it became silly not to—'

'You talked about discretion.'

'Because of Juan. She wants him to feel sure about her loyalty to his father. But that goes also for all her Chilean friends, so that means with everyone; there's no other way. People who know us probably assume it's happening but no one says it.'

'And Juan?'

'Juan comes to me as he would to a father; but he never sees me and Teresa together in that way.' His voice presses now, urgent for me to understand. 'The part Juan sees is the part that matters. It's an arrangement of loving friendship, Jennie. Becoming lovers just eventually happened, but it's never been—what you evoked in me was something quite different. But incompatible with what I'd already committed myself to.'

He waits. 'Say something,' he says. There seems nothing to say. He says, trying to push through my blankness, 'Jennie, I couldn't have withdrawn without damage. It was crucial to her, in dealing with the pain of what was happening to people she loved.'

Something is emerging now, some kind of feeling I can get hold of. 'I want to know not what you thought you *should* do, but what you wanted to do.'

'I wanted you, more than I liked to think about. I also wanted to be something positive in Teresa and Juan's lives, not the cause of further damage.'

'Are you telling me neither want was stronger than the other?'

He turns on me, puts his hands on both my shoulders, the tension breaking out of him now, 'That's a false question. She was already part of my personal life. You were new—I hadn't yet let you in. I couldn't see how we would all deal with the complications if I did. So I took evasive action.' His vehemence is comforting even though I am trying not to receive it, wanting to force him to admit to a confusion of emotions like those I am experiencing. He drops his hands and says, 'You were angry with me for saying I'd tried to protect you. OK, it was myself I was trying to protect as much as you. But you refused to see the barriers. I couldn't cope with your constant presence, constantly presenting yourself. By the end I couldn't wait to get away and be left alone.'

'And when you'd gone?'

'It was—' He turns away, distracted by some present feeling. 'I was in a sort of retreat, keeping things as simple as possible. Away from every one. You, Teresa. Juan. All my usual friends. Learning to accept that I wasn't going to have it—all that life and energy that was there while we worked together—'

I finish it. 'And that we could clearly have again, for the asking.' For a moment he doesn't speak. Then, slowly, 'It seems so.'

It ought to be joyous, what he's saying. Joyous to say, to receive. But it's hedged around with a knowledge of what is not going to be possible. I say, 'I can't bear this.' And now what I most cannot bear is the physical longing that has been let loose by the knowledge of being loved. I want to blot the world out and lie down right here, under this tree. I feel my knees going wobbly.

'Let's get home,' he says.

It's a different house—his own. I'm glad. No Tania or anyone else. I don't know why I would mind; just a fierce feeling about not wanting to share him with anyone tonight, not even for a few minutes.

His room, his bed. At first Neil is afraid, of causing more damage. But the damage has been done long ago. Loving now is the only way I know towards healing. I know there is no future in it. The constraints for him haven't changed, and in my life too much has already been decided. We have one night and then we will be gone in opposite directions and you can't throw lives over because of one night. But we have this night and we have had nothing else. It is obvious that despite his fear he wants it as much as I. For the moment that's all the reassurance I need.

We hardly slept, but the night was not long enough. He hadn't eaten before the concert and when we had made love the first time he was suddenly ravenously hungry. We went downstairs together to see what was in the fridge, then sat up in bed while he ate and I nibbled at the edges. We talked for hours more, made love again, and slipped down into sleep, holding each other close. Then drifting up out of it again—to find his warm, naked body still there next to mine, to have him turn and hold me so that every bit of me seemed to touch every bit of him, down the whole length. Within a few minutes he was looking down on me again, moving deliciously. Then I remember nothing till we woke to find each other in the first morning light.

There was an unreal lightness about the whole thing, as if neither of us could take seriously the fact that this complete oneness was going to be brought to an abrupt end. Once I said, like something one could joke about, 'Let's rewrite the script. Start again, with no Teresa.' He laid his hand lightly over each of my eyes in turn—a gesture so loving, so specific, colluding with me in closing off what we did not want to see. Then he lifted them off again. 'And no return to Africa, Jennie?'

The script had run too long, for both of us.

There's too much we never talked about, for all that we talked most of the night. Too much that couldn't be understood and that in the end just had to be accepted as done. Why he had never tried to contact me—

It seemed the only way. For me, and I presumed for you. To let things dissipate.' And then, 'Was I wrong?'

Of course he was wrong. And of course he was right.

'There was one time—I was working on a piece for a quartet, a few months after I'd come back from Manchester. I'd been feeling dead-endish about a lot of things and then I got this commission. I realised half way through working on it, everything I was trying to express had got caught in a specific kind of tension—almost getting there, but not quite. Not being willing to risk going for the thing that really matters. I went around for days thinking about you, and about how badly I had handled the whole thing.'

'Neil, if you knew that, why—?'

'I don't know. It seemed done, like it couldn't be undone. And I wasn't any nearer knowing how I would have handled all the other things.' I pull away, unable to keep still while I'm hearing this. He says, 'I also assumed you'd have transferred your energies to someone else. It didn't seem reasonable to expect anything else.'

'You're way out. It took a year and a half before I found anyone I could remotely contemplate.'

He is silent. Then, 'Does that mean, a difficult year and a half?'

'No. Two or three extremely difficult months. Followed by a long period of lying fallow. To recover.'

He says nothing but keeps holding me, stroking my back. Not a trailing, arousing touch now, but slow whole-hand stroking, from the shoulder, all the way down, and again, and again, trying to stroke the remembered pain out of me. Eventually he says, 'Were you angry?'

'Paula used to say it would be better if I could be. I couldn't manage it. Except—'

'Except what?'

I pull away from his stroking hand. 'The dishonesty of it. Not being prepared to admit what was happening. I kept trying to excuse you by telling myself it hadn't happened for you, so how could I expect you to acknowledge it. But I *knew*, I couldn't have done all that alone. You remember you used to talk about music as a shared consciousness. We did develop a shared consciousness, of an incredibly special kind. That's why we can be like this instantly, years later. You were making love to me the whole bloody time with your spirit and telling yourself you were protecting us both from it, just because you never actually put it into words.'

'Or touch. If I'd cared less, that would've been quite easy to do.'

'Thank you for nothing. What mattered to me was just being acknowledged. If you had just *once* been prepared to treat me as an equal, instead of thinking you had to make all the decisions—'

'And done what?'

'Told me what the hell was going on for you.'

'And then?'

'And then I could have learnt to accept that it was impossible, for the same reasons you had to. As we are doing now. But at least I wouldn't have felt *wiped out* as a person.'

He has gone still. Almost rigid. I wait, and still he doesn't move. I become afraid. 'Neil—I didn't mean to be so vehement.'

He says, with difficulty, 'Let's just lie quiet for a few moments.' No point. No point going over it any more. It's finished.

It is almost time. It's been light for hours and he has to get ready to go to Glasgow. By the time he comes back I'll be on the plane heading for Nairobi. I lie in bed and watch as he gets dressed. I'm holding on till the last minute. I can get myself ready after he's gone, and pull the door locked behind me.

He pauses, shirt half on, and stands watching me watching him. 'When you get there, will you write?'

'I don't know. I'll have to see what's manageable.'

His eyes are difficult to read. Loving. Troubled. Something more, connecting with the tiredness I saw in his face last night before he knew I was watching. Something he finds hard to deal with, in himself, not me. But all he says is, 'Don't be sad, Jennie. Just be glad we've had this.'

'I'm no good at half measures. I never have been.'

'The Lord be praised,' he says. And stays looking at me steadily.

Stay as you are, forever, his face says. Be forever a person who is no good at half measures, who does not accept limits, who cares passionately. His eyes say that to me, and mine to him. Stay as you are, for I love that very thing in you. We will each have to find out what is manageable; but I know already that he will have to do as he did last time and try to think about it as little as possible. Because he too is no good at half measures.

He stands up, to finish getting dressed.

2

I wanted to start clear, not carrying all that baggage like last time. But there will always be baggage, I've learnt that now. I check mine in, watch it bump along the belt and out of sight, to be loaded on the Nairobi plane, and while I wait to board I sit with my hand luggage and my viola and try to remember why I am going.

I wanted to go back to things unfinished. But now I understand, too late, that those things are so far away they scarcely matter, and the real unfinished business is what I have just recovered and lost again. Maybe it's not too late. Maybe I could still reverse time. Walk out of this anonymous glass cage where I wait with strangers to be loaded into a metal container and flown to a place I have never been. Just walk out, back to the life that has meaning—

And do what? Wait for phone calls that do not come? For Neil to extricate himself from a situation that has not changed?

I do up my seat belt and know that it is done. I am going.

3

Nairobi is before all else an onslaught on the senses. A riot of colour, smells, sounds, constant bright movement of people. Things that make me feel at home even though my spirit is still raw. Kenya is thousands of miles north of any Africa I have known, but each day I wake it is to the same sunlight, the same earth right there beneath my bare feet as I push open the door and go out on to the dew-covered grass, the same sense of space opening out in all directions. Brown faces and bodies everywhere, becoming within days the normal way for people to be, till when I catch sight of myself in the mirror I am surprised at how underdone I look. The friendliness and humour of even the most casual encounter. Men in cheerful short-sleeved shirts sitting about in the sun at all hours of day, time to stop and greet, time to stand and talk and laugh and slap each other's hands in laughter. Young women in provocative skirts, older ones with bright African print cloths wound round their waists, spreading over wide rumps as they bend to lift bundles on to their heads.

And the profusion of nature. The house I am to occupy is four times the size I need and I never feel comfortable with it, but the garden is paradise and I don't care that I am privileged to have it, I just rejoice. I come home to it each day at lunch and spend every last bit of daylight in it. I don't think of it as 'mine' , even temporarily. It is a bit of God's glory, there for me to tend, to make me whole again as once before the footpaths and wildflowers of the North Downs did. It rewards every half hour's work I put into it. Cuttings that I take from neighbours' gardens root and start spreading before my eyes. Mango and banana and pawpaw trees bear without anyone tending them. Mature flowering shrubs and trees tower over the house—a flourish of yellow trumpet flowers at my window as I wake, bougainvillaea in purple and red and orange over the patio pergola. Passion flowers, waxy and ornate, against a wall of dark green leaves. Red hibiscus with long yellow stamens, calling as I pass. A month after I arrive the jacaranda trees suddenly break out in a chorus of blue and purple, dropping blossoms to make dappled carpets on the driveway.

With the house comes not only the garden, but Ali—the houseservant, in the small building down at the back. That's less than comfortable. Ali receives me graciously and is cooking my first meal before I have unpacked. I try one of the Swahili greetings I learned from Muhib. 'You know our language!' he exclaims. 'Just a few words,' I say. 'I will teach you,' he announces. 'I am from the coast—kiSwahili is my language. These Nairobi people, they are Luos and Kikuyu, they can't speak it properly.'

By the end of the first week I have geared myself up to tell Ali as tactfully as I can that while he is an excellent teacher, I don't need a servant. His salary comes with my job, so he'll get that anyway, but he should feel free to take a holiday for the next couple of months—maybe go and visit his family at the coast? He can see for himself I have few needs. I love gardening, like doing my own cooking and I'm not used to anyone cleaning up after me. He is wasted on me and my simple lifestyle.

Ali is unimpressed. He has no desire to go anywhere. He is as attached to the garden as I am and he doesn't want a holiday. 'If I go to my family they will load a lot of trouble on my head.' He too likes a quiet life. We are well suited to each other.

Ali wins. I am a temporary incident in his established life pattern; my preferences are incidental. And I do well out of the exchange—I lose the right to wash my own clothes but my stock of Swahili phrases increases steadily. And Ali gives me company, undemanding and reliable. Someone there, as I make the transition.

New place, new people, new issues…and underneath it all a trail of miserable argument runs through my head. I tell myself Neil is a coward, afraid of causing Teresa a limited hurt and so ending up by causing me, and himself, a greater one. As soon as I've finished thinking that, I know that his commitment to Teresa is part of a quality in him that I love, though I can't find a word for it. Then I have a violent swing of emotion—he is just using Teresa as a protection because he is afraid of the strength of what there would be between us. She doesn't intrude on his aloneness and I would. He is thirty-eight and used to being in control of his own time and space. He wants the challenge I offer—an equal and opposite force—but he doesn't want to let it too near. A half relationship suits him better than a real one—

My indignation collapses. I haven't the least idea about what he needs or what he might be feeling. Everything I am thinking comes out of my own need. Anyway, it's pointless castigating him for what he is not prepared to give up. We neither of us even suggested it was a realistic option. If there'd been more time—But there wasn't. And it was my plans that stopped there being time. If he had said, 'Cancel your flight and your contract and stay'—would I have put aside the thinking and studying of two years? And if I wouldn't, how did I expect we could be together? His life is the music he can only make there, in his own cultural environment. How could he drop that, to follow me? And how could I want him to, when it's essential to the person he is?

Nothing has changed except a recognition of what it is not possible to change. Wisdom, in fact. Growing slowly.

The notice over the office entrance announces LCP International. It's symptomatic that the only word that's spelt out is the one that has nothing to do with Kenya—Local, Community and Projects have all been reduced to incomprehensible letters. I spend most of my time paper-shuffling in an office where European professionals on short-term contracts slip easily into the privileges of the post-colonial life. Everything happens in English—the expatriates fluent and competent, the Kenyans at various levels of disadvantage. Expatriates are attended by African menials who bring their tea, carry their messages, chauffeur their cars. Individual attitudes make scarcely any difference, there seems no getting away from how everyone expects a white person to live. I think nostalgically of my life in London, being part of the bus queue along with everyone else.

Out in the streets of central Nairobi bronzed men in shorts come in from the farms in dusty landrovers, and barefoot black boys scurry to wash the windscreen. Backpackers hang about in the park in jeans and long hair, swopping addresses of cheap places to stay up-country. A group of American tourists wait for their coach at the entrance to a large hotel, cameras slung from their necks, oozing suntan lotion and mosquito repellent—passionately interested in rhinos, oblivious of people. From the tenth-floor windows of the new office buildings that are going up everywhere, managers of international corporations glance down on the Africans milling about in the streets below, and make plans for the exploitation of the country's natural resources—how to turn some of the world's most beautiful unspoilt beaches into mile upon mile of tourist hotels. International financiers fly in to oversee the process of development, and make sure the exchange rate is pegged at the right level. Right for investors, right for the banks Edward's city, maybe, not mine. Already my manager has offered me a two-year contract once my initial stint is over. Higher pay, of course. I say thank you, but I have other plans.

After work I try to find places where Kenyans spend their time. But of course that means men—the women spend their time at home, doing all the things that make it possible for their men to spend their time out. Stephen, the accountant, takes me to a bar where electric guitars combine with traditional drums to turn out hour after hour of dance music that gets into your legs and won't let you stop. A couple of young women, dressed to an awe-inspiring level of sophistication, take me in hand to show me how to get some real movement into my hips and shoulders. Then they return to the more serious business of looking for or avoiding male attention.

Selina, the receptionist, shows me pictures of her children. 'And your family?' she asks. So I bring in my photos, the women in the house, Mom and Dad in the garden with the grandchildren I haven't ever seen. My divided life, summarised in those small rectangles of paper. After work she takes me home to the suburb of small box-like houses an hour's bus journey away where, alone, she supports her own children, two nieces and an elderly mother. Her husband decided several years ago that family responsibilities didn't suit him. He visits when he feels like it, to see the children, or when he's run out of money, or to claim his sexual rights with Selina. She's his wife, after all.

'Why don't you tell him to get lost?' I ask.

She laughs. 'He needs a woman, I need a man. It is better to accept him than start with a new one, a whole new lot of problems.' She turns to me, her eyes returning the challenge. 'And you?'

And she's got me, for we each make our own compromises. 'I want to be free to make my own life,' I say. 'Which man would follow me?'

A few days later someone arrives to see me at work while I'm out at a meeting. When I get back Selina says, 'Your friend came, from London, but he did not want to give his name. He is coming back at three o'clock.' She laughs, as if my face is exposing me. 'So he followed you anyway!'—

But when he arrives his name is Muhib.

Muhib, here on his home ground, looking even more sure of his place in the world. Eight months since we last lay together, but we have kept the friendship going through the complications of disentangling. It feels now oddly comforting that we put our arms around each other to hug hello.

'What happened to your travel plans?' I ask—the last time I heard he was going to spend the summer in Europe.

'Nairobi seemed a more attractive option. I changed my mind.'
'I haven't,' I say, taking his arm off my shoulder.

He laughs and says, 'You're still going to need someone to show you around.'

It's his home, he's perfectly entitled to be here. I can choose to spend time with him, or not spend time with him...Selina says, 'If you don't want that one, you are very choosy.'...Actually I am surprised at how pleased I am that he has arrived. Life needs some continuities; despite all the stimulus, I'm still internally disoriented. It's good to have a friend from a time before and we have more in common still than I have with anyone I've met here.

I take to dropping in at his home. I like being around his mother. She is unaffected by the change in my relationship to Muhib, continues talking to me woman to woman, and includes me easily in the broad sweep of family comings and goings. That gets to a part of me I thought I had lost years ago. There is also something about her I find calming, the sense that she has survived as herself, despite all the expectations and possessions she's lumbered herself with.

Muhib says, 'You have to see more than Nairobi, Jennie,' and we set off in his family's comfortable fourwheel drive. The Rift Valley…the national parks…

My spirit expands under the impact of all that space and grandeur, first home of humankind, still the natural environment of herds of animals. Muhib is an easy companion—that doesn't change. He makes all the arrangements. We stay in old colonial-style hotels with spreading lawns, views up to mountains edged against the sky, and almost unbelievable clarity of air.

For the first few weekends he sticks to our contract. Then his eyes start asking again. I say, 'No, Muhib. You know it's No.'

He says, 'It's a lovely thing to do, Jennie, just for itself. We both know that. And it hurts no one.'

The logic seems unanswerable, so I don't try to answer it. He says, 'Think of a good reason why not.'

I can't. But I won't.

I *am* very choosy. Still.

'Will you write?' Neil asked—wanting me to want to, afraid that I wouldn't, perhaps also afraid that I would. I wrote, in the first few weeks, letters of extraordinary length. I tore each one up. I could hear Neil's voice saying, 'It's the other bit I backed away from—the need.' Once you've posted a long outpouring of emotion you can't change your mind and take it back. It's not like talking, where other words—moments of laughing and sparring—can balance the effect of too much intense emotion, leave a different memory of the quality of the time. The letter is all there is and if it's too much and he backs away, I'm facing that shut door again and I can't bear it. Keep the door open, even if all we send through it are the things that matter least.

I write postcards. Frequent postcards, but just postcards. Brilliant colour photos—the market in Nairobi, the white-sand beaches near Mombasa, the stark lines of a savannah sunset. Postcards avoid the need to talk seriously but if you write small they allow just enough length to keep that thread of intimacy going. A shared reference no one else would understand. A light challenge, of the kind that only happens between us. Even moments of awe at the beauty I have discovered—that connect, and he will know they connect, with other kinds of beauty we have touched together.

Neil has devised his own strategy—he sends me short pieces of music he has composed. That too avoids the need for many words. Songs, pieces for solo viola. These magic pieces of paper arrive in an envelope for me to turn into sound, to have his spirit here with me in the room. I know his mind is constantly producing and transforming patterns of sound, that he can dash things like that off in a few hours. But still. Once the envelope contains just a couple of fragments—'An idea,' says his scribbled handwriting—'came to me this morning, with your name on it. See what you can do with it.' The challenge fires me, the offhand tone delights me, for it is a better signal that I am part of his inner existence than any attempt to describe it could have been. For all of one weekend I improvise intensely around those phrases with the tape recorder on, then I laboriously transcribe some of the bits that seemed to work best and send them back with my next postcard. Three weeks later they are back, transformed into a viola and cello duet. The note attached to it says, 'For when you next get back.'

We write nothing about our work, other people, what we might be planning to do. That in itself is an admission. However sensible our decisions, what there has been between us still lives, and powerfully. Why wouldn't it? It survived two years with no encouragement and was there, instantly, the moment we met again.

'For when you next get back,' says the note. It could happen again and we both know it—

Muhib is talking about another weekend. 'I'll be away,' I say—

—Overnight train on Friday, going to sleep with the open savannah slipping silently past the train window, then waking to the bustle of the station in Mombasa. Ali's family welcomes me, feeds me. The neighbourhood children gather round to stare and touch. Ali's sisters-in-law teach me to prepare fish soup. His brothers guide me through old towns created by the first Arab traders, where the call for prayer sails out from the minarets, Allahu akbar, God is great. Eventually I persuade them to let me go out alone…I want people, but no connections that pose obligations. To be out, and not in a hurry, and wait and see… Children who gather curiously, shopkeepers in the old town, women selling vegetables, young men hanging about…You are very choosy, Selina said. Why? Why not settle, for company, even if it's not the perfect company? Jaswinder's done it, surprising us all before I left by finding her own man, and not Indian either—Irish, with wispy pale hair and a wispy pale personality to go with it. None of us could see what they had in common, but he was male, marriageable, and he appeared to want her. She lives now surrounded by his family; a mother-in-law who cooks for them all, a father-in-law who dominates the household, and three married sisters who live within a few miles and keep popping back and depositing babies for their mum to take care of. Jaswinder slots into all that as easily as if she were born to it, which in a sense she was. They live in Mile End where racism is rife but his family seem free of it. They've absorbed her as she is, commenting freely on everything that's different about her, no middle-class tact about it.

Everything's a compromise. I choose to live alone, I say, and it's easy enough by day, with the unfailing African light—colours—sounds. But dusk falls suddenly, and it's dark from seven, every day; the nights can be long. And what I said about the freedom to make my own life—so easy to say, and such an oversimplification. Free yourself from the constraints others impose on you, and you lose also the shape that contains, the struts that support. And you don't know what it feels like without them until you've cut yourself loose.

The life I have left has disintegrated, no longer there to go back to even if I chose. My university friends have scattered, and the house—Paula's there for me as I am here for her, that doesn't change, and her letters are long, regular and satisfying; but in the house itself there's only Paula and Jane left, the others are women I scarcely know. And that earlier home—we still keep writing, their unquestioning acceptance is still there and I never doubt its value. But imperceptibly it has become harder to tell the most significant things, and by not telling I have become as distant as Edward from their everyday concerns. Loved, but increasingly unreal. I try to flip the picture and think about how it must feel at their end. A family so close, and now look at us...Edward in Geneva, working for a UN agency, constantly travelling. Trevor in Connecticut, with a child Mom and Dad have not seen. Me, choosing to take myself back into a drifting life. Peter, whose only consistent message is 'Keep away, I can't handle you getting near.' They know he works in a quantity surveyor's office and has become an intermittent church attender—beyond that, nothing. It's only Richard who is left. That life too is gone, unrecognisable now from the vivid, populated one I last knew.

And now Paula writes that the theatre group is breaking up. Jane has gone to Manchester to work with an all-women company, Paula is off to Bristol, joining a theatre-in-education group she got to know when touring. The women's house has ceased to be.

No going back. It's done. It's scary, at times, facing that. I belong nowhere—and I've helped make that the case. Why? Why couldn't I just have stayed, like Paula told me to?

At other times I know it was right, that I'd have nagged away at myself uselessly if I hadn't done it. It's done, just be positive about it. Keep open, keep trusting the instinct that led me this far, to find the new place—or not so much the place as the thing I can do, that'll make sense of life—

Listen, really listen. Create within yourself
an echo of the drum—then you will start to dance.

Dance means more than a dance, said Derek, and the drum more than a drum. Together they form the most powerful metaphor of African society—finding your individuality through being part of the whole. But I know even while I am trying to keep open that I cannot be part of this, not of Ali's people, nor Selina's suburb of box houses, nor Muhib's family of beautifully dressed women, and servants carrying trays, and at least three cars per household. Let alone the expatriates, talking only to each other.

Of all the people I knew in Nairobi, only Ali knew that I was dealing with loss and loneliness. He knew from the way I played the viola, and I knew he knew because on those evenings he didn't go back to his room when he'd finished producing my meal, but found small things to do that kept him in the house. He said nothing but it was helpful just having another person there.

Just once he talked about it. It was daytime, and I was full of pragmatism and activity. He was dusting around where the viola lay in its case. He stood near it for a moment, then touched the wood and asked if it needed polishing. I was moved watching him do that—he touched it gently, almost with awe, the way I did the first time I had held it. I asked if he wanted to have a go. He laughed and backed away—it is a thing for Europeans, he said. But he asked me to play, and I played a simple dance, vigorous and cheerful, to balance what he had heard me do in the evenings. He listened, head cocked. 'How was that?' I asked. '*Nzuri,*' he said, '*nzuri sana,*' good, very good; and he told me there was a man he worked for once who played a pipe kind of thing, 'but this one of yours is better. When it sings I hear many things.' The Swahili for 'to hear', *ku-sikia,* seems to cover things we couldn't say in English without being deliberately poetic. Ali just said it straight—'When you play, I hear cold, and the heat of fire.'

I hear things I would like to be simple, but aren't.

4

Time to move on, to another tune, one that has been dancing just ahead of me since earliest childhood, Richard's flute playing a strange rhythmic melody that they were dancing to in a village near where he camped. Now I am setting out myself to travel south to Nyika where once Richard travelled north, then on to Zambia and that border of all borders, the front line between independent Africa and the white-controlled south. I pack my modest collection of possessions into a couple of boxes, to stay in Muhib's mother's garage until I can tell her where to send them on. My viola—

I have never been parted from it since the day Neil first put it in my hands. But how can I take it when I set off with only a rucksack, to wait at the roadside, sleep where I find myself, no way to protect it from fierce sun—dust—rain? Violas belong to the settled life. I entrust mine to Ali, who promises to keep it away from extreme heat and termites till I can arrange to collect it. So it's back to the mbira and penny whistle.

And no address. So no more songs through the post. Another stage in letting go, when I thought I had let go already of all there was. Out beyond where it's possible to hold on to even that thin line that links me to the life I can't have. Push out on your own, girl, and swim.

'When you travel with the mbira you will never be alone,' said the old man who gave it to me. This is the place to rediscover it—here, on the dusty bus route down to Dar es Salaam, with the African bush stretching for miles in all directions. Playing it becomes like busking, but for company rather than money. The bus stops in a small town. I clamber off, amidst the clamour of people pushing, calling, the sweaty bodies of young men and the women who call instructions to children as they lift on to their heads bundles of possessions tied in cloth. I create a stir just by being there, a white person, and with baggage in this strange contraption on my back instead of on my head. I move a little away from the crowd and find a place under a tree to sit and watch, and see what kind of a place this is. A group of children gather round, staring at me curiously. They point to my rucksack and ask me to open it. I zip open the side pocket and pull out the mbira. The excitement level rises. 'Play it,' they say, 'play it!' As soon as I begin, others gather. There's a small crowd now, people exclaiming, clapping. I offer it to one of the children to have a go—the young men take it from them. They all seem to know what it is. 'Where did you get it?' they want to know. 'Where did you learn to play?' They discuss vigorously what it's called—the word mbira means nothing to them. An old man is summoned to give an opinion. It's clear I'm not going to get it back for a while so I open the next zip pocket and get out my penny whistle. Up another notch of excitement. A newly arrived young man has taken over the mbira, expertly picking out a rhythm pattern that goes with my tune.

Now I am being led off to a group of houses, the children hovering around us like bees. It's going to be night soon, and I ask, 'Where can I find a hotel?' They say, 'Stay here, with us.' A man brings out a drum and sets up a brisk rhythm, challenging me. The clapping begins—the drum rhythm takes over—my mbira can't keep up, but they've forgotten about me as the dancing and singing begin.

The miles of scrubby savannah begin to turn into hills—getting nearer...Across the border into Malawi, and here I am among pine trees, high and cool...The bus lumbers on, to the lake, an astonishing inland sea that stretches from steep hills on this side to mountains blue and misty on the far horizon...Now beyond the nearest hills the land rises, and goes on rising, and becomes a wall of mountain that continues for miles as we wind our way through the hills, never going towards it, always skirting round—

And on top and beyond is Nyika, the roof of the world.

'No one lives there,' say the people on the bus. 'Too cold. And dangerous.' I ask what kind of dangers, but they are vague. People go up and do not come back again, they say.'What is there on top?' I ask. 'Grass,' says one. 'Plenty of grass!' And they laugh. *Wyama,*' says another—animals, meat. The laughter spreads. The bus sways around yet another corner. I hold on to the woman next to me, looking up at the land that for half my life has been beyond reach, beyond comprehension—and is that still, even now I am so close.

A night in Rumphi. Then hours waiting as the heat builds up and the markets slowly get into action. Another bus ride, this time even more alert, not to miss the stop-off point from Derek's instructions. The fields change as we climb, fewer bananas, more forested Small fields of sugar cane, now, and tobacco. Villages closer together, roadside stands selling Nyika honey—

There's the sudden bend in the road, the place with the two small tobacco barns made of wobbly tree trunks. I squeeze my way to the front, get off the bus along with two large women with chickens in grass cages. The bus rumbles off, coating us with dust.

I am standing at the roadside. The inevitable small crowd has gathered. The faces are staring at me, waiting for me to do something. I try to summon the Chichewa for 'Can you tell me the way?', which I learnt in lesson three over two years ago, and must have used dozens of times since then in exercises—it is gone, simply gone from my brain. I produce the name of the village and my arms and head move to indicate helplessness. A babble of speculation breaks out.

Now a couple of schoolboys have joined the group. One starts speaking in English—I feel like hugging him 'You know Mr. Derek?' he asks. No one is surprised that I do—two English people, why wouldn't we know each other? 'I know him,' says the boy proudly. 'He speaks our language.' And within minutes it has been decided—the boy sets off with me, guide for the three hours' walk.

The place didn't seem a village so much as a straggling collection of homesteads. The huts grew out of the earth—walls of mud, roofs of thatch—and blended continuously into it in a way that made it impossible to keep hold of what was where. They were grouped around clearings edged by trees and a patchwork of small fields, leading by little paths through the grass to more walls of mud, roofs of thatch, another clearing surrounded by an almost identical patchwork of fields. I had no way of telling whether a particular group of huts constituted one household or several.

The boy told them I was Derek's sister. 'Friend,' I said. 'Sister,' he said, 'it is the same.' I presented the elders with the gifts Derek had commissioned me to buy. By some collective process I didn't follow it was agreed that a woman called Kiluleli was the appropriate person to be responsible for Derek's sister, and I was led off to her hut. Apart from Kiluleli and one or two of the young girls who stuck around me the whole time, everyone else merged into a blur of curious humanity—faces always towards me, eyes following whatever I did, talking and laughing at things I did not understand. I learnt names and forgot them again, for each time I looked there seemed to be more people or different people, or in confusingly different combinations. I wished I had got Derek to brief me more adequately—getting here was only the first kind of map I needed.

My rucksack turned out to be a more useful asset than anything I had studied about kinship systems. The women gathered pointedly, waiting for me to unpack it. Each item of clothing was examined with intense interest, the expressions on their faces indicating puzzlement, envy or ribald amusement. The boys pointed to my watch and mimed that they would like to try it on. It instantly became a focus of intense negotiation, like a war trophy. I caught sight of it in the days that followed, each time on the wrist of another youth. I assumed it was coming back to me eventually but I had lost any sense of why one needed a watch. I'd have happily left it but it was clear it would cause serious problems if it stayed.

Tumbuka was their language, and all I knew of it was the words of the songs from Derek's tapes, which didn't take me far for practical communication. My stumbling Chichewa helped—most of the men knew it, but they didn't speak it to each other so I didn't hear enough to model mine on. I gave up trying to form sentences, retreating to a sort of baby-language of single words, hopefully produced—and when that didn't work, relying on gesture. Collectively they had about as much English as I had Chichewa—a couple of lads who had been to school for a few years, men who had been away to work.

I took refuge, as I had done in Swaziland, in practical activity. I walked with the young girls to the stream where they fetched water, and was a source of high entertainment because I failed to carry even the smallest jar on my head without spilling it. I squatted and watched an old woman who sat with her legs splayed, surrounded by neat piles of grass that she was weaving into a mat. She ignored me and went on. Then quite suddenly she began to talk to me, a long story of which of course I understood nothing. She either couldn't grasp that I didn't understand or possibly didn't mind—it might simply have been self-expression prompted by an interested face, one step away from talking to herself. After a while she pushed the bit of mat she was working on towards me and gestured for me to have a go.

Mostly I attached myself to Kiluleli, like a mute daughter-in-law. She was the mother of several almost grown-up children and some already married—I never managed to work out the details. There was no sign of a husband but she had much more status than a widow, so presumably he was a person of significance, currently away. She too talked at me as she instructed, moving vigorously through the day's tasks, till I began to latch on to a handful of phrases that kept coming at me. Each time I got hold of a new one I felt a surge of competence, only to be dumped a few minutes later back into the shadows at the side, watching while others moved the action on.

When you don't have words, the rhythm of every day does your communicating for you. It was obvious when we were to sleep, to rise, to prepare food, to eat. But it was exhausting being so fundamentally deskilled, losing all capacity to initiate or decide. In Swaziland I had had Charity to interpret—that gave me unparalleled access, but it also gave me a false sense of knowing what was going on. In fact I had seen only what impinged on me, and could understand its significance only through my own eyes. This time I was more aware of my own limitations. The people in the village were getting on with their normal lives, facing in towards each other in relationships of which I was only dimly aware, doing or not doing things because of unwritten rules whose force I could hardly have understood even if I had known what they were. I felt stripped of layers of instinctive self-protection—my own kind of knowledge, my accustomed way of being—leaving me naked, vulnerable.

By the end of the third day I was running out of stamina. They showed no impatience for me to be gone but my novelty value was beginning to diminish and it felt time to move. The world beyond this had lost reality, but the idea of reaching Zambia hovered, my own new life still to make happen. I signalled my imminent departure by packing my rucksack, watched of course by a group of young women, babies on hips, children hovering. One was sent off to find the boy who was currently wearing my watch. Time being given back to me, in this place where there is more of it than anyone would think of counting. No house to live in unless you build it, no food to eat unless you grow it, no water to wash or cook with unless you fetch it—yet no one hurries, no one calculates how long a task will take. Time is *there*, an underlying measure of the seasons. People move within it. Times for hoeing, for planting; weeding and harvesting; threshing and storing; and all connected to a more fundamental pulse, the slowly changing stages of life, birth, childhood, puberty, marriage, then starting all over again with childbirth...Yet these same people in their music instinctively divide time so fast, so energetically, that it takes years for precise-timing city-dwellers like me to learn to really hear it...It seemed wonderful to them that I, who could say nothing of any practical use, could nevertheless sing their songs; and wonderful to me that all those hours of what in London had seemed esoteric, private activity was now transformed into something that connected me with these people who had taken me in though they had never seen me before, and to whom I could only speak with my body or in song. And now that I was about to go, the women started up singing again, for me, with me, turning each song into a dance—and confusing me by singing versions that didn't fit what I had learnt from the tapes. But there was no way I could ask about it, let alone understand the answers.

A young man presented himself to accompany me on the three hours' walk back to the bus. Had he been volunteered for this task, or would he have been going anyway? But the question was meaningless. I was going, he was going.

South to the border, squashed in buses; then west towards Lusaka, bumping in lorries; and all the way I was followed by the sounds I could no longer hear. Of sitting each evening with Kiluleli on the mat she spread on the stamped earth outside her hut, while the sounds of the women's quiet talking washed over me and the dark released me from the need to try and communicate; and receiving through the darkness the sound of drumming from some other village—or perhaps some other part of this one? I could not tell, as I could not yet tell what kind of drumming it was—whether it signified some special event or was simply someone who liked to drum, practising now that the day's tasks were over…The light of one small brazier holding us in a space edged by the shapes of trees. The distant pulse connecting us beyond—

—The nights and days blur, overtaken now by other village days and nights. But I remember with the clarity of a separate, significant moment that first walk to the village behind the young boy, hours striding along rough paths, pushing aside tall scratchy grass. The boy never hesitated about the path, pausing only to turn every now and then to see that I was still following, and to ask, 'It is good?'

'It is good,' I replied. He turned back, leaving me to the contemplation of the small maize fields, the banana fronds dancing in slow arcs. It was the first time since setting out from Nairobi that I had been left in all essentials alone, without people pressing around me, asking questions. My eyes absorbed the shapes of the trees against the huge dome of sky, trees of whose names and functions I had no idea, while my mind travelled in time and place, spiralling back to the first reluctant border crossing that had marked one life from another, as this one was doing. And the sounds of songs that belonged to other places, other times, moved through me…

The water is wide, I can't get o'er
Neither have I wings to fly,
Give me a boat that can carry two—

I strode out, feeling the energy and stamina in my own legs, and knew that I was stuck no longer on someone else's shore.

5

It is a shock re-encountering urban life. The lorry that has given me my last lift drops me in the town centre—I dozed through the last twenty minutes and saw nothing as we drove in. Now I stand looking about me in a bemused way. Mud puddles everywhere, air heavy with suspended moisture...The town centre seems to exist in isolation, no sign of the rest of the city. Just three parallel streets in descending order of modernity. Three-storey buildings in the first, with glass-fronted shops. The road itself enormously wide, an island with flowering trees running down the middle. Cairo Road—at least that has a familiar ring—a vague memory from history lessons at school—*the Cape to Cairo route*. What goes north to Cairo also goes south to the Cape. One step nearer home... Through to the street parallel—buildings lower, a definite small-town air. By the third street all city pretensions had been dropped. The buildings are scattered, paint peeling, tarmac washed away at the edges. And beyond that, tall grass. Where does everyone live?

What am I doing here? I have lived so long with the idea of arriving in Lusaka as a moment of significance, the place that will open up possibilities, a pull strong enough to steady me against the counterpull of what I know I must teach myself to put behind me. And now I am here it is nothing but three uninspired rows of buildings, dumped for no apparent reason in the open savannah.

I am sticky with sweat and the grime of travel. Before anything I want to be rid of my rucksack and get washed.

A decaying hotel, but a room that locks and running water—enough. A small lizard scurries upside down across the ceiling and then drops alarmingly on to the floor at my wet feet. A large spider lours at me from the corner...Strange, in the village no one bothered about keeping other creatures out—they had been there before us and would be there after. It's only here in town that it feels unnerving.

I emerge, wearing my coolest clothes. Now what?

I wander over to a couple of young men who are hanging about doing nothing—the standard occupation of young men in African cities, it seems. They are curious, friendly, laugh a lot. That too is standard—I begin to feel better about Lusaka. 'Which way should I go to see the city?' I ask.

They fall about with laughter. 'You are *in* the city,' they say. 'This is where we come when we want to see life!'

'Go on,' I say, 'there must be other places. I'm an ignorant tourist—you tell me.'

One says hopefully, 'You got money for taxis?' Ignorant maybe, but not that ignorant. 'Only for buses,' I say firmly.

'Taxis are better,' he says even more firmly. 'You will never see the city if you wait for a bus. People's taxis—not expensive.' He points to one passing—a car with three rows of seats, crammed to capacity. 'Come, we can go together and show you.'

By midnight we have done the city, the complete guided tour. The mansions and high security fences of the elite—Zambian and expatriate. The rows of identical small houses of Kamwala, uniformed schoolboys and girls walking home tired and hot—older girls sitting outside the houses plaiting each other's hair. The hospital where wives and mothers of those who are ill sit on the ground under the trees, preparing food for them. My companions vie with each other in suggesting our next destination and together we squash into and tumble out of people's taxis. They can't believe their luck at having found someone to pay their fares for such an extended jaunt, and I am indulging in a heady sense of irresponsibility. Tomorrow I will have to go back to making sensible decisions—for now I am having fun.

We pass the copper dome of Parliament, symbol of the wealth that is disappearing. They launch into a diatribe against all politicians. They are all corrupt—they take bribes and give jobs only to people of their tribes—government offices are filled with half-educated middle-aged men, while they, young men who have finished secondary school, have no opportunities. 'And women go only with the men who have money and cars.' They laugh as they laugh at everything, but their eyes check my reaction. 'How is it in England?' they ask longingly—Britain, Europe, America—those meccas of the easy life. That I should be choosing Lusaka over London seems to them extraordinary. They exclaim when they hear I have just come from a Malawian village. 'Village life is boring,' they insist. Then within minutes they are disputing the merits of their own home areas.

At the university everyone gets out—our fellow passengers are all students, it seems. Clement, one of my companions, says he has a friend in one of the residences, so we get out too. We walk across landscaped gardens, past a lake that curves through green expanses and massed splashes of purple and red bougainvillaea, to a collection of concrete buildings some Western architect has foisted on an unsuspecting Zambian public. None of it seems possible, here in the middle of the savannah, neither the concrete towers nor the artificial lake and lawns. We talk with Clement's friend and the other students who join the spontaneous seminar, and eventually make our way back to the main road, to take another taxi across the muddy tracks of Kalingalinga, a depressed village stuck in the middle of waste land with the city encroaching from all sides.

Finally it is night, and our latest taxi deposits us at a beer hall. Thump of Zairean dance rhythms, raucous laughter, sickly sweet smell of *chibuku* beer, pressure of sweaty bodies. I am beginning to be tired, and to wonder whether I am going to be able to get myself out of here at a time of my own choosing. Two of my mates have disappeared in the crowd but Clement has appointed himself my protector. As he gets more inebriated he tells me I should never have trusted myself to the others—Bembas are notoriously unreliable where women are concerned. In *his* hands I am safe. Then he sees a friend across the hall and is gone. His place is taken by a heavy middle-aged man, brown face shiny with sweat, breath heavy. He has been listening to us, he says, and can tell I am South African. 'We are home boys, you and I,' he announces, oblivious of gender. Through the deep-gut thumping of loudspeakers we shout at each other—when I ask his name he says, 'I have no name anymore. I am a liberation fighter.' All concept of security has dissipated in a haze of *chibuku*. That I too have fled across a border is enough of a passport to immediate brother-and-sisterhood. He wants to tell me about his wife and children, left behind like the name, and he wants to put his face very close as he does so. The *chibuku* is evoking a sense of cosmic sorrow…Then he suddenly pulls me to my feet to start dancing. Despite his weight and the beer his body moves with unexpected grace, an upwards lift of the foot on each beat, and a sideways sway—till he is hauled off, protesting, by his more sober companions.

A voice from behind me. 'Those ANC relics, they're pathetic.' I turn, to see a young man with a face that—

—That whips me back nine years, to Cape Town, and Jonas standing opposite me saying, 'You can't escape it, Jennie.'

But of course it is not Jonas looking at me now with those part-challenging, part-assessing eyes. It is a man I have never seen before who yet has Jonas's forehead and cheekbones, and who must have been listening to me shouting my answers across the blare, for he is saying, 'A couple of my friends also ran to Swaziland.'

Another South African. 'Do *you* have a name?' I ask.

He grins. 'I'm Winston.'

'You look just like a friend of mine.'

'I do? Maybe he's my brother.'

He's joking but I'm excited anyway. I glance across the smoke-filled, pulsating hall in the direction Clement was last seen moving, and hope he stays occupied wherever he is for a good long time. I turn back to Winston and the details trip over themselves in their hurry to be let loose, pushing up from some long-forgotten part of my being. 'Jonas Nkosane. He should have been out over a year now.'

It is ridiculous to be suddenly so full of a sense of possibilities. Why would this man know him, just because he has the same look about his face? But my linked history to Jonas is yet another password, and though Winston was so scathing about the drunken liberation fighter's lack of discretion, it's not long before I am hearing his own story...The uprisings in Soweto...The demonstrations, friends shot down by the police, funerals, more shooting, arrests...Escaping when they were being transferred from one police van to another—getting to the border—crossing into Botswana, Rhodesia, keeping low. Finally Zambia...His eyes monitor mine as he talks, checking my reaction.

'I saw you,' I say. 'On television. When you'd got to Botswana.'

'I was never on television!'

'I don't mean you, as you.'

But his eyes, tense even when he is laughing, are the same as those that looked directly out of the television screen at mine and summoned me here, following a crazy impulse. We have met, finally—Winston coming from the south, I from the north. He's stuck, can't go any further. And I have arrived.

I have never been in a place where it is easier to meet people. With my companions from the first night's jaunt I learn the social geography of the townships, passing from one casual contact to another till within a few weeks I am bumping into people I know wherever I go. I tell Clement I can afford no more people's taxis—he finds someone who helps me get hold of an old bike and I fix it up, privately thanking Paula that I know how. I need to get out of the hotel—and in the queue where I wait with other foreigners to report my arrival to the police I meet the American wife of a sociology professor, who says, 'Use our spare room until you can fix up your own place.' At her house I meet the wife of the Italian consul, who has little English but plenty of money, the reverse of my state. We agree an exchange, and I begin to replenish my dwindling savings.

Everywhere I encounter exiles—Angolans, Namibians, people with a dramatic past, an insecure present, a doubtful future, arguing over divisions in the liberation movements as if their lives depend on it, which they possibly do. They are alienated twice over, from the country they have left and from the one they have arrived in. I belong no more than they do, but these are not rational processes. Each day I spend here convinces me that Lusaka has what is for me the essential quality—it challenges; to see what I will make of living here, the point on the map at which the two Africas I know meet.

Chapter 3

The first challenge is to survive the bureaucracy. The officials are bored or hostile. They have only to say 'No' and it's the end of Lusaka for me. All I want is a piece of paper which says I can continue to exist where I am. All they want is not to have to make a decision that someone might subsequently blame them for. Their strategy is not telling anyone till they have queued for four hours which pieces of paper they need to present. Before I can get my visa extended I need a certificate to show I have registered with the police…to the police. But they need a certificate from the bank to show I have money to support myself…to the bank…Where is my evidence that I have an address?…Back to my American friend, then the bank, the police, the immigration officer…He sifts gloomily through my pile of precious papers and pushes them back at me. Why have I no receipt from the city officials? For what? I ask. For something, it transpires, that everyone new to the city has to pay to prove that they exist. I don't dare ask about work permits; time enough when I've discovered if I can persuade someone to employ me.

Out on my bike, learning Lusaka by cycling it, revisiting over days and weeks each of the places we crammed into that first mad taxi tour. The city is so scattered that walking from one part to another would take half the day. On my bike I have the freedom to move yet I am still open to the air, right at people's level, and I can stop any time and tune in to the sounds of the lives around me. Young children chatter their way out of school, high-pitched as cicadas. Buxom secondary school girls run to catch up with the overcrowded people's taxi that has slowed down for them. They yell uninhibitedly to each other, bags flying, short skirts barely covering their tight round bottoms. One squeezes in—the taxi carries her off but she is leaning out still, calling to her friends, the sound of her voice sailing clear above the traffic…

Stop at the post office. 'I have an address,' I announce in a flurry of postcards—Mom and Dad, Paula, Neil. For good measure I throw in the university's telephone number so someone could get a message to me if they really needed to…Stop it, I tell myself, no one needs to send you urgent messages, their lives are carrying on fine without you. Too fine…It will be weeks before I can hope for replies. I send a few more cards—Jaswinder, Jane, Derek, Megan. Then Edward in Geneva—he is the only person I know who might find himself travelling unexpectedly within my range.

I keep expecting to encounter Winston again but he's nowhere. That night in the beer hall he disappeared while I was talking to Clement, as if to make sure he would not be followed. Now I have an odd feeling *he* might be following *me*, and keeping out of my way till he's checked me out. But I'm not asking. I try to remember his face, exactly *how* much like Jonas he was; but it's gone.

On past the university, to the open-air theatre. I lean my bike against the tall grass outer fence that encloses a cleared space. Inside you could imagine yourself in a village, with mud walls and thatch; and perhaps for the group of students who are rehearsing in this space it is like the homes they grew up in, they who live now in the concrete tower residences of the campus. They posture and declaim, acting out the tensions of the divided life they have inherited. The vigour breaks into dance, the satire into song.

Back to the house. There are people standing about on the patio and in the garden, eating as they talk. The friends who have given me a room are hosts also to a constant round of lunch and dinner guests. I go into the kitchen to see if I can help. I carry a tray of food around, listening in as I move between the groups of people...An ethno-musician doing research on the Nau dances of Eastern Province...Some Zimbabweans arguing about the murder of a liberation leader. He must have been a Rhodesian agent, says one. But then why did the Zambian government arrest half the liberation movement's leadership at the funeral?...Through the munching of chicken and rice, rumour scatters light as chaff. If I were a Rhodesian agent, I think, I'd learn all I needed to know just by being here.

My eye strays through the glass doors into the living room—and there is Winston. I go to greet him—

—To be cut off by eyes totally unresponsive.

I retreat, confused, to the kitchen. When I return he has gone.

My first letter—a penny whistle piece. I take it off into the open land behind the house and play to the tall waving grass, a tune quirky and humourous, wistful and delicate. The sounds lift and fly off like birds that call to each other as they migrate. When I come to the end there's a weight in my arms. They have almost forgotten what it feels like to hold a viola. By the time I get back to the house I am crying—

No point. Shut away the feelings I can do nothing about. I want a life that is *centred*, not lived in absence. Get out, do something.

Do something about getting more work, that's the main thing. The wife of the Italian consul has begun to bring her friends along. They like my lessons; I could be on to a growth industry—

Is it to be English teaching after all, then? But I know this is not work I could sustain. They pay me to listen to them talk about the lives they have left behind. They never move outside their circle of spacious homes or the receptions at the Intercontinental Hotel, so no wonder they feel alien. I try to bring a little more than correct English to my role, sharing the things I am learning here. They are curious momentarily, but cannot connect—

Besides, to stay past the end of my tourist visa I need a full-time job, a contract, a work permit. Schoolteaching? But there my obstinacy sticks. I have tested the possibilities by doing odd days substituting for teachers who are ill. The children are beguiling, but to try to fit within those structures for more than the occasional day would be for me a cage. I am holding out for something that will let my spirit fly.

Meanwhile I cycle off to different homes each day, and with no one telling me what to teach or how, I earn enough to cover food and other essentials.

Like postcards.

2

The grass that I walk through is taller than my head, waving to welcome me each day. I am up with the first light and out before the heat builds up, out onto the path that passes behind the house, straggling across open land. African women with *chitenge* cloths wound round their waists stride past on feet cracked hard as mud in the dry season. Their worn blouses strain against full breasts, an arm stretched up to steady a wide enamel basin that balances on the head.

They sway in unconscious grace, a measured, perfectly balanced dance. They are heading for the market where they will bend their knees with upright backs to lower the basin to the ground, then unwind the cloth that has been cushioning the load on their heads and spread it out under the flame trees. Carefully they pile on it small pyramids of tomatoes and onions, or tobacco rolled in coils, to sit behind them for the rest of the day, while the sun climbs higher and the heat gets more intolerable. Once in twenty minutes someone might stop, but probably not buy. The women tie their small earnings in a knot at the end of their *chitenge*, and then untie another cloth that binds the no-longer-sleeping baby to the back, swivel the child round and shift a blouse to pull out a breast. The baby latches on frantically and snuffles into a quiet contentment. The women keep talking, hardly noticing.

I squat down in front of those piles of tomatoes and we chat. That is to say, I try out my slowly increasing repertoire of town Chinyanja. It is subtly different from the Chichewa I have learnt, and in any case that was all book-language, nothing by ear. The women laugh openly at my mistakes, vying with each other to correct me. Market days are long and I am an interesting diversion. They cross-question me about what I am doing here or why I have no husband. I miss most of the words but they leave me in no doubt of the meaning. One hands over a baby and motions me to put her to the breast. They rock with laughter, knowing I have no milk. They are taunting me—Hurry up, life is passing and you're not doing what a woman should do. There is no malice to the laughter, in fact it's a compliment. By joining them down at ground level I have opened myself to being one of them; and among themselves no one expects to be able to make unconventional choices without evoking comment.

They become curious about the habits of white women. Is it true they lie with any man? they ask.

'I lie with no one,' I tell them, sticking to the present tense.

That lets me off the hook of immorality, but leaves me dangling on another—am I not normal? They change tack—'You are different from other *mzungus*,' they say. 'See, you are learning our language. You are going to stay here?'

To answer that too is problematic. They know only two kinds of *mzungus*—the old colonial settlers, who stayed and some of whom learnt their language but usually only to command; and the new type, who don't get out of their cars long enough to get dusty. I say, 'I want to stay but I don't know if I'll be allowed to.' That puts us on the same level, for bureaucracies get in their way as much as mine, declaring illegal the homes they have made from scrap material at the edges of the city.

'Stay,' they say.

I'm on my bike heading for my next encounter with officials when I arrive, without having realised I was going to, at the station. There's a train lurching into action, off on the journey south. I stop to watch till it has gone…South to cross the Zambezi River into Rhodesia, down through Bulawayo, across into the Transvaal. The same train that carried Richard and his friend on that first journey north…

Perhaps I could take it and meet Mom and Dad in Rhodesia, they travelling north, I travelling south? But I cannot risk it. My right to stay here is tenuous enough; if I once crossed that border into hostile territory I'd have little chance of getting back.

Back on my bike—and here walking on the pavement towards me is Winston, that unmistakable taut vigour in his body, like action waiting to be released. He hasn't seen me yet. I wait for him to get nearer, not sure if…

He makes no attempt to get away. He is disarmingly relaxed; it's I who am cautious. 'I'm glad to see you friendly today,' I say. He grins but ignores the challenge. 'Where are you going?' he asks.

'Yet another queue, another official piece of paper.'

'I'll give you a bit of solidarity,' he says, and he turns to walk along beside me as I push the bike. Young-maleness expresses itself in every movement of his limbs. I'm thinking, this guy will get through life on sheer bull, but despite myself it's having an effect on me. I say, 'Winston, what happened the other day?'

'I didn't expect to see you there.'

'So what difference does that make?' No response. 'And what's different now?'

'You ask too many questions,' he says—which shuts me up, because if I go on asking he's likely to disappear again. We join the queue, it snakes slowly on, and he's telling me stories of other bureaucracies. Then we swop life plans, the ones we made before and had to abandon, and then laboriously try to reassemble in different combinations somewhere else—

Without warning he stops. His eyes flick, assessing all over again. He says, voice hard, challenging, 'You think *you've* got problems with these buggers!' His head gestures towards the officials. 'You with your white skin and British passport.'

For a moment I am angry. Why turn on me, when a moment ago we were together? It's panic pushing him to test me, making him mistrust the instinct that told him I was OK; but we're not going to get far if he thinks he can bully me. 'Cut it out,' I say. 'This is who I am and I can't spend my life apologising.'

For a second or two we stare at each other. Then he starts laughing and puts his hand out, inviting mine to meet his in a slap of acknowledgement. He says, 'This place gets to me. See you around,' and he's off, freewheeling out, that tightly sprung energy just beneath the surface. I watch him go, thinking, 'Thank God he hasn't let anyone beat it out of him.'

A few letters start coming. From Paula, excited—

'Love rules OK. I'm moving in with a woman called Bea. Come back soon and meet her. This is not another Eva! I'll write more when I stop feeling so over the top'—

'Paula, write now,' I scribble back. 'I *want* the over the top bit'—

Come back, she said, and I know it means only, 'Nothing changes the fact that we are home to each other.' But I want not to need her home, I want to make my own.

A letter from Mom, one of her long, satisfying catalogues of detail; but she ends with, 'Dad gets tired easily these days,' and I don't want to hear. Their role is to stay the *same*, to be the secure base that I do not yet have here. Why did I land myself here, in a place where I knew no one, where once again a life has to be constructed from scratch? 'You can't go back where you came from,' Paula said, years ago, 'so why go somewhere else?' It's nearer, that's why.

Winston's companionship comes and goes, jerky, unpredictable. This I am beginning to learn is the normal mode of exile life. He is alert as a creature who senses traps on all sides, ready at any moment to leap away; yet release that mysterious spring of trust, and he becomes appealingly boyish, easy going and spontaneous. 'That time,' he says, without preface, 'it wasn't you. There were too many people. I didn't want them jumping to conclusions.' I laugh and say, 'There aren't any conclusions to jump to. Let them think what they want.' But it's impossible to tell whether he means politics or sex. Both, possibly. His mood shifts restlessly. 'I have to be careful,' he says. 'There are things going on—I can't talk'—as if it's me pushing him. I say, 'Leave it, I don't want to know,' but he keeps wheeling back, unable to let go. 'There's this guy on the central committee, he calls us the Soweto kids and he treats us like we know nothing—'

'Listen, you said you couldn't—'

But the saga twists out, tortuous histories of rivalries between people I have never heard of. There is a compulsion in the telling, an awful claustrophobia—'There are people who'd be happy to get me,' he says, slicing his hand across his throat. Then immediately he laughs, so I am left not knowing how seriously he means it.

He has not even a temporary home, sleeping for a few weeks on the floor of this house, then of that; spreading out a blanket at night, rolling it up by day. No job, dependent on the Movement for his very sustenance, it is difficult to see what else he could do, but I get the feeling he would choose it anyway—safer with no fixed address.

Now I too am on the move again, constructing a new home with each new season, it seems, like the towers of mud the termites build. A Dutch engineer and his wife have gone back home on two months' leave; would I caretake their house? And who am I to decline, though there's a Zambian watchman living out at the back who patrols the length of the fence each night, wielding a lethal stick that will keep off intruders far more effectively than my sleeping presence. But I have become as pragmatic as my Zambian friends; I need a place to live, this house comes free. I move in, pack away the beautiful rugs so no one can spill coffee on them, and celebrate the quirk of fate that has placed me, homeless as I am, in a position to provide Winston and his friends with what Charity's aunt in Mbabane once gave me.

There are four bedrooms. I treat myself to the biggest, double bed and all, and tell Winston he can put who he likes in the others, provided they stick to some basic house rules.

'Like what?'—instinctive resistance.

'Like I'm not handing it back with cigarette burns all over the floor.'

They arrive each with their small collection of possessions. There seem to be more of them than beds. While the others move in and stake claims Winston dumps his bags on the kitchen floor, as if waiting on a decision from me about where he is to put himself. I ignore what he will not say, and carry on opening cupboards to find where things are kept. He stands there talking about other things. And all the time his bags are in the middle of the floor, challenging me.

The kitchen fills up. Together we make a scratch meal. The others take themselves off to a meeting in someone else's house. Winston says he's not going. The door shuts behind them and we have the house to ourselves. We stand looking at each other for a moment. His eyes are unreadable but the tension in his body is obvious. In all the weeks we've known each other this is the first moment of privacy—and I realise with absolute clarity that I am not ready for it. I say, 'I'm keeping my room to myself.'

He stares a moment longer, then walks out, angry.

Let him be angry. I hump his things into one of the other rooms and go out into the garden to dig. But I see his eyes still, staring. It was more than desire, he needs someone to love him. Proper love, trustworthy, strong enough to banish the mistrust he has learnt as the only way to handle a life intolerable. I want to feel detached and clear but compassion is getting at me, insidious…

The watchman's children squat near me as I work in the mud-packed earth. They watch, ask questions, straight and uncomplicated. I am grateful. They are clearly going to be the best of language teachers, tolerant and unselfconscious. Their eyes are like Winston's might have been before everything happened that made him as he is. They follow me as once I followed my mother, pulling up the occasional weed while she transplanted.

3

A car pulls in at the drive. It's Gerald, the American friend whose house I have been living in, now driving over to see how I am settling in; also to say that he has had a phone call at his office in the university, from someone who wants to get in touch with me. He pauses fractionally too long for comfort before he says, 'Your brother. From Geneva.'

Edward? My imagination starts zooming ahead, Edward's capital-hopping lifestyle—But it's not that. Gerald says, 'There's some kind of trouble at home, Jennie. But he said to call him first.'

Mom's letter, warning me, and I didn't want to hear—'Dad gets tired more easily these days'….

Driving back with Gerald to use his phone…trying to get my mind to focus. But it has blanked out.

Dial Geneva. Edward's voice—'Jennie, thank God. What kind of a place have you put yourself in that you don't have a phone?'

'Edward, tell me—'

'It's Richard.'

Richard! What on earth—My mind is stuck on Dad, I can't switch. 'He's been panned.'

The line isn't good. 'Panned?'

'Banned, Jennie, banned. Served with a banning order.'

It isn't just the line, my mind is refusing to hear because it makes no sense. A banning order—a kind of imprisonment, at home. *Richard?* But he hasn't been politically active for years—

'Apparently he has,' Edward says. 'But he never talked about it.'

Banned. Confined to the area around his home, and place of work. Not allowed to attend any meetings, no gathering of more than two people, apart from his own lectures and tutorials. Nothing he writes can be published…'For how long?'

'Five years.'

'Christ.' I can't react. Richard, with his quiet family life. 'Edward, what's been going on?'

'All sorts of things we never dreamed of. Including hiding a group of the Soweto students in his house when they were on the run. But that in itself suggests other things—how did they know to go to *his* house? And since then it seems he's been the mover behind an alternative school for the kids who were expelled. The police say it's a breeding ground for revolutionaries. Several of the teachers have been arrested—they're all ex-students or friends of Richard's.'

'But why not arrest him too then?'

'The newspapers are saying it's because of his international reputation. Did you know he had one?'

'I had no idea.'

'No, nor did any of us. No one reads linguistics journals.'

'Then how the hell did the police know?'

Edward laughs, a short, unhumorous laugh. 'There's some advantage in having your letters opened. Apparently he's been in correspondence with academics all over Europe and the States. Including your hero Chomsky.' His voice suddenly changes. 'I don't know why I'm laughing. It's bloody terrible.'

After that the days blurred into a surreal succession of international calls, knocking up bills I didn't know how I was going to pay—Bloemfontein, Geneva, Connecticut, Johannesburg... Finally Richard at the other end of the line, and the blankness gone, feelings surging now inside me. And Patricia, Richard's wife, whom I scarcely knew—we talked in those few minutes as if we had been real sisters to each other, holding on now to love wherever it was offered...Mom's voice choking, Dad's unnaturally old and grey. I said, over and over like a litany, 'I wish I could be there with you.' The old, urgent need to hold on, ignored for so long...Then phone down, cut off again.

Even Peter—three minutes with Peter, after years of silence. 'I don't know why I didn't write back,' he said. 'At least I suppose I do, but it's too complicated to explain.'

'Forget about explaining,' I said. 'If you can't, you can't. I just want to know whether I should go on writing or leave it.'

'Don't stop. I'll have another go.'

'Peter,'—I could not keep it back, even though I knew I should not push for more—'I can't go and be with Mom and Dad. You can. Even if it's complicated. We've all left it to Richard.'

There was a moment of silence. He was going to hang up on me—He said, 'There is also Trevor and Edward. They can and they don't choose to.'

'They're further away. OK, I know they chose that too but that's the fact as it now stands. You're there. Mom and Dad need one of us there, to be able to talk about it.' Silence. I suddenly couldn't bear it any more. 'Peter. Just *do it*. This is a crisis. When it's over you can do what you like.'

His voice was cold. 'You're a pain in the arse, Jennie. You always were.' And then the phone cut out.

I sat down to write, with no idea what I was going to say to any of them. I felt planets removed from everyone who mattered. For those few minutes they were all so *immediate*, after years of so little contact. Edward—our differences unchanged but set to one side, each there for the other. Trevor—reduced for so long to a set of facts—marriage, career; somewhere in amongst them Trevor the person got lost. I had been carrying around for years a view of how he conducted his life, based, I now realised, on almost nothing—one vivid moment in history when I last saw him. Now his voice reminded me of all his larger-than-life qualities, his capacity for enthusiasm, for spontaneous warmth. I felt again what it had been like to ride on his generous shoulders, and felt glad in the knowledge that he carried on them now his own child. For the rest, no point in having an opinion.

Peter—tension hanging over me, childish instinct wanting to fight back, to say, 'And what *you* were was a brother who played with me when no one else was around, and then shut me out when you lost interest'...But it hardly mattered. He was there, real.

Richard, I should write first to him. Why had we written so little before? We *knew* there was something special that linked us, but we had both just left it to Mom to give us news of the other. Now I needed to send my own message, that would mean something to him in the strange new cage they had constructed around him; a message from my own half-formed life here, in which he and I were so intimately linked though he didn't know it and I couldn't tell him—I with the Soweto kids who got away, he with those who were left behind. Both groups trapped, but differently. I summoned again the words of his letter to Swaziland, which in my loneliness and need I once memorised. 'None of us knows whether the little we are able to do makes any difference but we need to do it just the same. If there are consequences that we couldn't have foreseen, well, that just has to be accepted.' He was telling me about himself when he wrote that, and I had been too preoccupied with myself to understand...'The important thing is to live, as a whole human being, not to let anyone stop you responding fully to the people and the situations around you'...

Half an hour later I was still sitting there, not having got beyond 'Dear Richard.' I hadn't even been thinking, just being absorbed in all the things he had symbolised for me over the years.

Well, let me tell him that.

Richard's banning put the seal on my credentials with Winston's friends. Perhaps the change wasn't so much in them as in me. Several of them had started correspondence courses, trying to rebuild their interrupted education. They had been getting me to check the English of their essays; now that slipped into something wider, till I realised one day I was doing here what Richard had been doing in Johannesburg; until they shut him in a cage.

Winston listened to us discussing history and politics and literature, hardly admitting he was taking part. His mind had a kind of streetchild quickness, intolerant of the solitary discipline booklearning required. He gutted the prescribed books in no time, couldn't take the essays seriously. There were days when I felt, This man has gone through two lives in the time I've lived one, he's had no chance to finish being young. Then he would whip around 180 degrees, cutting across my own tension with sudden ease sprung from God knows where—fun to be with again.

Between us there was now an uneasy balance; intimacy hovered like an over-sensitive barometer, now pressing for more, now swinging back to a position more pragmatic. In any case there was seldom a moment when the house was clear of other people. His movements were erratic as ever. He would disappear for days, as once I used to from Tom's house. Once it was over two weeks, and detachment became impossible. If the others knew, they weren't telling. I could think of only two possibilities, that he had been sent to one of the Movement's training camps to keep him from getting troublesome, or that he had really had his throat slit.

I arrived back one day to find him lying on the sofa reading. 'Don't ask me where I went,' he said.

'You could have just said, I'll be away.'

'I'd have been in trouble for that too.'

But his body spoke, in its restlessness, the air of suppressed violence. Too much violence in his own childhood and youth for him to have survived without anger. I just wished there was something constructive he could *do* with it. He needs some real-life challenge, I wrote to Paula. A war to fight, a country to run, either would suit him. Sitting around in Lusaka waiting for both to happen does not.

'And you?' she asked in reply. 'Does it suit you?' That was harder to put words around. I was still cut off from the people who mattered most to me. Being here had brought one of my lost lives back into present reality. I was part of a landscape recognisably related, surrounded by faces and histories that connected. On the other side the link had become so tenuous I had nothing more substantial to hold on to than notes that lifted into the air and were gone. But learning that you can't hold on to the things you long for creates its own kind of freedom. You become more open to where you are, to things that present themselves once you stop trying to force a plan on life—

—The headteacher of the school where I have done occasional days teaching sends a message. A staffing crisis—one of the English teachers has had to leave before the end of her contract. Am I available to replace her? I was going to say 'Yes,' because it's time to settle. Then I was going to say 'No,' because that is not worth settling for. Then I thought, I'll do it part time, so I can keep my options open for taking on other things. Then I had a thought about what one of those other things might be—here, offering itself to me.

I went to talk to the headteacher. I would do it, I said, 'If you let me do something other than English as well.' He looked wary. 'I'd like to do some music with the children.'

Whatever he was expecting, it wasn't that. 'Music's not in the syllabus,' he said. I knew that, I said, that's why I thought it would be a good idea. An after-school club, maybe? But for that I couldn't pay you, he said. I wasn't thinking about money, I said—

—The school yard, a crowd of hopeful faces, no instruments except their voices. *The original and best*...I pack the voice away firmly where it can't distract me, and begin by getting the children to teach each other songs and dances they know. The range is extraordinary—six or seven languages, and for once the children more recently arrived from villages are at an advantage over their city-wise friends. We set about collecting instruments. Long dry seed pods that rattle, from a tree in the school yard. Sticks to beat together. An odd assortment of Western instruments from the back of a school cupboard, unused since the days when this was a school for the children of white settlers—and now these brown children crowd round, heads of tight springy hair bumping up against each other in their intense competition to have a turn. 'See if there's anything you can bring from home,' I say, and I show them my mbira.

The next day there are two more, the keys differently arranged. Everyone gathers round. 'This small one is called *kalimba*,' says one of the older boys, 'this other is *ndimba*.'

'Why are the keys different?' I ask. Different parts of the country, maybe? They all have theories, and none of the theories agree. But at school-ending time next day a chauffeur-driven car pulls up at the gate—an uncle, arriving to put us right. It was he who sent the *ndimba* mbira; a man with a waistline expansive from city living but he takes pleasure in telling me that he is from a village in Eastern Province, the only one of his family to go right through school. 'This is the *real* one,' he says. 'That *kalimba* is just for boys to amuse themselves with. It is easier for the thumbs. But for real Nsenga music, for singing when everyone is together, the *ndimba* is better. And you have to know the tunes. Not like on the *kalimba*—the boys just play what they want.'

'Can you teach them?' I ask. 'The real tunes?'

He laughs. 'I only know them to hear, not to play.'

But his cook is from the same village, and he knows. So next week we get a real teacher.

Now we're getting somewhere—

—Caught by a moment of awe…The children's face crowding expectantly around me, and I positioned as Neil once was for me, the person who might open up to them their own music…But this is not something for which I can get a work permit, and the months of my visa are running out. Having begun, I may have to leave too suddenly. Am I to spend my life starting again, working my way cautiously nearer—till suddenly love has grabbed me? I need to stay; and if they won't let me I will be leaving another part of myself here. It's the fear of letting that happen again that's holding me, just that last inner bit of me, in reserve.

4

The rhythm of earth and sky works quietly within me, helping me to know that I am part of this place. Through the morning the muggy heat builds up, till by early afternoon it is intolerable. A moment comes when you look up and see there's a strange shiny-grey light—a distant rumbling, like bowels that threaten action but produce only wind—then maybe half an hour later the first shafts of lightning slash the sky and the land trembles with thunder, serious this time. A pause, like gathering breath, then it buckets down, a great orchestrated crash. Bright clothes flash as people run for shelter and gather under trees. Cars pull up and hunch motionless as beetles inside their shells. Huge drops hammer on corrugated iron roofs, the roads turn in minutes to brown rushing rivers. The onslaught is so deafening that all normal sound is blotted out…Gradually the first uncontrolled violence subsides, the rain settles into a steady rhythmic descent. The cars begin to edge their way back into movement, sloshing through the water to find the higher ground in the middle. People risk leaving the shelter of the trees and run for the nearest buildings.

In half an hour it's over. The trees drip. The land steams. Banana fronds shift, released from the weight of water. Insects emerge from their holes. The earth crawls.

I am feeling strange today. Heavy, like everything's an effort. A headache looming, maybe that's all it is. The Dutch engineer and his wife are coming back, our time in this house is coming to an end. I have no plan for what happens next.

The house seems over-full of people, a Babel of languages from all the homes to the south that they have left—Xhosa, Shona, English sentences breaking through. Louder than usual, almost oppressive. It could be a meeting, could be just socialising; they talk about the same things on both occasions, and in almost the same way…From the kitchen the smell of cooking; they're clearly planning on being here several hours.

The watchman's children come to find me. 'Come and see,' they say—a strange insect they have found. I am glad to get away from the noise in the house. I squat with the children out at the back and soon I have begun telling them how, long ago, in a dusty village miles south from here, my father learnt from African children to catch and fry grasshoppers. But the headache presses. I'm struggling to find the Chinyanja words.

A woman I've not seen before comes out to join us; in her early forties probably, short and solidly built. She squats down to our level and motions to me to go on with my story. After a few minutes she asks, in Chinyanja, 'So how long have you been here?'

'Nearly four months now.'

'In four months you've learnt to speak like that?'

'I learnt some before I came.'

She doesn't comment, but turns to the children. 'Grasshoppers are one thing, but have you ever seen *locusts?*' 'Tell us,' they demand. 'When I was your size,' she begins, and launches into such a vivid description that despite my headache I become a child with the others, listening to a grandmother's stories. She interrupts herself and laughs at us, 'You made me forget—I was supposed to tell this one the food is ready!'

I follow her back to the house. She gets caught up in the milling group of people around the cooker. I realise I didn't even ask her name. She gestures with the ladle as she passes plates around, stiff maize porridge with a slosh of meat-and-vegetable relish at the side. Her movements are emphatic, no-nonsense. I listen for the language, trying to place her. Shona? So she's Zimbabwean?

I have no appetite. My headache is cracking me up, pressing at the back. 'I'm going to lie down,' I say, to whoever might be listening.

Now I'm starting to shiver…Time loses definition…Someone comes in to see how I am and piles blankets on me. It's the same woman, but I'm beyond thinking about her. 'The noise—' I say. She goes…Later I realise it's gone quiet—she must have shut doors, or sent some of them away…I'm unbelievably hot now, and throw all the blankets off. She's back again. 'I feel terrible,' I say.

'You've got malaria,' she says.

Winston appears a few feet from my bed, hovers awkwardly, leaves. The woman is back, bringing me paracetamol and telling me to drink lots. I half sleep, but with terrifying nightmares. The paracetamol is useless, my head has a metal band circling it, constantly tightening. I think it's night but I don't know which, or how many days it's been.

The woman reappears with the doctor. The doctor goes, the woman stays. Whatever he gave me must have been magic for the fevers and headache gradually depart. I finally sleep; real sleep.

She is in the room when I wake. I blink, taking her in as if for the first time. 'You're a miracle. And I don't even know your name.'

'I'm Ntombi.'

The name is South African. 'I thought you were speaking Shona.'

'Shona, Zulu—you know us. My grandfather was a worker in South Africa—he brought back a wife from Johannesburg. It was her mother who named me.' She's putting fresh fruit juice next to my bed. I say, 'I don't know what I'd have done without you.'

She won't take praise. 'That same grandmother used to tell us, *Umuntu ungumuntu nga bantu*. You know Zulu?'

'No. But a little Swazi. *Umuntu*—that's a person, isn't it?'

'It says: You become a person by being with people.'

I start trying to get up. '*You stay there*,' she scolds.

'I'm better,' I protest. 'And you've been doing everything.'

'This house is full of useless men. I've been making them work.'

I lie back—it is delightful to be told, and to submit. 'Sit and talk a little,' I say.

She looks sceptical. 'You're tired.'

'The locusts. Which country was that?'

'Which country?' She laughs. 'Zambia, Zimbabwe, how would I know? I was a child, it was all Rhodesia then. These stupid lines the Europeans drew on maps to make trouble for us all. These people belong *here*, they said'—arms gesturing one side of the bed—'and those ones *there*'—arms sweep across to the other side—'and we'll put a border betweeen them'—down the length of the bed—'to make them stay there. If they'd just asked the old people they'd have found out, no one stays still in Africa.'

I think of the anthropology books I studied—they did ask the old people. 'Our people moved into this land from the north,' they say, 'five generations ago.' Or up from the south, fleeing from Chaka's wars. Ntombi carries them in her own history, the ones who moved south and the ones who moved north. And now? Her mother is south across the uncrossable border, her husband and children north in Ndola. 'And I'm stuck here, without any of them. But that's another story.'

I plead, as children do—more stories—'Just tell me about your children, why they're not with you.'

'You sleep,' she says firmly.

The fever diminishes, anxiety returns to take its place. I have lost a week, it's almost time to be gone from this house. Winston has gone missing again, the others take no responsibility—they'll shift for themselves when they're actually thrown out. I haven't the energy to think of what I will do, only to listen to Ntombi's stories. Her husband, it seems, brought a new woman home and wouldn't move her out again. Ntombi gave him a month, then moved out herself. That meant leaving the children too—by Zambian law they belong to their father. She sees them now only in school holidays. 'It's all the fault of the missionaries,' she says, self-mocking even about her pain. 'They're the ones who taught us to think a woman should expect to keep her man just for herself. In our grandmothers' time everyone accepted being a co-wife.'

I am thinking, I want to stay near this woman and learn her resilience. Learn to look life straight in the eye and get on with the next thing.

Ntombi says, 'Where are you going to live when these people come back?'

I try her light tone. 'I'm hoping to make a career as a house-sitter.' She says, 'I hate living alone. Come and house-sit me.'

Ntombi's house is older than most in Lusaka, and slightly ramshackle. The gauze on the windows is coming away at the edges and doesn't keep out the insects, the bath leaks on to the bathroom floor. The house stands on a big plot of land that's more a yard than a garden—collections of pawpaw and mango trees out at the back, and in the front a miscellany of cannas and shrubs that some early white settler must have had sent up from the south and planted years ago, now overgrown and shapeless. The best is a flowering creeper that trails over my window, giving off a heady scent through the night.

She employs neither gardener nor house servant. 'And you're not filling the house with all those men,' she says. 'They want looking after, whatever they say.' So Winston has gone back to sleeping on the floor he was occupying before. I am glad to have a little distance. A week after I moved he arrived, mid-morning when he knew Ntombi would be at work. He hung about and it was clear what was on his mind. My mind was on other things. 'I need time,' I said. 'There are things I need to work out for myself first.'

'No one's talking about a permanent relationship,' he said. 'We're all temporary.' But that's the point; I don't want to slip casually into a succession of temporary encounters. Winston said, 'Why am I suddenly a temporary encounter?'

'You just said we all are,' I said.

But I know as well as he that I'm evading the real issue. He's hurt; I hate that but it's not reason enough to give in. 'I need time,' I said again, 'to work out what I'm doing here.' He said, 'You're too complicated,' and left.

Now I'm restless. Did I *want* to be pushed, despite all I said?

Ntombi will take nothing for my rent. 'Stop arguing,' she says, 'or I'll throw you out. I get the house with my job.' We compromise. No rent, but I contribute to what she sends her mother. 'Extended family obligations,' I say. 'You've become my family by taking me in.' She can't resist the logic. 'I'd feel better if you had a full-time job,' she says. So would I. She says, 'What's so bad about school-teaching?'

She's a teacher herself, she knows. The answer is there in what she brings home, piles of books every evening, filled with useless grammar exercises. List the parts of speech. Fill in the gaps. Ntombi gets fed up with marking but she doesn't query the absolute importance of filling in the gaps. That's what they pay us to do, she says; she doesn't waste energy thinking about the purpose.

But what purpose have I, hanging on for some mythical job that won't materialise? Paula writes, 'I get the feeling that you're not so much staying there, as staying away.' But I don't want to hear what she's saying…

I saw Ntombi watching me when I was playing the penny whistle, a look on her face I couldn't work out. The nearest I can get is that it was protective. No use asking her, she simply won't be lured into talking about anything that touches the personal too closely. For all I know it might have been a thought about her mother or her children. She casts me in their roles sometimes, fussing over me to eat properly, but she accepts it quite practically when I resist. There's a ruthless realism about her that leaves nothing to fester. I know she misses her children passionately but she doesn't persuade herself that they are badly treated by the new wife. And her husband? He's a man, nothing more can be expected of him; if the other wife weren't there, she'd be back.

'That song you were playing,' she asked. 'What is it?'

'Something a friend of mine wrote,' I said.

So she's not the only one who won't be lured.

Through my uncertainties the children's music grows and binds, winding round me like tendrils of a creeper—

One of the girls brought an older brother who knows how to make reed flutes. He was casting longing eyes on my penny whistle, so we've put him on that as the lead voice, with the reed flutes for the responses. So that's in one corner of the yard and in another the *kalimba–ndimba* players experimenting, metallic sounds plinking busily. When each group's ready they call the rest of us to do rhythm accompaniment on our strange collection of rattles.

The sounds keep reaching out beyond the school, pulling people in. Passers-by stop to listen and applaud. One of the boys who helps out at the petrol station down the road hovered at the gate a couple of weeks in a row till he finally got up the courage to come in and take a turn on our only real drum—which he plays far better than any of us. Now there's a group of his mates. Anything hollow they turn into a drum—upturned metal buckets, plastic containers—and their rhythms are powerful. We've had to start a parallel group to stop them drowning the younger ones.

Then some older girls started hanging about to listen. They were there to collect the smaller ones after school, and had that awkward longing in their bodies of almost-adults who see children having fun but feel they'll lose status by joining them. They contented themselves with calling out challenges to the boys, then that slipped into snatches of song, the kind of girl–boy rivalry songs they sing in the villages…and then they were there with us, the clapping, the dancing.

Ntombi comes by on her way home from the school where she teaches, 'Just to see what you're all up to,' she says. She starts telling the mbira players about how in Zimbabwe people use them to summon the spirits of the ancestors. Soon she has a crowd around her, and she herself is linking these children to those who went before—

—All this energy, this creativity, we need to find a way of bringing it together—

I summon the boys with their drums, the girls with their dances, the children with their scratch orchestra. We all sit down in an enormous circle on the dusty ground and begin to plan a musical story that will include everyone. The boys say, Let it be a story of a fight between two town gangs. The girls say, But we want the village dances. The children say, There should be some magic. Then someone says, Make it about all of them—village people, come to town, caught up in fights and people putting spells on other people—

*Extraordinary fusion music, in the middle of Africa…*So there you are, we're doing it.

5

The rains are showing signs of slowing down, the gaps between storms lengthening. The mud puddles are drying out and with them the weeks and months of my visa, and then—? There are days when I wake up thinking, I don't know how I got myself into this stupid position; then other days when I am alive to the life around me, and it seems only a practical matter to find a way to stay.

I don't know why, but as the months pass I find it harder rather than easier to put aside the things I have lost. Ntombi helps me without my needing to talk about it, by helping me understand that my case is not special. She lives with me rather than with *her* husband; Teresa with Neil rather than *her* husband; Neil with Teresa rather than with me. These arrangements indicate nothing about which loves are strongest, only about the constraints of history. All our histories.

A job arrived this week without my having to go and find it. A short term job only, but it jolted me out of inertia into realising that I still have a chance to make a go of this. Winston came to find me with a story about the Zambian army picking up a group of young women who had been found wandering in the bush north of the Victoria Falls, almost starving. 'No one can find out their story. Someone from the UN's asking for an interpreter.'

'What's the language?'

'Ovambo. Seems they came across the Zambezi from Namibia. But the Namibians here have all gone to Tanzania, some big *ndaba*. This UN bloke said, Find us *someone*. And they pay, UN rates.'

I can't see what this story has to do with me. Winston says, 'I told them you could do it.'

'*Me?*' He is grinning now. 'Thank those Boer ancestors of yours. The only other language these girls know is what they had to learn at school—Afrikaans.' It's unreal—even *this* bit of my past is being dragged out, brought into use after so many years lying redundant. '*You* could do it,' I tell Winston. But I know he won't. Afrikaans is too much a symbol of all he threw over the day they burnt the schools; he learnt it under protest and pretends he hardly knows it. 'Anyway, they want a woman,' he says.

The UN official is Spanish, called Fernando, and he has just arrived in Lusaka from some other refugee crisis. I climb into the landrover with him and we head for a camp twenty miles outside Lusaka, along roads that scarcely merit the name. 'As far as we can find out they're runaway schoolgirls,' he says, 'but you know how it is around here, half the kids don't get to school till they're almost grown. These are young women really.' The landscape jumps drunkenly before us, trees tilting as we hit potholes. 'They were in a bad way when the army found them. They must have been out in the bush a couple of weeks. Incredible journey. And they're suspicious as hell. Who knows what's happened to them on the way.'

He starts asking me what I've been doing here. 'Very little, paid,' I say. 'And unpaid?' I tell him about Winston and his friends. 'I help them with their studies, and negotiating their way through the bureaucracy. I'm an expert on regulations governing the movement of foreigners.' He smiles and says, 'I could use that.' He asks me a few more questions about things I've done before, listens quietly, then starts telling me about the office he has inherited from his predecessor. 'It hardly functions. The expatriate staff have changed too often and the Zambian staff are mostly secretaries and drivers. I need someone to set up a few systems, in between whatever interpreting this group of women are going to need.'

'Are we talking about a real job? With a work permit?'

He smiles again and says, 'What would you say to two months?' I say, 'Let's meet the women, and then see.'

Fernando slows the landrover to a halt. The camp looks like a prison. Barbed wire fence, recently erected, enclosing a village of makeshift huts. Fernando glances at me; the shock must be evident.

'Why the hell?' I say. 'They're not prisoners of war!'

'That's why we're here. Till someone can get their story out of them, they're illegal immigrants.'

We pass armed guards. Sign documents, like crossing a border. Once inside we make for the army hut, where we disturb a camp official who seems to have just woken up. Fifty yards away at the first of the huts a group of young women stand eyeing us. Fernando and the official get into a long discussion about technicalities. I walk towards the women, thinking, What are they seeing as I come? And when I speak? This white woman who comes speaking Afrikaans, language of the oppressor they have just fled from?... '*Goeie more*,' I say—good morning...How formal it sounds, and out of place. They stare, saying nothing. I tell them my name, and why I have come. Still nothing. I say, 'I don't understand why they've put you in this place, with barbed wire.'

Eventually one speaks. 'It's the third camp,' she says, dully.

'Even if they let us out, no one can understand us,' says another. 'What will we do?' Her eyes hold mine. She looks younger than the rest of them, the body of a girl, light-boned, small child breasts; eyes hard. 'At least here we eat,' she says.

What else happened on their journey apart from not eating, they will not say. Nor about what precipitated it. But that they have questions of their own is evident in the eyes that stare hungrily at me, torn between suspicion and need. Only the young one speaks. 'What's going to happen to us now?' she asks.

'*Ek weet nie*,' I hear myself saying. I don't know. But I'll find out, and tell you.

'You *have* to come with me,' I tell Winston. 'Let them see you trust me, then they might.'

We sit together in the dust, among scraps of debris blown by the wind and clinging to the scratchy tufts of grass. The young women look at us both, assessing. Winston behaves in a way that makes me forgive him all the insensitivity and aggression I've ever seen in him These young women are where he has once been, and instinctively he knows what they need. He is respectful, quiet, creating an air of being there to use if they wish, but no pressure. Once he even succeeds in making them laugh. There is a thread of personal history running through from them to him to me, linking all of us. With him there we find that part of human experience we have all shared. The story begins to come out, in dribbles at first, then a confusing flood, all the things they have been unable to say to those who loaded them on to trucks and dumped them here. They ran, they say, because the soldiers were attacking the villages, saying they were hiding Angolan terrorists. They were in school at the time. Winston asks, 'Where are the boys?' They shrug. 'The boys' school was one place, the girls' school another place, we did not see when we ran.'

'They are dead,' says the girl with the child-body. She speaks with certainty, no illusions to protect. 'The soldiers, they kill the young men first, so there is no one to fight when they start on the women.'

The journey—that too they begin finally to talk about. The land they were travelling through was hardly inhabited by people, but known to be home to elephants and lions. For days they ate only wild fruits. They were lucky it was this time of year otherwise they might have starved...But the journey is past, what obsesses them now is their present frustration. Their lives are being settled over their heads. It is a matter of survival that they be able to make their needs and intentions clear.

Winston and I convey all this to Fernando on the way back to Lusaka. In response he lets off his own frustrations. The Zambian officials won't budge. Too many disgruntled exiles drifting about Lusaka already, taking out their tensions in drunken fights with the locals. The Zambians are demanding that this lot be moved on, to Tanzania, Kenya, anywhere else but here. But no one will agree to take them...

He is doing too good a job explaining what isn't going to be possible. Winston becomes hostile. I feel now for the first time what interpreting is going to involve. The words are only the start.

I take the job.

The dry season has a grip on the land. It happened so gradually I hardly noticed. For a while the grass was still green, then one day I saw it had begun to look tired, and within a couple of weeks it had changed to yellow. I had been cycling the same paths each day and I thought I was looking, but there came a day when I realised, This is thatching grass, ready to cut. They'll be repairing the roofs in Nyika.

In the camp, time moves incredibly slowly. Not just the natural pace of Africa, for here there is no rhythm of the seasons—they sit at all times with nothing to do. Give them a hoe and some seeds and they could be feeding themselves next year, but no one will do it lest they think they are being allowed to settle. I have a strange sensation that I am in the same state, that no one will give me a hoe.

Paula writes, 'Tell me what it is you stay for, Jennie.' 'For the women in the camp,' I say. I have to keep pushing Fernando to make another journey to the camp so we can tell them where things have got to. Nothing's decided,' he said last time. 'What's the point?' The point is it's their lives.

I have started teaching them English. It just seemed the obvious thing to do. Fernando is trying to fix up for them to get out to other countries on UN scholarships, but they won't be able to cope with that, or even with Zambia, till they get past their dependence on an interpreter. I've started getting them to practise saying in simple English the things they need me to say for them. They learn faster than I learnt the viola, and for the same reason—it answers a real need. *This* is the kind of English teaching that makes perfect sense to me. But the times in the camp are so short. Now if someone would offer me a job doing *this* longer-term—

I suggest it to Fernando. He thinks I am joking. When he discovers I am not, he gets alarmed. 'Once we start running classes we'll never extricate ourselves,' he says.

'Then get the government to do it,' I say. 'Someone has to.'

Fernando rambles on assessing the political possibilities. Just hang on a while, he says, it might happen. He has heard talk of the Ministry of Education arranging to truck the girls in to Lusaka schools. I say, 'Fernando, they're *adults*, with incredible life experience. You can't put them in with a lot of young children, plodding through Book One! They need to learn *fast*, things they want to say and do now.'

He says, 'I could probably find the money to extend your contract another month.'

'*No one* learns a language in a month, especially sitting in a vacuum like they have to.'

He says, 'Just give me a break, Jennie.'

We rumble on, bumping over potholes. I can't do this forever, just lurching from one hole to the next, no clear prospect. For several days now I have woken up with my arms empty, and the feel of a viola just having left them…I glance at Fernando, wondering what moves *him*, in the private areas that have nothing to do with this job. 'Tell me about Spain,' I say. He looks surprised but starts in willingly enough; his boyhood, his passionate interest in flamenco…Before I realise it I am telling him about the viola that I have not seen for almost a year, still waiting to be fetched in Nairobi; about the aching hole it has left in my life. 'Why didn't you tell me?' he demands, suddenly decisive. 'My wife has one. She brought it thinking she might play, and she hasn't even opened the case since we came.'

He takes me straight home; middle of the working day, walking out as if this is an emergency. His wife fetches out the viola—

Open the case. The wood shines softly. Three of the strings have sprung loose—it's a miracle the bridge is still standing…

I hold it in my lap like an injured bird, carefully set the strings back in position. Tune it up. Tighten the bow, rub on resin. Lift the viola to my chin, feel its precise weight and shape. Left hand fingers poised above the strings, right hand settling into a bowhold light yet flexible. Bow on string. Breathe. Begin—

And it's done now, the feelings that for too long I have kept unhappily caged cavort wildly. Fernando and his wife go quietly out of the room. I play for hours, crazily at first, as loud as I can and as soft as I can, faster than my fingers will go and making a havoc of tunes I am trying to recapture. Eventually the urgency calms down and I am ready to start again, moderately. My hands, arms, back, breath, they have all forgotten and are absurdly tense with overuse. Start again. Learn to stand. To breathe. To know this viola, which has its own personality and does not do quite what my hands expect it to. Listen, really listen to the echo of the sound inside…

And with the listening comes clarity. That evening I tell Fernando, 'You've helped me sort something out. If you're going to have work for me after this month, I need to know now; and I'll need a contract for a year. Otherwise I'm going back.'

And almost, I don't know which I want it to be.

Chapter 4

November is not the recommended time to arrive back in London. Streets grey and wet and dirty, with cloud cover that never lifts. Dark setting in before the afternoon has had a chance. People looking tired and peaky, though we're only a month into winter. All I have to do is get myself from Heathrow to Victoria, and then hang about for a few hours till I can get a coach to Bristol. But that's enough to make me feel oppressed by the noise and greyness, and too many people on the underground not even noticing who they are standing next to.

While I'm waiting for the coach I start phoning. That too leaves me depressed. There's something insecure-making about trying to reconnect with people who used to be part of your daily life, who in their letters say it'll be great to see you, your new job sounds amazing, want to hear all about it—and then when you phone they aren't in. Half my SOAS friends are back in the countries they came from; the English ones have gone to jobs in other cities or are married and living in Surrey. A phone call is all we're going to get unless I spend my whole four weeks traipsing around from one to the next.

Muhib's here but he shouldn't be—his MA is over, he's now doing a PhD. 'Easier than thinking out what to do next,' he says, with characteristic candour. 'And why are you back, if you're starting a new job?'

'The contract comes with a return fare—home leave. It suits them for me to take it now because it's going to be weeks wading through red tape before I can start doing anything useful. And it means I can go back via Nairobi to get my viola.'

'So what are you going to be doing?'

'Organising what they're calling Transition Courses for refugees, so they can cope if they get moved on, or the policies change and they're allowed to stay. And to put something in place so if new ones arrive they don't land in the same awful situation.'

—Strange, to be describing it in this detached way, to someone who's my friend yet doesn't begin to understand what motivates me.

We make a date to go to some Indian music when I come back from Paula's. One concert will be enough.

Jaswinder is still living with her mother-in-law, now with a child of her own plus two that her sisters-in-law hand over to her while they're out at work. She sounds pleased to hear my voice but overwhelmed with domesticity. The call ends abruptly when a child's scream announces that someone has fallen off a chair.

And there's no answer from Neil's phone.

Bristol. Paula's home is always mine and mine hers, that's how it was going to be when I left. Paula won't have changed but I am apprehensive about the new lover. Bea may find it less than comfortable to see Paula leaping up to greet me when I arrive at the door, her hair flying all over the place as her arms go around me.

But it isn't at the door that it happens, it's at the coach station. I'm just climbing off with my thoughts somewhere else when suddenly there is Paula swooping down on me, grabbing the bags out of my hands to throw down right there and whirling me round in a wild dance. It's only when I've stopped whooping and laughing with her that I see she's not alone. A woman tall as Paula, standing a couple of paces back. My first impression is of someone steady and calm—which is a surprise because it's so much the opposite of Eva. Bea is watching us with an amused expression, apparently quite unthreatened. 'Hi,' she says, and comes forward to give me a hug. The kind you give people you don't yet know well but are going to.

We're putting the bags in the car. 'Paula, you with a car!'

'Paula pretends it's mine,' Bea says. 'She maintains her purity on a bike—except when she lets me drive her around.'

Paula says, 'Bristol's hard work on a bike. See for yourself!' Their enjoyment of each other is obvious, and delightful. We're heading up a steep hill and then dipping down to views over the harbour. Trees everywhere—and instead of the dull grey blanket of the London sky, a pile up of clouds with patches of sky breaking through. 'I'd put up with the hills,' I say. 'This feels a whole lot better than London.'

We have arrived. A terrace of small houses stepping down the hill, each door a different colour. I follow Bea in. Paula has her hands up ruffling her hair as she watches me take it in. My eye is still accustomed to the space of Lusaka—this room feels too small to contain someone of Paula's expansive energy. But they've made it full of colour, and it's light, with a glass door at the far end opening on to a tiny garden. Paula says, 'There's a room been waiting for you to inhabit. Not an attic but the next best thing.'

She leaves Bea to take me up and goes to the kitchen to start getting a meal. The stairs are steep, slightly rickety. I climb carefully, like a child exploring. Paula's right—the room has the feel of an attic. It seems full with only a single bed and a desk, and has an old sash window. Like my window in the women's house it looks out over the tops of the rows of houses that slope away down the hill. I move towards it, to open it and see if I can peer down on to the garden. Bea's voice behind me says, 'Take it easy—it tends to slip. Paula's always about to fix it but she never gets round to it.'

I turn. We smile, not a smile of strangers this time but something simple and real. A recognition of the things we both know about Paula, from living with her and loving her. I say, 'Thanks, Bea. The room's lovely,' and I know for certain it's going to be OK.

Paula has taken four days' leave. In the daytime while Bea's at work we talk—the longest continuous time we've ever had together, even longer than the couple of days when we went walking in the country—and as satisfying. I feel known, accepted, challenged, all those essential things Paula does for me. It still works both ways, but the balance is different now that she has a partner. That too we talk about, knowing the change makes no difference to our closeness.

She's asking me about my job. When I've finished she says, 'So holding out for the real thing sometimes works.' I glance quickly, to see what she's implying. There are things that didn't get into letters, and Paula notices what I don't say just as much as what I do. She asks, 'So are you going to see Neil?'

I don't know why I don't feel ready for her to ask it. I say, 'I want to, but I don't yet know when. Or how much.' She waits for more. 'I haven't fixed anything,' I say. She is beginning to look disbelieving. 'I didn't want him to feel pressured,' I say, but it sounds feeble, even to me. It was fear—*It's the other bit I backed away from—your need.* But I can't say this, even to Paula. I say instead, 'I tried to phone when I was in London but he wasn't in. So I sent him a card. I said I'd be staying with Megan and he could leave a message with her.'

She points to the telephone. 'I can teach you how to lift the receiver if you like.'

I don't want to phone Megan and say, 'Has Neil phoned?' I even more don't want to phone Neil and have Teresa answer. It's like my apprehension about Bea but vastly magnified. And with better cause.

It's impossible to hide from Paula. With her looking at me like that I too can't believe that I was so stupid as not to let him know earlier. I'm going to have only two weeks in London—what if he's out of town all that time? If he is and could have told me in time I could have moved around the dates with Paula. I hear myself explaining to her now, rationally, that I was trying to let it be a natural meeting like with any of my other friends. Not to make it seem too charged, which would only make us both over-conscious—set up defences—

She waits for me to finish and says, 'That was a long speech.' Then she relents and says, more gently, 'If it's that complicated maybe you shouldn't be seeing him.'

But Neil represents life and energy and I don't know how to say no to that.

Night. Paula and Bea have been in bed a while. I'm not asleep. The door opens, Paula comes in, to sit crosslegged on my bed. 'I thought so,' she says.

'What?'

'Still awake. I heard small sounds.'

She starts telling me about something that happened with the kids she works with, making me laugh. When I'm relaxed and feeling luxurious at having her here, entertaining me, she suddenly changes tone—'I don't like the signs, Jennie.'

I say, 'OK then, tell me what to do.'

'Phone and be done with it. You've come too far with your life to sit around like a vulnerable adolescent.'

I phone. A boy answers—Juan.

Immediately I feel an intruder. Neil's out, he says, at the hospital. He doesn't know when he'll be back. I don't want to ask who is ill and he doesn't offer anything that isn't asked. I leave my name and Paula's number, and try and forget about it.

It must be Teresa.

That's ridiculous, it could be anyone.

But Juan is there.

Juan's probably there most of the time.

I know nothing, nothing still about the details of his daily life.

Now I really am like an adolescent, waiting for the phone to ring. And it doesn't. I wish I had never phoned.

I don't know why but I am thinking of Peter. Perhaps it's the vulnerability, back again. Mine. Teresa's? Maybe also Neil's—who knows? Maybe it's the temporary loss of centre, being poised between two lives—this one that can't really be home, however welcoming Paula and Bea are, because there's nothing here for me to do, and the new one in Lusaka that has only just begun to formulate itself. The awareness of how I am supported by a few central continuities in a life perpetually full of change. Sadness at Peter's life, which never seems to have got past the mess caused by that one traumatic experience.

I wake one morning knowing I should make another attempt to write to him. But this time, I decide, there is no point in treading carefully around whatever he might be feeling. Either he has the capacity to be jolted out of old patterns, or he hasn't. If he hasn't, there isn't much point going on trying. If he has, I want the kind of relationship where we can be honest with each other.

'Peter,' I begin, 'I've been trying to talk to you ever since I had to leave, and you're never there. Whatever has happened since, the first twenty years still count, they're part of us. But if you don't reply to this letter I'm quitting.'

And perhaps the vehemence is not just for Peter.

Megan phones. We fix plans for my coming to London. She says, 'All sorts of people are leaving messages for you.'

'Like who?'

'Someone called Derek from SOAS. Your friend Jaswinder. And Neil's been trying to find you. He got a half message, but whoever took it lost Paula's number.'

He's got it now. But still no call.

Paula goes back to work. I do some more phoning. Derek, Jaswinder. We fix dates. Michael's parents. Jane, in Manchester.

'What's Manchester like?' I ask.

'It rains the whole time,' she says. 'And when it isn't raining there's a low mist that hangs over everything.'

'Come and see me in Zambia. Heat and light guaranteed.'

'You serious?'

'Why not? I'd love it if you came. We could go travelling together. Game Reserves, Victoria Falls.'

'Done,' she says. 'I'll start saving. I've just spent a week with Maria. Did you know she was an MP now? She hardly touched down she was so busy. And Paula—I'm still reeling at the thought of *Paula* buying a house. Not to mention you teaching English. There's nothing to be relied on.'

'And there you are, the only upholder of the true faith.'

'You got it. Women's household, socialist feminist group, the lot. Why don't you come up for a couple of days, Jennie? I need a bit of stimulus.'

'What's your women's household doing for you then?'

'No one takes the piss out of me the way you and Paula used to.'

And no one lifts me the way she and Paula do. But I don't want to commit myself to taking time out to go to Manchester, until I know what else is happening.

The phone rings. Paula answers. Hands it to me. 'Neil,' she says.

His voice is tense, trying to explain ten things at the same time. 'Jennie, I'm sorry it took so long. Things have been difficult. I've only just managed to get your number from Megan. Juan lost the envelope he'd written it on. There's been too much going on.'

I register the tension, and the fact that there are too many excuses—one good one would have done the job better. But it's impossible not to feel joy at his voice. I say, 'Juan said you were at the hospital. Is it Teresa?'

'Yes. I'll tell you when we meet.'

I start saying something asinine about there being no hurry, if he's too busy—He interrupts. 'Jennie, please. I'm too tired to faff about. Tell me when you're coming.'

We meet in a cafe near the hospital, for an hour, between his visiting Teresa and a rehearsal. He tells me, abruptly, it's cancer.

She has just had a breast removed. It was discovered less than a month ago. He meant to write to tell me but there's been too much going on. Juan is living with him for the moment. She seems to be doing OK but there's no question of her going back to a flat on her own—she will come from the hospital to his house until she is strong. They're assuming she will get strong again—but it's going to be months of treatment in any case. Depending on how she is, they'll see what to do next. It may turn out she's moving in long-term. He doesn't sound as if it's a decision he will be involved in, rather that this may be what life presents him with, as it presented her with cancer.

I sit opposite him, holding his hands across the cafe table as I listen. All thought of what might have been possible for us at this time is gone in minutes of seeing the strain in his face. And gone also are the anxieties that oppressed me while I was at Paula's waiting for him to phone. They vanished the instant he was physically here—to be replaced by a quiet sureness that comes from I don't know where. I want only that Teresa be well, and that he be calm again and free from care. I know that however little time we get, my being with him will help him. That is enough.

But *he* doesn't yet know that. He is unnaturally tense. The anxiety about Teresa, the tiredness, they are natural enough—but the abruptness is something more than that. Perhaps he thinks I won't want to hear him speak of her in a way that makes it so clear that feeling responsible for her is his unquestioned first priority. I want to say something simple to remove at least that tension—I understand, I accept it, I have accepted it for a year, I have made my own life, I am not asking you to change anything in yours—but it's difficult to get through to him. He is like someone living on too much coffee, over-speedy. Giving out messages, not taking them in. The tired look that I remember from a year ago is there again but this time it hardly lifts. If I hadn't seen it then I'd have read it as anxiety for Teresa. That's part of it, I'm sure, but there must be longer-term things he isn't dealing with. I don't know what they are and don't need to know. Seeing the tiredness in this man I love, and have loved for four years, and am clearly always going to love, I feel a compassion it isn't possible to put in words.

The impersonality of the cafe begins to oppress me. He'll never let me near enough to help if we stay here. I say, 'Neil, can't we go somewhere quiet?'

His eyes look defensive. 'Not my house—Juan's there.'

'When he's at school?'

But then Neil has music commitments. We can perhaps meet tomorrow at the end of the day for a short time, but he doesn't want to leave Juan alone too long. Before I have a chance to say anything he says he knows Juan is fourteen, it's not a question of needing anyone there, he's used to letting himself in and getting on with it—'It's just being *there* for him while Teresa's not around.' I want to say, 'Neil, you don't need to explain things like that to me,' but he isn't giving me the space. It's going to be difficult, he is saying. In the evenings it's hospital visiting time. He happens to have a particularly busy couple of weeks in terms of work. There's Juan, they need quiet time together each day. He keeps explaining, defending himself against the emotional demands he expects me to make. The truth is that if Teresa had not been ill I might have. I give up trying to get through to him. I just sit there, holding his hands across the table, listening.

Towards the end of the hour he pauses from his constant talking and looks at me as if taking me in properly for the first time. He says, 'I'm glad you're here. I was afraid-'

'Of?'

'I don't know.'

'Pressure?'

He moves his head slightly in acknowledgement—self-deprecating.

I acknowledge too. 'I haven't been feeling that calm myself.' He looks wary again. I say, 'There's no pressure, Neil. Let's just take it quietly, as it comes.'

'Your cards—that one after the music-making—it was your voice, really talking—it made me—I don't know how to say it. Churning. For weeks. And now—it's extraordinary what seeing you does.' He stops. I nod. He sees it isn't necessary to go on trying to put it into words. We both know. He says, simply, 'I don't know what we're going to do Jennie. I can't think past the present.'

'Leave it, Neil. There's no need to work anything out. We've managed, we'll go on managing. Let's just be together for the moment and try not to think too much.'

He is silent for a moment, just looking at me. Then he says, 'We could meet after I've been to the hospital this evening.'

2

A succession of cafes, stations, parks. Snatched hours between work, the hospital and Juan. Tentatively at first—he has recurrent anxieties about it being more difficult for me afterwards if we spend too much time together now. But he can't say 'No' any more than I can. Tiredness wins; he gives up fighting and slips into assuming, as I do, that I will be with him whenever he isn't needed elsewhere. Then having opened up that far, he holds on to every moment. I go with him wherever he has to be next, then do whatever can be done in that part of town until he emerges from the building again.

Each day I wake to joy, knowing I will be with him. It does not matter that he begins tensely, or that the tensions keep recurring. We are together. Together we get past them.

Together, but never alone. Teresa is there constantly. He has just come from seeing her or is about to see her. The twice daily bulletin—how she feels, what the hospital staff said. Things he needs to get for her before the next visit—suddenly remembered small responsibilities for Juan—a promise to phone someone, forgotten until this moment. The immediacy of her illness has blotted out anything else he might have wanted to share about the past year. The future doesn't stretch past the next couple of weeks.

In other circumstances I would have found it difficult to have to be so constantly talking about her. But I just listen, and the more complicated feelings mercifully hold themselves in abeyance. I am a strange appendage on the lives of these two people, one of whom I love and one I scarcely know—as she doesn't know me, or even that I exist as a feature of Neil's life. My days revolve for the moment as his do around what is happening to her—but in my case not from knowing her, but from wanting to be with Neil in whatever is happening to him. What he needs most is simply for me to be there for him, as he is being there for Teresa. All he can handle is the step right in front of him. I have landed out of nowhere and for a few of those steps I can be with him and help sustain him. Then I'll be gone. That's the summary of my relevance, and my irrelevance.

By now Megan knows. I could not have disguised it, living in her home. The night of his concert when she helped to make possible what has since happened, she did not know about Teresa. Now that she does it's obvious that she is worried for me and feels a responsibility to try to help me keep things in perspective. I am not worried for myself, but that's because, like Neil, I can't think past the present moment.

I don't think Neil knows what he's feeling. He's too tired to work anything out. He says he isn't sleeping much and I can believe it. That when he can't sleep he composes. It's an intense kind of concentration but different from what's required of him by day, and restoring—gives him a sort of space.

'Tell me about it—what you're working on,' I say, to help him take some of that space now.

It's a cello concerto, he says—and for the short time he is speaking about it the tiredness lifts. He's steered clear of that kind of format till now but he's ready—reclaiming something, in fact. Sometimes things he's working on take ages to get right but this is coming out at a rush—the only question is can he catch it fast enough before that clarity is muffled; then working out the detail that gives life to the overall intention. That kind of intensity probably has something to do with all the upheaval. There's so little time—the music is working itself out in his mind all the time—when he finally gets a couple of hours to give to it, it comes out under pressure. But the music's not *about* what's happening to Teresa—'I've never understood those things about the links between events in composer's lives and the music they're composing at that time. With me things don't come out in any direct way until months after—a kind of lag effect. My system has to have time to digest them without pressure. When I'm working now I never think about Teresa—it's the opposite—I'm letting myself be free of it, for that time. And it's an absolute necessity to *keep* free, to be alone. I mean necessary for me, not just for the music.'

But he's worked himself back to talking again about the thing he wishes he could block out.

'She's been afraid, Jennie. It's the first time I've ever seen that in her. She has such courage, about everything. But not being sure you're going to keep living is—It's almost certain now that she will, but once you've faced that fear, it changes everything—For me too, watching her deal with it.' He is silent for a moment, his eyes vague. Then he pulls himself back to telling me—'For a few weeks she couldn't get past being afraid for Juan. She knows I'll always be there, but they're very close—He's fourteen, Jennie—'

'Are *you* afraid?'

He looks startled, then immediately wary. I think he is going to close off and not be able to talk about it. But he says, in that steady voice that I now know means he is not feeling in the least calm, 'Only that I won't have done all I could to help her know it's worth going on living. And given Juan what he needs from me.'

In the times I can't be with Neil I am seeing other friends, stretching their tolerance by rearranging times so that they fit around when he and I can meet. Jaswinder and I talk as we fold nappies, and she interrupts herself to wipe a mess on the carpet and pick up a crying child, holding him on her hips as she stirs *dal* on the stove with the free hand. 'Give him to me,' I say, and she hands the child over. But there's another up to fill the space in no time and the *dal* is burning. I want to yank her out of there for just one hour, for her own sake. I say, 'Why don't you let me babysit for you, and you and Sean go out?' But she says, 'He's mostly down the pub with his mates.' I say, 'Could his Mom take care of the baby, and we do something together?' She says, 'Jennie, it's not like that any more. Wait till you've got kids, you'll see.'

By the end of the fourth day Neil has cancelled an appointment to make himself free in the morning while Juan is at school. I have not asked him to, and would not have, but I am glad he got there. We both need it. It is wearing us down, snatched hours—never finishing a conversation, having to talk about highly personal things over the noise of the underground. Never being able to do more than touch.

The first lovemaking is as tense as the first cafe meeting. He is reticent, apparently unable or unwilling to tell me what he is feeling. I can guess, but that's not the same thing. I can't make love with the body only, even with Neil. He senses my lack of response and pulls away, to lie silently next to me, cutting me out even further.

For some reason his withdrawal doesn't make me feel rejected. Perhaps because I know it means he could sense what I was feeling. Perhaps simply because my primary feeling for him at the moment is compassion. I prop myself up on my elbow and start stroking his hair. He lies still, letting me, and eventually turns over on to his side to hold me. He says nothing but after a while begins caressing my back, sending shivers down my whole body. We are both suddenly alive to each other again, unable to stop touching, holding—

—We lie together, quiet now, and for the first time in four days without that undertone of tension. He says, 'It's extraordinary that at a time like this it should still be possible to feel joy.'

He is choosing to let it happen—too much in need to be able to refuse what I so consistently offer and what he too longs for. But he cannot get past the feeling that we ought to try to limit what we allow ourselves—that if we don't, we are creating a situation I will find unmanageably painful after this time is over. There is never any question but that I will return and that he will stay. He will deal with that by blotting it out, immersing himself in his work, his responsibilities. He knows I will not be able to do that as easily.

I say, 'Neil, *I'm* choosing this too. It's not you deciding for me. You don't have to feel responsible.'

But he does. For me the question of protecting myself doesn't arise. If he had allowed his fear to deny us this time together, I would have been bereft of part of myself.

He stops trying to do the impossible and gives in to joy. His diary is further adjusted—more of the morning appointments are postponed until after I will have gone. We laugh about it, remembering the time four years ago when he cancelled half his preplanned life to make space for me and the workshops. He says wryly, 'It's a lot more difficult to do these days. Quite aside from Teresa and Juan.'

'The penalties of fame!'

'Hardly fame. Getting a reasonable amount of work is the highest I'd put it.'

We have hardly spoken about his work or mine. But his is around us each day—teaching commitments, rehearsing for a performance, meeting people. Now he begins to be conscious that I am about to leave, he plies me with questions as he did on our one night together a year ago—all the things of which the postcards gave only the barest indication. The more he hears, the more relaxed he becomes. He wants to think of me as active, involved, self-motivated. If I say anything that indicates I have thought about him, his eyes become wary—he does not want the responsibility of feeling that I might be unhappy and that he might have anything to do with it.

Mostly he avoids putting words around this kind of feeling. But the days are going fast. The moment of departure looms and we stumble into talking about it, despite ourselves. He says once, 'You have beautiful rejoicing eyes'—and then, 'Promise me you'll keep rejoicing. Not greet for what we can't have.'

'Greet?'

'Weep. Mourn. It's a word I hardly use anymore—I don't know what evoked it. Most of those words dropped out of my speech as soon as I left Scotland. Maybe just too close to the bits of my past I didn't want to be confined by.'

I want to hear more but he brushes past it. 'I've long since stopped bothering,' he says. 'I am who I am and the bits'll just have to joggle about together.'

'I love it.'

He looks amused. 'Oh? And what's it?'

'You being you. The Scots in your voice.'

'I can do a wee display if you like.' And he starts singing,

'0 y'cannae throw y'r granny off a bus—'

For a moment we have reclaimed the ability to be frivolous.

Another time—'Jennie, you've told me nothing about any lovers.'

'One. Very brief.'

'Why brief?'

'It was a mistake. There's not the love to sustain it.' He is waiting for more. I say, 'He's a South African exile. We're friends, we were both lonely, it seemed silly not to. But it doesn't work for me, that.'

'No one else?'

'Not unless you count an offer I refused. The man I told you about before. Muhib. He followed me to Nairobi, bearing gifts of weekends in the Rift Valley.'

He is entertained. 'How long did that one last?'

'It didn't happen.' Then, 'Neil, you're asking like you *want* me to have had lots of lovers.'

'I want to know you're living your life fully, not limiting yourself pointlessly because of something I can't give you.'

And later again, unable to let it go, 'Jennie, your Rift Valley lover—how long were you with him, in the post-Manchester time?'

'A few months only.'

'And you ended it?'

'Yes. We get on easily—he's fun and we like some of the same things. For a while I was swept up with loving him. But there wasn't enough substance.'

'What kind of substance?'

I laugh at his insistence. 'Now it's you wanting the whole thing.' But he's not being dislodged. 'Tell me.'

OK then, he can have it. 'I was measuring him against you, Neil. He didn't get past the starting line.'

He has the answer he did not want—it is immediately obvious that he feels it as a pressure. Partly to relieve it, I say, 'He wasn't enough like me either. In the ways you and I are the same.'

Curiosity distracts him. 'Specify.'

I know exactly what I mean—I always have known. But it's a question of how to fit it to words. I say slowly, 'Maybe, that even when we're having most fun, it comes from the fact that we both have a serious involvement with life.'

He considers. 'I like that.'

'It's true, isn't it?'

'Yes.' He has more to say. Now it's me tensing slightly, getting ready for I don't know what. He says quietly, 'It also defines neatly what I've always liked in Teresa.'

She is with us again, and constantly. I am glad at least that I saw her those couple of times and have some image of this woman who is so central to him. I see her full, definite figure on the stage, telling the audience about Victor Jara. Telling it straight, no attempt to manipulate our feelings, but just because of that, choking us all up...And then those few minutes I saw her when she came to collect Juan. I am glad of those too, that I saw the warmth in her, the humour, courage, all the things Neil is telling me about her. It makes it easier to be with him in what he is feeling, rather than excluded by it. But it is difficult for all that. Her constant presence. Having to learn that there is no way to be close to Neil without incorporating her—more than that, without giving her needs first place. And it is difficult to admit to these feelings in myself when I know that her needs are for the moment by every humane consideration more urgent than mine.

What is most difficult is not being open with Neil about how I am reacting. The pleasure of being with him is above all of being a *whole* person—mind, spirit, body, emotions, all equally and fully engaged.

But we have so little time. I am afraid now to say anything that will push him back into tension.

Just once, I tried. We were lying together in that slow, relaxed closeness that comes after lovemaking. Half an hour still before we would have to get up...the illusion of time enough...

'Neil, before Teresa was ill—what was it like?'

'What was what like?'

'I mean, how much together were you?'

'Not as together as this. Not anything like.'

I don't want to press him but he knows himself that isn't enough of an answer. He says, 'Ask me questions, Jennie. I don't know what you want to know.'

'Is it every day, spending time together?'

'Depends. Some weeks. Others maybe only once in the week.

We both travel a lot—we try not to be away together so one of us is here for Juan. That means it can be weeks with hardly seeing each other.'

'And when you are both here? The separate houses thing—how does that work, for meals and things?'

'We assume we each have our own space, and time. Our work times are all over the place, neither of us has regular meals. We see each other odd half hours, between coming and going. Occasionally if we feel it's a long time since we had a real conversation we'll try and organise to both be free for a morning.'

'And the sleeping together?'

His tone becomes vaguer. He says, elliptically, 'It just developed, like I told you when we first talked about it. And not that often.'

'How often?'

'Jennie

'Neil, please—'

Reluctantly he says, 'Maybe once a month, at the height.' Then, some vehemence in his voice now, 'I told you, we don't either of us feel driven to find opportunities. If we're spending time together anyway and it happens, it happens. In the last year there's been very little. Nothing to do with her illness—that's come on suddenly. Just—it hasn't happened much. We've both been busy. And it's never in the least like you and me.'

The vehemence has an anxious tinge—defending himself against the charge of causing me pain. His charge, against himself. I say, 'Take it easy, Neil. I'm OK.'

He looks at me sharply, as if he finds it intrusive to be known so well. Then his eyes gradually relax. We lie quietly together for a few minutes, simply absorbing the other's presence. Becoming safe again. He says, gently now, 'You've no need to feel that kind of jealousy, Jennie—it's a different kind of love altogether.'

The gentleness makes me want to cry. My instinct tells me that would be disastrous. I say—tentatively, because I am still afraid he will retreat, 'Neil, I'm not coping as well as I thought I was. We don't have much time left. For the rest of today I want to be alone with you. Without Teresa.'

I should have known better. For the rest of the day he does not talk about Teresa again, but she is still there, for both of us. Asking him to close her off was like saying, There's a part of *you* I want you to keep out of sight, because I can't handle it.

Separate lives, to which we must return. We practise each time he goes off to teach or visit Teresa or be with Juan. I fill the spaces with my own people—taking Michael to the swings, phoning Paula, a concert with Muhib, talking to Megan and her children as we get a meal ready.

Derek is the only one of my friends who has any success in lifting me out of preoccupation. It's obvious why—he alone has some idea of that other life of mine and therefore of what motivates me to want to go back to it. We talk animatedly about Nyika as we take advantage of a rare spell of thin sun to sit in Russell Square and drink coffee from the kiosk. We watch a party of schoolchildren on an outing, taking their lunch break in the square. A group of girls playing a counting game—One potato, two potato, three potato, four—and talk flippantly about its ritual significance—initiation into the circle of belonging (take care or you're out)—ring-a-ring-o-roses (we all fall down.) 'They play the same games in Lusaka,' I say. It's a children's culture, leaping continents—it just takes a couple of English children in the school. No adult teaches them.'

He says, 'I may get to Lusaka next year. There's a possibility of a research grant to do more work in Nyika over the summer. Maybe I'll detour to see you.'

'Forget Lusaka, I'll join you in Nyika. You promised to take me as your assistant—remember?'

He meets me half way in fantasy creation. 'You find time to learn chiTumbuka fluently between now and July, and it's a deal.

With two African languages already I'm sure it'll be no problem.'

It's a help to be talking in this light way about the future—what he'll be doing, what I'll be doing. On an impulse that surprises me I say, 'Derek, I think I've got myself into a mess.' And I tell him, unemotionally. There's someone I love. There's someone else he is with who needs him. His work is here. I'm going back, and at the moments when I'm not totally absorbed in him I want to go back. Each statement makes sense on its own, and none of it makes any sense together.

Three days left. Two days. It is almost over and we have only just begun. I do not seem able to make good departures. I am once again glued by emotional need, half my skin coming away as I prepare to wrench myself free to go.

This time it is obvious that he is going to find it as painful as I. Normally he is so practised at protecting himself against what he cannot have, but this has not been a normal time. Two weeks is not long but in two weeks as we have used them you travel a great distance. We come home to something basic in ourselves each time we come together again after each small separation. The light is expressed always in his face, increasingly in his words, and I feel it in the lightness of my whole being. We are awed at the depth of feeling we have each evoked in the other. We touch each other's naked bodies with delight and tenderness and longing, learning to know, awakening to subtle changes, celebrating the desire for union of the spirit. We hold up mirrors to each other's inner self, and see ourselves reflected not as we know we are—full of insecurities and imperfections—but as we know we can be, made perfect by love.

Nothing remotely like this has ever happened to either of us. We know it is an experience potentially available to every human being, and also that we are fortunate beyond what either of us could have hoped for that it has been given to us. And now we are about to lose it again.

We begin to talk about what will happen when I have gone. He does not want to, neither do I. There is nothing to say that can make any difference. But we do it because we know we must.

He says, 'All this last year, I've known we were just putting it on ice. But I didn't want to think about what that meant, because I couldn't see what to do about it. Not ever being able to talk—Being so aware of you, and knowing I still knew so little about huge areas of your life—You there, me here—And now—'

And now it's going to be the same. Except that Teresa is ill and will need him more than before. And that I am starting a longer-term commitment to a life I have chosen and that makes sense of much of who I am. And that we now know far better than before the power of what there is between us, and can find no way of incorporating into these already allocated lives.

I say, 'There's no question of going back to postcards.'

But that's about all it's possible to sort out.

3

I stand on the pavement across from the hospital and watch him disappear into it for the last time before I leave. Any serenity that I have schooled myself to achieve has deserted me. I feel I am watching a strong swimmer being pulled further out to sea by a current he does not seem able to escape. It is the very thing I love most in him that weighs him down, so that he is pulled each moment further away. I don't even know if Teresa will really need him in the way he thinks once she is well again, or if it is his own fear that makes him feel this is a commitment which excludes all others. But either way he cannot extricate himself. I have no option but to let go, and stand on the shore, and watch him battle against the current that drags him out.

I speak to no one on the flight. Nairobi is scarcely manageable. I open the viola case to check it's still there, but don't even try to play. Ali watches, disappointed. I make myself go through the motions with the people I had promised to see. Then I lie awake most of the night, tense with misery. I go to the airport earlier than I need next morning, so no one can phone me.

It is only as the plane begins to come down over Lusaka that I feel the first stirrings of some response other than trying to blank out life. I press my face close to the window. The land is so vast, so empty, the small signs of human settlement so insignificant. Can this really be where I have chosen to put myself? But the hugeness of space is comforting. A place where you can be left alone, without other people pressing in on you...We are coming in lower...Can see the trees now, each separate...I left a landscape brown and dusty at the end of a long dry season—I return to one transformed by a month of rain—the earth waterlogged, green tangles of growth rushing up to meet us.

We land. It is done. I am here, and he is there.

I have begun to cry.

I wait till everyone else has got off the plane before I get up and follow them. Ntombi is waiting to greet me. Her hug is warm, unavoidably alive. I am hugging back, and crying again. She doesn't ask why, she just strokes my hair, packs me into the car, and we set off for town.

Flamboyant trees line the road in red, flowers above, fallen petals below. The gardens slip past the car window, cream silk of frangipani blossoms dancing between a light blue haze of jacaranda and the dense red velvet of poinsettia. But the road is crumbling, mud packs of debris washed up to the sides.

'You didn't hear?' Ntombi asks. 'Floods. Terrible floods. Cairo Road is like a river every time it rains. Kanyama's half washed away. People drowning—we were wading through all the shit from the pit latrines trying to get their bodies.' We pass the show grounds; it's like a refugee camp, covered in tents.

'There's something about this place,' I say, the first thing I've volunteered. 'The sense of crisis is built-in.'

'That's not this place,' she says. 'That's life.'

We pull up outside her house. Cassia trees with yellow tulip flowers, weeping wattle with yellow candles. We carry out small wooden stools, hollowed out bits of tree. Their legs sink into the mud and we wobble precariously. The banana fronds drip still from last night's rain, the bougainvillaea calls loud and purple from over the kitchen door, sensual pleasure, wooing me out of sadness. We drink fresh lemonade Ntombi's made.

People start popping in to see if I have arrived. Winston, with stories of what's been happening to thc people we used to share a house with. Someone from the school—'The children keep asking when you're coming back,' she says…

Beyond the circle of people the pawpaw trees are silhouetted against the sky. The light is metallic, building up for the afternoon's downpour…Fernando arrives, news of the camp. Saved from the worst flooding because it's on high ground, but the temporary huts half washed away. People too demoralised to rebuild—they're crowding into the couple of buildings that have survived intact. 'There's an emergency meeting tomorrow,' he says, 'we need you to be there'…

My people, my work, my place.

BOOK THREE

Listen, really listen

Create within yourself an echo of the drum—

then *you will start to dance*

Chapter 1

After midnight. The house quiet. Deep dark through the window above my desk—curtain open so I can feel the warm night air, sticky with humidity. Scent of flowering shrubs, too many to disentangle. Sounds of night insects.

Ntombi wakes and stumbles in to see what I am doing, here at my typewriter at such an hour. 'Go to bed,' she says.

'It's cool at night,' I tell her.

She looks unimpressed. I say lamely, 'It wakes me, wanting to be written.'

She grunts. The real question, as we both know, is: What is 'it'? But I'm not talking about it, and she's not asking.

She stomps out to the bathroom. Sound of peeing, water running, footsteps back to her bed. Just me again with the night air.

> —Time's lost shape since you left, Jennie. I do all the same things, but nothing is the same. Our times together have all been so *short*, and never normal time. Always intense, with you about to fly off somewhere, off the map. Your presence illuminates everything. When you take it away, it's a struggle to find my own light again—

Daylight, and back to my work, my people; no time for useless reflection.

Post takes at least a week between London and Lusaka, more often ten days. It is collected from the post office by a driver, who then goes off on a round of other chores before bringing it back. Sorted by a secretary who sees no cause to hurry. If there's nothing in my in-tray by lunchtime I'm still not sure something hasn't come because she may not have got round to sorting it yet, so I go back again at the end of the day. When there is a letter I can always tell even before I get near enough to see the handwriting on the envelope. There's an office-full of eyes watching—I put it in my bag, and the moment I'm out of the door I stop to open it, reading it twice before I can move on—

> —Teresa came home yesterday. I take my useless anxieties for her out in constantly boiling kettles. Hot water bottles, more cups of tea than she could possibly want. I remember now that this is what my mother used to do. Certain things you can't escape. Teresa just laughs at me and tells me to drink the tea myself—

His life, his people. I want to know it all, but it churns up feelings like the wheels of the landrover that gets stuck in the mud on almost every journey to the camp—

I want a life that is centred, I have been telling myself for so long, not one lived primarily in absence. Yet I have gone and stuck myself here and he is there. I hump blankets into vehicles and challenge bureaucrats to account for the money that has been collected for people displaced by the floods, and nothing could be more involving. Yet more than ever it is somewhere else that my real life moves. I go to bed exhausted then wake three hours later, completely awake and needing to talk to Neil through my typewriter, to write him my life, as thousands of miles away in the midwinter night he writes me his—

> —Her Chilean friends are constantly around her, wearing her out with depressing news about the situation back home. I feel like booting them out, the lot of them. She says I'm not culturally attuned. She'll have them sitting on her bed and talking for hours and be tired as a result, rather than not have them. So I leave them to it and retire to my own room, feeling rebelliously Celtic. Or Viking Or whatever. Juan is

> sufficiently a product of having grown up in Britain to share my point of view so we have a bit of male solidarity in the kitchen.

I can hardly believe it, Jennie, you've got me laughing again—

The floods have had one good result—the camp is being closed. Ntombi's house has become like a refugee camp itself, but she and Winston and I are gradually finding places for each of them—mostly as living-in baby sitters in the homes of expatriates. Winston calls it the refugee version of house-sitting. They're with other people, they can practise English, and they eat. Now it's the college administration I'm doing battle with, to get them to make space for students who have passed no exams and constantly break the rules because they don't understand them. They'd forgive us anything if we could keep our class registers neat, like pinning down moths so you know exactly how many you have. But the numbers in the classes float up and down chaotically, a barometer of the intensity of the crises in countries all around us. News of renewed fighting in Tete—and two weeks later we have a new group of Mozambicans, as tense as the Ovambo women were when I first met them. The war in Rhodesia/Zimbabwe seems to have peaked—the Zimbabweans are restless, making plans to return, but no one knows if it will be half a year or three. They are gone from the classes, then return two weeks later.

One last trip to the camp. By next week it will be abandoned by all except the guards, whom no one has yet got round to ordering off somewhere else. I'm going to miss it—not the camp, but the time alone getting there, watching the space constantly open up in front of me. The road has disintegrated. Two hours of struggling and the left back wheel is spinning uselessly as I rev the engine, sinking further on each attempt. No villages nearby; too far from the main road to walk and hitch. I spend the night in the vehicle, which rocks as the rain batters against it. The dark is darker than I have ever experienced, clouds blocking the moon.

I am not afraid, for when it's so obvious there is nothing to be done you just accept things. I huddle in the blanket that we keep always in the back for emergencies, and move to avoid the places where the roof leaks. One stage closer to the people whose homes are eroding around them.

First light. Fernando arrives in another vehicle, with two men and ropes and a thermos of coffee. 'I'd have come last night,' he says, 'but there was no point trying. Couldn't move till the rain stopped.' When they've pulled me out he says, 'Enoch can drive that one back—you come back with me.'

Alone now together on this road we have travelled so many times, he takes a hand off the steering wheel to take mine and say quietly, 'Jennie, your mother phoned. Your father has had a heart attack.'

'He's OK,' Fernando says, and he has to repeat it several times on the journey back. 'She said he's OK, Jennie, just weak.' But it takes Mom's voice on the phone to shift the panic. 'He's looking very old,' she says, and she sounds old herself. 'We were about to go to see Richard. Now the doctor says there's no question of travelling.'

He can't get to Richard, Richard can't get to him That makes two of us unreachable now. Three, if you count Peter.

I read through piles of Mom's old letters, immersing myself in the detail of her life, focusing properly for the first time. I have hardly any from Dad—he left Mom to do the writing for both of them. And I? I wrote, but to Mom-and-Dad as if they were a single entity. I need to break the habit of years, to find out, so belatedly, who *each* of them is, what we might have been to the other as fellow adults if we had been able to continue in each other's lives. To value Dad properly while I still have the chance. And Mom, facing the possibility of being alone—what kind of life will she be able to make for herself? More alone than me, because starting so late.

I pick my way through the debris of washed-away homes, and I see her in Bloemfontein, moving now always in fear of loss. I have never had that shared life with the person I love but I have touched it briefly and I know for sure it is what I want. I become intensely aware of her, as if she were somewhere near, but just out of sight—round the corner, maybe. I feel I am beginning to know her, just by the strength of my imagining. Her sadness gets right inside me, till I can no longer tell it from my own.

2

It's a strange many-layered awareness I move in. The glaring light of Lusaka, the satisfying demands of work I know I do well. The house where Ntombi and I make our second-best partnership, each grateful for the other but each here only because we cannot be with the person we would have chosen first. And then the other life that no one around me sees, the one that makes its demands on Neil, and whose details I follow as intensely as if they were my own, for ultimately they may determine my own—

> —Teresa wants to move back to her flat. She's not ready, and it'll make life unnecessarily complicated. Here I can do things for her when they're needed, and get on with my work in between. When she moves I'll have to keep making journeys down the road, only to arrive when she doesn't need me. But I can't get her to see it—

I search beneath the words for clues, as once in Swaziland I scoured the pages of each day's newspaper to find where my future might lie—

> —Juan doesn't say much, but he's apprehensive about the responsibility. Him coming back here after school suits us all. I position myself in the kitchen, he makes a preliminary raid on the fridge, and once he's concluded that he won't starve after all, out come the things that have happened in his day. If I don't see him till later all I get is a large

teenage body slumped in front of the telly, with as much to communicate as a box of cornflakes—

He is *afraid* of life moving him on, afraid of losing his excuse for going on as he is. Afraid of what the demands of real intimacy might do to his daily life. 'Neil,' I write, 'you're building dams to block out thought. Teresa herself is saying she needs space, and you're backing away from even *asking* where that would leave us'—

—Of course I ask the question, and constantly. What's troubling you is that I haven't yet come up with the *answer* you want, and I still can't see how to without unacceptable levels of damage. And if you don't know that I long for it to be simple just as you do, I don't know how to make you know—

The rhythms cut across each other, a future that can't be kickstarted into happening, a present that demands attention and in doing so distracts me from the things I cannot resolve. 'Transition Courses' is what they call our classes and that about sums up my state. 'Some transitions last a long time,' I tell Fernando. He smiles; no comment.

Transition, but to what? Through all the negotiations no one, neither UN official nor Zambian bureaucrat, seems to ask. They see only that political exiles need to have their time filled so they will not brew discontent. I am here with my budget for part-time tutors; what we do with it, no one cares.

We do the obvious thing, which is what the refugees themselves decide. Ntombi does an evening class in Grammar (filling in the gaps)—little relationship to life, but everyone wants certificates. Anyway grammar is comforting, rules to follow when everything else is shifting around you. Motor mechanics' training—a sure income-earner in a city that imports too many vehicles and doesn't know what to do with them when they break down. A group starts producing a newsletter, a world of news gleaned just from interviewing each other. I persuade Radio Zambia to send someone to train them to make radio programmes. Another group says they want to study international law—preparing to run the independent states that still have to come into being. I fix up for them to use the university library and get a couple of the lecturers producing reading lists. The rest is taken care of by the thirst engendered by years spent in schools with only one interpretation of history, and that one manifestly false.

I suppose it could have been any work, any people, but these are special. They have been in prison, have run before gunfire, have watched people they love being killed. They carry the guilt of still living and have walked over more borders of the spirit than I have ever had to deal with. Daily they present me with a level of personal crisis that puts my own dilemmas, Neil's and mine, in humbling perspective. Here am I landed among them, and I seem to have manoeuvred myself into a position where I can do at least small things to make some difference. Not of course to the scale of the crises, but to their ability to be resilient.

Getting even the simplest things set up involves skirmishes with institutional rules and bureaucratic inertia, but that suits me excellently. I am in need of a fight. Too much practice of serenity in my private life. I am on the side of courage, for changing the things that so *obviously* needed to be changed.

It was a time of generous spending, of life, of energy, of time itself. I loved it, every day of it, loved the giving away of love in so many directions. I stopped trying to reconcile it with the idea of being with Neil. He was there in the midnight hours when I sat alone in the still dark, sharing with him anything I thought or felt at that moment. Knowing I was loved and received gave me zest and fortified me with humour in the daily life in which he had no part. I had never given up on the vision of a permanence in which I would sleep each night as we had on that one night before I first left for Nairobi, our bodies touching all the way down, and wake to find each other, would go to daily lives that were independent and full but never essentially separate, and come back each day to the pleasure of small shared domesticities. Would challenge and become indignant and make up, eyes laughing and reading each other's, windows into the shared consciousness that fuelled it all—

But he was thousands of miles away sharing his domesticities with two other people, and I was here, spending life generously—

—Watching a group of children play in the mudpools as I cycle through Kalingalinga, my viola case strapped to my back. They turn and stare, clothes ragged, hair matted, and call out as I get near. I skid to a halt, they gather round and ask the inevitable questions. How is it I speak their language? What's that thing on my back? A thing to make music with, I said. Where are you going? To my friend's house. She has one of these too, and we play together sometimes. 'Take it out and play,' they said. But their hands were grubby from never having enough water to wash with, and I pleaded needing to be off or I would be late. I cycled away, and felt mean-spirited all afternoon as I made music with Fernando's wife, Ana, in her spacious, comfortable living room. It would take so little to stimulate them—

> —But now I might have found a way. The headmaster has been asking if I'll revive the music group, on Saturdays. My conditions are, one, I'm really busy so I'll need a group of parents to help; and two, the Kalingalinga children come too. Let's see what he makes of that. He's not going to be so keen on letting in children with sores on their legs. But I'm in a good bargaining position and enjoying it.

The answer came back,

—I'm afraid the headmaster hasn't a chance.

—You clearly have small experience of headmasters.

—But large experience of your capacity to move immovable objects.

But I was not managing to move Neil. He couldn't think further than my coming back to London on leave at the end of my year's contract. He had marked the whole of November and December clear in his diary, he said. He had done that the day after I left, he said, and he would keep it free of bookings till he knew my dates—

So that's the best he can do, I thought, plan a holiday. I put the letter back in its envelope, feeling suddenly hurt, angry, abandoned, not knowing what I was holding on for—

The phone rang. It was the headmaster, to say 'Yes' to the Kalingalinga children. A balance lurched within me—

Fernando came in, carrying budget papers. Would I be willing to add four months to my contract? The work was obviously going to continue, and it would be easier to extend now while he was doing budgets through to the end of the financial year. The balance took another lurch—There was a life here that kept offering itself and I was tired of saying 'Maybe', while I waited for Neil to sort himself out. *Something* needed to move.

I said 'Yes' to Fernando, feeling momentarily defiant and clear; and in that clarity I wrote to tell Neil.

It took me less than a day to realise that I had gone too far. What had I been *thinking* of, to add, unilaterally, four more months to the time we must necessarily be apart? I, who had constantly told him he had no business making decisions on behalf of both of us? What if I had tipped a balance in *him*, but the wrong way?

I watched the post for a reply the way I had done in my first weeks back...Nothing. Days overdue...Now a week... Two...I faced, perhaps for the first time, a recognition of how untenable our situation was. His silence was lacerating me, as presumably my confrontation had lacerated him.

A letter, finally—

—I didn't want to write while I was angry, and it took me a while to realise I had no right to be. The responsibility to find a way out of this is mine; that I always knew. But you have faced me with what should already have been obvious, that if I take too long about it, you will get on with your own life without me.

But there was no undoing what had been done; on both sides. The weeks went by and he wrote no more about ways out. Last November was beginning to seem a long time ago.

3

I watch a messenger on a bicycle wobble to a halt at the gate of Ntombi's garden. Watch him prop up his bike against the fence, see the words *British Council* on the side of his bag. He walks towards me to hand me a piece of paper…A telex. For *me?* I've never even seen a telex before…From Derek—

> —Jennie excuse pigeon post, this is urgent. Research grant came through. Will be in Nyika July to September. Research assistant can only do two months. Can you take off month of July and join me? Your chance to observe music in action. Telex answer soonest via British Council. ChiTumbuka grammar already sent. Money regrettably not great but Nyika should make up for it—

It's madness. My job is more than full-time, I need nothing extra to keep me fulfilled. Anyway, Derek's out of his mind—how does he think I can learn chiTumbuka in three months?

April to June—Intense preparation for Nyika. Getting up at dawn for two hours' language study before the work day begins. Searching for a chiTumbuka speaker to practise with—eventually finding one, a night watchman who sleeps by day but is pleased to have company at night…A cocoon-like experience, sitting huddled in the dark over his little brazier, face and hands chafing in the cold dry-season nights that have followed the unusually heavy rains, speaking haltingly in a language that I use with just this one person…

And then home, to start in earnest to analyse the songs on Derek's tapes that have crossed the continent with me. The rhythms are no longer elusive—I can't any more see what the problem was. But the tunes—there's still something there I know I'm missing, the thing that would have made sense of what I was confronted with in the village—songs that to me seemed different but to them were variations on the same tune. Ntombi comes in, listens for a few moments, says, 'Play that last one again.' Then she sings along, casually. It's not even her music but she knows instinctively what will work as an answering phrase to what the lead singer has called.

'*How* do you know?' I ask. She thinks that's an absurd question. There's a Zimbabwean saying, she says—

If you can walk, you can dance
If you can talk, you can sing.

So simple. But I can't get there her way. I need a way of notating this music more accurately, then I'll be able to take my time over studying it, see how the patterns relate to each other. I post off to Neil one of my attempted transcriptions with a copy of the tape—'See what you can do with this for me.' Three weeks, and I have his transcription. It cuts through one of my main problems by giving each line of the tune its own time signature rather than trying to fit them into one. I would never have thought of that. I become excited and try the same technique on other tapes. I copy those and send them off to him for checking. They're always back again within three weeks—whatever else is going on in his work, he's making time for the transcriptions the moment they arrive. 'I could get hooked on this,' he writes—

We are back to the high of working together.

A moment of childish panic when my birthday reminds me

I am twenty-nine. Being in a still-transitional state of life in your twenties is OK, but approach thirty and you see the sand dribbling steadily through the narrow waist of the egg-timer. I take a roll-call of my friends—all settled, in chosen lives. That's what I thought I was doing when I found Lusaka, found this work—*This* is my life, I told them all. At some moments it is, at others it is still a stage on the way to the real thing. When I don't know which it is I get confused and temporarily anxious. But then I am beguiled by the light and the sounds and the colours, all the things that have assailed my senses and made me glad to be alive each day I wake to the African sun, ever since the day I had to flee and discovered that the good things you have always taken for granted can be suddenly taken from you.

July. Flying to Lilongwe, being met by Derek in a landrover covered in dust. Heading north…Arriving—to the women singing the songs they know I know. Being adopted by Kiluleli again, followed by the young girls and children, who are amazed that I have forgotten their names, and who immediately want to start unpacking my rucksack. The old woman who showed me how to weave mats—she talks at me again, a long speech—*and this time I understand!* She is scolding me, saying, 'It's time somebody found you a man, a grown woman like you.' And this time I can reply—take her hands and say, 'Ma, if I had a man I wouldn't be here learning from you.'

She announces that she will tell one of the old stories, for us to record on that black box. Night, and we gather round, not just us but half the village. *Panangotele*, she begins—this is what they told; the others answer, *tili tonse*—we are with you, we are listening—

There was a certain man (We are listening)
Who married with a woman (We are listening)

An ancient tale, the standard ingredients. A man with two wives, jealousy, magic—

And this man was very powerful (We are listening)
He could take thunder and put it in a pot—

Is she trying to tell me something?

'Focus on children's songs,' Derek says. 'They're a simple measure of changing times. Any song children have learnt is by definition still in active use.' The children follow me and never tire. Adult voices call after them, commanding. They have work to do like anyone else, but they are back as soon as they are let loose, for my presence offers rare licence. The girls chatter animatedly, reminding each other of new songs they can give me—snatches of what the women sing at weddings, or their older sisters at initiation ceremonies; and the boys, songs of fighting and heroes. They love nothing more than repetition, and make the most of having found an adult who lets them instruct her instead of instructing. Those who have been to school come out with what they have been taught—songs in Chichewa, and one so strange in words and tune that I assume it must be in the language of a neighbouring tribe—then suddenly realise it is *Jingle bells*. They sing it with gusto, offering me my own music. Do I sound as strange when I sing theirs? And what can they possibly make of a one-horse open sleigh here in the middle of Africa?

We move beyond borrowed songs, to what they call and sing when no one listens. I play back what I have recorded, while they cluster around, close as they can get. They take turns to press the pause and reverse buttons while I begin to note down tentative drafts. They peer over my writing. Those who can read a little exclaim at finding it is nothing but a series of dots and lines rather than words. I sing it back to them, testing tune or rhythm by making deliberate changes. They vie with each other to correct me when I haven't got it right; if they let it pass, I know it's another way you can sing that tune…

Finding my way beneath the surface differences of another musical tradition, to touch again a music that is part of the tasks and emotions of daily life—And here, so far from my own daily work, I look back at what I have been doing in Lusaka, and ask myself how it is possible that I have never thought of using music in my work with the exile students?...The end of a month of absorption, and I emerge from the cocoon of the village to travel back in the dusty landrover to Lilongwe, thinking, All of the people I am going back to have within them the music they have been hearing from childhood, and using to mark all significant events in their lives... They knew, the teachers knew, I knew—how was it we all boxed it off, as if that connection of life and music was now broken?...I fly into Lusaka, thinking, The *whole point* of the classes is to give a voice to people whose disrupted lives have left them with so much they need to express—

It's all coming together. *This* will be my real work.

We start making music. The motor mechanics trainees and the international law students and the beginners in the English classes, the kind of music they have known all their lives how to make—but they use it now to express what they feel about exile, war, life and death; the longing for what is lost, hope for what may still be possible. 'What the composer chiefly does is create the space,' Neil once said—and into the space they bring the songs of Ovamboland, the dances of Zambezia...We search for instruments. My ethnomusicologist friend at the university helps us track down some *timbila* xylophones from Mozambique, big ones with gourds below each wooden slat, the kind I once told Neil I wanted to play. Ntombi uncovers an incredible singing voice—I've heard it in fragments before but never till now in sustained song. It isn't particularly special when she speaks, but now she lets it loose to teach us liberation songs that knock us all over.

Hoihere mambo—Vaitamba chigendeya—

Yes, our people used to dance the joy dance—
You can't believe it, but they used to.

She spends her weekends gathering the women to practise dances—

War unleashes suffering, swallows the innocent
I cannot keep these happenings from my mind…

I learn with them. It's like Swaziland and Nyika but better, because there's more equality, somehow. Ntombi's songs are liberating something in me, bringing it home.

Some of the men begin talking about needing guitars. There's a whole strand of music they can't make without them. I badger a director of one of the mining companies into donating funds, and suddenly we are listening to the songs of the people in towns—the *kizomba* sound from Angola, Zimbabwean *chimurenga* music that the white Rhodesian officials have tried to ban, but that pulses undaunted over the night air, its messages hidden in allusive 'deep' Shona that the censors wouldn't understand even if they got someone to translate…while the people just keep dancing, to the sound of acoustic guitars playing ancient mbira rhythms…

The concept takes shape. A liberation celebration, that's what we're moving towards. An event to celebrate the life that is in us and sent us into exile. To sing of the homes that are lost, and of those whose lives have been squandered; and of the courage we will still have to find, to change what remains unchanged.

4

November. The earth is parched, temperatures boiling. The rains are late. In the open-air theatre dust rises wherever people move. Trucks arrive with equipment, buses with students. Engineers from Radio Zambia set up loudspeakers. Now the children start to arrive—the Saturday scratch orchestra—children from the school ferried by the parents with cars, the Kalingalinga children in twos and threes on foot. The mbira group, the penny whistle band. The trees are ahead of the rains and have broken out already into their annual celebration of colour—as if they have sniffed the still distant humidity moving in slowly from the far away ocean, and they know before we do that it is time to celebrate. Flamboyant, frangipani, jacaranda, cassia, the same flourish that greeted me almost a year ago when I had wrenched myself away from Neil and felt as if nothing could ever make me smile again. Well here I am, rejoicing with the trees, without even having to try.

There are groups now practising under trees. Publicly this is a celebration of unity—behind the scenes it has been a Pandora's box of national and factional rivalry. The Zambian national dance troupe is miffed that its now tired traditional dances are being upstaged by the Zimbabwean band's more dynamic guitars and saxophones. Agreeing the final line-up required the negotiating skill of a political conference table. It's a major achievement that we're all here, milling about together, laughing, talking. We have given up all idea of a final run through; this is an African celebration—the music will take off spontaneously, whatever the programme says. I stand at one side, and let it happen.

Almost over. Ntombi is teaching all the hundreds of people gathered here the response that we will sing after each line of her song—*ndopatigere pano*—'So this is our home now' . It's a song of the townships, she says, of exile; of people who have left behind homes in the villages and now squat at the edges of affluence—

The scorching sun comes and fries us—ndopatigere pano
The rains beat down and we have no shelter—ndopatigere pano

A group of women from the classes files singing and clapping in to join her, in the dusty space surrounded by people. Her voice sings the line, they call the response, their bodies bending and clapping and twisting as they move round in a circle, the ancient women's dance of all Africa, maybe of the whole world. As she passes where I am standing Ntombi reaches out to grab my hand and pulls me in so I too become part of the dance—

The wind tosses us about like dry leaves—ndopatigere pano
The cold is in us and we are numb—ndopatigere pano

The words pull with pain but the singing is loud, strong, no trace of sentimentality, rooting me here among uprooted people. Someone from the crowd calls out a new response—same meaning, but in Zulu instead of Shona. The women call it back, voices lifting it out of the dust our feet are making. Now Ovambo—Xhosa—Ndebele—all of us using each others' languages—

Until finally even Ntombi is tired. She turns, gives a wide gesture with her arms; the moving circle slows down. Someone ululates; the place breaks out in a chaos of noise and cheering. Ntombi turns to me, and we are hugging each other, laughing and crying at the same time. I disengage—look up—and there is Neil.

Chapter 2

He is standing to one side watching, a look on his face that stills all sensation—I can only describe it as loving. Loving what has been happening, loving that I have been part of making it. I am so stunned to see him that I do not move, but just stare. The moment stops, takes forever. I notice in a detached way that he is with someone I vaguely recognise—Adrian, that's it, the man from the British Council from whom I collected the language course books for Nyika. Then Adrian is dismissed from my mind and the question of how Neil got here and why becomes marginal. He is here, that is enough.

He moves forward towards me, breaking the frozen moment. Time shifts into normal gear again. He says, 'We seem to make a habit of appearing at each other's performances.'

I feel suddenly light headed. 'Did you hear the mbiras? It's what you said, remember? Extraordinary fusion music—the middle of Africa!'

'I heard it all,' he says. 'I'm bowled over.'

We are surrounded by hundreds of people milling about, and we are alone. I am learning his face again, the way his eyes hold laughter, which is only another form of love. Watching my face to read it, as I am reading his. I say, urgently, 'Tell me—how did you get here?'

'The British Council offered me a fellowship.' His head gestures towards Adrian, who has been standing discreetly a few paces away and is now in conversation with someone else.

'Neil, how—?'

We are standing so near, yet not even touching. He's aware of being in a strange place, all the people around us, not knowing what's possible. Keeping his tone light, detached as the words we speak—'Working on your transcriptions tempted me. I decided it was time I took learning about African music a little more seriously.'

'They *offered* it to you? Out of the blue?'

The laughter in his eyes strengthens. 'Not quite. I made enquiries and applied. Along with a lot of other people. I was lucky.'

'And they offered you *Zambia?*'

'They offered me a cultural exchange. The choice of country was mine.' He is laughing now, outright. 'I would not have been interested in going just anywhere, Jennie.'

'Why didn't you *tell* me?'

'You were off in Nyika when I heard I'd got it. By the time you came back the Zambian government was doing its best to louse the whole thing up. This classifies as research and they couldn't get organised to give me research clearance. Until almost the last minute it looked like it wasn't going to happen. I didn't want to risk setting you up and not being able to deliver. Again.' He pauses, watching my face. Then, vehemently, 'You've no idea what the bureaucracy's like.'

The absurdity of this statement sends me into giggles. 'I do, Neil, that's how I earn my daily bread!' I am airy with excitement, unreal, as if I might take off. I reach out for his hands—firm and material. 'You've just arrived?'

'This morning. I've spent the day getting Adrian to drive me around trying to find you. I should have known better on today of all days but I couldn't stand it—having finally arrived and still you weren't anywhere. In the end Adrian struck and told me I'd just have to wait till tonight.'

'You're staying with him?'

'For tonight. Then in a place called Roma—a house the British Council uses for visitors.'

The words pass between us. Vital, but almost irrelevant. It's still our eyes doing the essential checking out. I am almost afraid to ask the most important question of all. He does it for me. Tightening his hold on my hands he says, 'I have two months, Jennie. The two months I marked clear for you the day after you left London.'

Two months he will be here and then he will be gone again. Nothing will have changed. But it does not matter what happens afterwards. Neil is here, I am here. Now is enough.

Sounds of vehicles starting up. The crowd beginning to thin. We need to get somewhere quiet. Again he seems to know what I'm about to say before I say it. 'Adrian's expecting me back tonight but we could take an hour or two now. If you're not too tired.'

The idea that I might say I was too tired is so ridiculous that we both start laughing. He says, 'I've got the use of a British Council car. You say where.'

'Just wait while I find Ntombi.' I turn to look for her—then turn back again, caught by a childlike fear that if I leave him for a moment he will disappear as suddenly as he came. 'Stay *exactly* there,' I say.

'It was a long way to come. I'm not likely to think better of it now!'

Ntombi is packing drums into the back of a van. I say, 'The most extraordinary thing has happened.' She too is laughing. 'I saw,' she says. She turns to lift one of the heavier drums. I become aware that I'm just standing there, letting her do it all. 'Here, let me,' I say and we lift it together. She says, 'And if he's the one who's responsible for all that midnight writing, tell him I say why did he take so long getting here?'

She's going back with some of the others, she says, and she'll come on later. Neil and I go to his car. 'You drive,' he says. 'You know where we're going.'

So slight a remark, but it stuck.

'Neil,' I say, as we drive off, 'Teresa—'

'She's fine.' A slight tension in his voice, but only slight. 'I wouldn't be here if she weren't.'

I know that. But still I need to ask. Everything needs to be asked—his coming here has changed all that I thought I understood and had to learn to accept. I want him to say more but I don't know how to frame the question. He says, 'I told you in my letters—she's had almost her normal energy back for a couple of months now. We're back to how we were before—Teresa in her flat, I in mine.' Then, lightly, 'And Juan commuting between them.'

I want to watch his face but I have to keep looking at the road. 'Does she know—why you chose Zambia?'

'No. I saw no point in telling her. At this stage.' We have pulled up at a traffic light. I turn to look at him. 'What I mean is, I didn't know what I would be telling her until I'd been here and we could work it out together.'

Now for the first time I am afraid. Too much to lose, if it goes wrong. All these months of writing and the letters have said nothing that can take us past this point. The traffic lights change, my eyes are back on the road. 'I need to understand *exactly* what you're saying.'

He touches my cheek lightly. 'We need time together, Jennie, normal time. We need to live in the same place for a while, with no crises going on. Neither of us just about to leave.' His hand has moved to the back of my neck, sending shivers down my back. 'The things we're not dealing with—I couldn't see how we could get any further with them unless we had time to at least have a conversation. Sensible time, without undue pressure. And I knew this time it had to be on your ground.'

We are in the house. My entire body is alert, desire surging. I show him round—this is the desk at which I've sat writing to you after midnight. That's the trumpet flower outside the window, the one I told you fills the night air with its heady scent. My bed—

I want to lie down. *Now*, to hold him. I turn to look at him. His eyes say the same. I say, 'Ntombi will be back soon—'

He says, 'Five minutes. Just to lie close, nothing else.'

Half an hour. And even after we have both come we cannot stop touching each other, checking that it is real. Then I feel something strange welling up in me and I begin to cry. I have no idea why, or where it came from, but I sob as if I will never stop sobbing, and his arms fold round me and he strokes my hair and makes small inarticulate noises that move me so that they set me off crying again. Gradually the sobbing turns to a sort of gasping laugh, and then we are both laughing, in relief that it is over. We sit up and he fetches me a handkerchief from his trouser pocket, and comes to sit next to me on the bed, holding me again as I wipe my sodden face. I say, 'Ntombi—' and before I can get further I realise I am tired. More than tired—so tired it feels I will not be able to make the effort to get up off the bed and get myself dressed and into the living room, ready for when Ntombi will return.

Neil says, 'You stay there.' He is up, pulling on underpants.

'I don't know why we're bothering. Ntombi will know.'

'Still,' he smiles, 'it'll be the first time I'm meeting her and it might be simpler if I'm dressed.'

Fully clothed now, he comes to sit next to me on the bed. I sit up against him, letting his arms keep me upright. So tired. From all the weeks of build-up to the performance. Up since five this morning with last minute preparations. All the excitement of the event. Now this—all these rapid swings of intense feeling…Neil has started talking again. 'The programme Adrian's prepared for me is packed. Too packed. But it means we'll both be busy. That'll help it be normal, too. Not one of us waiting around till the other has time.'

He's trying so hard to package it safely, and it can't be done. 'Neil, there's *nothing* normal about your being here. It changes everything.'

'I'm trying not to assume that yet. That's what the two months are for.'

The words flip me back to the time when he insisted I take his viola. Another large gesture, like coming here. 'We'll see how we're going by the time the children's workshops finish,' he said. And when they were over, he left. I can't go through all that again. Three times is enough. The tiredness is taking over, like a temperature. My eyes travel vaguely over the room—Ntombi's home, but now also mine. I feel confused, it has all been too much. I lean up against him like a child asking for comfort. He folds his arms around me, his hand strokes my hair, lightly, touching again that awe that we have tried year after year to keep manageable. I want his hand to go on forever.

Eventually he makes himself stand up to go, shaking his arms unconsciously to loosen out the tension. The familiar movement wakes another memory. I sit up, energy momentarily returning.

'Tomorrow—bring your cello!'

Tomorrow—today—now. Saturday morning, and we have the house to ourselves, for Ntombi did not come back last night after all. We sit facing each other, bows poised: The sun streams in, lighting the wood of Neil's cello. Neither of us moves to start.

He drops his bow arm and says, 'I want to hear. You go.'

'I play on my own every day. Today we start together.'

We stare at each other, then both start laughing. He says, 'What're we playing?'

'What kind of a question is that? Play, and we'll find out.' 'Jennie—' He wants to talk.

I say nothing, my bow still poised. I am not ready to talk. He will have to wait.

He decides. I can almost feel him saying, 'OK then, if that's the way you want it,'—lifts his bow on to the string, and before I can react he is off—a huge crash of sound that blots out all possibility of me joining him Suppressed force let out, and now resisting being brought under control. It is a side of him I have never seen, or heard through his cello, and it shocks me into immobility—

—Eventually the sound calms down. I enter, cautiously at first. I do not feel safe. The notes wind tentatively around each other but keep jostling uncomfortably. I can't work out what he is doing. He stayed with me briefly but now has taken off—fast, complex, no way I can join him. Not communicating with me at all, still asserting parts of himself I don't connect with. Then that too runs its course. Gradually he stops doing all the pushing and begins to play responsively, ready now to listen to me and adapt. I feel his cello line moving more sensitively beneath mine, and it becomes possible again for me to move. My bow gets lighter, begins to explore...He picks up a phrase of mine, offers it back to me... We are moving together now, beginning to pattern things through each other...Then he slips deliberately back, forming a rhythmic foundation, creating a space for me above it. My bow feels the freedom and begins to travel more lightly—I am playing now the way I can when I am alone and I have mentally closed off from all that has been preoccupying me during the day; that facility I discovered through such pain and need in the first days after he had gone, when I could not look at written music nor even cope with the dominance of rhythm, but went right back to pure sound, unpatterned, unstructured...Now something new is happening, something beyond what has been possible alone. With a surge of confidence I realise that all the learning and becoming of the years since we first played together—the hours on the viola, the challenge and stimulus of other music, other lives, the choices I have made with my own—*all* of it is as if gathered together in my mind and body and spirit, there for my fingers and bowing arm to draw on—

This is why I want this man, for all the things he makes possible in me, in both of us. It was *not* deluded to hold out for this—on the contrary, my tenacity has been the sanest choice I have made, even though it happened beneath the level of choice...

And now I too have calmed down. I have finished playing all the things I needed to get out, as he released his force and complexity when we first started. He feels it, and his cello line begins to move again, to initiate things to which I respond and then to take the cue from me. It feels as though we are telling each other things quietly now and both able to listen, making real at last that simple inner conversation we have been prevented from having for years.

His bow is moving towards stopping. I slow down with him. We stop together.

Silence. The sun coming through the window lights the dust particles in the air between us.

2

Ntombi arrives, but she's heading off for a week in Ndola to a curriculum workshop, which also means she gets to see her children. She and Neil start talking about last night's celebration. 'My head's still whirling,' he says. 'I've never seen energy like it.'

'This is the one with the energy,' Ntombi says, putting her arm around me briefly, then starting to move around the house gathering what she needs to take. She instructs Neil to follow her. 'I'm off in an hour and you can have all the time you want with Jennie then. I want to find out who you are.' Neil follows her, bemused but entertained. She plies him with questions as if she's my mother and he's a son-in-law who hasn't been taking his duties seriously. I get on with clearing up the kitchen and leave them to enjoy each other.

When she's gone he says, 'She's amazing. Maybe you've told me but I've forgotten—what's the story with her children?'

'They live with their father. There's a new woman, brought to live in the house. The husband can't see the problem—he'd like to have them both.'

The parallels are too close for comfort. We share it with our eyes but don't want to put it into words. Then something gets into me—maybe anger for Ntombi, tripping off into anxiety in case this is what I am about to do to Teresa—then turning that against Neil because I don't want to carry it myself. I say, 'Most Zambian men I know assume a natural right to more than one woman. The only thing that's unusual about Ntombi's husband is that he does it openly.'

He says steadily, 'I'm not assuming anything, Jennie.'

I am immediately sorry, knowing I've been grossly unfair, and grateful that he is calming me with that steady voice. 'I know you don't. I don't know why I said that. I just seem to keep swinging between feeling wonderful that you're here and insecure in case you go away again.'

Perhaps to distract me he says, 'There's a viola and cello duet I've been waiting for a couple of years to play'—and so have I, from Nairobi days. I only have one music stand so we peg the cello part to the curtain, and the breeze lifts it as we play. After that we pull out a pile of sheet music, and we're laughing now as we play because I still can't read music anything like as well as I improvise. When we stop he leans back in his chair, legs stretched out, and surveys me in amusement. 'You look highly pleased with yourself.'

'I am. I've done it. I can play with you, the Holy Books. And at a level that isn't boring for you.'

'Jennie, I've felt many things in your company, but never boredom.'

We stroll out to the shops, for Neil to try his first Zambian mangoes. We pass a man mending his puncture by the roadside. A Zairean rhythm crackles from his radio perched on a couple of stones. Two children—three or four years old at the most—jive away in time to it. 'Watch,' I say quietly. 'See which beat they move on?'

He watches, listens—and turns to me. 'They're syncopating!'

'You can hardly call it that, it's how people feel the beat. The kids learn it almost before they can walk. Listen next time you hear women sing, what they clap to.'

'Jennie, that celebration of yours. I want to know how you did it.'

'They did it. I just created the space.'

'Do you think my head buttons up the back?' His words are laughing, but there's more than amusement beneath them. 'All that didn't just happen. I want to know how you got yourself into a position to release it in them.'

That's half my life story...We keep walking, arms around each other and still there is more he wants to know, has never had a chance to ask. He interrupts only if he thinks I'm leaving anything out. I tell him about the teacher who made me do hours of mindless exercises. The idea of me meekly obeying entertains him—'What's she got that I haven't?'

'How can you say that?' I demand. 'I practised every single thing you gave me, till my housemates went mad.'

'But I designed them for an independent-minded musician. It took me two minutes to see that if I offered you the standard curriculum, you'd walk out'—

—Laughing at the smallest things, at nothing. He is right, this is what we need, time to talk like this, the getting-to-know lovers do when they are first together, that we have never had a chance to do—

He is asking about my own music now, what I play when I'm alone, how that developed. Where to start? 'It began after you left,' I say, then I realise that he doesn't know what I mean, that I have a vocabulary for our personal history which he doesn't yet share. 'After the children's workshops,' I say. 'For you that was going to Manchester. For me it was you leaving me.' His arm has moved from my waist, creating a small distance. He doesn't like to be reminded, even though it's so long past. I see it, but I'm not going to stop, it's too important that we say everything now that has never been said. '*The water is wide*—you remember? I was trying to play it after you'd gone, and my hands just wouldn't. Like a survival instinct—they were telling me I'd go down the plughole if I kept trying to play your music without you being there to be part of it, that I had to make the viola my own or lose it altogether. So I packed away everything you'd prepared for me and started again.'

His eyes have relaxed. With emphatic approval he says, 'That's the way. That's the *only* way.'

I start singing the tune. I've always loved it, even at the time my hands wouldn't play it—

I leaned my back against an oak
Thinking it was a mighty tree
But first it bent and then it broke'—

I break off to say what has only just occurred to me, 'Extraordinary when you think of it, you *choosing* to set words like that for me, at a time like that.'

I look up, to realise too late that he's much less secure than I had assumed. It was a stupid thing to say, so long ago anyway. I put my arm around him and we walk silently together, but he's not shaking it off easily. After a minute or two he moves my arm away, saying, 'This heat's incredible. I'm melting away to a greasy spot.'

Together we get lunch. He washes the lettuce leaves, I cut up green peppers and tomatoes and mix salad dressing. I say, 'This is absolutely the best, having a house to ourselves and doing something so simple and domestic together.'

He says lightly, 'If you didn't think I was making assumptions I'd say there's one thing better.'

I stop in the midst of squeezing a lemon—look up to see him watching me as he shakes water off lettuce leaves—shaking it all over the floor. I say, 'I think we'd better postpone lunch'—

Mid-afternoon. Lying next to each other, bodies hot, sweaty, just a sheet on the bed, covers on the floor. Watching the closed curtains lift slightly as a stray wind passes. That peaceful drifting sensation that comes only after lovemaking, secure lovemaking, completely mutual. Too hot to lie close now but his fingers are still moving over me, lightly, lazily. He says, 'What you were saying about your hands refusing to play—'

'Mmm?'

'Mine are refusing to stop.'

And refusing still as we stand together in the shower, and his hands soap me. Breasts, belly, legs. Time for this too, sheer indulgence. No one coming that we have to hurry to get dressed for, nowhere either of us has to go. The water is icy against our hot bodies, and unpredictable

—the shower squirts sideways in fierce bursts or doesn't run at all. I travel with the water over his chest, his hips, his balls. Touching and moving on, learning every part—

—Making love, making music, making up for all the time that never was…Asking, listening, challenging, exploring everything—except the one thing that really needed to be discussed.

'Later,' I said, whenever he got near it. It's enough that you're here.'

'Jennie—' his voice was edgy. 'The whole *point* of coming was—'

'To have normal time.'

He was caught, by the honesty that made him laugh at himself, by the desire that was sparked off when I challenged. We rolled on to the bed, both laughing now, but we both knew this one wouldn't be easily rolled away. He had come to sort things out, and I was still refusing to think beyond the present. With a sudden movement he turned me on to my back and sat astride me, pinning my arms down. 'What's got into you?' he demanded. 'It's always been you telling me not to block.'

I knew very well what had got into me, it was the need to keep Teresa out. *All* our times together had had her shadow on them. This was our time. I was claiming space for us to evolve our own way of being, without constantly working out how that would affect her. Through the mock-wrestling of arms and legs we acted out the struggle—what he needed was to get beyond the tension by talking, what I needed was to avoid it by not talking. But I knew even as I fought back that he was right, and I only trapped myself by my refusal. If I wouldn't let him talk, how would I learn what had changed to make possible now what he had thought impossible before?

I was afraid, that was the truth of it, afraid of hearing from his own voice what I was going to have to give up, or share, or accept, so that in our being together he could keep being to Teresa what she needed of him.

'I just need more time,' I said. 'Not negotiating, just being.'

But there was a price to having it my way—a reflex withdrawal of the openness he was offering.

3

His programme of visits has begun; I am back at work. We meet for lunch and again as soon as his afternoon's appointments are over. He puts in a brief daily appearance at the Roma house so they won't think he's absconded, and then is back and we are together all evening, all night. Within days the warmth of his body next to mine becomes so familiar that I lose all sense of how extraordinary this time is, and feel it has always been this way, will always be. Having my life and him, all to myself, no need to choose—

And then I remember that this is but a moment in time, and after that for sure I will be losing one of them.

This is the week the rains break, even the weather announcing that everything has changed. Usually it takes a week or two getting into action—rumblings in the distance, producing nothing but short spatterings that hardly wet you, then back to dust and heat till a couple of days later. This year the sky cracks open on Neil's second day, drenching us in minutes—and that's it, the rainy season is here.

Winston drops by to see me—late afternoon, just as Neil is emerging from the shower. I introduce them; Neil chats for a few minutes holding on to his towel and then goes off to my bedroom to get dressed. Hostility steams off Winston, like moisture rising from the trees after rain. A man in my life who can suddenly appear, and move in to my bedroom...Neil comes back, dressed. Winston is at his edgiest, deliberately making it impossible for Neil to like him. I can read the thoughts behind Neil's non-commenting, observing manner—Is *this* the friend you value so much?...

Of course Neil *can't see* what lies behind all that over-assertiveness, you'd need second sight for that, the kind you only get if you've *seen* the damage it does to live under the indignities that have constructed his experience since he first breathed. Unless you understand that, you can't see what a cause for celebration it is that he is obstinate, and determined never to let anyone sit on him...

Winston takes himself off, and I try to explain, but somehow it comes out all wrong—like I'm telling Neil he doesn't share enough of my background, and will never understand *me*. I can feel him withdrawing—

There is an odd change in the balance between us. Balance of confidence, almost. This time it is I who have my friends around me, he who is the outsider in a new place, wanting to be part of a kind of music I can open up to him. He has introductions to all the people from whom he can be expected to learn something about Zambian music. I know them all, and can see why it isn't getting through. The ethno-musicologist, who can't speak except in anthropological jargon...A day spent with a local band...He uses his cello like a double bass, *learns* Zairean rhythms from them and teaches them Latin American ones. 'They probably came from Africa anyway,' he says. But a day is enough. 'They have no musical voice of their own,' he says, 'it's all rehashing what they've heard on Zairean radio.'...The national dance troupe—they've been doing it so long, and in such artificial contexts, performing for visiting heads of state who stand politely when they get off the plane and couldn't care less; so the dancers have stopped caring too. 'It's not just that,' Neil says. It's that I know there are things I'm not hearing, and they won't take me seriously enough to help me learn. I feel as if I'm just another tourist with a camera, asking inane questions that they're bored answering.'

Each evening he produces scraps of paper from his pockets, scribbled fragments of things he's heard, and starts writing them out, pondering over forgotten elements. I watch him and think, it's never going to work. This is participation music, you don't get it just by listening. And what kind of sense can he make of it anyway, he who has never seen an African village?

I ask, 'Do you want to have a go at a few mbira patterns?'

The rhythms are no problem—he's far more versatile than I. But he's trying to pick out some pattern of notes that's in his head and he keeps getting tripped up because the keys aren't tuned as he expects. 'Forget the sound, Neil, think about patterning the *movement*. Like a dance of the thumbs'—and when he's settled into a couple of alternating patterns I start on top with the penny whistle, my tune pulling against his...He gives up, laughing, needing a break. But it has opened up some channel in him and he starts asking me about Nyika, and we end up talking into the early hours, me telling him stories...About how music is for them simply part of the expression of everyday experiences, but also something beyond...how Ntombi's people use the mbira to lift consciousness away from the detail of every day, and connect with the world of the spirit...As he uses his own music. An awareness, a way of being...

He says, 'With you it's so accessible. But what Adrian has set up for me—the music's out there somewhere, but I can't get to it. And I hear myself sounding so bloody negative—' He moves tensely, the restlessness expressing itself in a body that can't get used to the heat.

He's late back, nearly midnight. I've been waiting for hours, wondering why he was so late. It turns out he's been with the band, and they went on to a night's session at a beer hall.

'And you played too?'

'Part of the time,' he says, but short—obvious that it's he now who doesn't want to talk. 'Dead loss of an evening,' he says. 'Watching people drink themselves silly.'

'You asked for a cultural exchange!'

He won't be drawn into laughing. 'Drunken male culture I would rather do without. Reminds me too much of my dad.'

'Your dad? I didn't know.'

But he's not offering any more.

I give up—there are practical things we need to sort out. Tomorrow Ntombi is due back from Ndola, so Neil will have to move back to the British Council guest house.

'And you?' he asks

'I can come there some nights, but I can't walk out on Ntombi totally.'

'This is absurd,' he says. 'This is your home as well as hers. Why can't we go on as we are?'

'When I moved in there was only one condition. She said, You're not filling the house with all those men.'

'And who were all those men?'

'Winston and his friends. As long as there's a woman in the house they hang around waiting for meals to appear.'

'Jennie, what has that to do with us?'

'Nothing. But—'

'But what?' he asks again; and he's pushing now, with the pent up frustration of not being able to move our situation forward. But I won't compromise on Ntombi, like he wouldn't on Teresa. I say,

'She looks tough, but this hits her vulnerable spot. I don't want to shove what's going on between us in her face.'

Ntombi gets back. Despite what I said I have been hoping she would say to Neil, 'Stay, for heaven's sake.' But she seems harried from dealing with wife number two, intolerant at finding things in different places from where they were when she left; no spare energy for noticing anyone else's needs. An hour or so after Neil has gone she calms down and starts asking me about him. From the first mention of Teresa she ferrets out my insecurities, which are like an inverted mirror of her own. 'And he thinks he can go on with her just the same if you go and join him?'

I become defensive. 'We haven't—Ntombi, it's not as simple as that.'

But to her it is. 'Tell him straight, he has to choose. And don't you move until he does.'

Week two, and it's already clear that Adrian's programme is not working—time I took action. Neil cancels a couple of things and comes with me to the college, where I introduce him to some of the students who sang in the liberation celebration. With the smallest encouragement they sing for him and he sees for himself that casual ability to create overlapping lines of melody as they go along. 'There's never even any discussion, Jennie, they just sing, and out comes four-part harmony. You can't imagine a group of British people who're not trained musicians doing that. And that xylophone player—'

'Themba. He's good, isn't he?'

'I've seldom seen hands move that fast.'

'There's a lot needs letting out.'

'Whatever you're letting out, your hands don't co-ordinate like that without years of training. I asked him where he learnt. He said from his uncle, in the village.'

'Get him to tell you what happened to that village. You and he have more in common than music.'

He presses me, but I won't tell him. He needs to make his own connections.

Winston arrives at the time he knows I usually finish work. He hangs about chatting while I stack books in a cupboard. From a building across the open yard there's the sound of Themba teaching Neil the xylophone. Winston says, 'I see you even bring that musician of yours to work.'

'Winston, take it easy.'

He doesn't answer, but follows me out to my bike. I try to talk about other things, to get back to a more normal level. I perch on my saddle, toes balancing the bike, ready to push off. He says, 'So are you going back to London with him?'

'Nothing's fixed. And my contract goes until March anyway.'

'And then?'

'I told you, I don't know yet.'

But that's less than honest and he knows it. We both feel so out of kilter—with ourselves, with each other—that all I can think of to say is, 'Come over and eat with Ntombi and me.'

His eyes are suspicious. More is required.

'Neil's busy tonight,' I say.

'OK,' he says, 'I'll come.'

He is in a bad mood all evening. He just wants things to stay the same—and it gets to the part of me that wants that too. *This time it has to be on your ground,* Neil said when he came, but we both know that if we are going to be together longer than two months it will have to be on his. I am vulnerable at the thought of losing who I have become here, of abandoning my people—and in exchange? Pushing myself into a space Teresa has had to herself for years, and will resent me for taking away? Trying to attach myself to his musician friends? What do I even know of them? Tania—'You're a wizard, Neil'—when what she meant was, 'Why are you bothering with this person?' Now here is this person coming back as Neil's partner, and I can just see how Tania's going to take that. Another Winston, but less tolerable because less to excuse her—

Saturday. Heat building up for the afternoon storm. Ntombi's out, house to ourselves again. Neil carries a tray with salad and bread out under the trees at the back while I go to get a rug. When I join him he is staring into an acacia tree, at a line of huge red ants that marches up one side of the trunk and down the other, like Michael's Grand Old Duke of York, determinedly heading nowhere. 'The mindlessness is terrifying,' he says. Then, as we settle to lunch, 'So you grew up with creatures like these?'

'Not quite like those. They're a Zambian speciality. But sharing the earth with crawling creatures, yes.'

He starts getting me to tell him about my childhood, and then back even further, to Dad growing up barefoot in the veld, passing that ease and groundedness on to me without words, just by the way he was. And from that to Mom and her stories of Scotland—

'So you're half Scots!'

'More than half. On Dad's side, missionaries from Aberdeen, three generations ago. The clan is crawling with dominies. He was one of the first to break.'

'From?'

'Religion, puritanism, the conviction of being part of an elite. Everything except the social conscience. He's a special person, my Dad. You'd like each other.' It feels strange, Neil and Dad suddenly in the same space, these two so separate parts of my life coming together, and in Lusaka.

'You remember that Swazi song you sang me, years ago?' he says. 'The quality of feeling behind it was—I should have known, that came from real experience—' He breaks off. 'I'm amazed at my own lack of imagination.'

'You were afraid to let yourself think. Like you were afraid of me knowing about you.' The memory of our viola lessons, and those sudden moments of cutting out…'Tell me about your family,' I say. 'Your brother, the one you said I was like.'

Instantly, that same defensiveness—but I'm not having it any more. 'Neil, we've passed the point where you can keep me out.'

'I'm not keeping you out. There's nothing to say about my family. Except that it was minimal; of minimal use to each other.'

'*Neil—*'

'OK then. I have an older sister and brother whom I hardly know. They were adolescents when my younger brother and I were still toddlers. My father wasn't available to be known; in the pub most of the time. My mother suffered it unhappily, which meant she had little energy for us. We grew up despite them. That's about it.'

I take his hands, moved by the obvious difficulty which making even these bare statements has caused. His own hands press on mine, asking for a break. 'These things are old. I can tell you more later but it's not relevant to now. There are things we need to be talking about and it's *you* who is stopping it happen.'

'The really stupid thing is,' I say, 'I think I'm scared.'—

—Scared? Of moving forward to the very thing that I have known so surely for years I wanted? I want it, of course I want it, but as one would want the sense of floating free that comes after the parachute jump. But that moment of stepping out into space—

And this man was very powerful

He could take thunder and put it in a pot—

—He is sitting absolutely still, saying nothing. I want him to say, 'There's nothing to be scared of,' but he won't. What difference would it make, anyway? But his silence adds to the fear, because I don't know where he is withdrawing to—

He has let go of my hands. He gets up and without speaking goes inside. I stare after him, waiting for him to come back. He does not.

I don't know how long it has been. Ten minutes? An hour? And still I am sitting here. His walking away was like an act of violence, his silence more dangerous than angry words. I sit numb, trying to accept it, trying not to give way to panic at what it may mean. Eventually I make myself get up and go into the house to find him...He's not in the living room, not in the bedroom. The bathroom door is open...The panic slips out from where I have been controlling it. The kitchen? Ntombi's room? Has he gone from the house?

Then I find him, in the small spare room where Ntombi piles things she's not using. He's on a chair, back to the door, reading. I stand for a moment watching his back. He must have heard me but he does not turn. My emotions have been swinging wildly, but now that I have found him a new feeling takes over, unexpected—compassion. He's a large man but he looks at that moment very like a child who has looked for a part of the house where no one will think of finding him.

I have no right to be here, watching him from behind. I am intruding on an aloneness that is necessary to him. For one last moment I watch his back, trying to read in it the things I am sure he will not say when eventually he returns. It hunches, blocking out something intolerable.

The afternoon is long, and silent. No sound of movement from the room where Neil still sits and reads; or maybe just sits. The air is close, heat building up intolerably. I stand at the kitchen door waiting for the storm that will not break, and I feel it like the unadmitted things between us. 'I am scared,' that's all I said, but my admission of fear must have triggered off his own. I see now that this moment has been lurking, from that crash on the cello—no, from long before that. From the first time we worked together, that unresolved tension that he keeps so well out of sight most of the time, but that suddenly makes him take protective action just when we seem closest to intimacy; and that when really pushed, will lash out, out of control, telling me, This man does not even understand what he is feeling, let alone know how to handle it.

The lightning comes, a stupendous crack of electricity leaping jagged across the sky, banging the clouds against each other, resounding...Footsteps behind me...I feel his body now, arms coming round to hold me, his breath on my head. We stand together silently, waiting for the next roll of thunder.

4

I am staring at the calendar that has caught my eye as I chop onions, discovering to my horror that I had forgotten—Jane is about to arrive for a week's holiday. Four months ago she booked it, so many months ahead that all I did was circle the week on the calendar. I was really looking forward to her coming, and thinking how extraordinary it would be to have someone from that other life join me in this one—and then Neil arrived, and Jane's holiday went clean out of my consciousness. Now it's about to happen, and it's going to take up an entire week. I was large in my promises—my home, my company, all at her disposal. I'll take leave, I said. The Victoria Falls—

Maybe Neil could come with us? But that's not what Jane has in mind. Anyway, there's Adrian's carefully planned programme.

She climbs off the plane into our tangled lives, her agile body full of the stored-up energy of someone who has been waiting for this holiday and intends to enjoy it. On the way back from the airport I tell her about Neil. To the house, and she meets Ntombi. Winston arrives, and she's listening to rumours about South African government agents. Neil arrives, and Winston does his usual male territorial bit. I see by the light in Jane's quick eye that she has sized the whole situation up. When we're finally alone again she says, 'Have I walked into the middle of Act Three?'

'We could do with a new character,' I say.

On day two I take her around Lusaka. In the market she listens delighted as I chat in Chinyanja with the market women, and we buy vegetables she's never seen before and small dried *kapenta* fish. Back home to cook a vast meal, for the word has gone out to my friends. 'How many?' she asks. 'Lots,' I say. We talk non-stop while we chop and stir, and she brings back into sudden focus the life I left to come here, Paula and Bea in the terraced house in Bristol, Jaswinder and the children who clamber around her while she cooks, Maria leading a women's caucus in Parliament, too busy now to write poems, Jane's own life in Manchester, street theatre, socialist feminist conferences, off to join the Greenham Common protests—I had almost forgotten, it's *that* I'll be going back to, not just Neil's musician friends…The party goes on late into the night and Jane bridges the parts of my divided life—woman-to-woman ease with Ntombi, animated political discussions with Winston, concepts of improvisation with Neil.

On day three she and I set off in the car Ntombi has lent us, and we're hardly out of Lusaka before she starts cross-examining me. The whole story, she wants, right from the beginning. When I have done she says, 'And how's the sex?'

I laugh, at the pleasure of having her back just the way she always was. 'Great,' I say. 'One of our definitely uncomplicated areas.'

'Seriously?'

'Seriously. Or rather, not seriously, delightfully.'

She shifts in the seat next to me, getting into a better position to study this interesting phenomenon. 'Well, who would have thought it, after all your celibate years.'

'Doesn't feel odd to me.'

She asks, curiosity growing, 'Don't you get pissed off with things like having his clobber on the bedroom floor?'

'We did have an argument about his dirty socks the other day,' I admit. 'But we argue lots. It's part of the dynamic that fuels it.'

'Tell me,' she insists. 'About the socks.'

'I said, If you leave them on the floor the servant feels he has to pick them up. Neil said, I can't take responsibility for post-colonial subservience. I said, If you don't pick them up, *I'm* going to have to.'

'And?'

'Then we both realised we didn't care who won, we just wanted to go to bed together. So we did.'

'With the socks still on the floor?'

'With the socks still on the floor.'

She shakes her head. 'Can't last. The glory of sex wears thin and you begin to realise it's the socks that really matter.'

And now we stand and look out together over the slow brown crocodile river. It travels innocuously till the plate of rock on which it moves comes to an abrupt end; then the river is transformed into an awesome sweep of white falling water, force untamed, disappearing over the edge—to swirl angrily in the narrow crevice way below, hardly visible through the spray. We stand for a long time, silenced, all other sound drowned by the noise of the crashing water. Eventually we move a little further away so we can hear each other. Jane says, 'It sure makes you realise your insignificance.'

'For me it's—I don't know. But different from that.'

'Try.'

'Release, almost. Like I'm part of that natural force, suddenly let loose.' My eyes lift from the shooting spray, back to the land stretching endlessly beyond the river. 'It's the size of the place,' I say. 'I feel different the moment I get out into it. I was going round in small circles in Lusaka before you came. Just being here gets things in proportion. I've even got a little distance on Teresa!'

'To what effect?'

'I've been trying to take myself back to what I felt the couple of times I saw her, before I knew what she was in Neil's life. It's obvious she's a really *live* woman, strong and warm. Someone I would love to get to know, if she had nothing to do with him.'

It seems you're going to.'

'I just hope I can hold on to that. It's bizarre when you think of it, both of us landing in Britain from political traumas half way across the world, and each latching on to the same person as the one who could help build a meaning from the wreckage.'

'Twice can't be an accident.'

'No. It's something in him.'

She is thoughtful for a few moments, then says, 'You ought to get Neil out of Lusaka. To some place like this.'

I start telling her about the village near Nyika, and how I have been thinking that he could learn about music in a totally different way if I could take him there. 'Forget about music,' she says. 'All sorts of things about *you* make sense here.' Her arm sweeps the vast plunging water, the wide savannah landscape, the dotted umbrella trees. 'I can see you now, walking across your border. When I get back I'm going to issue instructions to Paula and the rest—qualification for continued sisterhood, one week in Zambia. And potential life partners, at least two months.'

To the airport, waving Jane goodbye…Then straight off to see Fernando.

'I've come to ask a favour,' I say. 'I want to take unpaid leave. It's really important.' Fernando raises his eyebrows, but it's obvious that the idea of passion and spontaneity appeals. When he hears where we're going he says, 'You'd better take the landrover.'

To Adrian—can we cancel the next three weeks of Neil's programme? Adrian hesitates but there's not much he can say. 'The point of the fellowship is for you to learn what you want to. If you're sure you can do it better that way—' But then he registers that the village in question is Derek's. 'That's in Malawi, isn't it? Now *that's* a problem. This exchange is hosted by Zambia.'

'That's absurd, Adrian,' I say. 'Derek's village is about ten miles the other side of the border. The music isn't any different.'

'It's not the music I'm thinking of, it's the diplomatic considerations.'

Neil says drily, 'That's not what you just said the point of the fellowship was.'

Adrian looks startled, then laughs. 'There are two points—as seen by the British Council, and as seen by the Zambian government.'

Neil says mildly, 'Three, actually. There's also mine.'

Telex to Derek:

Real musician willing to spend time in Nyika. Only available immediately. I can interpret. How do we get messages there?

The answer, next day:

Have phoned Nathaniel in Lilongwe to take message. They'll be expecting you. Impossible to get research permit at short notice. Rely on stout denial if questioned. Give everyone my greetings you lucky sod.

Adrian says, 'I'm going for stout denial too. If anyone asks me, that village is ten miles *this* side of the border.'—

Done! We're free—absconding properly this time, shedding all constraints, just us. When? Tomorrow—can we do it, so soon? Come on, let's just *do* it. An evening to pack the landrover and go round to people handing over work. Get to my place tomorrow before it's light, I want you to see a real savannah sunrise—

Spare tyre, tools, petrol can, breakdown manual. Tent, sleeping bags—oh shoot, the only ones in the house are singles. Into the landrover again, over to friends to borrow a double. Food, in case we get stuck somewhere. Water. Thermos flasks of cold lemonade, tea.

Clothes, shoved into a bag. Set the alarm…Wake at four-thirty, pull on clothes, pack my toothbrush, sunblock cream—condoms. Christ, I never thought. Neil has some—but to last three weeks? Wait—where's that diaphragm I used to have? Scrabble around in drawers…Ludicrous, I've carried it halfway across Africa with me, used it once, now when I need it I can't find it. I don't even like to think about that time with Winston, that's probably why I've forgotten where—Damn, the rubber's perished. Lain at the back of my drawer and gone crumbly—

My mind whirrs. The chemists won't open for hours. The Intercontinental Hotel? They have jet-setting travellers coming and going at all hours. Maybe there's an all-night chemist.

I leave the door unlocked, and a note, 'Back in a few minutes. Make yourself some coffee,' and I rev off to the hotel.

Neil is standing in the kitchen doorway as I get back. Mug of coffee in his hands, looking out into the still-dark yard of pawpaw and mango trees. The light's on in the kitchen, framing him. The usual, involuntary flush of joy I feel each time he reappears.

He comes down the steps to stand next to the landrover as I get out. His eyes have the suggestion of amusement in them. 'Where were you, so early?'

'The Intercontinental,' I say. 'For essential supplies.'

'I thought so. I saw you come into the car park as I was leaving.' It takes me a moment to connect. 'You too?'

He nods, the amusement now escaping from his eyes and all over his face. 'I'd say we're probably equipped now.'—

Into the driver's seat. Neil gets in the other side, settles himself next to me. Doors closed. Start up. On the road, finally.

Chapter 3

Straight the road stretches ahead of us, east to where the sky is already beginning to lighten. We drive towards it, watching as the edging of earth and sky gradually appears clearer and clearer out of the dark. There is an awe that affects us both—we are about to be present at a miracle. I pull up, so the engine noise will not get in the way. The sun breaks out, sudden and tremendous in its power. For the moment, the power only of light; in a few hours it will be murderous heat.

Move off again. I am driving with one hand on the steering wheel, the other in Neil's lap. He's running his fingers softly around the palm. One bit of my mind receives it, luxuriating; the rest is absorbed in a meditation of trees, boulders, grass; earth, sky. The inner journey we are making together becomes the real one, the visible road a symbol.

Eventually Neil breaks the silence to say, 'There's something about the endlessness of this road. Never getting anywhere.'

'It gets somewhere all right. But African roads have a long breath.' 'How long, this one?'

'Three hundred miles to the border. Then another day's driving in Malawi.'

'I thought the village was ten miles from the border!'

'But a long way north from where we cross, and the road goes further east than we want to be—we have to swing back again on small tracks.'

'If the landrover breaks down, you'll know what to do?'

'Now he asks! You shouldn't have trusted yourself to this journey at all if you weren't sure of that!' I swerve slightly to avoid a place where the road has been eroded. 'Actually the more likely problem is getting stuck. Three more weeks of rain, and the roads are quite likely to disappear in mud. Getting out of that just takes brute force, so you'll be more use than me.'

'I take that as a compliment, do I?'

'Well, you are larger.'

'Maybe you should start briefing me for the village. I feel like a child being taken off to boarding school, and I've no idea what the rules are going to be.'

'The first is that privacy is an unknown concept. We will both be openly observed every minute of the day. At close quarters. It takes a bit of getting used to.'

'I can imagine,' he says drily. 'Is three weeks enough?'

'The second is that public expressions of affection between men and women are out.'

'And this is the ideal lovers' retreat?'

'It's a retreat, all right, you'll feel we're away from the world. But it's a world in itself, and there's no choice but to fit into it.'

'Do I get to see you at all?'

'We'll be within a few hundred yards of each other most of the time. Men and women occupy the same spaces, but separately. It's hard to explain. They get into repartee with each other but it's like gangs in a school playground, you know which group you're part of and you don't step out of it.'

'Jennie, what *are* you taking me into?'

We're both laughing, but it's all true. 'Don't worry, we'll get nights together—we'll have the tent to ourselves. But that's another thing. Since we're sharing it, we will have to be married, for the purposes of the village.'

'*That I* can cope with!'

'Me too. But we're going to need a good story. They all saw

me single four months ago and cross-questioned me endlessly. Offering to fix me up with a husband.'

'And you said?'

'My usual line. Freedom to decide where I live and work.'

He says nothing. The mood has changed, our own reality trapping us again.

The land stretches in all directions, greening already after just a couple of weeks of rain. The sun moved upwards fast for the first hour after sunrise, now seems to be slowing down. We pass the occasional large farmhouse, collections of scattered huts. The plain begins to break up into hills with rocky outcrops. The road winds around them, then straightens out again.

I say, 'I think I'm ready to talk.'

He looks wary, but also a little amused. 'You mean, there's a long road ahead, so I can't get away once you've started?'

'Something like that. Neil—' But now I hardly know where to begin. 'You charmed Fernando the other day, talking about that flamenco player. I'd almost forgotten about your Spanish. Where did that come from? It was before Teresa, wasn't it?'

It's the first voluntary mention of her name since the night he arrived, and his face has an expression that I read as gratitude, that I am prepared to speak of her. I am moved by it and wish I could have got here sooner. But he says only, 'Long before Teresa. A year of grape-picking and bumming about in Spain, after I left college. When music had given up on me.'

'You never told me what made that happen.'

'I did—we talked about it, I remember precisely.'

'Only about your violin, and reacting against being pushed into mindless technique. There must have been something more—to stop you composing, and for years?'

'It happens. Artistic block, quite common.'

His detached tone holds a notice—Landmines: take care where you walk...I give up, try another tack. 'I need to understand more about you and Teresa. Tell me her story. How she got out.'

For some reason this seems safer. 'She and her group were touring when the coup happened. She had Juan with her because they knew it could be any time.' He stops, checking it's OK to go on. 'When I first met her she was raw with it all. You know that stadium, that the military turned into a human slaugherhouse? People she knew were there. Not her husband—he was out of Santiago, but it was weeks before she knew that. Meanwhile all those terrible stories—she dealt with it by doubling what she expected of herself, telling it through her music; but inside she was breaking up.'

It's like everything he ever tells me about her, it gets to me in a place where I'm defenceless. I have tried to contain the thought of her by reducing her to a concept, a fact in his situation. But each time he speaks about her he shows me this real person and it's obvious why they love each other. Then panic grows insidiously, the feeling that it's *they* who are fundamentally together, and I am outside that charmed circle of intimacy—

I glance quickly and see that he is watching my face. He says, 'This isn't what we need to be talking about.'

But it is. It's facing me with the parts of his life I haven't wanted to think about, because they exclude me. 'Tell me how it was for you, being with her.'

He looks cautious still, but starts again. 'I used to think sometimes it was like being responsible for an injured bird that won't accept its wings are damaged. You can see it's not going to be able to fly again without first receiving care and attention, but if you handle it too much you might undermine the very quality that could help it survive. So you become very watchful, not saying much, but constantly looking out for what might be required of you.'

There is something of that watchfulness in his eyes now, and I wish I didn't evoke it. 'Neil, you said it was always agreed that—if Teresa's husband were released—you'd—' I can't find the words for talking about their relationship, it slips sideways of all the categories.

'That we'd stop being lovers?'

'Yes.' I hope he might do the rest too, but he waits for me to frame the question. 'Did you never talk about what would happen if *you* found someone else?'

'She did, often.'

My foot on the accelerator jerks involuntarily. Something so vital and he never told me—

'She kept saying, This can't be permanent for you. You have to feel free to find what you need.'

'So *why*—?' I am overtaken by indignation. 'You knew Teresa felt that, all these years, and still—? *Why?*'

'Because people say the things they like to think they feel. It's not always what they do feel. It was all bound up with her own sense of disloyalty to her husband. She kept saying for herself, this is temporary, conditional, so she felt she had to say it for me. But there was so much despair, and it was only with me that—It didn't matter what she said, I knew what it would have done to her if I'd taken her literally.'

I remember now the time of Teresa's operation, asking him if he were afraid; and he said, Only that I won't have done all I could to help her know it's worth going on living...So he's done it twice.

'Jennie, we keep coming at this from the wrong end. It's now we have to deal with. She senses things have shifted in me, even if she doesn't know why. It's become a burden not to tell her; damage or not.

It just got so overlaid by what's happened to her this last year I couldn't—'

'I know.'

'Neil—'

'Go on.'

'What are you going to say when you get back?'

'Jennie, we haven't even—'

'Assume I'll be following. What are you going to tell her?'

'That I've been here with you. That it's been years waiting to happen.' I wait for more. 'And that I don't expect it to change the substance of what she and I will continue to be for each other.'

Insecurity flares. He must see it in my face for he says, immediately, 'Jennie, she has half done it herself already. Ever since the operation she's begun to let go—not just from me, from Juan too. Like she's saying, I'm not going to be here forever so we all need to loosen up—'

I can't handle this, each thing he says makes it harder. Too emotionally confusing trying to think simultaneously of Teresa's needs and Neil's and mine. There are two people speaking inside me. The calm one that knows I am loved says, 'There is nothing to sort out. We can have what we need and he can still be there for Teresa.' The one that is afraid of what I am going into says, 'I won't feel safe unless I can be sure he's going to tell her straight'—

Anxiety wins. 'Neil, you *can't* be so simple as to think she's not going to feel it. What happens when she next has a crisis? Will you be on call for her, as totally as you have been before?' He is pushing me to put into words what I hoped I wouldn't have to. 'And *I* need to know she understands the boundaries.'

'Which are?'

'That you're no longer her lover. Even an occasional one.'

'If you knew her, you'd have no need to say that.' His voice is sharp—defensive, as I felt for Winston. 'When she understands I have the possibility of a life with you, she herself will make whatever changes are needed.'

My insecurity flips over into anger. 'You're backing off again and it's just storing up trouble for later.'

'For Christ's sake Jennie, she's a grown woman. I am not going to diminish her dignity by making speeches about it.'

I can't stand this. I turn towards him, pushed by the urgency to make him understand. The landrover swerves, one wheel off the tarmac to the gravel at the side, starting a skid—

Hold frantically against the sideways pull—

—Straightening up. Slow down, over to the side of the road. Pull off. Switch off. Stare straight ahead.

I make myself breathe slowly. We could have been dead by now. Neil's hand is on my thigh, firm pressure, no words…Get out, look at the tyre track, just to make sure it's registered emotionally. This is madness. No more risks. Back into the driver's seat. Adjust mirror. Check the road is clear—like doing a driving test again. Start carefully, drive off. Very sedate pace.

Through all this Neil has been sitting quiet, leaving me to sort myself out. Once we've driven a little way with no incidents I say, 'Thanks. I couldn't have dealt with you saying anything.'

I can feel he's smiling. He says, 'If it's relevant for you to know, I feel completely safe in your hands.'

I laugh, but still shakily. 'And no amount of evidence is going to change your mind?'

'But maybe we talk about something less emotional for a bit?'

I am about to say, 'There's *no way* we can stop now.' Then I too back off, staring at the road ahead that keeps coming towards us, to be swallowed up under us, while in the silence of my own mind the thoughts churn. I've pushed, and he won't budge. Until he does, I can't feel secure. But if the concession has to be screwed out of him, I'm still not going to feel secure…*You need to know her,* he says—Why am I afraid of knowing her? 'She is more governed by principle than anyone I know,' he said once. 'A Catholic childhood, a revolutionary communist adulthood'… What he doesn't understand is how principle will work with me. I will be so aware of what I am taking away from her, that it's going to be impossible to be natural. My principles will tell me that it's reasonable, right, for the two of them to continue to be what they are to each other. There has been no quarrel, no dynamic of their own to make Neil put artificial distance between them. But vulnerability stirs tenaciously below the realm of principle…

I shift sideways—'How is Juan going to react to me moving in?'

'The house is big enough. What I do doesn't particularly interest him as long as I'm around when he wants me, and the kitchen's well-stocked.'

'Come *on*, Neil—'

'It's a non-issue, I assure you. You've maybe forgotten how self-concerned teenagers are.' His voice says, Don't think you know him better than I do…'Stop trying to imagine problems, Jennie. The real one's enough.' His hand touches my cheek, moving the tone. 'We have reached the point where we both know that being together would transform life, and it would be madness not to act on that. But my life's not transportable. I had naively assumed yours was. Just a couple of weeks here and I now can't see further than everything you've created, and that you shouldn't even have to think about leaving. So I'm stuck.'

And I have nothing to say, because I too am stuck.

There will be things I can do anywhere, I tell myself. I didn't know what I'd be doing when I first came here, it just evolved. I can do that again somewhere else…I'm a migrant, I tell myself, I have moved more times than I can count, I will survive another. My life has been waiting for this change. I don't understand why part of me is fighting what the other part longs for—

'Ntombi and I have been making plans,' I say, 'for after I've gone. She's going to build a regular music group from the people who took part in the liberation celebration, and I'll organise a solidarity tour in Britain. We'll get Fernando to find funding'—

He waits. I can't go on. I am deluding myself. They'd never get travel documents. I'm breaking contract, that's the truth of it—the never-stated contracts with Ntombi, with Winston, the students in the classes, the Kalingalinga children. They have been second-level intimacies, but those too have their rights. They have sustained me when I had no prospect of Neil's companionship, and given my life shape, purpose. I committed myself, not to any of them individually, but to all of them together, to a kind of life that draws no boundaries between the people who matter to you and the work you do, personal commitments and political ones. And now I am about to walk out on all of that, and all of them.

2

Near the Luangwa River bridge now. We've had the road almost to ourselves, but now there's a build-up ahead—a couple of overloaded trucks stuck on a steep climb. Beyond them there's an army checkpoint—makeshift barriers of barrels and poles.

Neil asks, 'What's all that about?'

'We're near the border. Two borders, actually, and fighting the other side of both. It may look like empty bush out there but there's a lot going on.' There are soldiers poking rifles in at the windows of vehicles. 'And regrettably we have the skin colour to be mistaken for Rhodesian spies. Let's get out of here while they sort out those trucks.' I backtrack to a turnoff that heads south along the river. Pull up. Neil climbs out stiffly. 'My legs need unfolding,' he says, kicking them out each in turn and waving his arms about. 'Come,' I take his hand, 'Let's go and take a look at Mozambique. Where Themba comes from.'

We walk to a point where the land suddenly drops to the river valley, and stand looking out south and east over an endless vista, green and innocuous; trees and distance hide the burnt out villages. Neil says, 'That man's amazing. I think of him growing up somewhere in there and—you should have seen him handling my cello. First time he's ever seen one, and the sound he produced!'

'Did you get him to tell you his story?'

'I tried. All I got was that he was a teacher in a village school, and had to leave suddenly because the soldiers came.'

'He was in the middle of a lesson and most of the adults were out in the fields. Then suddenly the place was on fire—they just had to run, he, the children—scattering in all directions, but a group of about eight stayed with him. They walked three weeks getting out, and a couple of them didn't make it. The others he has taken on as his own.'

'Jesus.' Then, 'What did you mean, about what we have in common?'

'His children, and what you are for Juan.'

He says, sharply. 'Don't elevate me, woman. My role doesn't compare.'

'Not the getting-them-out bit. But being prepared to be there forever after. There are plenty of people who do amazing things at moments of crisis, but not so many who take on that level of long-term responsibility.' But still he does not want what I am saying—almost, I think in surprise, that I expose some failure in him by giving him praise he feels he does not deserve.

Back to the landrover, to join the line of vehicles crawling towards the bridge…Our turn. The soldiers come towards us, handling their rifles too casually for our comfort. They motion to us to get out and open up the back. One of them pokes his rifle at the tent. 'Take it out,' he orders. Neil takes out the tent. 'All of it,' says the soldier. Neil gets going handing things out to me. I think, I hope to God he's not going to say something rational and British, like 'Is this really necessary?' He lifts up the viola case, that hours ago in the Lusaka dark a last minute impulse made me add to our equipment. 'You brought this?' he asks, distracted by surprise. 'For the *village?'*

'For you,' I say. 'I thought you shouldn't be without an instrument.'

'I'm not—' he begins. But the soldiers are pressing around us, suspicions now clearly aroused. Neil is instructed to open the case; they stand back cautiously as if it might go off. One of them peers inside. Neil preempts further investigation by demonstrating what it is for, a perky flourish of sound—and the soldiers grin delightedly. 'Play some more,' urges the one who a few moments ago was ordering him around so brusquely—and Neil flings off an impromptu jig. A crowd gathers, other drivers, soldiers abandoning their posts further along the road. Uniforms and rifles momentarily irrelevant, just the faces of boys and young men, eyes loving the dance, bodies moving, pressing for more, more—'Enough,' Neil says laughing. They watch regretfully as he packs it up again, then take themselves back to the boredom of checking vehicles.

'Tell Adrian about that one,' I say as we repack and climb back in. 'That was worth any number of embassy receptions.'

Moving now slowly nearer the bridge that straddles the wide gorge. Across, one vehicle at a time…looking down to the brown water moving way below…We pick up speed on the other side. Neil says, 'I might as well warn you, I'm not playing the viola once we get to the village.'

'Why not?'

'I don't want to be cast in the role of performer. Look what just happened—I could have kept them there for hours if I'd chosen to.'

'So? If they would love it, why not?'

'I'm coming to learn *their* music.'

'And them? What are they going to get out of that? They're just as curious about difference as you are. Look at Themba and your cello.'

'He's different.'

'Why?'

'Woman, lay off. You're cornering me, and I've run out of reasons. But that's my line and I'm sticking to it!'

A town, finally, Katete. I watch Neil taking it in as we drive slowly in. It's hardly a town—a bus station, a market, a straggling collection of houses. We park, climb out, bemused at finding ourselves again among other people. At a small general store we down a couple of cokes and load up with supplies of candles, soap, tinned goods, to take to the village as our contribution to our keep. Then on a rough track that leads out of the town, to find some minimal shade for a picnic.

'I've just been working something out,' I say, as we eat. 'You were in your mid-thirties when you met Teresa.'

'I was.'

'Tell me what happened before that.'

'You mean women? Nothing that amounted to anything.'

'That's not possible.'

He sounds amused. 'Fact, I'm afraid. Denial will get you nowhere.'

'What about Tania?'

'Briefly. OK, there have been a fair number of those. I thought you meant living with someone.'

'Tania had that look of someone who has once been in possession. And she sure didn't want me getting in there.'

'You don't want to pay any attention to her. She's like that till she gets used to people. Anyway, we were disastrous as a couple.'

'Who ended it?'

'I did.'

'Why?'

'Jennie, this is like an inquisition.'

'I want to understand, that's all. Why is it a problem to tell me?'

'It isn't. I just can't see the point.' There's a definite edge of defensiveness in his voice but he carries on. 'What happened with Tania was essentially what happened with all of them. She wanted more, I felt invaded. Like she was trapping me into feeling responsible for her unhappiness. When I see that coming, it's not that I think, 'I need to get away,' I've gone before I know I'm doing it.' He reaches across me for another coke. 'Where is all this leading?'

'You once said it was my need you backed away from. Was it like that?'

'Yes. But with you it was more complicated because *I* wanted more. That was terrifying—like standing on a precipice knowing you might voluntarily throw yourself over. I'd have been running away from you even if there had been no Teresa.'

'*Why?* It makes no sense, someone with your capacity for loving.'

'Ah, but I've have an even stronger instinct for avoiding intensity.'

'That's an absurd thing to say. Look at your music!'

'My music's different. That's *me*, how I feel inside, about life, about meaning. People are another matter.'

'How can you separate the two? Your music is a way of sharing yourself.'

'But a way *I* channel, on my own. It's for communicating ultimately, but while it's coming out of me I am communing only with myself. That creates an immense freedom. I'm not aware of anyone watching over my shoulder, and if I were the thing would dry up instantly.' He hesitates, as if he's reluctant to put into words something he knows about himself but doesn't like. 'Of course I wanted intimacy. But as soon as anyone I was with began to show signs that they wanted something more, I began to feel—unbearably intruded on, is the only way I can describe it. Then a survival instinct takes over, building walls to protect myself.'

'So you directed your passion into your music?'

'Jennie, don't mock.'

I am startled by the tone. But it's true that I've been listening with a kind of detachment, the interest of a complex jigsaw, trying to fit the pieces together. For him it's no intellectual puzzle, it's his own difficult feelings that have trapped him for years. 'I'm sorry. I didn't mean it that way.'

He covers my hand with his and holds it for a few minutes quietly. Then he gets up, gives me a hug and starts packing up the lunch things.

He takes a turn driving. It's a relief for both of us—gives his body something to do, leaves me free to just let the world come towards me. Trees, grass, sky…Elephant and giraffe country around here, Luangwa game reserve off somewhere to the north. He asks where we will camp for the night. Chipata, I say, just this side of the border. 'The road to Chipata,' he says, turning over the sound, making of it a rhythm that fits the mesmeric movement past our windows…Trees, boulders, grass…He puts an arm around me. I say, reluctantly, 'You'd better take it back. One near-miss is enough.'

He says firmly, 'I drive perfectly safely with one hand.'

I lean up against his shoulder, savouring the moment…'I want to ask you something. The kind of question that might make you build a wall.'

'Try me. I'll do my best to stay visible.'

'There are things that make me afraid when I think of us being together all the time.'

'Like?'

'What you were saying about intimacy. *I* demand, don't I?'

'Yes, but I want you to.' He turns to look at me briefly, smiling. 'It seems you've broken the cycle.'

'Keep your eyes on the road. And I'm not sure about breaking the cycle. Some things I ask, and it's like I've pressed the wrong button—whoops, you've gone. There's no pattern I can predict, it just ups and slaps me in the face. It makes no sense, when we're as close as we are.' I wait to see if he wants to say anything. Apparently he doesn't. 'And you'll never talk about it afterwards, it just gets buried, like we're pretending it never happened.' Still nothing. I sit upright. 'Neil, we *have* to find a way to talk about these things—When I extended my contract and you didn't write—I've still no idea what was going on. Tell me what happened. What you felt and did.'

'Why?'

'You shut me out for *two weeks*.'

He says nothing. I begin to feel rebellious. There's no reason why he shouldn't tell me. 'Whenever things get a little close to the bone you slip back into this defensive silence. And then I hear myself dragging it out of you—I hate having to do that, you hate me doing it, but it's your backing away that *makes* me, like I constantly have to stop you removing yourself.'

'Now hold on—'

'It's *true*. If I'd left it to you a year ago, the time Teresa was ill, we'd have had three half-hours in a bloody cafe! I wasn't just pushing for myself, it was for both of us. God knows how I've known it was what you needed all along because you certainly weren't helping.' I am working myself up into a self-pitying state. I can feel it, and I can't stop it. Still so much that's never been processed—

His voice has a carefully controlled steadiness as he says, 'When we talk about difficult things, it's extraordinary how differently we have experienced them. Do you want to hear—what I was feeling, that time in London?'

'You know I do.'

'I was overcome with longing, all those first few days in cafes. You sitting there, offering something I wanted so much. Something quiet and real and strong and forever. And me not seeing how I could accept it without buggering us all up.' He has to stop. 'And now you tell me all you could see was I was trying to get away.'

'Of course I saw the rest. It's just—Neil, all that's past, we got past it and we're here together. I don't want to go over it just for the sake of going over it. But I need to understand. Especially if you're going to keep cutting yourself off even now.'

But my flow of words has dried him up. Wisdom, Jennie, you could do with a little wisdom. Accept the things you can't change.

The sun is coming at us from behind now, bearing relentlessly down on the roof, through the windows. It's like travelling in a moving greenhouse, with the land opening out ahead of us, its features changing so slowly that we are lulled into timelessness...

I pass him the water bottle. 'Thanks.' He drinks, passes it back...Cool trickling down my throat, moisture on the lips...He says, 'I could talk now.'

I glance at him. 'About?'

'What you were asking me. What happened when I got the letter saying you'd extended your contract. If you still want me to, that is.'

'What do you think?'

He begins, 'I'd got in late. Been rehearsing and sat around talking afterwards.' Amazing, half an hour's notice of the question, and the thing he couldn't find a way even to talk about before, he can now tell in this simple, detached way…

'Letter from Jennie. Drop my things, open it there in the hall. I always scan them quick, then go back and read every word.' I love this story. 'I was already overwound. You'd been saying for several letters past, it's up to *you* to make the future happen, and because I couldn't see how to do it I was feeling trapped. Responsible for you, and failing you. Then this letter, 'November's cancelled.' I remember thinking, It's *me* she's cancelling. She's doing what makes sense in *her* life.' He stops. Then, 'That's all I remember.'

'You *must* remember more.'

'Just a blankness. An inability to feel.' Pause. 'And that I walked out.'

'Out? Of the house? Why?'

'I was trapped. Primitive escape instinct, I suppose.'

'Where did you go?'

'I found myself about two hours later, several miles from home. It seems I'd just been walking off the blankness.'

I found myself—

He says quietly, 'It's a thing that has occasionally happened to me. Once early in life in an extreme form. Not often since, because I try to avoid situations that will provoke it. When it's over I am exhausted for days.' He pulls up, switches the engine off, and turns to me. 'The thing you maybe don't understand, Jennie, is that you're the first person for a very long time that I've allowed myself to become vulnerable to.'

We sit quietly, saying nothing. I take his face in my hands, pull it towards me, kiss each eye. He lifts his head, takes my hands. We are receiving quietness from a source we have tapped into rather than from ourselves…Then the moment comes to a natural end. We both feel it, slip together but wordlessly to a more mundane level. He says, 'Come, let's move a little.' Only now do I become aware of the stillness since the engine was switched off, and of the place we have stopped in—a long straight stretch, trees straggly and thin, nothing between them but grass and stones. We climb out to the blanketing sound of cicadas—cricket legs rubbing, invisible. We walk a few paces but the heat presses in, discouraging movement. We find a couple of stones to sit on and watch the build up of the elements for the afternoon storm—clouds lowering rapidly, that strange metallic light.

He says, 'This place is so *extreme*. Extreme heat. Intense glare. Endless vistas. Absolutely no sense of moderation.'

'It unnerves you?'

'I feel I've lost all ability to control what's going to happen to me.'

A crack of thunder, so close it is instantly deafening. The first hard drops hit us like hail, and in seconds have become a downpour. We scramble back into the landrover, sodden from just that minute's exposure. Laughing, panting, sitting close together to watch the violence that has been unleashed, and that if we had not had a vehicle to retreat to would have flattened us in minutes. The deafening battery on the roof, making the whole landrover vibrate. Dense curtains of water lashing the windscreen, jagged shafts of uncontrolled energy tearing the dark sky, lighting up the world for an instant and then whipped away.

3

On the pawpaw trees fruits dangle like old women's breasts. Banana fronds sway in the wind our landrover creates as it passes.

Men stand talking in the stamped earth clearings or sit on rickety chairs under shelters held up by crooked poles—simply branches of trees, put to use. Women bend over cooking utensils or walk tall with buckets of water on their heads. Women carrying, fetching, calling—always in movement.

The road winds round a corner, climbs a rise. The banana groves thin out—and there is the lake. We climb out and stand together, taking it in. Midday heat. The water is still, and more beautiful even than I had remembered. On the far shore the line of mountains runs, blue and hazy. We can't see the nearest shore—the land must drop down to it—but there are signs of the life of the people who live on the lake's edge—small boats out, apparently stationary, fishing. In the distance a ferry makes a thin white smear on the water as it moves slowly down towards the southern end. A bird circles after it. Somewhere nearer, but out of sight, another bird calls insistently.

We become aware of another sound, behind us. We turn to find it—a path through the banana trees to a couple of huts, just visible—an offbeat but rhythmic *doump-doump*, *doump-doump*, wood landing on something that muffles the impact. For me the sound is warm and familiar, announcing that we have almost arrived. Neil?—I turn to see what he is hearing. He has seen them now, the two women who stand on opposite sides of a deep wooden bowl, pounding whatever is in it with long poles, arms raised to beat on the world's oldest drum. One pole rises, the other drops, to thud. Though their movements follow so close on each other's that the slightest pause would cause their poles to collide, they seem not to need to concentrate for they talk as they lift and drop, the pattern of their voices cutting across the rhythm. One of them starts to sing, the other responds—voices alternating like the thudding poles. Then the two voices together, winding round each other.

The song comes to an end. The poles are laid down. One woman bends over to sift her hands through the grain, the other moves off to other work.

Back in the landrover, Neil taking a turn to drive. He says, 'It's clear who does all the work.'

I laugh. 'The men do things too.'

'Such as?'

'Discuss the state of the crops. Eat the meals the women prepare.' Then, at my fairest, 'And they repair houses, when termites eat the poles and the mud plaster crumbles from rain and the thatch starts leaking. Which happens every year. When I arrived in the village Derek spent two days fixing up a house with the men. I was really envious—I've always wanted to learn to thatch.'

He is amused. 'What did you get to do?'

'Winnow grain. But I'd learnt that already in Swaziland. And stir *nsima*—maize porridge. It's a case for divorce if you get lumps in it.'

'Serious?'

'No! That's one of the women's jokes. They have a good line in jokes. I didn't understand half of them, but I could see they were good and earthy, by the reactions.'

'Derek couldn't translate them for you?'

'Derek is immune from acquiring that kind of vocabulary! Maybe they're special female words anyway.'

There's an expression on his face I can't read. He says, 'I'm not sure how well I'm going to cope, Jennie. Being with men who assume their right to be waited on is not my idea of a good time.'

'We'll get you drumming as soon as we can, that'll give you common ground. And we can laugh about it in the tent at night.'

But there is something in his mood that won't shift.

The dusk, and dark falling quickly, as it always does. We are driving through a tunnel of vegetation, on roads that are scarcely more than tracks, winding endlessly, getting nowhere. There seems to be no clearing big enough to pitch a tent. Time has lost shape since the light went. Neil says, 'This could go on forever. Let's just put the tent up here, on the edge of the road.'

'It's all someone's back yard. They'll wake in the morning to find we've dumped ourselves in it without even greeting them.'

'OK ma'am, I leave it to you.'

The meek tone does not deceive me. 'It's character-forming, being out of your depth,' I say.

'I'm not out of my depth, I'm just hungry.'

Small lights dance ahead of us, moving up and down as the landrover bumps—a fire, a group of people sitting around it. Huts loom from the darkness behind them. I bring the landrover to a halt.

'I'll go and talk to them,' I say. 'You want to come?'

But he's leaving that to me too. 'I'll start unloading,' he says.

Tent up, fire going. And around the edges of the circle of light, at least fifteen small faces, big dark eyes solemnly observing our every move. The children.

Neil pauses, tin-opener in his hand. 'I can't possibly eat with all of them watching.'

'They'll have eaten. They're not hungry, just curious.'

'Still.'

So the baked bean tin multiplies like the loaves and fishes. The children may not be hungry but the tins we intended to last three weeks are scraped empty. And when there are no more, the children stay watching, till the fire is out and we have retired into our tent.

Neil says, 'I had a feeling we might be sharing the tent too. Now that would have been *really* character-forming.'

The village. The excitement of returning, and Neil here, about to live it with me...If I had a man I wouldn't be here, I told the old woman last time. But here I am arriving, man and all. Maybe you don't have to choose after all.

People gather as the landrover bumps to a halt. The men closest, women a little way behind and to one side, children wriggling in between to get a better view. I climb out into the middle of them. Greetings, laughter—the children calling, hands stretched out to touch—'Jennie, Jennie!'—the little one I used to play silly games with, pushing to the front to be lifted up and put on my hip. I glance over to Neil, who has the whole landrover between him and the welcome party. He hovers on the edge, not part of this. For an instant I see him standing in just that way at the first children's workshop, letting Megan and me do it all, till without notice he seemed to decide it was OK and shed the detachment like an unnecessary jacket…

Everyone is staring at him in undisguised curiosity. To give him time I say, 'This is my husband, Neil.' Despite myself, the words are hard to say. A babble breaks out. One of the children touches his T-shirt. Neil smiles and stretches out his hand but the child backs into a giggling group of those less brave. There is a sudden bustle through the crowd and a large woman pushes towards me—Kiluleli. We embrace, laughing in pleasure. She makes some ribald comment about me having acquired a husband, that sends everyone into convulsive laughter. 'You will cook on my fire again,' she announces. I point to the landrover full of camping equipment. 'Surely I should be cooking for my husband now?' She launches into speech so voluble that I lose all grip on the words. Then she slows down and says emphatically, *Nyoko ni nyoko*—your mother is still your mother—They all laugh again—'It's a saying she taught me last time,' I tell Neil, 'reminding the young of their duty to care for their elders'—*nanga wapendere*—even though she may be lame. Kiluleli is far from lame, still vigorously in command of an unmarried daughter and two daughters-in-law. But she's making sure no other woman gets the kudos of our presence.

I turn to Neil. 'It seems we've been adopted,' I say.

One of the men says, 'Nathaniel sent a message that a man was coming who knows how to make music. Your husband is this man?'

'He is.' To Neil I say, 'They're asking if you're the musician.'

The detachment in his eyes has become more pronounced. He says, 'You handle it, Jennie.' I turn back and say, 'He is a teacher.

It is from him I learnt music, but the kind of music Europeans play. He wants to learn to make music with you. To play the drums, if someone can teach him.' The discussion leaps off, faster than I can follow, let alone translate. Neil watches, riveted but wary. The words spin over us, meaning nothing to him.

A decision is reached, and I pass it on to him. 'Mwene will teach you. He's the old man, that one over by the tree. He doesn't drum much any more but he knows more rhythms than the younger men. And he only teaches those who really want to learn.'

'Tell them I'm very honoured.'

I translate, then turn back to Neil. 'I wouldn't get too humble. You probably got Mwene because the others have better things to do!'

His eyes suddenly come alive, flickering amusement. 'You stick to the words, Jennie. I'll do my own interpreting of motives.'

Slow days under a tree that scarcely shades, looking out to where the land drops away to the west. Steamy heat, muddy earth. Barefoot children constantly following me and my little black box that plays their songs back to them. Neil on the far side of the village, out of sight—

Mwene is in no hurry to start teaching. He demonstrates briefly on the drum, lets Neil have a go as he let me four months ago, but then puts the drum aside. 'First let us talk,' he says. For an hour or more he savours the pleasure. He asks a question. I translate. Neil answers. I translate. Mwene ponders Neil's answer. Neil's eyes laugh with mine as he submits. Mwene gets tired and says, 'Tomorrow we will start.' We are dismissed.

When tomorrow comes I make myself busy with the children. If there is no interpreter they will have to use the drums. I get out my cassette recorder and in no time the children are round me like wasps. We set off to find a clear space away from the huts. From across the compound we hear a short rhythm being beaten, then repeated on another drum. On and on, for hours…

Another day, and two drums are playing together. Another, and now there are at least three, with Neil somewhere in the middle of all those overlapping rhythms. He returns to Kiluleli's at meal times, tired, but his face alive—

—A great squawking in the clearing, children running, calling excitedly. Neil comes to stand near enough so I can give him a running commentary. The women stop in their work, laughing at the sight of this grown man who is seeing for the first time the catching and killing of a chicken—

Caught. Wings flap wildly. Throat slit. The flapping continues, then drops suddenly. Kiluleli holds up the limp corpse by the legs. The headless neck dangles. She makes a drama of the plucking—earthy jokes fly with the feathers. Neil says, 'I think I'm off chicken.'

But he doesn't have an option, for this chicken died in our honour.

Slipping back into life among the women, as if I have never been away. To the stream with the older girls, who ply me with questions. Who chose my husband, if my father is far away? Where is my mother-in-law? Do I not have to live with her? Is it true that Europeans don't give cattle or even money for a bride? What kind of celebration did we have, if our families were not there? It is all incomprehensible—what is a marriage, without these things?

Then returning, to find Neil standing at a respectable distance from a group of women, listening as they pound and sing—

A Jere, ehi!

Manyi nivwalenji nawo…

Kiluleli summons me to explain to him what the song is about, and Neil takes this as permission to come nearer. They sing it again, and I tell him, 'It's a complaint against a husband. A lot of the pounding songs are like that.' They have stopped pounding to listen. They understand none of my words but the phenomenon itself is interesting—a woman instructing her husband. 'They choose songs that say things they can't accuse their men of directly. People will know who is being got at, and if he wants the women to stop embarrassing him, he has to do something about it.'

'So what's this song say?' Neil asks.

'That her man's not ambitious enough. The woman says, How will he clothe me? His friends go to Johannesburg to work and buy suits and all he does is take a hoe and tries to catch mice!'

'She'd prefer him gone?'

'She'd prefer not to be poor!'

Kiluleli asks what he has asked. The question and my answer get relayed around the group and cause an outburst of comment and joking. They all start chipping in with things the man needs to have explained to him. Tell him, they say, we women are the ones who have to make sure something grows, and that there is food cooked every day, and that the man has sons to follow him. Tell him it is only the men who have a chance to go somewhere and earn money. Tell him if your man is lazy and just wants to stay in the village so he can visit your hut at night, you have to watch other women's children with bought clothes and money for school books while yours have nothing—

Neil puts his hands to his ears, pleading for peace. 'Tell them they've given me the answer to our problem,' he says. 'You stay in Lusaka, and I'll go back to the big city to find someone who will pay for my music.'

'Sorry, no good. My minimum requirement is a shared bed.'

'What are you saying?' demands Kiluleli. But she's not getting that one.

Back to a different sense of time, regular repeated patterns. The fundamental thing about music is that it structures time, he said once—and now the pace of village life structures it for us. The noontime buzz of insects. Afternoon rain. Standing by our tent to watch the sun set, the land fired. Evening noise of cicadas. Deep darkness of the night, lit only by stars and the flickering glow of the little fires with people sitting round them, the huts looming darkly behind.

Back into the tent, our own enclosing space. Making love and waking to find each other again. Sleep, Neil's body warm and large and real, right there, part of that sleep always.

Each day I wake in the still-dark. I shift myself quietly out of the sleeping bag, open the tent flap, wrap myself up against the damp morning air, and sit to watch the dawn slip silently towards me. I turn, hearing Neil move. Now he is here, sitting beside me. We sit with arms around each other, not speaking, letting the early morning noises from the village float over to us. Cocks crow. Dogs bark. Voices call. Utensils clang. The light gets stronger. The new day, like every other day, moving at the same pace. Time stretching, limitless.

4

What the village gains from our presence, apart from entertainment, is access to a vehicle. Mwene's son needs to go to the Boma office in Rumphi. By the time I am ready to set off, there's a group of six men waiting at the landrover for a ride. We leave Neil drumming and off we go, and while I'm there I load up with more supplies of food to contribute to Kiluleli's household. Two days later her daughter-in-law needs to be taken to the hospital in Livingstonia; she is large with her first pregnancy and has strange pains in her belly. It's a long drive, and a beautiful one, skirting Nyika itself. By the time we are nearing Livingstonia she no longer has pains, and she tells me her own parents' home is in a village just a few miles away. At her parents house she settles in, clearly intending to stay. We are too late for the hospital today, she says, but I need not wait, from nearby here she can get a bus any day. Now I am confused—if I go back without her, am I in trouble with Kiluleli? But who's side am I on, anyway? It's fine for me to assume filial obedience for a couple of weeks, but if I had Kiluleli deciding all the important questions in my life I'd need a break too, no doubt about it.

When I return alone no one seems surprised. Maybe they meant me to leave her there? Maybe she has to go back to her own family for the baby's birth? Perhaps that's what 'strange pains in the belly' means? Or perhaps they had an argument, and they're sending her back, but didn't want to burden me with the unpleasantness of knowing? There's no way I can attempt subtlety, at my level of language.

We are every minute aware of our difference, but what excites is the illusion that we are transcending it. And it is clear the people in the village feel it too. The children will not let me go, the young girls wait in little groups for chances to get me alone, Kiluleli claims me against other corners. There are always a couple of men standing near where Neil practices with Mwene, and when Mwene thinks it is time for a break a group gathers in no time, squatting on their haunches, and I am summoned to translate. Any visitor represents a rare chance to find out about a world they have no means of reaching, and they question him closely. 'How do you know about these things?' he asks. 'There's hardly a newspaper reaches this village.' They laugh and say, 'When one goes to town he listens to the radio in someone's shop, and when he comes back everyone will learn what that one man has found out.'

We use a bizarre combination of my limited chiTumbuka, their limited English, with sideways swipes into Chichewa to plug the gaps. The younger men who know some English monitor my interpreting. '*Ufumu nkhuwoko*,' Mwene says to Neil, and I translate, 'It's an old saying—it means something like, Your worth is in your own hands. He can show you rhythms, but it's up to you how well you learn.' But one young man thinks I have not properly understood. Mwene wanted to say that he may be a famous musician in his country but we know nothing about that. Only if we hear the drumming is good, then we will know. Neil responds in kind—'Tell them there's a poet in our language who said *How can we know the dancer from the dance?*' I attempt an explanation but in my clumsy chiTumbuka it's becoming a long paragraph. 'Choose something simpler!' I say; but Neil insists. 'He means, if the dancing or drumming is good, it does not matter who is doing it, it is the *music* that we hear.'

Debate breaks out again. Mwene nods approval and announces that this man understands music. The younger men start telling Neil about the *vimbuza* dance that drives out the illness caused by spirits—they jump up to demonstrate the ankle-bell stamping, the headdress whisking at every shake of his head. 'The power of the dance is not really in the dancer,' they say, 'but in the spirit working through him. And if the drumming is not right, the man who dances will never have the power he needs.'

Mwene asks, 'This poet, he is from your country?'

'Irish,' says Neil. Discussion breaks out on the exact nature of the Irish—are they British or are they not? One says they are a tribe like we Tumbuka, dominated by a larger tribe. That seems good enough. 'And I am from another minority tribe,' says Neil.

Mwene disputes. The Scots are not a real tribe, he says. He has had many opportunities to learn about them, because there have been Scots missionaries in the area since his grandfather's time. They cannot be a tribe for they do not have their own language.

'We used to,' says Neil, 'but the English punished people who used it. Now the language is only there in our songs.' And they are off again, mulling over this new but entirely plausible idea that tribal dominance exists also among the British.

It is some days before their own stories begin to come out, days of sizing us up. Derek they trust; I came with Derek but I am a woman; Neil comes with me, but he doesn't know Derek—it's all getting a bit tenuous. They have welcomed us because we provide a diversion in life, but anything beyond that requires testing. But gradually we start hearing stories of the Youth Pioneers who arrive to round the men up into the back of a truck and drive them off to town to appear at political rallies, where they have to sing praise songs to the President. Compulsory lift there, but by the time the rally is over the truck has disappeared…find your own way back. A man in the neighbouring village refused to go…sudden attack in the night, a hut on fire; the man crippled for life.

We retreat to our tent, and listen in a new way to the night sounds.

Nights are our only guaranteed times alone, but there are unexpected interludes when it rains and people scatter for shelter. Then we run for the tent, to fall laughing together on to the sleeping bag—released again to closeness, to touch, body to body, still celebrating the newness of this constant possibility. I say, 'How long do you think we can keep up this level of activity?' He says, 'A couple of decades?' We listen to the rain, willing it to keep going—

—Sounds of people moving about. If we stay too long the children will be here, not quite peering in but the sounds of their moving and whispering right next to the tent. We emerge, to an earth steaming. It is like a second awakening of the day—the plants shake off their moisture, the grass begins to lift where it has been flattened. Neil goes back to Mwene and his drumming, the children return to find me.

Away from his world and mine, we make the shape of our first days of coupled life with the eyes of this other world constantly on us, noting any departure from a set of restrictions that in any other context would seem to us arbitrary, absurd. But it is only an intensified version of what all new lovers must experience—the world blown open inside you, while the 'you' other people see gets on with practical things, and everyone seems to collude in behaving as if that extraordinary inner life does not exist. We are alert to the nuances that edge each separate consciousness, carried by the urge to make of them one…From across the clearing I watch Neil's absorption as he drums. There is a compulsive quality in the long cycles of repetition, changing so subtly that unless you are part of the making of them you aren't aware of the moment of change, only that it is now different from the last time you noticed. The concentration it demands of him, body and mind, are like a meditation, his medium for regaining the solitude that is necessary to him.

Early evening, and he sits now with a group around a brazier. Nothing very active going on. Someone drums idly; someone says something, but there's not enough energy in it to bother to summon me to interpret. The ease with which he sits there makes me think, he's ready, to share something of himself that is more than they will discover if he meets them only on their ground. I go to get the viola that he has not played since the soldiers thought it might carry explosives, and go over to the group and put it in his hands—

—They gather closer to see this instrument that at first they think is a type of guitar. Neil's eyes are laughing at me—You don't give up, do you? But his hands are tuning it up already, and he plucks absent-mindedly as he thinks what he will play. His fingers find a tune the women were singing earlier today. There's a buzz of recognition. He smiles but he's hardly noticing them or what his fingers are doing. Suddenly he has decided—he picks up the bow, and the viola bursts into sound. It has become a gipsy fiddle, swirling music to dance to, rhythm that drives the feet to move, the hands to clap. The tunes change, become Scottish reels—notes and rhythms circling, speeding up, beoming now incredibly rapid, raw. The wild highlands, the hills of Nyika, it calls to something in all of us—

'You can say what you like about that early training in technique,' I say when he pauses, 'but look what it lets you do now!'

'You're wrong, my girl. I had to go to Nova Scotia to learn that.' And later in the tent, lying together watching the flickering shadows from the kerosene lamp, he tells me about the summer he spent there, escaping from music college to try to find something more real…'Someone told me there was a Scots community that had been there for generations, and passed on to their children a way of fiddling that stayed close to the dance—moving from what moves inside you.'

He wears it so lightly, but I know that what moves in him is something quite exceptional; a depth of lived experience beneath the mind that forms his music, the hands that set the reels flinging furiously off his bow—

He says, 'It's what I tried to show you years ago, when you were lamenting not having learnt an instrument as a child. You were lucky to come to it fresh, simply following your own desire. I had to fight my way free to try to find my own musical impulse, to get my mother's hands off my soul—You asked about my family, Jennie. I've been trying to work out ever since why can't I just tell you.'

I lie still, aware that almost anything I say now could halt him.

'My mother—'

But now he cannot find a way in. I prompt, 'All you've ever told me is that she played Handel.'

He takes the lead gratefully. 'She was a frustrated musician. She taught piano in a girls' school but she'd never got past lessons at school herself and no one thought it important that she should. What she needed was a lover who would recognise her as a real person, and all she got was my dad who couldn't tell a real person from a bottle of scotch. She used me to make up for what she didn't get from him. She tried to turn me into her life's companion, receiver of all her confidences, the one who would always love her best.'

'And you?'

'I was embarrassed, and out of my depth, and I felt I was being used. And most of all I couldn't handle knowing that I hurt her every time I pushed her away. So I escaped, by shutting myself in my room and practising my violin.'

'Why your violin? There are other escapes.'

'None my mother recognised. I was her wish-fulfilment musically as well. All those hours practising, she was leaving me to it because she felt it bound me closer to her. And all the time I was burrowing down my own tunnel to get away.'

'And that's how you got to be a prodigy?'

'Prodigy's a trifle strong! A *lad o' pairts*, maybe.' I have beguiled him into laughing at himself. 'But that too was a trap. Even going to music college, I thought I was getting away—I hardly went back in holidays, I made sure I was travelling all the time, but she had manipulated her way into my very hands on the violin, the tension was always there, I had to keep finding new ways to come at it to try to free them, setting myself insane technical challenges. And I was so blocked emotionally I didn't even understand what was going on.'

'It was just you she used that way? Not your sister? Your brothers?'

'I don't know about the others, they were so much older. I told you, we weren't a family, just a collection of people trapped by each other.'

'Neil, what I said about you and Juan, and Themba—you didn't like it, did you?'

'I find it difficult to hear,' he admits.

'Why? You must know it's true.'

'You're seeing the end result of a rather long process. There have been other people earlier in life whom I failed. You don't undo those failures, however you try to move beyond them.'

'Perhaps it was trying that made you.'

'Perhaps. In my music, certainly. But getting to that point took reversing all I'd imbibed as a child about how you handle tension. In our house the standard thing was, you walked out.'

'Your father?'

'Perpetually. And I *wanted* him gone because I hated what he was like with my mother. I couldn't understand why she kept taking him back. But it wasn't just him My older brother and sister were leaving home from the time I can remember. They'd come back, get into an argument with my dad, and leave again. No one took any responsibility for anyone else. I learnt to eventually out of deep necessity, but I had to work out how you did it entirely on my own. You *have* to understand, that's why it matters so much, not walking out on Juan.'

'I understand,' I say, almost automatically, for he needs me to say it; but I am registering that it is Juan he talks of in this way, not Teresa—

—Bodies touching, all the way down. Skin coming alive to sensation, but content to hold it quietly for a while yet, knowing we have time. He says, 'There's less than a week left, and I'm not yet ready to leave the tent.'

The tent has become our metaphor for a state of being in which we can shut out the world and feel we have been new created, the first man and woman, the first ever to love; can sleep safe in each other's arms, and stir in the night to the knowledge of that loving presence and the small night noises outside. Wake to the new day's first glimmerings of light, and sit with the tent flaps open and feel the dew in the air—

But in this moment of birth I am saying goodbye to all that I look out on. Neither of us is quite ready.

5

Kiluleli has just understood that we are staying only a few days more. It seems an extraordinarily short visit—we cannot go so soon, she insists. I explain that we have no choice, I have work to get back to and Neil his final recital to prepare for. She summons some of the other women to confer, and announces that we cannot leave until the village has celebrated our marriage. People would carry the burden of something badly done, and that would bring them trouble from the ancestors.

'In other words, it's a while since there was an excuse for a party,' I tell Neil. The ancestors probably also have in mind that a wedding celebration will up the stakes on my next trip to town to lay in supplies, but that suits me well. It's a puzzle still to know what level of gift people will see as appropriate. Too much can be insulting, implying that their hospitality was not freely given. Too little would be worse. Kiluleli has taken it upon herself to provide a formula.

Everyone gets involved. The younger women bustle, preparing food, calling instructions to the children. The boys compete with each other in demonstrating the jumping dance of the men of the bridegroom's family. There is a dispute over whether Neil will be drumming—some say he's the bridegroom, how can he? But Mwene supports him. The men summon me to interpret while they explain to Neil which dances will be used, but they can't agree among themselves for the roles are too confusing. There are songs to be used by the village the bride is from, and others by the groom's. We are both but neither…We all know we're play-acting but people get worked up about it anyway, , and everyone has a different breaking point at which they laugh and say, What does it matter? They are different—

—Across the milling people my eyes find Neil's, and in the brief moment before he gets drawn off by the drummers we share a flash of amusement, but something more—an awareness that we are being carried on their wave, that the thing is out of our hands now. It is oddly less problematic to submit to someone else's ritual than your own. You are free to regard it with scepticism, but still it takes you through certain paces, across unseen borders that might have taken a long time by more ordinary routes…Now the entire village has assembled. The girls pick up the smaller children, sitting them on their hips as they crowd nearer, not to miss out as the line of women comes dancing into the space in the centre, bodies squashing closer together until the last one is in. The music accelerates. Breasts swell and heave as they bend forward, or fall back and flatten as they fling their heads back. A woman hip-sways her way into the centre, to dance alone while the others keep up their accompaniment of voice and body. Someone begins to ululate—*u-lu-lu-lu-lu-lu-lu*, the sound more bird than human, and I feel Paula with me, dancing in my attic. The circle of hypnotically moving bodies begins to wheel its way round again. One of the young girls who first taught me to dance breaks the rules to move into the centre. The crowd exclaims and calls, and for a few minutes they give her licence—small firm breasts that shiver as she shakes her shoulders, slim hips rotating—till an older woman pulls her away from everyone's premature attention. The whole thing is so overtly sexual it leaves me almost breathless—the women's bodies heaving, the men's intense involvement as they watch, the passionate energy of the drummers, sweating faces, arms pounding; the girl's unconscious grace and conscious awareness of the effect she is creating with her bare, shaking shoulders…The provocation and longing, given free reign to celebrate within the safety of the dance those instincts that in the steady rhythm of every day are hedged round with rules and penalties—

—Finally alone. Neil comes into the tent, sweaty from all that drumming as I am from the dancing. Too late to find water to wash with till the morning. The sweat has become part of the intimacy, part of living in a tent, of walking into the fields to find a place to squat, of rolling into the same crumpled sleeping bag each night, his body and mine, his day's sweat and mine, baptism into a life in which separation is unthinkable. Eyes laughing, he says, 'So we're married. That saves a lot of bother and expense.'

We wake to an atmosphere of torpor. The men are either sleeping off hangovers or sitting about lethargically. Mwene is uninterested in drumming. Kiluleli is not in her hut. Her daughters are there, but uncommunicative.

The hangovers and tiredness are natural, but it gradually becomes clear that something more is going on. 'Have we broken some fearsome taboo?' Neil asks. But it's probably nothing to do with us, just something they don't want us to know.

Later I walk around the village again, asking the other women where Kiluleli is. I notice now that while everyone is behaving oddly, there's something specific about the way the women avert their eyes—as if they are collectively deciding to be sullen. I go back to Neil. 'I'm beginning to think some woman got beaten up last night, and Kiluleli's bathing the wounds.'

Neil is looking cooped up, too large for the tent, too large for the village. 'Let's get out of here till they sort it out. If we can do it without setting off a great stramash.'

'Stramash—I like that!'

'You can have it. It's wearing me down. We won't get three yards before we'll have a trail of children joining us.'

'I'll have another go at finding Kiluleli. She'll sort the children out.' He looks sceptical. I say, 'I'll tell her it's an inviolable European custom to let a newly married couple have time alone, without anyone watching.'

Kiluleli is there this time. Neither of us mention what's going on in the village. She says, 'Go, the children will not trouble you.'

When I tell Neil he says, 'They're glad to be rid of us.'

And it's true, our exclusion feels like rejection. There's no reason why they should tell us but it breaks something that was growing, and tender.

'Maybe just as well,' I say. 'Simplistic notions help no one.'

Off in the landrover, to make sure the children don't follow. Us excluding them—it's working both ways. We park on an isolated stretch of track leading up into a forest of pines. We walk through them, arms round each other in our new freedom, climbing up towards a rocky outcrop we could see from where we parked. When we reach the level where the pines give up, we find a bit of overhang that shades us, and sit soaking in the view over towards the mountains in the east. It's a buzzy day, nothing here but us and the insects, and an occasional lizard.

He says eventually, 'So much for last night's celebration.' His voice sounds burdened, more personally than it need be. I say, 'Leave it, Neil. It's nothing to do with us.'

'I know,' he says, but it's got to him anyway. 'I've been remembering—the way we've been talking, Jennie, I keep coming up against things I haven't thought about for years, and don't want to start remembering. But they're pushing themselves at me now. Thinking about last night—weddings, and the fuss people make of them, and what they're landed with afterwards. My mother used to tell me the things my father said to her when they were first together. She fed on those words, and they kept her a slave. I've never been able to bring myself to say things like that to any woman.'

'Or cope with it when they ask for it.'

He smiles, ruefully. 'No.'

'Where is she now?'

He looks surprised, as if he can't see why I ask. 'Edinburgh.'

'And your father?'

'Dead long since.'

'Do you see her ever?'

He shrugs. 'When I have to be in Edinburgh for other reasons.'

'How often is that?'

'Maybe three times in the last fifteen years.'

'Your brothers and sister?'

'No.'

'Never?'

'We have nothing in common, except the things we all wanted to get away from.' He shifts abruptly, warning that something is beginning to trap him again. 'I told you, Jennie, the only way to survive was to cut, to start again. My mother's view of it is that she loved me and that for some inexplicable reason I turned against her. But I'd never experienced a kind of love that wasn't a threat. You don't get away from what growing up like that leaves unresolved in you.'

'I am amazed we ever got started, Neil.'

'So was I. You just walked in, that's the thing. You didn't ask for intimacy, you assumed it. We were already in it before I could get a hold on myself—and once I was there, I knew this was what I had always wanted, but always tried to evade. It's your vigour that makes it possible, Jennie. When you're stroppy and not letting me put anything over you, I couldn't stop myself delighting in you if I were under threat of death for it. It's only when—'

'Only when I *need* something from you?'

Something difficult is stirring in me now. We're getting near the crux of what goes wrong between us and it's making me feel vulnerable just listening. 'Like when I told you I was scared—then you can't stop yourself cutting off, is that it?'

'I am telling you that this is a history I'm landed with.' He speaks quietly, deliberately. 'I'm trying to explain that the way I react has nothing to do with you. But it will be easier for both of us if we can get to a situation where you'll not be feeling that too often.'

That flips me into indignation. 'And you think I don't want that? Do you think I have *liked* feeling insecure?'

His voice gets steadier as mine gets angrier. 'All I am trying to say is I want to move on from where we are, as quick as we can, to something emotionally more stable. For both of us.'

'Well go right ahead,' I say, the indignation fully in its stride. 'It's in your hands as much as mine.'

'Your solutions are always very simple, Jennie.'

I hardly hear him. 'And it makes me *wild*, this *I like you when you're angry* bit. It's so bloody sexist. And patronising. It's like saying the anger isn't real.' I pause for breath. 'And what makes me more furious is that I can't stop myself feeling furious when you say it, and that plays into your hands!'

'Jennie, *stop*.' The voice is that of a father ordering a child, and I am surprised into obeying. He takes my hands firmly, not giving me a chance to refuse. It is obvious that he is completely unperturbed by my outburst—proof of what he has just said. The waves of indignation begin to subside, till I am quiet from inside myself. The pressure of his hands has steadied me, making me safer than if he had tried to put reassurance in words. He's not letting go, that's the essential thing.

6

One last meal with Kiluleli, then tomorrow we pack up the tent and leave. I have been left in charge of stirring the nsima while she has gone off to see a neighbour. A little way away Neil is chatting to a group of the older boys, just returned from school in Rumphi. They pride themselves on being able to talk without an interpreter but the questions are limited to Books One to Four of the English syllabus—'Where do you live? What is your father's name?'...The words drift over me as I watch the thick glug-glugging that follows my wooden stirrer through the porridge. Such simple family questions, and they're within inches of a minefield...

'How old are you?'

'How old do you think I am?'

They discuss it vigorously in chiTumbuka. The spokesman announces the verdict. 'We think you are like our fathers. But you are only just married!'

Neil laughs. 'I'm forty.'

'And you never married before?'

'In my country a man and a woman can be together even if they're not married.'

Rapid conversation breaks out again. What exactly did he say? They check that they have heard it right. 'You had a woman but she was not your wife?'

'Yes.' He laughs at their amazement. 'Almost a wife.'

'You have children by her?'

'One son. He is not really my son but I feel he is.

They move to the next question. 'How many brothers have you got?'

'Two,' he says—and then corrects himself. 'One now. One died.' My stirring hand stops.

'When did he die?' they ask.

'A long time ago. Fifteen years.'

They lose interest in the brother, so long dead.

Kiluleli comes back to check on the porridge. Neil and the boys are still talking, but I hear no more.

Night, and we sit outside the tent—dark shapes of trees and grass just beyond where we can see—

'Neil, I heard you talking to the boys.'

'I saw.'

I take that in. 'Did you *want* me to hear?'

'It wasn't a conversation I planned. It happened.'

'But still you tell them, and you couldn't tell me?'

'It's not so strange. Their questions are idle. They've no real interest in the answers.'

'This has been going on too long, Neil. We need to move past whatever else you're holding on to, and tonight. You lay traps for us both, blocking off chunks of yourself like this.'

'You measure it by the things I still don't know how to share. I measure it by the enormous amount I've already shared with you, as with no one else.'

'Not even Teresa?'

His voice is suddenly sharp. 'I said no one. And Teresa wouldn't ask. She takes me as I am.'

That hurts. He sees it and says, even sharper, 'Jennie, if we're going to get anywhere sorting out how to accommodate Teresa, you have to decide not to misinterpret what I say. She takes what I offer and has no curiosity beyond. That suits me, from her. You're entirely different.'

Cut. Cut talking about it. Leave it, and get up and get busy with practical things. I move things about in the tent, vehemently and uselessly, while Neil continues to sit outside alone. I can't believe I was so stupid as to say that about Teresa, it was my own absurd insecurity resurfacing now that we're having to go back to all that. But I'm sure he seized on it, because it gave him an escape route.

I get into the sleeping bag, waiting for him to come. After a long time I turn the lamp down and lie in the dark, curled up as if asleep. Eventually he comes. I wait for him to get in, then I turn towards him. He says, 'I'm tired,' and rolls over, back to me. I put an arm over him but he just lets it lie there. It is so obviously unwelcome that I take it away again, and turn over.

It is hours before I sleep, and then fitfully. Each time I sift back up into semi-consciousness it is to the knowledge of something deeply amiss, and a feeling of urgency that it has to be sorted out before we go back. Then I sink back into a sleep that is full of anxious doubtings. I dream it is Juan who is dead, and Neil is so full of grief that it seems he will never find again the ability to love without fear. His words come back at me, all the things he has only half said and then backed away from, and they move in and out of my dreams, now in his voice, now in other people's, swelling and fading like orchestrated sound.

Eventually it seems safer not to let myself be a prey to any more dreams, so I edge my way out of the sleeping bag trying not to wake him, and go and sit at the tent door, though it's deep night, many hours till dawn. I look out into the shapeless dark. I am finally beginning to understand, This man is in trouble. Longstanding, ongoing trouble. He has walled it up so effectively that even I was deceived. I have seen and heard the signs, but I did not know how to listen to them, did not consider what depth of trouble could render a man of generous spirit unable to trust himself even to someone of whose constant love he had no doubt.

I become aware that he is awake. No sound from behind me, but I am sure he is lying watching me in the dark. I turn, and see that it is so. I go back to lie with him. He folds me to him in a simple movement, arms encompassing. After a while he says quietly, 'You didn't sleep?'

'Not much. You?'

'Same. Jennie, I want to talk.'

'I'm here.'

'I hate what happened last night. If I could change, I would. But there's a lot of life gone into making me this way.'

'It's not me you need to change for, it's for yourself. To free you from the things that are trapping you, still.'

'Ever since I got to Lusaka—'

'Go on.'

'I feel like you've been *digging*, and I'm constantly trying to put back the soil, to keep him buried. It's over fifteen years ago, I don't know why it should be following me now—'

'Neil, we can't be as we are, and you still keep part of you buried.' 'I know. But it's terrifying.' He laughs, shakily. 'It sounds absurd, but I've known it would come to this, and that's been part of the fear of letting things happen between us. I'd found a way to handle it on my own, long ago, it's years since it got in the way of anything. But there was something about you that made me know you would strip me naked, and I couldn't face going back into all that again'—he stops. 'I don't suppose this makes any sense to you, there's nothing about yourself that frightens you.'

'There has been. I have been frightened each time I had to learn to do without you. Frightened that alone I wouldn't be enough.'

He says nothing. For a few moments I let the silence lie with us. Then I say, 'Is it OK if we have a light?'

'Go ahead,' he says, and sits up watching while I pump the lamp into action. I sit cross-legged facing him, taking his hands in mine. 'I don't want to dig now, Neil. It's for you to find a way.'

He is silent a few moments longer. Then he says, 'His name was Ben.'

'Ben.' We both hold the name, carefully, getting used to it being there with us.

I used to think he was like Benjamin in the Old Testament, the youngest brother, beloved boy. And the jealousy of the oldest brother, that fitted too.'

'He's the one you said I was like?'

'It's only occasional things, like the way you get incensed if you think I am treating you like a child. The connection wasn't really that—something about what you evoke in *me*. It was constantly there, constantly having to be shut away. And then the day you sang—the song of the woman in the stream your voice got *inside* me, to the part only Ben connected with. It was so painful I could hardly bear to listen, and at the same time I wanted you never to stop.'

'Shall I tell you what that song says?'

He looks surprised.

'*Catch the sun before it sets, you who are mourned.*

I loved a young man but they took him…'

We look at each other, not speaking. Eventually he says, 'I don't understand how you are possible.'

'We.'

'We.' Then, rebellious, 'But *you*, as you.' Then, as if something is just becoming clear to him, 'What's the same between you and Ben is the complete absence of guile. My older brother and sister were crusted over with it, you couldn't find the person underneath. Ben was just himself, he didn't know how to hide. But he didn't have your—' he searches for the word—'conviction. What you said about being sure you are enough. Life never gave him the chance to develop that.'

'You did, from the same starting point.'

'It wasn't the same, it was disintegrating each year, and he was four years younger than me. By the time I was seven my mother had already fixed her remaining energy on me. It was like the love of a leech, but what Ben got was worse, it was nothing. I remember watching him when he was little, wondering how babies got from being so small and helpless to being children who could run about, and feeling that our house wasn't a safe enough place for a baby. I wanted to give him things all the time, to make up for it. When I was at school and he was a toddler, I used to come home to him, like I imagined real fathers doing—' He cuts out, the memory too much for him. 'It wasn't just that I was his big brother and responsible for him, he was the only person *I* had to love. When he died—when he died it snapped something in me about the rest of them. I gave up pretending it mattered if I had anything to do with them. I've never forgiven them, for not valuing him properly when he lived, and then the ready tears when he died. Especially my mother. She gave him *nothing* when he was alive, he had nothing to take away from her.' The vehemence shakes him so that he has to wait for it to calm before he goes on, cold. 'You asked me if I ever see her, Jennie. It was four years after the funeral before I even told her where I was living. When I reappeared she started in about what she'd suffered, losing us both. I knew she had a right to feel that about me, but I couldn't take her saying it about Ben. After that I made sure she didn't ever have the chance to talk to me about him again.'

I wait, but he is stuck, needing help past the point. 'How old was he, Neil?'

'Just turned twenty.' Then, 'You haven't asked me how he died.'

'No.' And I wait for him to be ready to hear his own voice saying the words that have hovered unstated through all he has said—'He hanged himself.'

He begins to rock involuntarily, forward and back, forward and back. I circle him with my arms, holding him, letting the movement come from both of us. 'My mother—' He stops. He is crying now, trying to talk through it. I follow his breathing, willing it to become less tense…'My mother insisted I play at the funeral. One of my own pieces. That was all to do with *her* needs, nothing to do with Ben. I was too stunned, I hadn't the psychic energy to refuse. But every note was false. I felt it was being extracted from me by her self-pity and her awful power of manipulation—'

The rocking starts again, but his voice pushes on—'I took myself off where I hoped none of them could ever follow me, and sat alone in a dreadful room in London until my money ran out and I was driven out to earn some, and I couldn't touch the violin without terrible tension and had no music coming through me. I nearly went crazy—What you've told me about your home, Jennie—There's something you seem to have been given, that I've had to work to find. Without my violin I'd have made no sense of why I was here. Despite my mother, despite everything, it was my meditation, and my relationships, and my way of exploring life. And without it I—'

'Were there no friends?'

'A few from music college who'd also come south. But they were all pushing to find work and start careers—most of them had no other point of connection with life. At the college people had made a fuss of some of my stuff, that's all they knew of me, someone who had succeeded in getting launched young composing. With the musician in me incapacitated, they had no idea how to respond—we'd had no practice being *people*. Eventually I met up with someone who was going grape-picking in Spain. I went with him because I had nothing else to do, and I needed to get further away from myself. At least there was no one from my past there, no one who could expect me to make the kind of music I no longer could. Grape-picking's hard—hot, physical work, that stops you thinking. And when the harvest was over, I did what I could find, as long as I could keep away from English-speakers. Not to have to talk, or be provoked into feeling. It was like a negation of living, seeking nothingness, like Ben—'

The outpouring comes to a sudden halt. He takes my face in both hands, looking straight at me, no trace of evasion. 'Do you know this is a very strange experience for me, talking about it?'

I nod. 'And you're managing fine.'

'If you come out the other side of that kind of isolation, Jennie, you are different, fundamentally. I knew no Spanish when I went—for months I hardly used words except for unavoidable practical purposes. When I started speaking again it was in Spanish and everything came out differently, not just the words, but what I thought or felt with them. I didn't know I had been learning it, but my ears had just gone on while all the rest cut out. But I wasn't just learning a language, I was listening to *human sound*, trying to work out how people used their voices to break out of their separateness and connect with each other, and their fingers on the guitar, and their bodies in the dance. I began to understand that music exists because people *need* it, to express energy, and pathos, and humour, and all the things that come organically from living—and I could see now why the music I was trying to make had given up on me, it had nothing to do with me. And then I began to think, if I could learn a new way of being musical, like I've learnt a new way of using language, it won't ever desert me again, because it won't be external to me.' He stops again. 'And you see if I could only have understood any of those things before Ben—he had nothing that—I don't know how to tell you, Jennie, he was intelligent and sensitive, yet nothing ever lit his imagination enough to make him want to work at it. I was the only person who made life real for him, but I kept trying to shield him. I couldn't bear him to be dragged down into the mess. I saw too late, I had done all his fielding of tension for him. You have to deal with those things yourself—He had a kind of desperation about sex, Jennie, a feeling he'd never get it together to find a girl. He'd a group of mates, older than him mostly, but useless to him, all surface buddiness, talking about their sexual conquests when he was paralysed about how he would ever get a girl. They hung about near the pub before opening time to show they were going to be the first in—Ben was under age, but tall enough to get away with it. But he wanted to say no, he was afraid of becoming like our dad—those things happen to lots of lads that age, it's only afterwards you look back and think, I could see all that, and I walked out on the problem, just like our dad used to.'

'Neil, don't—'

'It's true, Jennie, I know, you don't. Everything was going wrong for him, and I didn't know what to do, so I left. The day I heard I'd got a music scholarship I told him I wasn't coming back, ever, that when he left school he could come to me and we could share a place. But he had years still to go, and he only came to Glasgow a couple of times in my first year, and then he stopped.'

'You were writing to him?'

'I don't know. It's hard to believe, but I can't remember. Not what I did, nor what I thought I was doing. I was blanking out, playing my violin till I was squiff-eyed and composing pieces based on medieval fragments.' The hardness is back, painful. 'There must have been some specific trigger. My mother knows, I'm sure.'

'She didn't say?'

'Because it had something to do with her. I was gone, who did she have left? And if she was draping herself over him asking for comfort—maybe more than just comfort, who knows?' He shifts tensely, to dislodge the thought. 'It's only a guess, I've nothing to go on. Except her voice when she phoned that last couple of times. She was worried about him, she said. She was worried all right, but it was like all my mother's emotions, it was entirely to do with herself, not him. She sounded—panicky, like she knew she'd gone too far. Pleading with me to come back. Ben needs you, she said, you're the only one who could get through to him. But all I could hear was *her* voice and all I could feel was that I had to shut her out.'

The light splutters and dies.

Dark, sudden and intense. I move to relight the lamp. Neil holds me back—leave it, the movement says. And he begins again to rock in the cradling dark, moaning softly, 'I didn't go…I didn't go.'

Rocking, rocking, body to body, till his voice dries up and he is motionless against me and it is my body that rocks his. And the rhythm of my rocking arms says, I have seen now the pit of hell from which you fled, and flee from still…Rocking, holding…and now the rhythm moves within me, and I am in a room with light glancing off a cello and the child Juan coming up to talk to him, and his arm rests lightly, easily on the boy's shoulder. *'You have to understand,'* he said, 'that's why it matters so much, not walking out on Juan'…Beloved boy, one more chance…

Back, back through a dark tunnel, and it is myself I am rocking, the self that once huddled alone in the night in the hills and was lost and cast out, and there was nothing to defend me against the knowledge of those I had failed…And the rhythm goes on so long that it carries me beyond self, to an attic where I lay holding Paula's sobbing head against my chest, and rocked her against the fear of aloneness, the death of love…Hold her, rock her, this woman who has held me and lifted me. Hold him, rock him, this man who has given meaning to what I have tried to become.

Be still, my love. What has happened has happened. It is finished.

7

Outside the tent, the first sounds of the village waking. We need to get up and fetch water and wash, and go out and be part of the life which cannot be avoided and so must be danced. Another round, another round.

Pack up the tent, pack up the landrover. Goodbye to the children, the men drumming, Kiluleli stirring, the early mornings watching the dawn. Back on to the rough road, past rickety stalls selling Nyika honey. Through banana groves, past groups of women pounding, bending, carrying, arms raised to steady the pot of water on the head.

Stopping one more time to see the lake, miracle of light and water and stillness, the haze of heat on the distant line of mountains.

On to the town, Lilongwe, to find Derek's friend Nathaniel who sent the message to the village to say we were coming. Now it is our turn to take him a message from his mother, and some rolls of tobacco from home. Nathaniel welcomes us, summons his wife to prepare food for us. That's several hours. Stupid to be back counting time again, but we're ready to be gone, back to that other life, ready to start the future. Nathaniel says if we're not in a hurry can we give his friend a lift to the hospital? His uncle is having an operation. Nathaniel comes too. At the hospital he meets another friend, who needs a lift to the airport to collect a package that has been sent by his cousin who is working in Johannesburg. At the airport—

At the airport the most extraordinary thing happens.

We are hot, tired, and beginning to feel we will never escape from Lilongwe. Nathaniel's friend is taking forever with some official who will not release the package without going painfully through several sets of forms in triplicate. While we wait for him we watch idly as the passengers assemble for the flight to Johannesburg. Neil says, 'I didn't know there were flights from here to South Africa. I thought there was a boycott.'

'This is the only African airport that does them,' I say, 'So the planes from Europe stop over here to refuel.'...Idle chat, no energy in it, just letting time tick over till we can set off—

And then I see through the plate glass windows the passengers from the transit lounge file slowly out on to the tarmac, back to their plane to take off for South Africa, and one of them is Kevin.

It's not possible.

But it is him, there is absolutely no doubt about it. Some people you can mistake, Kevin's body I know, every movement of it. It is Kevin in a suit, looking scarcely any different from the last time we ate together in a restaurant in London. If Kevin is going back to South Africa, something extremely strange is happening.

Out of Lilongwe, at last. West, to the border. Neil tries to distract me, unsuccessfully. Eventually he says, 'Jennie, *leave* it now. If there's some implication for you, you'll find out. If there isn't, it doesn't matter if you never do.'

'The only thing that could make sense,' I say, undeterred, 'is that Kevin has done some kind of a deal. Being a go-between to fix up secret trade deals, maybe, to get past sanctions. But *Kevin*—I can't believe it of him. I know he was changing, but not *that* far.'

I feel Neil's eyes watching me. I glance up and ask, 'What are you thinking?'

'That it's not just me that has trouble with unfinished bits of history.'

We arrive back, to Ntombi and Winston, and the news that the day after we set off for the village the South African Minister of Justice made a public announcement. There has been a reconsideration of the circumstances surrounding our case. It is now understood that the students involved were young and misguided, not aware of the seriousness of their offence. Those still serving sentences have been released. Those who fled the country can return, and there will be no charges brought against them.

I can go back.

Chapter 4

No, no, NO—

So many things floating across my brain, most of them irrelevant. I can't think, it's just bits of debris swirling into my dreams, surfacing, lost again…Standing on a stone bridge with Paula, looking down at the slowly moving water, telling her I wanted to get back to Africa, and Paula saying, 'You can't go back where you came from—why go somewhere else?' Now I can, but I am already somewhere else…Muhib, telling me that in Urdu the words for yesterday and tomorrow are the same—*kal*. It makes sense, I said, both are just one step away from today. The only reality, a constantly moving present moment; while around us swirl circles of yesterday and tomorrow all mixed up, and they keep redefining each other. Things that have happened, which themselves create the possibilities for what may still happen—

My past is offering itself back to me, changing the future I thought I had finally made.

'It's irrelevant,' I tell Neil. Because I want it to be.

'It's far from irrelevant,' he says. 'It's part of your life. A big part.' And a part he has no connection with. His voice is ordinary but his eyes have that I-might-remove-myself look that I thought I was never going to see again, not seriously. Insecurity, just hovering, but needing to be thoroughly squashed before it can grow. I say, 'I'm not going anywhere. I told you, you're stuck with me for life.'

But it's he who has to calm me. I do not want to speak about it but I cannot sleep, and he does for me what I tried to do for him, to hold me against my irrational fear, stroking my hair in the dark and saying sensibly, 'Jennie it's not anything to feel churned up about, just unexpected. Take your time. Work out what it means for you.'

It means I can go and see them again, Mom and Dad, Richard, Peter. I should be jumping about in celebration—what's wrong with me? It changes nothing about where I live or who I am with. The only thing that's different is I can go back and see them, after years of thinking it would never be possible.

Yes, I can see it now, it's quite simple. Neil goes back to London, I stay here and finish up. Then before I go to join him, a visit home—the kind anyone might make. What Kevin was doing, that's clear now. Then I fly from there to Neil, to start our new life. A few weeks' delay, that's all. Time for Mom and Dad to know I am really back, normal, for all the talking that's never been, to happen naturally now, in its own time. Like Neil and I have had these last few weeks, it's the same thing really. Three weeks should do it. But there's Richard—he can't move, so I would need to have time in Johannesburg. A week for that, maybe. OK, that's still not too—

Peter? He could come home while I'm there, but I bet he won't. Am I going to go to him? Crazy not to, it's the only way we're ever going to get past—

Jonas. That's a whole new possibility. Going back means I could try to find him again. Why has no one heard of him, in all the three years he's been out? Will he *want* me to find him? Do I want to?

Leave it, it's finished, we've all moved on. Why dig? Just the *thought* of him is disturbing. The picture, suddenly so vivid, of Jonas thinking, feeling, reacting to all those things I no longer have to think about and react to, thank God—

I'm afraid, even thinking about going back.

But they've promised, no charges. Kevin's gone, it must be safe—

It's more basic than that, I'm afraid of myself, of not being able to predict what I will feel when I get there. If I never go back I can't feel it, so there will be no confusion. I'll just go straight to London, maybe even cut my contract short, I'm sure Fernando will understand. Just get away from all this, quick, and start life with Neil before anything else can get in the way.

And know that Mom and Dad know that I could go and see them, and that I choose not to? There is no choice. I have to go.

'Yes, go,' says Neil, 'of course you must go.' And then, laughing at himself, 'Go quickly, and come back quickly!'

But he too is not feeling simple about it, I can tell, despite the calm tone, the gentle touch. He's afraid of that other life of mine of which he knows so little, of something in it claiming me once I get there. He's talking himself into staying calm, keeping at bay that old panic that once made him walk out of the house and wander blindly for hours before he knew where he was—'She's doing what makes sense in *her* life, I have no part in that'...

He's beyond walking out now, but he's shutting himself away in the Roma house, composing, and only coming to find me when the flow dries up. All that stimulus from Nyika, he says, waiting to get out. We're sleeping at Ntombi's—she seemed to assume that was going to happen this time—but it's late before he gets here, so bed is about the only time we have together. I'm happy for him to be composing again, very. There's just something about the way he shuts that door—

Winston says, 'You are out of your mind if you go. Those bastards don't keep promises.' Fernando says, 'Your country, not mine, but I'd say it's safe enough. Probably safer if you go quickly. They know the journalists will be watching.' Ntombi says nothing, but she doesn't like this kind of talk. 'What do you think?' I ask.

She shrugs and says, 'Some have gone already, and nothing's happened.' I know what she's thinking—There's your mother waiting. How can you hesitate?

Their voices surround me, blocking my ability to think. *I* have to decide, no one else's judgement is enough.

Work out if it's safe, that's the first thing. Winston's right, there is something very odd about it all. Why give an amnesty for this one case, that happened ten years ago? Why release a couple of minor prisoners when far more significant ones are still inside? Of course there's no real change of attitude, it's calculated—but for what purpose? To cause a distraction while they hammer harder somewhere else? Are we being used as some kind of decoy? Or maybe only some of us? Kevin's OK, he stayed in Britain with his neat suits and his respectable job, too scarred by experience to want to get involved in anything political again. Meanwhile I—I, who knew I could never go back, lost all sense of the need for caution. Liberation fighters are my friends and colleagues, we work together, eat together, discuss politics together, openly long for the same future. If I cross that border and let myself be trapped again for however short a time inside their crazy logic, these things are no longer a normal human response but a treasonable offence.

But that's ridiculous, I've done *nothing*—

But Winston has. Does. And all his friends, my friends. What are they doing each time they disappear for weeks, and can't say where they have been? I can guess, and so I don't ask. But it would be easy for anyone watching us to think I must know. Perhaps it will be useful to the police if I go back, and they can question me—

No way.

'I'm not going,' I tell Neil. 'They messed up my life once, I'm not letting them near enough to do it again.'

He says nothing. I get defensive, as if I'm being accused of cowardice. 'Lusaka is crawling with spies,' I say, 'and they're serious, there are cars blown up, letter bombs through people's doors. They know about everyone—'

I stop, and notice his face. I've been talking at myself, at my own fear. Neil needs no persuading.

Words are useless, so I stop. We lie together silently, while he strokes my hair, my face. Then he rolls over to sleep. I lie thinking, he's protecting himself. I have become dangerous to him again.

Sleep evades me. I lie in the dark composing a letter home. What do I say? I cannot even hint at why I am more nervous to go back than Kevin was. But if I don't find a way to tell them but just keep stalling, what can they think except that it doesn't matter much to me whether I see them again, so caught up am I in my own concerns? I can already hear Mom trying to persuade herself out of the longing she feels. 'Of course we would love so much to see you, but it's taken you a long time to find your life with Neil. You get on with making that now. It's what we want for you. There's plenty of time later.'

But there may not be. Not for Dad.

I wake, to the Lusaka sun and the trumpet flowers outside the window. Neil turns to hold me in his half-sleep. The fears of last night seem less convincing.

I go to work, and everything is as it always was. The people who in the night were my dangerous friends take on again the shape of ordinary people, and it seems absurd to think that anyone anywhere could want to question me to find out what they are doing, when it is so obvious that all they are doing is studying English or learning how to mend cars. I watch the afternoon thunderstorm, and know that it doesn't matter where I go or what I do, this place will always be part of me, so leaving it can take nothing away from me. And when the rain is over I walk back to Ntombi's house to wait for Neil to get back, and the trees that drip with after-rain moisture line my route, as the clipped pine trees lined the route that Dad walked to school every day of my childhood, while I sat on the dusty earth of the pavement and counted the trees as he passed them, growing smaller and smaller in the distance till he disappeared.

Life is offering me the chance to stop him disappearing for good, to have him walk back along that same pavement, back into my here-and-now—him and Mom and Aunt Ellie, and the apricot tree in the garden, and all the things that formed me and made me who I am. I have lived without them for ten years, thinking it had to be forever, and it would have been perfectly possible to carry on that way if I had never been given the option. But now that they are there for the asking I cannot say 'No' without damage, to them, to myself. *Certain* damage, balancing against the small possibility of trouble.

Dad is old, and not well. He might die any day, without my seeing him again. I have to go.

Neil hasn't seen the pine trees. He says, voice controlled, 'Last night you told me precisely why it is too dangerous for you to go. Today you're telling me you're going.'

'It was night. I got it out of proportion.'

'It'll be night again. Then?'

'Neil—'

But he has turned away, and I don't anyway know what I was going to say. Except that I can't stand him turning away when we're trying to talk about something important. 'Neil, *look* at me.'

He turns and we look at each other silently for a moment. I realise he is missing the whole first chapter of my life. I thought we could start together in the middle, but it isn't that simple. I say, 'I'm sorry. It's all a mess.'

He says, 'If you go, I'm coming with you.'

For once I laugh—I haven't felt like laughing since all this started. 'And what will you do if they arrest me? Beat them up?'

He is not laughing. He moves suddenly, swings his arms about and says, 'Jennie, I'm out of my depth. It's for you to decide.'

But his eyes are so wary, they don't talk of acceptance but of escape. He says, 'I don't want you to misunderstand this, but I need some space. This piece I'm working on—I have to be alone when I'm doing it. I'll be sleeping at the Roma house for a couple of nights.'

It takes me a long time to get to sleep each night. I think, perhaps we would have faced this anyway once we got back to London. I remember how he talked about the piece he was working on at the time of Teresa's illness, that it had nothing to do with any feelings he was then experiencing, but drew on quite other parts of him, holding him together by its very separateness. Perhaps this is just how he has to be. But I think of the tent, of lying close together watching the flickering shadows of the kerosene lamp; sitting with arms around each other to watch the dawn.

All the old voices are around me again. Charity's eyes sizing me up, saying, 'You're a political, aren't you?' Jaswinder in Leicester Square saying, 'I've been seeing you every day and wishing—but I wouldn't have had the courage.' Now *I* don't have the courage. Nothing is irrelevant any more, everything I have ever been seems to be trying to crowd in on this one crucial moment of transition in my life and claim its place.

And now Neil is keeping himself away, and I know it is out of fear of loving too much and losing again. We see each other each day, but never long enough to get past the person everyone else sees. The self that he opened to me has been withdrawn, instinctive defence against the possibility that he may have to face what Teresa faced when the person she loved was trapped in a prison thousands of miles away. Until I make a decision he's not going to let me near enough to help—But it's *I* who need help, I want to shout—

Let go, let go. I cannot hold on to him if he needs to be alone.

Alone—

Paula. I need Paula. And having let the thought in, I feel almost overwhelmed at all that's happened since I could last be with her, all of it life-changing. And even when I get her on the phone it takes ten minutes of outpouring to get to the point where I can say, 'Help me, Paula, I don't know what to do.'

'Take it slowly, Jennie. You don't have to decide now.'

'I *do*. I have to say something to Mom and Dad, one way or the other. And I can't go on in this state with Neil. I've hardly *seen* him for a week. He says it's this final performance thing he's been preparing—I don't mean he's faking, he really is totally absorbed in it, I've never seen concentration like it. But *he's* set himself the task of doing it this way. He could have just used a couple of his old cello pieces, they'd have been quite happy.'

'When's it happening?'

'Tomorrow night. But then it's only four days till he leaves.'

'Jennie, this is a temporary blip, it won't undo what's happened between you.'

Her voice is strong, definite, but my panic is running away with me now. 'You don't know what he's like. He *hides* inside himself where I can't get at him, and it's fear that makes him do it, and now it's me causing that fear. If I let him go back to London in that state he'll have built huge walls again before I can get there and we'll be back to his bloody limited relationship again.'

'If that's him, maybe you have to accept it. You can't go through life avoiding things because of how he might react.'

She's right, I know it. I'm fighting against hearing what she's saying but it calms me anyway. I say, quieter now, 'I've just remembered something.'

'What?'

'You saying you'd miss me if I drowned.'

'I would,' she says. 'Still. So you take care.' Then, 'And I'm remembering something you said, that time we went for the long walk. You said, I'm trying to make sense of my *whole* life, not just this part of it.'

That's it. That's so precisely it that I am stilled by gratitude, that I have Paula in my life, that she has been there so long, and that she can still do this for me.

Out, out on my bike. Out in the last hours of daylight, on the Leopard's Hill Road past the last houses of town, to find a rock still damp from the day's rain, and sit alone, looking out. Grass, boulders, trees, sky, the shape of my present land. And beyond, to the woods and fields where I walked with Paula—and tried to summon so she could imagine them those other hills, where once I sat in the dust and watched an old man's thumbs conjure worlds of his own from the strips of metal on a small box of wood. And beyond that, to the side of a mountain where once I stood arm in arm with Jonas, momentarily singing our defiance of a crazy world. And beyond that still, to a childhood unhurried, with time stretching endlessly before me like the veld, opening out to a vast dome of sky.

I am in the middle of Africa, and about to leave. Whichever direction I fly in, this is the end of a part of my life. Ntombi, Winston, the students in the classes. The women in the market who laughed as they put a baby to my milkless breast; the *ndimba-kalimba* playing children, the mudpools of Kalingalinga, the night watchman who let me squat next to his brazier and practise chiTumbuka...Each in turn they come before me, and each in turn I hold briefly—we take hands, and round together once in a circle dance, then on to the next—while somewhere in the wider group is the partner I started out with, and though I don't see him I never lose the awareness of him till eventually the dance brings us back opposite each other again—to touch, to hold, to circle each other, momentarily oblivious of all others. Then the music moves us on.

The others are circling back towards me again. They come in two sets, each waiting for me to join them but I can only go one way. Paula, Jane. Jaswinder, Derek, Megan. Michael, who will be at school now—what kind of a school, and what will it be doing to him, letting him become? Juan and Teresa, who don't yet know that I am coming, to be part of their daily life. And then the other set, Jonas, Richard, Peter, Mom, Dad…

Dad sitting on a chair under the maple tree, his shorts slipping below his brown belly, reading. Dad laughing at my indignation, but the laughter in his eyes loving me, as Neil's does when he is relaxed and not retreating from the things he cannot deal with. Dad waking me on a frozen July morning to go to the station to collect one of the boys. 'Are you sure you want to come?' he asks.

Are you sure you want to come? echoes his voice across the years, as he waits now for my answer.

Neil, my love, I say, but not to him, for I am here on a rock looking out at the land and he is behind his closed door—I am hearing your voice too, rocking in the dark and moaning, 'I didn't go'…The sound is so painful I can hardly bear to remember it, but I am making myself hold on to it because I want you to understand that I am going for both of us. I want to hold on to what we have, but see, in my trying to hold on we are losing each other already. Nothing ever stays still, the whole universe is dancing. We have to move with the dance, or lose part of ourselves.

2

The performance was—Extraordinary. Even I, knowing what he is capable of, had no conception beforehand of what it was he was working on all those intense hours when he was not with me. I realise now I didn't think about it musically at all, simply as an emotional state. Now I sat watching as his hands on the drums evoked the slowly repeating patterns of village time, the long unfolding road, and I understood that the door he had closed on me and the world was like an in-breath that makes possible the next out-breath. Each in turn the people he had been learning from moved into the spaces his moving hands shaped, and added their own music to his, which itself drew life entirely from theirs, and there was no way to tell the dancer from the dance. His cello he had put into the hands of Themba, his brother musician, who used it like a steady bass voice in African harmony, deep and full on open strings. Their complete awareness of each other as they played was so moving that I lost for a few moments the ache of loneliness that for the week past had settled in my gut, and that I had thought might never move again. To get to this point they must have been playing together for hours every day, and all I had seen was that Neil was avoiding me. He was, but it made a different kind of sense now. I saw that I had failed him as he had failed me. I had been so preoccupied with my own dilemmas that I had not even tried to imagine what all this was demanding of him, could not rejoice in what he was giving to others, and in giving, receiving. I saw only what I thought he was taking away from me.

—Let it go, let it go. It has happened, we have to move on. Just open up to the music—it is his voice, speaking through what he makes possible for others. Speaking also to me, perhaps, the things he can't say, about what being here has helped him to become. Accept that, and be glad.

I waited for him at the end, through all the packing up and goodbyes. He was flushed and tired, but the tension that had closed him up for so many days had drummed itself out, and he looked as he used to after a day with Mwene. Standing there waiting, I began to feel again something stirring between us, an awareness that he too was waiting, and wanting to be alone with me. When finally the hall was almost empty and there was no one near, he lifted his head to look at me—really looked at me properly for the first time for a week. I stood receiving it, so gratefully I could feel the tears starting, and I didn't bother to stop them.

I said, 'I feel like we're starting all over again.'

He nodded. 'I need to. I'm sorry, Jennie.'

'Forget it. It's over.' He nodded again, but he was waiting. 'Neil, I've decided. I have to go.'

'Yes.' As if he had known all along, and it was the obvious thing.

'Your music, tonight—'

He took my hands to stop me. 'I know,' his hands said, 'it doesn't need saying. Go back to what matters.'

'Fernando has released me from the rest of my contract. I'm leaving when you do, and I'll be back with you in London in six weeks.'

His hands tightened. 'Don't worry about the timing, Jennie, just do what you have to do.' And then he looked suddenly completely exhausted.

Chapter 5

The immigration officer pages slowly, too slowly, through my British passport, studying each page carefully. Place of birth, Bloemfontein, South Africa. He turns again to the cover, as if he can't quite believe the nationality. Then he lifts his head, and I hate his eyes. They look at me as a man does who mentally undresses a woman while he considers if it's worth having a serious go at her.

'So we weren't good enough for you?' he says. Voice supposedly jocular, but the tone is deliberately provocative. 'Or were you one of those who ran away?' *I don't have to reply*, I tell myself, but the adrenalin is pumping already. He continues to stare, idly tapping the passport as he waits for an answer.

'I was studying in Britain,' I say. Then, as that doesn't seem enough, 'My husband is British.' Now I really begin to panic—Why did I say that? They can so easily check. He's got me on the defensive already, there is nothing these people aren't going to be able to get out of me if they seriously try—

He is still staring at me, as if considering whether to challenge me. Silently I rehearse my defence. Kevin is a British citizen, I married him. It's all true, all legal. The staring eyes say, Don't think we don't know about that, young lady. And why did you get divorced the moment you got your own passport, may I ask?...I shift ground—I'm not talking about him, I say, 'I have a new husband now'—Oh, Christ, why did I get into this?

'Your husband, hey,' he says, turning the word over to examine its possibilities—he's really speaking now, it's not just my panic. 'But I see you're still calling yourself de Villiers?' His eyes leave me to deal with that one while he reaches over to get a sheet of paper and starts making notes on it. Passport number, name, date of issue.

'Lots of women keep their own name these days,' I say. It sounds unbelievably feeble. He keeps his head down, writing as he says, 'Not here, they don't.' I am waiting for him to ask, 'Have you got your marriage certificate?' But he's moving on, maybe saving that for later. He continues to turn the pages, noting the visas on to his sheet of paper. Kenya, Malawi, Zambia…It's all there, like a police dossier. Date of arrival, date of departure. It might as well list the names of my friends…Zambia, Malawi, Zambia, Malawi, Zambia…I watch the top of his bent head, trying to read what is going through it. Crossing and recrossing the same border. Carrying messages, perhaps?

He hands the passport back to me. A sudden, dismissive gesture. I take it and scurry through, a rabbit miraculously allowed to escape. I glance back before I turn the corner. He has not started on the next passenger yet; still noting things on his sheet of paper.

I hate this, I hate it—what am *I doing* here, back in their clutches? People stream past me, towards the where the baggage will arrive. I stand to one side and let them pass, trying to calm my pulse. Concentrate on breathing…let the breath come in without doing anything, just be aware of it, life continuing regardless…in, out…

Manageable now. I follow the stream of people. But there's some kind of unexpected delay in the luggage arriving. Paranoia flares yet again. Have I packed anything that—? I didn't even bring my mbira, I didn't want the customs officials pulling it out, turning it round suspiciously…A white woman *choosing* to carry one of the natives' instruments? Hide, hide—back to hiding who I really am—

Stop it. Just calm down and deal with what's actually happening.

What's actually happening, I calculate as I wait, is that Neil will have been back in London for over twelve hours, and may at this minute be talking to Teresa. If he's not backing away. He is in a volatile state, too much of his inner self has been exposed in the past couple of weeks, and there has been no time to assimilate it. He knows he needs to change things in his life, not get drawn back into the patterns of how he has been living—'Keeping myself from thinking by working too hard, and at the wrong things,' he said the night before he left. 'You should see my diary. The things I thought I was saying no to so I could come here—I didn't say no, I said, I'll do it in January.'

'Neil, you were saying things like this when I first met you—that you needed to make space for things that mattered.'

'I do it constantly. But there's something beyond my control that pushes me to overfill my life, to make sure it has meaning.'

Still running away...Leave it. I have no choice now but to leave to him what is his task, and get on with living mine.

Still no luggage...Hard to believe, but it's Johannesburg out there, outside this glass and concrete cage of an airport—I can say hello to Richard while I'm waiting. Find a phone. Damn, no South African coins...A man standing next to me says, 'Here, take these,' and hands me a couple of coins, smiling. I thank him but I'm thinking, he's been watching and I didn't even know. My every movement tells people things about me that I think are private.

I dial. Engaged. Wait a few minutes. Now no answer.

At the far end of the baggage hall a couple of policemen come in with an official, walking in this direction. I watch them, mesmerised, convinced they are heading for me...They pass me without stopping. To the phone again. Dial, each number deliberate.

Richard answers. Instantly I feel better. 'Where are you?' he asks. Where does he think I am? 'The airport,' I say. 'Where were *you*? I've been trying and you didn't answer.'

'Stuck on the lay.'

I start laughing, in pleasure at the familiarity. 'It's ten years since I heard anyone say that!'

'What do you do, in your circles?'

'We go to the loo.' We're right back in the middle, as if it's normal being in the same city, and we can witter on about nothing.

He asks, 'You haven't found Patricia?'

'I'm not through yet. She's here?'

'And the children. Don't say you've missed them?'

Here to meet me—or to ask questions if I should never appear. I feel held by a net of safety I had almost forgotten would be here.

He says, 'There's been a run on fatted calves this end. How long are you staying?'

'Just overnight this time. But I'll come for longer once I've had some time with Mom and Dad.'

'There's a set of viola and flute duets waiting.'

But my viola's gone back with Neil. Why? Sending that bit of myself ahead to make sure I followed?

'I'll borrow one,' Richard says.

No other official approaches me, not even customs. Out—

To Patricia coming towards me—a woman I know only from one brief shared Christmas when I was still part of a family and she a newcomer, overwhelmed. Now she represents the home group and I am the outsider. The reserve I remember is visible only in something about the way she holds her body, a slight space she keeps around herself—but not any more from me. Her arms are around me, assuming the intimacy that ten years would have brought if I could have stayed. At her side are the two children I have never seen, waiting for their turn to hug.

We walk out to the car park, the seven-year-old Joshua skidding on ahead to extract the last few minutes' challenge from the smooth airport floors. Claire walks with us, watching from the dignified height of her nine years, then suddenly slides off after him. In the car I tell them about the photos that were for so long on the wall in my attic in London, and how Kirsty used to ask me why they never came to see me. We laugh together at the absurdity of a world that has kept us apart, and gloat in having finally defeated it. Except that we haven't quite, for Richard is stuck at home, waiting.

He must have been listening for the car, for he is standing at the kitchen door as we pull in at the driveway. The casual ease of the phone conversation deserts me—the man standing here waiting as I climb out to go to him is more than a brother I haven't seen since I was scarcely out of childhood. The very sight of his body—tall, self-sufficient, utterly familiar—wakes within me a strange, painful longing, for things I have wanted to do and be and experience, beyond what I could ever reach. I move towards him, losing my adult self with every step. His arms are around me and he ruffles my hair as he used to when I was small enough to cuddle into his lap, and the smell of his body warmth enfolds the longing, containing it but making it more intense. I never want to grow up and have to go out and face the world again…Never want to feel again what I felt the night Neil arrived in Lusaka, when he held me like this while I cried and cried—relief that he had finally come, fear that it could not last…I am not crying now, but I make no move to lift myself. I am dimly aware of the others standing a few feet back, leaving a space around us, and no one is speaking, just Richard's hand ruffling my hair.

'Come,' he says eventually—summoning himself as well as me. 'In you come, and about time too.'

We lie on the lawn in the late afternoon shade, while the children get back to the making of a tree house that my arrival has interrupted. The moment of childhood longing has been absorbed now into something simpler. We talk about Chomsky, the best way to grow beans, the music of Nyika. I tell the children about Richard teaching me Xhosa clicks, and how shy Patricia was the first time she came to Bloemfontein. Claire says, 'Now it's always her doing things for Ouma and Oupa, and all the rest of you stuck in other places.'

Mom and Dad are on the phone within an hour of my arrival—'Wonderful to hear your voice,' they say—which means, Wonderful that you got through. 'No trouble?' Dad asks…'No trouble,' I say—but I wouldn't be here to answer if there had been…'See you tomorrow,' we say…Then each of the others takes a turn talking to them, bits of daily news. A regular ritual, ongoing family life.

No trouble…just walking back into the tension of trying to decide what constitutes trouble. No question of letting them in on the little scene with the immigration officer—it would set off a panic far greater than mine, and to no good purpose…I am aware suddenly how much energy has been released in me all these years by having got away from the need to constantly watch what I say, even what I think, lest I should think it aloud, in front of the wrong people.

The family gathering over the phone is over. I say, 'Can I make a quick call to London, just to say I got here?'

'Take it in the study,' Richard says, 'and forget about the "quick".'

Ridiculous, but the adrenalin is surging—as if I'm running, longing, but not quite able to trust that he'll be there—

'Wonderful to hear your voice…No trouble?'…Strange, we're saying the same things to each other that I did with Mom and Dad, and even more left unsaid. The 'no trouble' means only 'no trouble so far'; it will not set aside his fear of what might still lie ahead. 'This is worse than postcards,' I say, reaching instinctively for a private language. Not just the censors listening, already so much I am not going to know how to convey to him.

'We'll have to rely on shared consciousness,' he says.

'Have you and Teresa talked—?'

'She's away touring, I won't see her till tomorrow. But don't think about it, it's going to be OK.'

I'm not thinking about it, actually. I had asked because I thought it was what he was thinking about. All those issues feel far away. I summon myself to do better than this. 'How's the diary?'

'I've taken a red pen to what I can. But there's not much I can do without letting other people down. And while I was away they scheduled a performance of one of my pieces in Glasgow for next month—Will I come, and do a couple of workshops while I'm there?'

'And of course you said yes.'

'Of course. Wouldn't you?'

'Of course. Unless I had decided *definitely* to simplify my life.' The chemistry of challenge and laughter has got hold of us again. 'Jennie, this is my part. You get on with yours.'

'I was telling myself that while I was stuck in the airport.'

I realise after I have put the phone down, I let the word 'stuck' slip out. So he'll know something not quite ordinary happened.

The household functions normally, with a normal level of noise and small irritations. Perhaps I expected it to carry an atmosphere of semi-disablement, with three of them free to come and go while the fourth lives confined within a five mile radius that he can leave only to get to work and back. And within that space, no meetings of more than two people—checking before he sets out that the person he is going to see knows he is coming, and there will not be others present when he gets there; reporting every week to the police…Four years to go, but there's no relying on an end point—banning orders expire only to be immediately reissued. It has become a way of life; as little point in fretting as there would be over an amputation.

But there are signs of pressure. They're hardly greater than you'd find in any other family, but they don't fit with Richard as I remember him. He barks unnecessary commands at Joshua. Joshua stomps off, injured. A door slams. Patricia raises her eyebrows at me, and distracts attention by telling Richard something someone said to her yesterday. It's obvious he wants more, that if he had been there he would have asked different questions. She's his eyes and ears on the world, and he hasn't come to terms with the dependence. But the tension passes; and the calm, thoughtful person he is resurfaces. Half an hour later the offended Joshua is back, being cuddled and saying '*Dad*, you're so horrible,' in a tone which clearly means the opposite.

Curtains closed against the night, and it's a cocoon I have been taken into, not yet having to face the complexity outside. The voice of Richard's flute hovers once again—Bach, Telemann—rhythms reliable, secure, protection against a chaotic world—

We play the duets that have been waiting to happen since my earliest childhood. Then Richard says to Claire, who has been curled in an armchair listening, 'Get your clarinet,' and now I watch as the two of them play, and the absorption in the present moment lets his spirit escape from what confines it. Joshua appears, to climb silently on to my lap. I feel in his child's trusting body Michael—Charlie—the children in Lusaka. Richard and Claire are playing my life back to me, letting me hold it all together.

I ask Joshua, 'Do you play anything?'

'No,' he says. Claire says, 'He's learning the recorder. But these notes are too hard for him.' Joshua denies it vehemently, but what he is really denying is his sister's right to speak for him. I say, 'Why don't we play without notes then?' Richard says, 'Come on, Jennie,' as if I'm being a little thick. But to the children the idea that there are no wrong notes appeals so strongly that after a tentative start they both go wild. Richard looks appalled, then gives in, laughs across their heads at me, and starts holding a few long low notes under their confusion, instinctively trying to calm it. I slip in between them, echoing fragments. Patricia joins us, beating the rhythm on a tray—

'Bedtime,' announces Richard, too suddenly. Joshua objects, appeals to me. I say, '*Ek kuier lekker*'—I'm enjoying being a visitor, I'm not getting in the middle of a family argument. 'Joshua, *move*,' Richard orders. Joshua sits tight, cross-legged on the floor like someone at a sit-in. 'I bet in that house Jennie used to live in there weren't any rules about going to bed.' Richard says, 'You're living in this house, not that one,' and he lifts up the protesting small body and humps him across his shoulder like a sack of coal. Joshua kicks and says, 'I want a goodnight hug from Jennie.' Richard stops next to me to let Joshua lean his head forward like a seal to receive it. I say, 'You keep playing like that—you were great.'

'I will,' he says, grinning. 'Instead of that stupid Grade 1.'

Richard says, 'I had no idea I was letting such a subversive element into the house.'

Now to gear myself up to phone Peter. I have no idea how to handle this. No point going over the past, but there's not enough between us any more to start creating a present tense. And on the telephone—With anyone else the rules are clear—politics are dangerous, stick to the personal; with Peter the personal is even more dangerous. There's nothing left but the practical—when and how are we going to see each other? That I definitely don't want to do by phone—making it too easy for whoever is listening—but there's no way out. 'I'll be going to Cape Town,' I say—perhaps I can come via him on my way back to Bloemfontein? But he is not sure where I would sleep, his flat is small. That gets me. I say, 'I've just come from three weeks in a tent!' Then it seems pointless to go on edging around each other in this way. 'Peter, I want to see you and I don't care where we do it. You suggest somewhere.'

He fumbles on for a minute or two, then says, 'I have to go to Cape Town later this month. Maybe we can synchronise.'

I can see it—meeting for a meal. His panic is like Neil's, that if he lets me near I might open up things he would rather leave buried. Well, I've learnt something in the last couple of months—

it's a long and dangerous business, not to be embarked on unless you're going to be there to help pick up the pieces. I say, 'I'm quite harmless really,'—and that surprises him into laughing.

Morning. Children at school, Patricia out. Richard and I in his study. I say, 'There's a friend I've lost track of, Jonas Nkosani—did you ever hear of him?' Richard says, 'Don't think so'—an ordinary voice but he shakes his head as he says it, and waves a hand across in front of his chest, and starts talking about old friends of Mom and Dad's. A few minutes later he says, 'Come and I'll show you my beans.'

I follow him out. He says nothing until we're sitting on the lawn in the far corner of the garden, looking up into a huge avocado tree. Then, in the voice he uses with the children when they don't listen instantly, 'It's an absolute rule, you don't name names in that room. There have been tape recordings used as evidence in trials, conversations in people's homes when they've had no idea how the bugging devices had got in.'

I feel crushed by my own stupidity. But more than that—fear beginning to rise again—already, by that one small mention, I may have done something to damage Jonas. I try to push the panic away, knowing it is absurd. Richard is warning me well before any danger point. I say, almost to excuse myself, 'We were close, before I left.'

'Finding him now may be a luxury you can't afford to indulge in. If he's disappeared, there's almost certainly a reason. You'll do him no good by going around asking.'

Something in his tone—I realise, this is not a hypothetical case. I ask, 'You know him?'

'Listen, you've been away a long time. The first thing you have to get a grip on is that each of us is a potential problem for people we care about. Work it out. They let you in without too much hassle, and you sit in Bloemfontein for a couple of weeks and get lulled into thinking no one's following your movements. Then you set off to find someone that they have almost certainly got a continuing interest in—' Then, 'I'm sorry if I'm sounding like an older brother.'

'No, you're right.' Then, rebellious, 'I'm not good at accepting that there's nothing I can do.'

He puts out a hand to ruffle my hair again, lightly this time. 'Tell me what you've been doing in music.' A distraction—safe ground; but he's letting me answer my own restless feelings. He says, 'There are people here making a kind of music you'd be interested in. Patricia can introduce you to some of them.'

It's not the first time I hear Patricia mentioned in this way. 'I'm beginning to think they'd have done well to ban her too.'

'I keep telling her, they got the wrong one. But her style's unobtrusive.' And he's on his feet, pulling me up. 'Come, it's time we got you on to the next stage of the journey.'

2

The road stretches long, hot and absolutely straight, lined still with pine trees clipped round like the trees children draw. I stand on the dusty earth pavement under the tree nearest our gate, where twenty-five years ago I used to sit drawing patterns on the ground. I turn to walk the path from the gate to the *stoep*—the verandah where I sat on Mom's lap as she tried to teach me to read *Old Lob*. I feel again the frustration—see Dad arriving home, raising his eyebrows at my tears, looking over my head at Mom to ask, *Dink jy sy's dom?*—Do you think she's stupid?—thinking I wouldn't understand—as people thought Michael didn't. 'He's been listening since birth,' I told Neil indignantly. It has taken coming home to understand that my indignation started *here*, on this stoep—

Dad stands next to me now, laughing at me for being stuck here already, and we haven't even got inside the door.

Every detail of the house, the garden, the neighbourhood, is of compelling interest to me. All the things that are the same, all the things that have changed. The living room has been shifted around. Well, of course; moving furniture was Mom's way of dealing with the emptiness after each departure. 'All that leaving,' I say. 'One green bottle after another.' And now one of the bottles is back, pieces glued together. I settle back on the same wall and feel the world steady itself again around me.

'The garden,' I say, 'take me round it.' And together we survey each bit of it, stopping every few steps for her to tell me the stories behind the small changes that no one has thought to mention in letters. Dad sits nearby, enjoying my simple enthusiasm, as if he had expected I might have become blase from living in so many different countries. He doesn't understand that no other place has ever been as real for me as this. Later he and I take a slow walk down the lane. I adjust my pace as I once did with Michael. I am thinking, he walks like an old man, and I have to remind myself that that's what he is.

The lane is shamelessly domesticated. When Peter and I played there it was a tangle of bushes, hiding all sorts of possibilities; now it is simply an open space between the houses, no mystery whatever. 'They've cleared all the bushes,' I say indignantly to Mom.

'Yes,' she says, 'and a very good thing too.'

Here I am, getting ready for bed in the room that used to be mine. What a ridiculous way to describe it—in my room. My young girl's bed again. It feels odd, like cancelling everything that has happened since…I lie listening to the climbing rose scratching against my window pane as the wind works itself up for a storm, whining through the tops of trees. An outhouse door squeaks rhythmically—the garage? Somewhere beneath the other sounds there is a low shushing—continuous, familiar—what is it?

So much waking in me, things heard, seen, remembered, summoned. I roll over, in this narrow bed that comes from a time when alone was the normal way to sleep. The life I have left is aeons away, like a novel I've been immersed in that has come to an abrupt end, the characters still moving powerfully in my mind but in danger of losing their reality because the people around me don't see them.

No point thinking I'm going to sleep. I get up and go to kneel on the chair under the window, lifting the bottom of the curtain and letting it fall back behind my head. I wait for my eyes to adjust to the black outside, the strangely moving, swaying shapes. I can just make out the line of agapanthus swaying on their tall stems, stretching away to the corner at the bottom of the garden where—

Where once for a few months—how old was I? ten? twelve?—I used to creep out each morning before anyone else was awake, to sit on the still-damp grass and read from the Bible and pray to Jesus. Experimenting secretly with religion, guarding myself from questions, from almost certain teasing. Each of the boys had by then had his religious phase if he was going to have it, like measles that you then become immune to. In my friend Gwendolyn's house they said grace and gave each other texts written out on beautiful little bookmarks. They opened the Bible when they needed guidance—and got it, opening always at a page with something relevant. Jesus loved me, they said, *me*, personally. If I once took him into my heart I would never thirst again. *Was* I thirsting? Maybe I was too deadened by lack of religion even to realise it? This was something different from Aunt Ellie's Sunday School, where all we did was draw stupid pictures of people taking up their beds and walking. Me specifically? How did I find out if it was true? Not by asking anyone at home, that was clear. I had to do it alone. And outside. If Jesus existed surely he would make himself known to me through the natural world. Alone, with the grass damp and intimate beneath my bare legs, the early morning air sifting in the reeds that lined the bottom of the garden—

The reeds, of course. That's where the shushing noise is coming from. Bamboo, really, like a tall curtain, sheltering my earliest longing to be loved by someone other than those I had been born to…And I remember now a patch of reeds below Nyika, downstream from where the women fetch water, the kind they use for making mats but also for that strange private instrument the women call *nkangala*. A bow with a single string that she rests between an outstretched hand and her mouth, and as she plucks, her moving mouth shapes harmonics that can be heard only inside the sounding box of her own head. 'Not music like ours,' said Mwene when Neil asked him about it, 'it is just to soothe the spirit of a woman when she feels alone.'

The water is wide—we are alone again, each on opposite sides of that vast ocean that we have crossed and recrossed to find a way of being together. The aloneness has travelled with each of us, through all the dismantling of walls and becoming one flesh. We came into the world alone, and have travelled to meet each other by such different routes; and each alone we will leave it. In between we have been given this space to delight in each other, and to learn through loving and the knowledge of being loved how to become more ourselves.

The first shaft of lightning flashes to light up the garden, wild and strange with lashing branches. Then gone, and the night is back. The impersonal anger of the wind, the dance of surreal shapes. But in that moment of light I know I saw something move, something more than a tree. A person? Impossible to tell. I am hyper-aware, looking for signs of trouble, infiltrated by memories of nights pressing my face against this window, to follow in the dark the figures that appeared round the corner of the kitchen, moving like shadows. Then the noise of shouting and rough laughing, and the police, knocking at the door.

Our days are paced by the routine of Mom and Dad's slow-moving retired life, and the rhythms of the garden. I wake to early morning birdsong, and we sit out in the evening over supper to the low whirr of insect noises. When nothing else is required of him Dad still sits reading a large history book in a chair in his favourite corner of the garden, no shirt, while Mom gets back to her constant trail of small chores—letters, accounts, writing book reviews, sorting out the linen cupboard. The nearest she gets to doing nothing is a crossword puzzle. She still gets through a pile of library books every fortnight but you never catch her reading peacefully as Dad does. She must do hers late at night or early morning—she doesn't sleep as well as he does.

I make her sit with me at the piano. 'My fingers hardly work any more,' she protests, 'this stupid arthritis.' But I hear the sound as it always was, with all of us gathered round singing. 'I used to think it was a kind of magic only you could make,' I say, 'the way you make up the left hand.'

'Darling, you have a generous memory. They're such obvious tunes, and I could only ever do the simplest chord sequences.'

The house itself has a retired air. No boys strewing their clobber about, no Annie in the kitchen. What used to be her room out at the back is now a storage place for the books and university notes the boys have deposited at moments of departure, and never come back to claim. Mom treats the kitchen now like a library, spices alphabetically lined up, and there's no one to disturb the order. But no one to enliven it, either. I miss the daytime voices, Gertruida's and Annie's; listening to the pattern of sound as they chatted to the milkman, or called across the fence to the servant in the neighbouring house. I wonder vaguely about the Tswana that I heard in those earliest years of life. Where did it go? A language I must once have known, absorbed naturally from extra mothers, taken unnaturally away; a socially induced forgetting.

It's obvious that not having a servant suits Mom. She was never comfortable being an employer; too well developed a sense of fairness. And perhaps also the childhood memories? Fragments of overheard conversation by the aunts in Scotland who had gone into service, as she might have ended up doing had luck gone just a little the other way…I ask, 'Do you remember the time Trevor and his lot trooped through the kitchen in their hockey boots, just after Annie had scrubbed the floor?' They troop again before our remembering eyes as we sit in the garden. I hear Edward saying, '*I* didn't make the mess so why should I clear it up?'…Trevor saying, 'OK, OK, later,' and then he's off outside again, to find the ball that has gone missing in the reeds…Peter taking himself off to his room to read, hoping to escape attention. But that's not an easy memory, for it's hard to talk about Peter without raising present pain. Perhaps there was more going on even then than getting out of tidying up.

We return to the muddy boots, to a time less complicated than the present—or so we choose to remember it. Trevor is back, saying defensively, 'I thought Annie was paid to tidy up,' and Mom suddenly losing her patience—'That doesn't come into it, it's a question of elementary consideration for others. And *I resent* being turned into a nagger by your idleness'…

I too am relieved that Annie is gone.

Off to see Aunt Ellie, in her eighties now and in the old people's home. All the way down the corridor to her room we are stopped by people who edge their way along, backs humped. The old cracked voices are like thorns that catch at me lest I pass too briskly. 'I knew your grandfather, my dear, long before you were thought of.' There's nothing sentimental about it, they are putting me in my place, reminding me how little I have experienced of the world they have so long inhabited. They need an audience, and having found one even so briefly they use the moment with startling directness, too tired to pretend. 'Look how old I am,' they say, 'I don't know why the Lord doesn't take me.' They touch my skin, marvelling at how unwrinkled it is, at the spring of my step. My mere existence momentarily reaffirms the person they know themselves to be, invisible to outsiders, trapped inside the indignities of an aging body. We finally reach Aunt

Ellie's room. She shuffles round in her slippers, searching in her bottom drawer for something to give me, as if I were still a child needing entertaining. Outside the window the voices of a couple of African women drift towards us from where they sit up against the wall in the shade in their hour off. The mood takes them to sing rather than talk, a hymn, which should have pleased Aunt Ellie; but she has a painful mouth today—something wrong with her false teeth—and her tolerance is low. She says, 'I wish they wouldn't *yell* so. It drives me mad.' Extraordinary. To me it was a wonderful release of sound, full of simplicity and power.

It takes days to learn not to tense up when the phone rings. But it seems no one is following up on my arrival. Richard phones every couple of days, and chats to each of us. 'Your phone bill must be going off the graph,' I say. He says, 'It's been out of control anyway, the last year.' The rest of the time it's one of Mom and Dad's friends. I get called to the phone—'That's wonderful that you're back,' they say. 'When are we going to see you?' I chat a moment or two then pass it back to Dad, and go back to the garden burrowing in. I don't want to go anywhere. From the house Dad's voice drifts back to me, talking, laughing, switching languages effortlessly. I can do the other side of the conversation without hearing it…'What do you think about the new Free State hockey team? Did you hear Elsa and Jannie's son got a scholarship to study overseas?'…Then he goes to find Mom to tell her the details, and she makes quiet judgements that entertain him, or that he disagrees with, and either way they discuss it some more. They have so many friends, yet it seems always to be through Dad that their coupled relationship with the outside world is mediated. Was it always like that? Does Mom mind?

Everything happens in couples. I'd forgotten, my own life has been so differently structured. To their friends they are Catriona-and-Frank, a social entity like Elsa-and-Jannie, Jean-and-David. The getting together in each others' gardens for a drink before dinner is in couples, the going-to-lunch on Sunday. I am an oddity because I am just Jennie, the Jennie who has taken so long to get herself sorted out—poor girl, such a difficult start she had, and drifting around from one country to another. I am getting a taste of how constantly noticed one would feel to be a woman living here permanently and not part of a proper couple. To be a widow is problematic, long after the sorrow is absorbed, just because of having to enter rooms alone. To be divorced, a private tragedy everyone takes care not to mention. To be single, regrettable. What do you think is wrong with her? At best, she is unfortunate—it could not be a choice. I have started remembering the trail of women we had to have to Sunday lunch because they lived alone. Miss Stainton, Aunt Cecily—Do we have to have her again? Isn't it someone else's turn? It was always Mom who invited them, Dad who said, 'Do we have to?' All the years I was growing up the headmistress of the primary school shared a house with another teacher, Miss Fairweather, but it never occurred to me that *they* might be a couple—because I had never been given a word to clothe it in? Or was I reflecting what the adults themselves could not see?

Everyone makes friendly noises about the unknown Neil, but they are tentative, waiting for someone to make it clear whether we intend to be married or whether it's one of these uncomfortably vague situations the young in other countries go in for. Mom says, as we prepare for a visit to a couple of the aunts, 'I'm not saying anything,' as if it's none of their business how I arrange my life. But it's obvious she too needs a label they can relax with. I tell her about the village dancing us into a properly married state. She laughs at the story, but she's certainly not telling it to anyone else.

'You know that quotation you used to have stuck up inside your wardrobe door?' I ask. 'The one about serenity? It's gone.'

She's only half listening. 'That was a long time ago.'

'I've wanted to ask you for ages. Which was the one you needed?' She looks up, not having an idea what I'm talking about.

'Serenity, courage, wisdom. Which did you think you didn't have?'

'Good Lord, child. I can't even remember why I put it there. I just liked it, I suppose.'

A cousin comes by for tea, with a one-year-old called Amanda. While Dad and the cousin talk cricket, Amanda and I paddle about in the shallow lake made by the leak from the hose. I become a child myself in her delight, and then the pleasure slips into fantasy and I see her as a child of my own, mine and Neil's, and I have brought her home to have Dad watch her as she runs free across the lawn with no clothes to encumber her, squealing as I spray her with the hose, and the sun glints in the drops of water.... 'That child *lives*,' Dad says, and for a moment I'm not sure which child he's talking about.

I take Amanda off with me to sort through the boxes in what used to be Annie's room, to find my childhood books. The room is stuffed, dust so thick that Amanda is filthy within seconds, but she's in her element climbing over things, into things, pulling things out of shelves. Chaos definitely appeals to some instinct that civilised society relentlessly tries to train out of children. It's harder this time to enter into it with her because I am fighting a sense of being dragged down. How is it possible that Annie was expected to live in this appalling claustrophobic, dark hole, when the rest of us had the space of the whole house? OK, she had it too by day, but as a work place, not a place she could use for herself in any way...

Amanda clambers up next to me. Feeling the warmth of her small thighs I see again Annie's grandchildren, who spent a night with her here in this stuffy room once. A small boy who already knew his place; an even smaller girl who had not learnt hers, and please God, I hope she never did—

—A hot afternoon haze. I have arrived back from school on my bike, and the children are there, playing outside the kitchen door.

They've been brought by Annie's son Gabriel, who was left in charge of them while their mother was in hospital, and has decided he can not cope alone. Gabriel's arrival has provoked in Annie a spectacular display of bad temper and he has been set to do all the jobs in the house she least likes doing. The grandchildren are left to hang about the kitchen steps and make up games with a piece of string and some pebbles. I offer them things to play with—they hide behind Annie's skirt but eventually are persuaded to come and see what I have brought. By the end of the afternoon we are playing tickling games on the lawn and they are jumping up and down asking to be swung round once more.

Evening comes and Gabriel is sent home—to stay overnight in the white town with no permit would land him in jail. We all know that the children are in Annie's room but she makes sure they're quiet enough that the neighbours don't hear. The next morning when I wander into the kitchen in my pyjamas they're there again, playing on the steps just outside. The little girl—Thandi, she is called—attaches herself to me. It soon stops being flattering and makes me long for peace, but I can't say no, there's something too important about her absolute lack of fear of rebuttal. Her brother, only a year older, won't even come into the house further than the kitchen. I think, 'Let's try my room, she can find things there for herself.' She takes my hand and follows me down the passage. Once we reach my bedroom she stands still for a moment just inside the door, and then begins to touch things. She gives each object a quick, light touch, as if noting its presence, and then she moves on to the next. I sit at my dressing table to watch. She comes and climbs on to my lap and carries on her silent survey, touching each thing. The little box I keep safety pins in, a pile of homework books, a hairbrush—

—Amanda has fallen off a pile of books and is shrieking in the cloud of dust she has created. I scoop her up and carry her inside, to a bath which we both get into, washing all that old dust away.

3

Twelve days and no letter yet from Neil. I want to phone but I make myself wait. In this house phoning overseas requires an emergency; banning orders or heart attacks qualify, needing to be close does not, otherwise they would be on the phone to three continents every week.

Mom has begun to ask about him. Real things, trying to get a sense of the person. There is hardly an answer that wouldn't alarm or shock her friends—Teresa, sharing his bed all these years and her husband still living; Teresa still in place, and I about to arrive…I don't hide the things that aren't going to be simple. Too many years of censoring what I say in letters, I am not doing it now. Nor do her eyes hide the moments when she's anxious for me. But she makes no judgements, too instinctively compassionate not to see Teresa's side as well as mine. What really bothers her is Neil's mother. Perhaps there is something personal for her about the fact that it's Edinburgh where Neil's mother sits alone—the place where *her* own life started, her own mother's short life ended.

'Does his mother know about you?' she asks.

I feel irrationally defensive. 'Mom, I told you, he doesn't see her.'

The thought of Peter hovers; neither of us mention him. To rescue her I say, 'Neil's mother was different from anything you and I know about. He got away to salvage the possibility of being whole.'

She looks contrite, in case she has upset me. That irritates me more. 'Mom, *fight*—don't give up so easily!'

She is surprised out of her anxious look. 'Why would I want to fight you, when I'm so happy you're here?'

'I only mean, if you're thinking something, *say* it.'

She says, cautiously, 'Whatever you say about her, I can't bear to think of how she must feel now.' And then more boldly, 'And she must have loved him, or he would never have turned out the way you say he is. With Juan. And the children you were teaching.'

Finally a letter—written the day after we spoke on the phone, but it has taken two weeks to get here. I show Mom the postmark. We both know what it means; someone else has been having a turn before it got to me. I push the thought aside and take a quick skim through the pages, lost for the moment to everything except the private world only he and I share. His voice, warm and present…He has talked to Teresa—it's OK, he says, she reacted as I knew she would…I want to say, '*Neil*, I don't just want a press release!'…Juan's not around much, he says, the habit was temporarily broken, with me away.

I can't read beneath the tone. Is that all it is, or is Juan reacting to the idea of me coming? And does Neil feel as calm as his words suggest?

I look up to discover Mom watching me, her eyes a mirror to my concern. Protective privacy flares—I don't *want* her knowing me that well. She's looking at my hair that falls in my eyes when I bend forward. I say, before she can, 'I know, it needs cutting.'

'Do you want to get it done while you're here?'

'No, I'll cut it myself.'

Without thinking she has put out a hand to move it clear of my eyes. I pull away sharply, taken over now by an intense resentment at being invaded—*leave my hair alone*.I am shocked at the force of feeling. Mom looks contrite and anxious—that irritates me more—then something snaps and I realise how ridiculous I am being.

'Tell me about Neil's music,' she says. 'What kind does he compose?' And I have been talking for minutes before I realise, she's letting me touch base again with him, talking about things he and I understand together. And all without her having to say, 'I can see you're anxious. I want things to be well for you.'

She's clever, cleverer than I realised.

Time is running out. I feel it in the way Mom ticks off a mental list of all the people she feels I need to be taken to see. The remaining aunts, the family friends. I am toted around to be shown—See, Jennie has come back. They are all greyer and more stooped, and diminishing health is a constant topic, but otherwise it is like a time warp for they talk exactly as they always did and about almost the same things. They see only the Jennie they used to know, an unformed young person—and instinctively my voice becomes that person in talking to them. It is so easy I hardly notice I am doing it. When I catch myself at it, I think, This is ridiculous, just be yourself—but then I realise I don't any more know the ground rules. They have been hearing news of me over the years, but filtered, as if Mom and Dad are protecting them against infections to which they would have no natural immunity. Will the same things still shock them? What will Mom and Dad prefer me not to say, lest I upset them? Instinctively they bypass Africa—they ask only about my time in London. I collude, and talk about my work with the children. It does not occur to me to say that the children had parents from Africa and Asia as well as Britain, but now I see Mom is giving me openings, wanting me not to miss this chance to show how simple it could all be…

I take my cue and say my little piece. I don't mind, one way or the other. I am here to be with Mom and Dad and I want things to be the way they will feel comfortable. I spend enough of my life confronting stupid authorities and being indignant, I don't any longer feel a special need to do it here, with these old people whose lives are nearly over. But they are quick to sense a challenge. Things are changing here too, they tell me firmly. The fact that I am back is proof. And so much money being poured into the Bantustans, you'd never believe it. You should see the beautiful hospitals and schools that are being built for all these black people…For all that I have decided to be quiescent I can't resist asking them whether *they* have seen these things themselves. No, but someone knows someone who has a friend who is a doctor in one of those places—Bophuthatswana is it?—and he says, *nothing* is spared, all the latest equipment. And my dear, black sportsmen on the television news, all these young coloured women walking about town dressed up to the nines, absolutely the latest fashion, things our own children couldn't afford to buy. Things have changed a lot, you people overseas only ever hear the bad news…I say very little but they are fending off my challenge before I have worked out whether I am going to make it.

We move now to safer topics. How thankful we are there's been rain—have you seen the veld my dear? So dry you can count the blades of grass. We drink tea and they absorb like thirsty plants my pleasure at having homemade crunchies again and see that I still let Dad tease me. Imperceptibly we touch on my problematic life history, to get it safely out of the way. Every opinion is wholly positive—the subtext, which we all understand, is never stated. How nice it is that I am finally settling down. (It was a worry to your parents all those years.) How interesting that Neil is Scots. (We are so glad you didn't get stuck with one of those long-haired ones who got you into trouble in the first place.) 'And did you know Martie's boy is doing so well in America, and also something in music.' But they can't remember quite what it is that Martie's boy does, so we pass on to the photographs of their own children who went overseas and made good, who look out of their frames on the bureaux of these living rooms so calm and gracious, on to gardens so expansive…'And they manage without servants,' they say, these proud Bloemfontein parents who are so deeply trained in the importance of being positive. 'You're wonderful, you young people, the way you cope. But that's England, isn't it? We're very spoilt in South Africa.'

Silently the new Jennie is answering back. 'Some of us are, some of us aren't,' I say. Then, getting into my stride, 'And thank God I had to leave so I had nothing left to lose, and I was free to listen to what was going on around me.' But of course they don't hear, for I have not spoken.

Mom is saying, 'Time to move.' And we all get up and stand about for a few minutes saying thanks for the lovely crunchies and how nice it has been to see each other again, and how wonderful it is that I can be home—

—It's beginning to get to me, closing in on me, this warm, enveloping world that cushions one part of me and threatens to smother another in a kind of emotional ether. I have to get out, the house has become too small. But our simple daily routine that has delighted me until now has become a shape that can't be altered without hurt. That's nonsense, if I need to go somewhere, go—what restraint is anyone imposing on me? None. All I have to do is say, 'I'm going for a walk'—

Done. I am out, on the pavement, alone. And now where will I walk? These familiar close-to-home streets, we have driven down them so many times in the past couple of weeks, there is nothing in them I haven't already seen. I know none of the neighbours any more, no one to pop in on. The veld has gone. The lane takes two minutes and I'm out the other side. For the rest it's just houses, endless white suburbia, gardens perfectly maintained by underpaid black men, the spacious houses serviced still by Annies and Gertruidas who live in cramped rooms at the back. A group of them stand waiting for the bus, stout African women with thick legs and scarves tied round their hair, carrying baskets of things they are taking home to Bochebela, the African township, still off the edge of most white people's map, still that other troubling landscape of the mind A place from which servants were recruited by other servants, or where *tsotsies* controlled the dark streets at night with knives ready; untarred lanes where children played in the dust, a general store with almost no stock, one cinema hall with its advertisements for Coca Cola peeling off the walls. Streets identical, with house numbers that went up to thousands. Annie's was 3257, I remember…

Who do I know there now? The woman at the welfare centre? She had arthitic legs, I remember. Her son, who one year came to Dad to get help with his Maths...Did it take him anywhere, as his mother so hoped it would? Annie's gone to Vereeniging, Mom says, to live with her daughter. The grandchildren who once played at the kitchen steps will have grown up now, God knows to what future. Gertruida? Too long ago, no chance of tracking her. I hope she's still brewing *skokiaan* and that the bastards never got her. Who else is there to show for an entire childhood of growing up in what should have been the same town?—

—I come home from my walk. Dad says, 'Well? Find anything new?' His eyes are teasing, but for a second I wonder whether they are also insecure. His place, his life, under scrutiny.

4

'I'll be back,' I said, all three of us hugging as we did when I arrived, hugging and laughing. Back after four days with Richard, four in Cape Town. 'See you in eight days' time,' I said.

I dreamt, the second night I was back at Richard's, a dream so real it felt like memory—no, like something present that might be taken away from me. Patricia had spent half the day driving me around to meet people she knew who were involved in music making, and to pick up tapes they had copied for me to take back. An extraordinary net of people, partly caught up in, partly creating political change—and Patricia—the apparently conventional mother and wife—in the middle of it. Neither she nor the friends we collected tapes from asked, 'How will you use them?' There was a mood, a faith, that something would happen if others could hear these songs with which they were trying to shake their world—

When Sibongile sings
the breasts of rooftops kiss the southern cross
tiles tingle, metal shimmers, concrete shakes
and Hope sneaks through every shattered window with a hug—

We sat up late talking, and from music we got on to Neil. I had been keeping him down, deep, away from the uncomprehending eyes of the aunts and the Elsa-and-Jannie's of Bloemfontein. It felt strange now to be letting the real Neil out; and without meaning to I found I was telling them about him cutting off from me; and that I didn't know how to teach myself to accept that that might keep happening. And then I ended up telling them half his history, so they would understand the obstinate integrity that's at the root of all that's been problematic in his personal life but also all that's strongest. The rejection of what his father represented, the capacity to accept responsibility for the damage he has done, and to strive for a way beyond it; the inability to make easy statements of love and commitment unless he is absolutely sure he can live by them. It is the *absoluteness* of the man that causes him, and me, trouble; but it's also that which makes him so infinitely worth being in trouble for.

But after they had gone to bed, together, and I had climbed into mine, alone, the distance that cut me off from Neil came swooping back to engulf me. I saw it again as I used to when I was a child, listening to adult talk—us at the southern tip of Africa, unconnected to the rest of the continent, adrift in an ocean which could only be crossed by sailing north for weeks.

And that night I dreamt—impossible to recapture—At first the quality was like the warm smell of intimate bodies...of being a child, leaving my own bed to come and stand silently next to Dad's back, humped towards me in the dark. He and Mom were sleeping like coaches of a train, each hooked on to the next. I touched his shoulder. He woke instantly, eyelids flipping open; then he saw it was me, woken by another of my nightmares. He grunted a quiet acceptance...Climb in...then rolled over to present his back to me...But now that simple comfort of body to body eluded me. I realised it was not Dad's back but Neil's and he would not turn to face me. I felt insecure that everything could change so subtly and without my even noticing. Why was he cutting me out? I reached my arm over to fold around him, to soften that tense back, but my arm kept reaching out and never reached him, for he was lying now at the far edge of the bed, back to me, as Kevin and I once lay. I could not understand how it had come to this, after all these years of loving—

—I am awake now. Totally awake, to a sense of impending loss.

Breakfast. Patricia and the children scrabbling to get off to school. Richard doesn't have lectures until the afternoon... They're gone, and a quietness descends. Richard says, 'Phone Neil, Jennie. Just to talk.'

His voice answering the phone is casual, like he's three feet away. Just a tinge of, 'I was having a nice quiet breakfast—'

I say, 'This is an unknown admirer.'

A moment of shocked silence. Then, 'Jennie!'

'What's it like being single again?'

Now he's laughing. 'You trying to trap me?'

'Would I do such a thing? Go on, tell me exactly what you were doing when I phoned.'

'Reading.'

What?'

'Don Quixote.'

'*Don Quixote?* In Spanish or English?'

'A bit of both. The Spanish is beyond me, a bit like Shakespeare, but I like to dabble.'

'I had no idea you read things like that.'

'I haven't done for years. I'd forgotten how profound it is.'

I am thinking, I don't believe this—all the things I have been needing to say and ask, and here we are talking about *Don Quixote*. But the pleasure is carrying me along—'I once read a children's version. I remember it being ridiculous.'

'And ridiculous things can't be profound?'

'Go on then, what profundity did you discover?'

'A line I'm setting to music, pertinent to my state.'

Now this is something—but he refuses to tell. 'I'll send it to you when it's done,' he says.

'Neil, people here have been asking about your music. Do me a tape of some of your other pieces and send that too.'

'Who is people?'

'My mother, mainly. Also Richard.'

His voice closes over, protectively. 'I've no idea what your mother would like to hear.'

'Doesn't really matter. Just something to give her an idea. A couple of cello pieces maybe.'

An obstinacy gets into his voice. 'I'm no good on mothers, you know that.'

'Neil, come *on*.'

'I'm serious. The idea of trying to communicate musically with yours paralyses me.'

'You've never met. How can you be so pre-judging?'

'Jennie—' Something in his voice I seldom hear—it says, 'Take it easy, I'm not feeling very strong.' But I'm not stopping, not now I've got him again. I say, 'If you want me to, I can tell you what would help her understand.'

'Go ahead.' The voice is tight, giving away nothing.

'Musically she is what your mother could be, minus all the pressure and emotional blackmail.' I know I'm on dangerous ground, but what works with Neil, always, is the frontal attack. 'What you have to imagine is someone starting from a lifelong pleasure in conventional western music, no other exposure. She'd like to think you make wonderful music, but she's not going to understand it unless you lead her there, by gradual steps. Give her some clues what not to expect. Tell her why you did it the way you did.'

'You want all that on one cassette?'

'As many as you like. But do it quick, so I can listen to it with her and let her talk about what she makes of it.'

'You're a scheming woman. And I wish you were back.'

'Neil, I had a really strange dream. Is everything OK?'

He sounds suspicious. 'What kind of a dream?'

'I can hardly remember, just the feeling. You were there, and then I lost you. When I woke I was afraid. Is anything happening with you, that you haven't been able to write about?'

'Nothing worth getting into your dreams. I'm restless, that's all.' Then, 'All those last weeks were so intense, working ourselves up for huge changes, and now I'm back here and it's all the same. It feels as if life hit a barrier, and I ought to be doing something to shift it. I've had hardly a note in me that hasn't had to be dragged out. This *Don Quixote* line is the first thing that's happening on its own.'

'Tell me what it says. Please.'

'Love is too powerful to be overcome by anything but flight.'

I feel blocked, like I'm about to cry and speaking might set it off.

'Jennie—are you there?' Voice quiet now and serious. 'I can't believe I did that to you in Lusaka. It was like looking down into a precipice thinking, 'Don't fall, don't fall' until of course I fell. I had Ben so near the top of my consciousness—'

Another pause. I wait, sure he is about to say more. But he switches abruptly to something about the workshop he's preparing, to follow his Glasgow performance. I wait till he's finished, then I say, 'You were thinking something you didn't say just now.'

Silence. Then, voice over-controlled, 'Jennie, lay off. Take your damned antennae and go practise on someone else.'

And he puts the phone down.

I stand holding the blank receiver. What's going on?

Perhaps Juan? Perhaps things aren't coming right between them?

Richard's in the next room when I come out. He must have heard that I'd gone suddenly silent minutes ago. 'Did something happen?'

'What I was telling you. He's either larger than life, or he's gone.'

He puts an arm around me. 'Stick in there, girl.'

'I'm not budging. But I could do with some distraction, to stop me thinking about it.'

'You're not going to phone him back?'

'No point, till he's ready. Maybe this evening.'

'Come for a walk,' he says.

There's a park down the road, one of the only walking places within Richard's permitted orbit. To take my mind off Neil I start asking him about the tapes I'm taking back with me. How can people get away with singing songs like those? There's a strange kind of licence for performing arts at the moment, he says. The poetry of the songs is oblique—people know what's being referred to, but you can't pin it down. And there's too much of it, in too many languages, it would take an industry of translators. But no one can be sure how long it will last this way. If they suddenly do a swoop, there needs to be some place the music is stored, so it's there for people to claim back again when there is next a space…

A light has gone on in my head while he's been talking. 'Listen, before I left Lusaka my friend and I had this great plan for getting our liberation concert on tour. It's pure fantasy really—none of them can travel. But maybe—what are the chances of musicians here getting passports?'

'Can't tell. But not impossible.'

'And could they go on tour, and be safe when they came back?'

'Again, can't tell. But the chances are if they let them out, foreign media attention would act as a protection.' Then, almost casually he says, 'And if you did get it off the ground, it might serve a double purpose.'

'Meaning?'

'There's so much music around you would be spoilt for choice. We could slip in a couple of people who have other reasons for wanting to travel. The trade unions—they're needing to link up with unions elsewhere—they've been so cut off, but they'd never get permission if that was known to be the reason.'

'That's neat!'

'We've been trying to feel our way to something like this, but none of us thought of music.' He pauses. 'Soliciting funds abroad for political activities is illegal. It would make life considerably more complicated for you if you're planning on coming back.'

'I told you, I need a way to connect. I can't handle this state of dropping in and out and not being part of anything.' But there's Neil's tension, Dad's health—one more of us in trouble and his heart's going to give up on him…The restlessness that I have kept muted through the weeks in my cocoon with Mom and Dad breaks out…If I'm going to do this, I need to move now, to get Patricia to take me to meet some of the groups…

I feel Richard is waiting for my answer. 'I'll need to think,' I say—

—I'm holding on against time that moves constantly forward, a relentless rhythm…Holding on to that one conversation with Dad that came out of time, unconnected to anything that was happening. It was evening and he wasn't well; another angina attack. They happened almost every day for a few minutes, but this was a big one and I saw for the first time the fear they both lived with. They were both so adept at parental over-responsibility, keeping from the children anything that might worry them. But now for the ten minutes the angina lasted he sat like a ghost while Mom held his hand and I hovered, useless but wanting to be there. When the tablets began to take effect and the pain diminished, he looked up at me with something in his eyes that I could hardly bear to see—*Dad ashamed*. Ashamed—not of having shown his fear, but of having felt it. Then he moved carefully towards his bed. I sat next to him now while Mom was on the phone to the doctor. There was never anything new to ask, she told me afterwards, the attacks followed a predictable pattern. But Dr Cohen had made Mom promise to phone him when she was anxious; it wasn't just his sons that Dad had taught, but him too.

When the pain came on it was early evening; Mom and I were about to set off to a play she had to review for the local paper. There was no question now of us both going, only whether we would both stay. I said, 'Mom, *go*. You'll make him feel worse if you cancel. There's nothing you can do by staying that I can't.'

'It's not that.' She hesitated, then said, 'Dad doesn't like to show anyone else he's afraid.'

'Go,' I said. 'Give me a chance to feel useful. I've got years to make up for.'

She said, 'My darling girl.' And made herself go—

—I sit in a chair at Dad's bedside. I am writing to Neil, looking up every few minutes to check. Eyes closed, lying quite still, breathing shallow but even…Now he moves his arm so that the hand falls at the edge of the bed, inviting me to hold it. I put down my pen to take the hand. After a moment he says, eyes still closed, 'You think you're going to do everything differently with your own children. But I can't remember that we ever talked about sex when you were growing up. I don't know why. I meant to.'

'We didn't need to.'

His eyes open. 'Why not?'

'Because you made it all so natural.'

His lids drop again. I feel he wants to go on talking, but there simply isn't the physical energy. I sit holding his hand, waiting to see if he's going to sleep again. He shifts slightly. 'Your periods were late coming. I should have talked to you then.'

'Mom did.'

'I know. But I should have too. I meant to.'

'Stop it, Dad. There's nothing that would need doing differently if you had it all to do again.'

His eyes wake to a little of his normal vigour. 'That's not a philosophy that'll take you very far!'

I laugh. 'I'm talking about you, not me. Anyway, you did talk to me, more than anyone else's father. I remember when I had my first period, you asked me what words the girls at school used for it. The curse, they used to say—I can't come swimming, I've got the curse. You said, "It's a gift, not a curse. Even if it's uncomfortable, it means you're a woman and can lead a full woman's life."'

He is silent a while; then says, 'Aunt Ellie never had periods. Did you know?'

'No.'

'My mother never talked to her about it. She was never taken to a doctor. If she had been, there might have been something they could have done. I only found out years later.'

'Who told you?'

'Aunt Floss.' Aunt Floss, who stood with me to listen to the sound of moonlight…'She saw me being cross with Ellie once, I can't remember what about, something like her giving Edward some more cake when Mom had said he shouldn't. You know.' He rests a while. 'Aunt Floss got me alone afterwards and said, Ellie has given you and yours the love she would have given her own children if she could have had them. Have some compassion.'

The small spurt of energy has gone. His voice is tired again as he says, 'When you were spending so much time with other people's children, and didn't seem to want a partner, for all those years—'

I finish it for him—'You worried.'

He smiles slightly, acknowledging. Theoretically it is Mom who does the worrying, Dad who is calm and rational and tells her not to.

I say, 'There's nothing missing in my sex life. I wanted to be alone after Kevin. And I did have a partner before Neil.'

'You never said.'

'I did write about him, but I didn't say he was a lover. If I'd had any idea you were worried I would have.'

He says nothing, but I feel a different kind of awareness growing between us as he lies there watching me—me as I am now, grown woman with a sexual life of which he knows nothing, but in the same body the small girl who once lay cuddling into his back when she was woken by nightmares. He needs to be able to imagine the unseen man whose body I now choose to lie with. I ask quietly, 'Shall I talk to you a little about Neil?' His head moves slightly, a fractional nod, but his eyes tell me I am right. 'He's like you in lots of ways. I only realised it recently, but I'm sure it's part of why it's always felt so natural being with him.' He waits for more. 'I think about you meeting, sometimes. When I talk to him about you, he listens in a way that makes me feel moved, because I know he can hardly believe there's a father like that anywhere. But he's like it, by instinct.' I am watching his face as I talk. He wants more. 'And about lovemaking,' I say—The awareness has strengthened; I know now for sure that this is what he needs me to be talking about, though he couldn't ask directly. 'We've had other issues to sort out, but never that. He's a man you know you can trust, to be exactly who he is, and to take you for just who you are. There's no separation between expressing that with our bodies and our beings, they're the same thing. And both wonderful.'

A small movement of the head, a letting go. That's OK then, his eyes say.

I say, 'I wish you'd told me you worried. I could have said that long ago if I'd known.' Then, 'That's one thing I *would* do differently, if we could do it again. I'd make a rule that none of us try to protect the others by not saying things!'

He smiles, a closing down, tired smile. 'That was how your mother and I started. It's easier said than done. But you try.'

You and Neil, he's saying. Handing the mantle on—

Richard and I arrive back from the park. He is saying, 'There's a young woman I know, who remembers you,' when from inside the house we hear the phone ringing. Claire comes to the door. 'For you,' she says, eyes alive with curiosity. 'His *accent*—it's like out of a play!'

'Neil?'

His voice mild, calm. 'Next time you're going to make me lose my temper, give me your phone number first.'

I start giggling. 'How did you get it?'

'I had to phone your mother. And since it's the first time we've spoken, I could hardly say, "Give me Jennie's number," and put the phone down.'

'Go on! What did you talk about?'

'You mainly. How empty houses feel when you remove yourself.'

'Which house—yours or theirs?'

'She said it first, then I said it. We were remarkably in agreement.'

'You see, it's not so difficult. You build these things up ludicrously.'

He says, 'And it was ludicrous putting the phone down on you. It isn't even anything major—you just happened to step on one of my obstinate refusal buttons. There's something I'm worried about and I'd decided there was no point bothering you about it. I should have known nothing escapes you.'

'Tell me, Neil. That's what we're for. Is it Juan?'

'See? You know.'

'Only because you were talking about Ben again.'

'It's this bloody male need to test himself against the universe. He's determined to go mountain-climbing in Scotland in the half term, and it's completely the wrong time of year. The mists come up on those mountains with no notice. I blew up at him, which was stupid, and of course made no difference. I know I get too anxious about the danger, and he just sees it as over-controlling.' Then, 'He's just turned sixteen. That's how old Ben was when I left home.'

'*Neil*, this is completely different.'

'Of course I know that. Maybe it's just that I have no experience to draw on past this point. I don't understand it, why it's got so near the surface after years of being packed away.'

'You said yourself, those two months were like digging up—archeological layers of experience. Of course that's disturbing.'

'I don't regret a thing. I just don't want to land Juan with all this; or you. I have to find a way of burying Ben. Properly, this time.'

Was it before the phone call or after that—?

I can't go forward. My mind keeps jerking back, looking for that safety...The bed full of body heat and familiar night smell, bedclothes rumpling around me as I lie half awake, listening to Neil's breathing...Dad's breathing...Breath is life; while it moves, we live. Everything comes from the breath, Neil said as I held the viola the first time, start always with that...

Try again. Richard says, 'There's a young woman I know, who remembers you—'

But we hear from the garden that in the house the phone is ringing, and he never tells me who the young woman is, for this time Patricia calls him to the phone, saying, 'It's your Aunt Josie.' And because Aunt Josie never phones him, I follow him in, and stand with Patricia there right next to him, listening for what we do not want to hear. So near that we hear Aunt Josie's voice—

'My dear, I am so sorry. Your father...another heart attack'... Dad is dead.

Chapter 6

Mom's voice, strangled. Some inarticulate sounds. I say, 'Oh Mom, oh Mom,' again and again. And then, 'We're coming. Just know I'm hugging you, until I get there.' Her voice emerges from the sounds. She says, 'I'm so grateful you're here. And that he saw you.' But what does it matter now that he's dead?

At the funeral too, they all say, 'It's so good you came back. It meant so much to your father.' I want to scream, *Dad's dead, don't you understand? Nothing means anything to him now*.

Now it is not just me, we are all back. Summoned by death, when life was not enough to do it. Patricia and the children and me, driving down in her car, almost as soon as the phone is down. Peter from East London—finally left with no option. Edward from Bangkok, cutting short negotiations about interest rates or God knows what. 'If I come back the army will get me,' he said when he left. He's back now, protected by an American passport. Trevor, who could have come back but was too busy—now abandoning a medical conference at which he was to present a paper. Flying in from all over the globe, and all at the same time, together for the first time for sixteen years. Even Richard, granted twenty-four hours' release from his banning order. Funerals have their uses, it seems.

Dad is dead. Say it again and again, ritual incantation, to take in the thing that is impossible to comprehend. Dad is no more. Dad is not. And now it seems as if I wasted every minute that I was here, with all the things that were never said. With allowing myself to be subverted by the Bloemfontein lowest common denominator of acceptable interaction, and not pushing past that to the things Dad and I could have said to each other if we had not been so constantly doing our social duty to other people. I grab at fragments of memory, holding on to small shared moments like a final note I am not ready to let go of. Coming home from school, indignant at some injustice by a teacher, and Dad laughing lovingly down at my face, saying, before I've even started to tell him, 'What's not fair today?'—

Hold on to each other, since he is not here to hold on to. Peter, Trevor, Edward—hugging for what words won't do, arms around each other cancelling the small jealousies of childhood and the years with almost no contact. Then anything we might have said to each other is swamped by the arrival of aunts, uncles, cousins, people announcing themselves as cousins whom we don't even know, all driving down from Johannesburg, up from Cape Town—de Villiers, Donaldsons, Marais, McLeans, the whole Dutch–Scots melting pot down to the fourth generation. The small-town *dominees* with their hatted and gloved wives, who have hardly seen Dad since he became an adult. The teachers and lawyers with their city offspring, not so used to funerals—the boys awkward in their unaccustomed suits, the girls wondering if their dresses are right—

Submit, accept. I am in the village again and this is a ritual gathering of the clan. My village, my clan, no way of detaching myself this time and saying, these are other people's customs, I can watch but I don't have to join.

It had not occurred to me to think about what I would wear for the funeral. Aunt Josie surveyed my meagre collection and said, 'I'll take you to town tomorrow and we'll get you something.' She came with me into the changing room, as if I were eight years old and unable to decide anything for myself. She looked at my almost naked body as I took my summer dress off—pants, but no bra—and said, almost enviously, 'It must take you no time at all to dress in the morning.' Then she got busy doing up buttons and arranging the collar of the blouse. Through it all I stood there like a little girl and let her do it.

The funeral was—I don't know how to say it. It was not as I would have done it. But I was there, part of the group that let it happen that way…The announcement in the paper, the church decided on, hymns chosen. Dad was an atheist all his adult life—not just a vague agnostic, but a clear-thinking, definite atheist. He respected religious beliefs if they were sincerely held, but thought most people simply carried on what they had been born into and hadn't the intellectual courage to question; or perhaps the emotional courage to face up to their own mortality. When we die, we die, and that's it. The point is to use life well while we've got it…And here they were, the aunts, Patricia, Trevor, his own people, ignoring the very man he was and arranging a conventional religious funeral. But I was there and I did nothing to stop it.

And half way through the ceremony I realised they were right. Surrounded by the hundreds of people who had known him, been taught by him, loved him, each connecting with him in their own way, valid for them as mine was for me; and for almost all of them this was the only possible way to have a funeral. This funeral was for them, not for Dad.

Then the gathering afterwards. The aunts took over the arrangements for that too, explaining to those who hadn't been to Bloemfontein for a while how to get to Aunt Josie's new house, providing trays of food, relays of tea, coffee, a meal for those who hadn't gone by supper time. The only thing we had to do was be there, and somehow keep talking to everyone as if things were normal, when everyone knew that the only reason we were all milling around in Aunt Josie's living room was that they weren't.

Then they drove off, back to Johannesburg and Cape Town and wherever. The Bloemfontein ones took themselves back home to get on with the other things in life. Aunt Josie turned on Aunt Ellie as Dad used to do, saying, 'Ellie, *leave* the clearing up.' Aunt Ellie said, 'And what do you think I'm going to do with myself instead?' and went on carrying the trays back to the kitchen. For once everyone listened to her, and we all worked together to clear and wash up and put away, and were relieved that there was something practical to do. Then Peter said quietly, 'Look at Mom,' and we saw she was sitting on a sofa at the far end of the now deserted living room, looking finished. Peter said, 'I'm taking her back.' Then we were suddenly all ready, all finished, and we set off in convoy, Richard and his family in one car with Edward, and Peter, Trevor and me in the other, with Mom just lumped in her seat in the front. Home again, opening up the dead house, to our separate beds or borrowed mattresses on the floor. Aunt Josie had said Richard and his family should stay with her, because there couldn't possibly be room for us all in one house. But for that one night, there was.

No chance for the conversations I had imagined we might one day have if we ever got together again. Too many of us together, and all taking refuge in practical tasks. One fragment, when Peter, uninvited, put his arm round my shoulder and I leant up against his, saying nothing that might make him take his arm away. Then other people came into the room and I lifted my head to stand again separate and said, 'Thanks, brother.' That was all. A whole lot better than nothing, but so much less than it might have been if there had been more time.

And now we are about to go back. It seems obscene, we've only just arrived. But those other lives have crept in again with their insistent demands. Edward's interrupted financial negotiations, Trevor's work, Claire and Joshua's school, Peter's need for distance. Richard gone already, the law yanking him back. My life with Neil—but no deadlines on that.

We work out how to stagger the departures. Edward has urgent meetings coming up, but if I can stay a couple of weeks more he'll get back to deal with lawyers and money. Thank God one of us understands these things. Peter says he can probably come for a weekend sometime after that. Trevor says, perhaps in a couple of months—Probably. Perhaps. When it fits in around other things. All of us sitting at the kitchen table, with Mom looking so grey and with her eyes staring.

Four times over Mom and I climb into the car to drive the next brother out to the airport and wave him off. Mom looks smaller after each departure. Then we come home, to the house now empty and far too big, too many rooms, too many things, not enough people to use them. She says, in a dazed voice, as if noticing the house for the first time, 'It was wonderful to have everyone at once, but it was a pity it had to be now, when I can hardly take anything in.'

She is alone. More completely alone than she ever was in her childhood. Nearly half a century of a shared life, now starting again. All that love and thought and effort gone into making a family where once there was none, and now Dad is dead and we are scattered, thousands of miles away. To her coupled friends she will become poor Catriona, whom we must remember to invite for a meal, a drink, because she is alone. And some won't even do that, the ones who liked having Catriona-and-Frank because Dad got people talking and laughing, because he had known their father, taught their sons—the voice on the cricket commentary, the common-touch chat columnist on the local paper. Without her more extrovert half, will they remember to include her?

And she knows. Her eyes stare, like someone about to drown who has been taught it is impolite to mention it. She says, 'I'm going to find out who my real friends are.' I feel uncontrollably angry.

2

For the first few days we do very little. I make cups of tea, as Neil once said he did for Teresa. The phone rings often, and I begin to feel better about Mom's friends. People visit, bearing pre-cooked meals so we won't have to bother, staying for a cup of tea, but not long because they don't want Mom to feel she has to talk. A couple of friends come for even briefer times—'We were just passing,' they say, 'we thought we'd drop in, we're not staying.' I have wild swings of feeling, sometimes grateful to them for the tact, because she *is* exhausted, sometimes thinking furiously, what if she *needed* you to stay? How will she ever tell you? You're gone before you can listen. Just passing. Passing by each other's lives.

'I don't know how long I'll be staying,' I say to Neil on the phone. 'Just do what you need to,' he says.

'A couple of weeks at least. Mom's going to need help, learning to be alone.'

'You know I want you to be there for her.'

I do know. Neil has lost no one, for he never knew Dad, but I sense something has changed for him too. Scarcely a month ago he knew almost nothing of my family and would happily have relegated them to some point off the end of the world's map, as unreachable as he has made his own. Now he can say, 'I want you to be there,' and mean it.

'Your father wrote to me, Jennie. It came today.'

'*Dad?* To you?'

'He didn't tell you he was going to?'

'No! When did he write it?'

'A week ago.' After that last angina attack.

'Read it to me.'

—Just a note to welcome you as a son-in-law; or not in-law, but I'm sure you know what I mean. From all I have heard of you, you would be the last to want conventional expressions of sentiment. But I want you to know how glad we are for Jennie that she has found a partner with whom she has the kind of lively, equal and loving relationship she—

He's having difficulty keeping reading...Neil's voice speaking Dad's words, Dad speaking through him, literally now, handing on his mantle. *You try*, he said, you and Neil...And to Neil he is saying, Jennie has chosen you, so you are part of us already...A welcome so natural for Dad to give, so extraordinary for Neil to receive, this man who has never experienced anything as simple...

He says, 'I can't go on. You read it when you get back.'

'Neil, *please*—'

—I can well imagine the difficulties you must have felt at the prospect of her returning. We honour you for making it easy for her to come—

Silence. I manage, 'Neil, be gentle on yourself.'

He makes a noise, untranslatable.

'Things happen. We get past them.'

No sound. 'Neil, they had been married forty-five years. It gives you a different perspective thinking of that. We could have thirty years together before you're as old as Dad was. There's a lot that's going to happen in that time, and we can't let ourselves be thrown by one small setback.' A vast distance I am trying to reach across, and no clue whether I am getting through. 'Neil, what Dad said about honouring you. He didn't know how right he was. All I have to do is follow my instincts, it comes so easy, because of what I've had from them. You have to invent it, each new step. It's the people who *break* a damaging mould who deserve to be honoured.'

'Jennie, please—' His voice is crying, he can't handle any more words, especially praise. I wait, and I begin to feel he has quietened me, each of us there at the end of the silent line. Eventually he says, 'There's more to say, but I can't do it like this.' His voice steadies as he pulls himself back to the practical. 'I'll try and write before I go to Glasgow.'

The days drift on, and Mom and I with them. The questions that so short a time ago seemed urgent to decide on have been jettisoned. The crisis that loomed in my dream was nothing to do with Neil; it was this, this fundamental loss that I still cannot absorb. Jonas is part of the long-ago past, pointless to think I can reclaim it. Richard's plans for me seem now wildly unrealistic. I was beguiled, briefly, by the vision of salvaging something of wider significance from a life pattern that is personal, nothing more. There's a bigger story out there but I'm not part of it, and was never intended to be.

I take Mom out for drives. Something to do, to get out of the house. To Naval Hill where as children we were taken to see the zebras wander in the nature reserve at the top. Now it is I who take Mom, for she has lost the ability to decide anything for herself. We stand to look out over the town spread out below, stretching miles further than it did when I was last up here, over to what was once a no man's land between the white town and Bochabela. A funeral procession going on there, right now—three youths killed by the police a few days after Dad died. The mourners appeared briefly on the television news, hundreds, maybe thousands of people pushing through the streets, chanting, singing, *toyi-toyi* dancing—the whole-body music that is at once mourning and political protest, dancers weaving their way through the untarred streets to collect outside the police station...Then Mom came into the room and it was obvious that she couldn't handle it. Switch it off—

Where next? The new botanical garden at the north edge of town off the main road and along an untarred track, winding down to a dip in the land where the garden lies, protected by a low curved ridge. It is nothing like the gardens of the town, created in defiance of the veld; this grows out of it. The very shape is ancient, a shallow valley scraped out between the low hills before humans were thought of. The trees are indigenous, tough highveld species, but in this protected valley growing to unusual size and grace. The beds are filled with plants that know how to deal with drought and bloom despite it. We stand together, arms around each other, moved by their resilience, absorbing it for ourselves. We walk slowly along the edges of the beds. Mom looks at the botanical notices. For a moment the interest of discovering a plant she does not know distracts her from her pain.

We talk about Dad constantly. We go over each minute of his last day—the sudden pain in his chest, calling Doctor Cohen, the ambulance, the hospital; what each of the doctors and nurses said—as if there might be a loophole we have missed, and if we rerun it enough times we might change the outcome. We look again at all the letters, and wonder about the few who have not written. Surely Dennis and Madge would have written? Maybe they haven't heard. 'Perhaps you should phone them?' she says. She wants me to do it all for her, as if I have become her mother. I tell her things I remember that she has forgotten, or maybe never knew, things Dad said to me when I was a child. She soaks it up, and it leaves her dry again, thirsting.

Even in that terrible thirst she is incapable of being sentimental. I tell her I heard someone at the funeral say that for such a talented man Frank was always so humble. She turns her staring eyes on me and says fiercely, 'Never! He was sometimes so arrogant it drove me wild.' I am amazed at the vehemence, which uses more energy than she has been able to summon all week. But of course, it is even more important now to hold on to him as he was, and not to lose one iota of his reality in prettification. A few minutes later she says, almost to herself, 'He was a lovely man. But not humble.'

The house surrounds us, aching spaces. I see her as she will be once I and then Edward have finally gone—no one needing her, nothing required of her. The image is painfully confused with a memory of sitting in my attic with a meaningless box of papers, the lifeless remains of a life with Neil that I thought had come to an absolute end. For her it *is* the end.

She walks from room to room, unable to settle to any activity. 'It's time we began sorting out Dad's things,' she says. His clothes are simple; they will go, as our old clothes always have, to the welfare centre in Bochabela. She wants them gone, now. I phone someone, and they are collected. She keeps nothing. His papers take longer. Each one reminds her of something, and we talk about it. No question of throwing any of the papers out; they are the life of the mind, the spirit, all that remains of it. They go back into the boxes from which they came, in slightly reshuffled order.

And that's it. The books, the photographs, the letters were all shared. Nothing left of Dad's life to sort out, for that is done. It is her own that is the question.

She says, quietly, 'What am I going to do?'

What am I going to do?...Never in all our childhood was there a question of what she should do. She was always busy, always the next job waiting before this one was finished. The accounts to sort out, on Sundays while the rest of us relaxed. Letters to answer late at night, after everyone else had given up on the day. And never enough time for all the things she *wanted* to do. What has given her life substance is the quiet passion, the things of the mind that have engaged her intensity. All those years of producing plays, getting supper organised early three nights a week for the month rehearsals were on, shifting chess pieces around as she plotted the moves of her characters on a paper stage—

I pull myself back. What matters is *now*. A seventy-year-old woman sits staring at me, waiting for me to say something simple and practical that will rescue her. I say, 'You'll go on doing what you've been doing all these last years since you retired. Reading. Reviewing plays and books. Seeing your friends. A bit of gardening.' I ignore the arthritis, which has cut that 'bit' down further every year. 'You have more resources than almost anyone I know.'

Her face seems reduced to huge dark eyes, staring, and a pale surround. She does not bother to answer my pointless comfort. I am telling her it is going to be OK, when it manifestly isn't.

'Maybe,' I say, 'we should try to make a list. Of your options.'

One—Stay in the house alone.

Two—Find someone else to share it.

Three—Sell it, move into a flat. (Query—no garden?)

If three, sell most of the furniture. (Query—books?)

'Four,' I say, 'come and live with one of your children.' But I know she won't write it. 'You have your lives,' she says. 'I'm not landing myself on you.'

'You wouldn't be landing yourself on me. You'd be giving me back something I've been cut off from, and longed to have.' But that too is only a half-truth. If it was just me, we could make it work. But not with Neil, with his experience of mothers. She knows that, without discussing it. I summon all the people I have known who would think her refusal, and my acquiescence in it, unintelligible. Charity's aunt in Mbabane, whose house expanded always to accommodate the number of people who arrived, and who never asked when anyone was leaving. The village, where old people might be poor and powerless but went on being part of the whole—

Mom releases me from the pointless struggle. It is not possible, accept it. But the passion with which I want to sweep away her aloneness gets through to her momentarily. She says, 'Dear girl,' and then stares again at her list.

I have not given up on Four. If Neil and I can't do it, maybe one of the others? Peter is out. Edward moves all the time, and anyway has made a clear choice not to share his life with anyone. Trevor is too far from anyone and anything she knows; she would descend into being a dependent old lady in a foreign country, waiting for them to come home. Richard and Patricia are the only real possibility. 'They have enough to contend with,' she says.

I say, 'Maybe at least a flat in Johannesburg, to be nearer?' She looks confused for a moment, for this might be a real option. But it panics her, more than comforts. 'My life has been *here*,' she says—as if someone is trying to take away from her the one thing that remains.

3

Of all Mom's visitors only one stayed and talked, and that was someone she did not remember having seen before. A young black woman. She arrived at the front door—this in itself was a surprise—and introduced herself as Thandiwe Moletsane. The name conveyed nothing. I invited her in. Mom stood up from her armchair—almost to attention, the stimulus of the unexpected jolting her momentarily out of passivity. They shook hands. Mom said, 'Please sit down,' and looked to me as she would have done in my childhood, to say, 'We have guests, go and do something about tea.' I moved automatically towards the door, but I couldn't leave. In all the years I lived in this house I never saw a black person sit in one of these armchairs.

She moved over to the chair nearest Mom's, from where she could lean forward and take her hand. 'You don't remember me,' she said, 'but I have been in this house when I was a child.' She spoke confidently, her English fluent and relaxed, her manner that of one quite used to walking into other people's lives. Mom looked at her with big eyes, giving up her hand. Thandiwe said, 'I am the grandchild of Annie Moxetse.'—

The child who made herself at home in my bedroom, as she makes herself now at home holding Mom's hand. Touching everything in turn, the books, the collections of small china ornaments, the curtains, feeling the fabric, the texture—

Now looking at me, eyes smiling to acknowledge the memory. Then she nodded as if to say, 'We can talk later. She's the one who needs attention now,' and she turned back to Mom. I left them and went to make the tea. When I came back in with the tray Mom was listening like a child to a story, eyes following every movement in Thandiwe's face. I poured tea, passed the cups, and sat to listen.

She stayed more than two hours. A death pulls us momentarily out of time, and it is good not to resist that pull. I remember from childhood the complaints Mom and Dad's friends used to make about servants taking so many days off for every funeral; because they could not see it as another culture's response to death, they saw only people avoiding the work of living. To Thandiwe it must have seemed equally strange to come into an almost empty house so soon after a death. Nor was there any of the tactful avoidance of what was painful that had made Mom's friends tread so carefully. It was clear Thandiwe understood that the burden could not be lightened by pretending it was not there, only by sharing it. She had come to talk about my father, and that was what she did.

The effect was dramatic. Her directness freed Mom from the need to be anything other than what she was, a grieving woman, still stunned by what she could not take in. She listened greedily as Thandiwe told her everything she had ever heard people say about Dad. Things Annie had told her, that we would never have guessed Annie noticed. The cleaners at the school Dad taught at, where he once arranged for Annie's out-of-work son to be taken on as a messenger. The waiters at the cricket club—one of them Annie's neighbour in Bochebela…Listening to her I saw again Dad sitting on the cricket club verandah having a drink with friends—sociable, relaxed, looking out over the cricket pitch where a team of green-overalled gardeners pushed huge rollers up and down… What could they know of him, or he of them? How was it that they saw in him anything other than another white man who took their services and scarcely noticed?

'He was different,' Thandiwe said, answering the question I had not asked. 'To him everyone was a person. He used to stop and talk for a few minutes, make jokes, ask them about their families. These are not small things. I come bearing many people's sorrow.'

'Where do you live now?' Mom asked.

'Johannesburg. But I have friends still in Bochebela. My grandmother always used to tell me it was you and Mr de Villiers who paid my school fees, and I knew one day I should come back to tell you your kindness was not wasted.'

Mom said—surprising herself, I think—'My dear, you have no shyness, have you?' Thandiwe laughed and said, 'That's what they tell me! But it's also my job. I have to talk to a lot of people.'

'What do you do?'

'I'm a trade union organiser.' Then the slightest pause before she added, 'A union of domestic servants. My grandmother's trade.'—

—Suddenly, Richard's voice—There's a young woman I know, who remembers you... Thandi is watching me, nods slightly. Then she turns back to Mom. It is time she took her leave, she says. There are people in Bochebela too who are grieving, for their lost sons. It is time she got back; and before the evening curfew.

'I'm driving you,' I say.

'Just to the bus station,' she says, as we set off in the car. I want to take her all the way. I don't want to let her go, this first link I have been offered to the unreachable world where everyone else lives. But she won't let me. 'You've forgotten,' she says, 'you can't go into Bochebela without a permit.' I have not forgotten, I am just in a state of rebellion, having been let out momentarily from the tunnel in which only Mom and I exist. I can't sort out which things are worth taking risks for.

Thandi can. 'They're out on the streets again today,' she says. 'It's not a good time to be a white woman driving into the place.'

'Thandi—my brother Richard—'

'Yes,' she laughs. 'We have been friends since I first went to Johannesburg, long before he was banned. And Patricia.'

'They told you I was back?'

'And that maybe you will help us.'

'The funeral—they knew you were there? They must have—'

She laughs as each penny drops. 'Sometimes it is better if you don't show who your friends are where everyone can see.'

I feel suddenly overwhelmed at the simplicity of it. Someone walking into my life, offering me something that brings it all together, the unsorted out things from my childhood, the unfinished work I have left behind to start life with Neil. Then that is overtaken by frustration at all that stands in the way of our going forward from this moment—starting with the curfew that will soon be on us, after which it will be illegal for Thandi to be on the streets. She is about to get out of this car and go to where it's all happening, and I shall drive back to the carefully tended gardens of the white suburbs, and be trapped once more in inactivity. I say, 'Thandi, I don't know when we're even going to get together to talk properly. When do you go back?'

'Tomorrow. But you'll come to Johannesburg on your way back?'

'Yes. How do I get a message to you?'

'Patricia,' she says simply.

We have arrived at the bus station, surrounded by black people crowding to get a place. For a moment I could almost imagine I am back travelling, about to climb on myself. We sit talking for a few moments more in the parked car. Thandi is saying, 'Some of my white friends tell me about the black women they remember who looked after them. I remember *you* looking after *me!*'

'You were small,' I say. 'What can you remember?'

'Sitting on your lap, and all the things on your dressing table. That was the first white person's house I'd ever been into. Now every day I am with women who still only go in at the kitchen door. You see—' she takes my hand, laughing—'this thing between us goes back a long time. Keep at least a few days for Johannesburg. I want to take you where you can hear people sing.'

She lets go of my hand and climbs out of the car. I watch her move to join the crowd of people who try to push their way on to the last dilapidated bus that will make the journey to Bochebela—before dark makes them vulnerable to people with knives, before the curfew sends out its wailing siren, sounding the threat of arrest. For her, but not for me.

4

It takes a death to put things in perspective. I can't believe now how much energy I expended trying to work out whether to come back. Nor can I really remember the fear of Neil withdrawing. I remember of course that I felt it but I can't revisit how it felt, not now when I look at Mom and think: *That's* what it means to be alone, to be cut off from the person you love.

Now somewhere halfway across the world Neil has set off for Glasgow—the performance, the workshop—and he is out of reach, more surely through absorption than through distance. He either has or has not written the letter he promised but it hardly seems to matter. Whatever needs saying, we'll say it eventually. Until he left he had been phoning every couple of days since Dad died. I realise I have no idea if he can afford it—our lives are intertwined in all essentials but in practical terms we're just beginning. But it's obvious neither of us is into counting the cost. There are just times when it is more important than anything else to be able to talk, and later is when you start to work out how broke it has made you.

I have had to tell him twice that I am postponing my flight back. On the second time, for the censors who might have been listening I said simply, 'I'm still needed here,' but Neil will have picked up that it wasn't Mom I was talking about because he knew Edward was coming to take over from me. I need time with Thandiwe, not just to listen to people sing, but to work out in detail the plans we will not be able to write about once I have gone. This time I am choosing for myself the manner of my departure. And if the unstated things spark off Neil's tension again, only he can deal with that, as only he can find his way past the anxieties about Juan falling to his death in the mist of a

Scottish mountain. We can love each other through these things, and laugh at each other's fears, or hold each other rocking in the night. But the essential loving is to give each other space to be what we are, and rejoice.

Mom and I sit together in the living room. I am longing to get away and be quiet on my own, but there is panic in her eyes each time she thinks I am about to go. This has been building up for days now, her need becoming more obvious rather than less as the numbing effect of the death wears off. I try to wait for a good moment but there never is one. Eventually I have to do it anyway and ignore the eyes.

About the third night I find a form of words. 'I hope your night isn't too long,' I say. She replies quietly, 'Actually, I don't sleep.' The tone is that of someone admitting to a regrettable deficiency in herself, but her eyes have that drowning look again. I know exactly what I should say—'I'll come into your bed with you.' I know it from the dream I had before Dad died, that elemental need to be close to the other body. I know it from how I have felt when Neil has cut himself off from me—the need to touch and be touched, to be comforted beneath and beyond the words we can't say...This is a woman, I tell myself, who had her own mother taken away from her before she can remember and yet had the capacity to give each of us in turn a love unconditional, undemanding, enabling. All that is asked is that for the few nights more that I will be with her I should give her this one simple thing, to lie close to her so that her body is comforted from the aloneness no one can take away from her.

And I cannot do it. Anything else. All day I put her needs first, I do whatever is in my power. We hug, often and easily. But not nights. Not lying next to her in bed. I do not know why, but I cannot fight it. The part of me that said to her *leave my hair alone* holds tenaciously to this last corner of what keeps me separate from her. I think of Peter and of Neil, and of the simple things they could not do because they felt compelled to put distance between themselves and their mothers, and finally I am humbled into knowing that I am no different.

Jennie my love,

You'll see from the postmark I'm in Edinburgh…

—I have come to see my mother. I wanted to tell you when I last phoned but it seemed like tempting fate, so I made myself wait till I got here. It was your father's letter that jolted me into it; that, and the way you instantly dropped other things to stay with your mother when she needed you. The truth is I've been shamed into it.

It's five years since I was here, and that visit too may have been connected with you. I was in Manchester, the time after the end of the viola lessons, and I was in a tunnel of emotional withdrawal. God knows what impelled me out of it in her direction, but I was certainly in no state to handle it in a way that was any use to either of us. She started right in on self-pity, about how I'd thrown away all my talent and ruined her life, so I was out before she could get to brewing up the kettle a second time. I don't know what I expected to be different this time—certainly not her, but I suppose I had persuaded myself it might be possible for me to react differently.

She was in her dressing gown when I arrived, at four in the afternoon. I suspect she has given up bothering to dress for the day. If she'd known I was coming I'd never have seen that, and then perhaps not have seen the other things either. The gas stove was so dirty the flame didn't catch all the way round the ring so she's probably been gassing herself every time she lights it—she has no sense of smell. Even now that I've cleaned it she's quite likely to turn the thing on and forget she's done so before she puts a match to it. She can't cope, Jennie. Not with dressing, or with remembering where she has put anything, or with making plans to see friends. I can't find out for sure if she *has* friends, and I've been here two and a half days now. I've stayed so clear of any involvement all these years, and now I have walked into a situation that I'd have to be a monster to walk out of again. So I'm stuck with it for the rest of her life, in one form or another. I am feeling unspeakably trapped, as if she has finally won, manipulated me by her very aging into not being able to get away. I don't attempt to persuade myself that I should try to feel loving about her, or even like her. I can't. But whatever she once was she is now just a pathetic old woman, who has long since lost any power to control my life, and who will sink into increasing indignity unless I take minimal action to arrange things better.

We talked about my needing to bury Ben. *This* is what it took. But I went back to Dundee too, before I came here, the first time since the funeral. I thought *that* would be burying him, forcing myself to go back so I wouldn't forever be running away. In fact being there was nothing. The same places, with different people in them, people who never knew Ben. I stood on the pavement opposite our house and looked up at the window of the room where he hanged himself, and there was nothing left to feel, I've felt it all already. So I just took the next bus back and sat in McDonalds drinking coffee while I waited for the train to Edinburgh, and watched the people come and go. Maybe that was the most significant part of the whole apparently pointless journey, just sitting there for an hour feeling completely detached, watching people in constant movement. In at the doors and out, up the road and down, on to the bus and off. From home to the shops, from the shops back home. Women going their messages, pushing pushchairs, calling to their toddlers not to lag behind. Mesmerising, like one of those mbira rhythms, the changes so subtle you don't notice they're happening till after ten minutes the tune is something else yet still in the same pattern of time. Babies becoming children, children becoming adolescents, awkward young men coming to terms with adulthood, young girls becoming mothers, pushing pushchairs, calling to their toddlers not to lag behind. I ran away for fifteen years, and when I came back again the place was nothing but a stream of people doing their shopping on an ordinary day. By the end of that hour I understood that Ben has been released from the dance. There is no point even feeling defeat any more. It happened. The only thing to do is absorb it, make it part of the next step...

... Mom's eyes stare, holding on to each moment of the story as I retell it; almost as if it is she going back. She does not comment until the end, when she says, 'And now maybe it's too late for that poor woman.' Then she pulls herself up, almost physically pushing the feeling off. 'We just have to be grateful for what's here now.'

It is night, and I know now that I am going to say the thing that has been impossible, and that it will be Neil helping me do it, through having done the thing that was so much harder for him. I say, 'Mom, shall I come into your bed with you?'

She hesitates. Her face says, I shouldn't be burdening the child with my troubles...But she is driven now by a need stronger than the lifelong instincts of considerate motherhood.

I save her from having to answer. 'I'm coming,' I say. 'It's silly, each alone in our own room, and neither of us sleeping properly.'

She is tense and awkward at first. We lie parallel, not touching, in this double bed where I am usurping my father's place. I am no more relaxed than she. I am on duty but the task is beyond me. The more she lifts the edges of the curtain that hides her terrible aloneness, the more useless are my pathetic offerings of comfort. I consider moving closer and putting my arm around her, but I don't risk it. Why? Is it because it is night, and in bed, and it should not be me putting my arms around her, but Dad? I wish my time was over and Edward would come back, that I could return to the normality of life with Neil. 'Normal time'—but what is that? We had no time to form a pattern before all this intervened. There will be time, just hold on to that. Time to absorb the changing feelings and states of being that each of us continually brings into our joint life. Time to work out a way to give Neil the space he needs to be alone, and for me to find a way to give expression to the creativity that will certainly cause trouble for both of us if I let it be shut away, thunder in a pot…

Why is it harder to put my arm around my own mother in her need, than to mother each of the children I have held? I hold the thought of each of them, quietly, summoning their simple warm bodies to release mine—Charlie and his pile of stones. Kirstie and her stories. Michael and the banging of wooden spoons. The children of the village and of Kalingalinga, splashing in mudpools…The softness of small limbs, the way Michael's body cuddled into mine, fitting into whatever shape I provided. His child-breath lightly touching my skin. They blur into each other, the years of soft bodies touching, keeping each other company against the night, or the need to greet the day.

Jennie, do it. Just move close and put your arms around her—

Still something prevents me. I am grateful that she keeps this space between us. There is something too basic about her at the moment, a smell of grief, perhaps, an unloveliness about the flesh. Too great a need of the spirit, a nakedness that I am afraid to see. I turn over on my side, my back to the space that separates us. The bed moves—she too has turned, to face the other way, away from me. Schooling herself, not to burden me…

But that movement of acceptance gets to me. I feel a rush of protective love for her that surprises me in its intensity, and that sweeps aside my resistance to touching this old woman's body. I turn back and move myself right up to her, body to body, and I begin to stroke her hair as I once did Paula's, and Paula mine, when each of us had lost the person we loved.

She lies at first rigid beneath my moving hand. There is no question but that she is awake and receiving it, but no muscle moves to show it. After a long time I begin to sense a slight

- *Thunder in a pot* is from *Mphezi, mphezi* by Anasibeko, recorded in Blantyre district 1967, in *Malawian Music*, Gerhard Kubik, University of Malawi, 1987
- *Sibongile sings* is from *Hallucinations etched in song* by Heather Robertson, in *Under the sun*, 1991.

Many people shared their expertise during the writing of the book. James Harrison guided my listening in 20th century western classical music. Judith Weir, Michael Finnissy, Alasdair Nicholson and Stephan Montague talked to me about the process of composing. Greg Lanning located Paula's music. Ilse Mwanza stimulated my memory on all things Central African. John Parry Williams tracked Swazi sources. Lynette Mudekunya provided Shona translations. On musical participation I have drawn on the stimulating writing of Anthony Storr, Derek Bailey, John Miller Chernoff; on African music, of Paul Berliner, John Blacking, Gerhardt Kubi, A.M. Jones, Attach Mensah, Enoch Mvula, David Rycroft. I have done my best to track and acknowledge sources of quotations.

Author's note

This story is entirely fictional, but it grew out of real-life experiences. The strands of inspiration from other lives are by now impossible to disentangle, but a few stand out, and I want to record my gratitude. First to my parents, whose humane values enabled their children, growing up in a deeply divided society, to go into adult life knowing that we are all part of one another, wherever we live, whatever language we speak, whatever music we dance to. My aunt Louise ensured that I was exposed early to the conditions in which African children were growing up in my home town.Monica Wilson, eminent anthropologist, allowed me to become a friend when I was a young student, and inspired me by the respect with which she studied social change in African cultures. My brother Colin shared musical enthusiasms and helped friends cross a border to escape prison. My students at Kabulonga Girls School in Lusaka gave me my first introduction to Zambian life. The East London Late Starters Orchestra opened up the pleasure of shared music-making, and Wendy Giles, violin teacher extraordinaire, helped me discover the musician within. African colleagues working for Save the Children in East, Central and Southern Africa shared their stories. Robert, my husband, constantly sharpened my understanding of political contexts. My daughters, May and Star, inspired me by the resourcefulness with which they made their way as young women in a confusing world.

If you can walk, you can dance has travelled widely since it won a Commonwealth Writers Prize. It is rooted in its own particular past - the African lives it shares - but these are also universal stories, shared by millions who have been thrust unwillingly into exile, and by all who have been enriched through encounters with other cultures, and through making music. It is dedicated to the grandchildren and great-grandchildren of Davie and Kathleen Marquard, scattered across three continents. To their journeys.

